nice try, jane sinner

LIANNE OELKE

CLARION BOOKS

Houghton Mifflin Harcourt

BOSTON NEW YORK

Clarion Books

3 Park Avenue

New York, New York 10016

Copyright © 2018 by Lianne Oelke

All rights reserved. For information about permission to reproduce selections from this book, write to trade.permissions@hmhco.com or to Permissions, Houghton Mifflin Harcourt Publishing Company, 3 Park Avenue, 19th Floor, New York, New York 10016.

Clarion Books is an imprint of Houghton Mifflin Harcourt Publishing Company.

www.hmhco.com

The text was set in Minion Pro.

Library of Congress Cataloging-in-Publication Data

Names: Oelke, Lianne, author.

Title: Nice try, Jane Sinner / Lianne Oelke.

Description: Boston ; New York : Clarion Books, Houghton Mifflin Harcourt, [2018] | Summary: "Jane Sinner, a 17-year-old dropout, sets out to redefine herself through a series of schemes and stunts, including participating in a low-budget reality TV show at her local community college" — Provided by publisher.

Identifiers: LCCN 2016035569 | ISBN 9780544867857 (hardcover)

Subjects: | CYAC: High school dropouts — Fiction. | Universities and colleges — Fiction. | Reality television programs — Fiction. | Internet television — Fiction. | Diaries — Fiction.

Classification: LCC PZ7.1.O35 Ni 2018 | DDC [Fic] — dc23

LC record available at https://lccn.loc.gov/2016035569

Manufactured in the United States of America

DOC 10 9 8 7 6 5 4 3 2 1

4500689898

For Dana and Goose

nice try, jane sinner

NO TRESPASSING
VIOLATORS WILL BE SHOT
SURVIVORS WILL BE SHOT AGAIN

MARCH

FriMar4

I'm not a particularly good daughter, but I sat through a month of therapy for my parents' sake. I'd like to think they got more out of it than I did. Couldn't have been too hard. Any system that requires the patient's family to pay someone else to care about her is fundamentally flawed. But I digress. If my decision to stop attending therapy means James Fowler High School no longer welcomes me as a student, I guess that's on me.

The novelty of playing hooky has worn off, and I'm desperate to fill my time with something other than introspection, the occasional afternoon stocking groceries, and Mario Kart.

Bonnie just texted me. She wants me to burst through the clouds like the beautiful ray of sunshine that I am and come to a party tonight where everyone is apparently super super stoked to see me again. I told her it's too dangerous. I have been known to blind others with my relentlessly sunny disposition. I may be desperate for a change, but I'm not desperate enough to face a party full of ex-classmates. Bonnie is a better person than I will ever be, so she promised to stop by later for whatever garbage I'll be binge watching on my laptop.

So that's nice. It's also nice to write in here. I haven't written in this journal for months. It's kind of funny that the only time I don't write in here is when a therapist says I should. But I needed a break from myself. Understandably, I think.

SunMar6

Ditching school five months before grad isn't all it's cracked up to be. It's too late to catch up now. I dropped the ship, that ball has sailed, Jane Sinner has left the building. Everyone is still a little scared to ask what I'm going to do now because they know I have no fucking clue. The parents certainly didn't see this coming. They're still scrambling to find "the window God must have opened, since he closed this particular door." I'm old enough to close doors on my own, thank you very much. But the parents don't want to hear that. They want to hear me say, "Why yes, I'd love to come with you to church this morning." Not "I can't, I have to catch up on a variety of reality television shows."

They thought if Bonnie came over for lunch after the service, it would encourage me to at least shower and put on a bra by the time they got home. It didn't.

Apparently, Bonnie's fashion choices are rubbing off on Carol. They both decided to wear skinny jeans and fluorescent baggy sweaters to church, which annoyed the parents. Carol kept getting her sleeve caught in her lasagna while we ate.

DAD
I wish you would have come with us this morning, Jane.

MOM
You used to love going to church.

I also used to love running around half-naked with crayons up my nose because I thought they looked like fangs. I take comfort in knowing people can change.

DAD
You know, the best way to move on is to get back in the swing of things. There's nothing wrong with taking some more classes. You could use more structure in your life. Some order.

It's like he didn't even notice that I had divided my salad into a rainbow of vegetables.

JS

You're meowing up the wrong tree.

DAD

[Sigh.]

Barking, Jane. It's barking up the wrong tree.

BONNIE

Cats chase small animals up trees too, you know.

DAD

Yeah, well. You don't want to end up like your Aunt Gina, Jane. You can't make a decent living for your kids by sitting at home all day, "being funny" and writing Lord knows what for the internet.

JS

I don't have kids, Dad.

MOM

Oh, please. Can't we all just get along for one meal? Bonnie, how have you been lately? Is school going well for you?

I guess that's why they invited her over. Not only is she a conversational buffer, she's also a reminder that even bisexual girls with tattoos can have their shit together, so why don't I?

BONNIE

Yeah, school is going okay, I guess. We all miss Jane.

CAROL

Janie's gonna go to community college instead. That's what the guidance counselor thinks she should do, anyway.

BONNIE

Oh really? She didn't mention that to me.

JS

That's because I'm not going.

CAROL

[rolling her eyes]

Well, you can't just not go back to school!

JS

Thanks, Obvious McObviouspants.

DAD

Well. You can at least go to the information session tomorrow. It'll be good for you to explore your options.

MOM

We talked to Pastor Ron this morning, and he thinks that finishing your diploma at Elbow River is a good idea.

The parents are Pastor Ron's biggest fans, so if he thinks an idea is good, my parents think it's great. I think he's all right (for a pastor), but I'm not convinced he's the most qualified authority figure in my life, considering that my apathy toward his church was the domino that broke the camel's back. I'd tell the parents that, but they get frustrated when I use idioms incorrectly.

MonMar7

Carol told me I woke up on the wrong side of the bed this morning. I told her to bite me.

CAROL

No one says that anymore, Janie! And stop tagging embarrassing pics of me on Facebook. Mom always has to comment on each one. She's on a roll this morning.

I can do what I want.

I took Carol's Pop-Tart out of the toaster and ate it in front of her to drive the lesson home.

Respect your elders.

I'd like to say I'm going to the info meeting because I care about my parents' happiness. But really it's because I've racked my brain trying to answer the question *Well, what else are you going to do with yourself, Jane?* and I've got nothing. Just restlessness and understimulation and this constant hum in my body from energy wasted on Netflix. I need to run a marathon or something. I hate living in limbo.

From a distance, Elbow River Community College looked half-decent. Up close, it was just a fresh paint job and decorative glass designed to look like windows. I distrusted it already. It was bigger than I had imagined. Not that my imagination has been getting a chance to shine lately.

I stopped in the bathroom on my way to room 213. You can tell a lot about an establishment from its bathroom maintenance. This bathroom looked like it was recently renovated as cheaply as possible. Small, but cleanish. No GET OUT WHILE YOU CAN! Or JAKE S. IS FULL OF CHLAMYDIA N LIES! scrawled on the stalls. I did find a pamphlet tucked behind the tampon dispenser, featuring a girl with a perm and a turtleneck holding a pregnancy pee stick too close to her face. It was called *Tracy's in Trouble!* I would have stayed and learned a thing or two, but I was late as it was.

The classroom had twenty other potential students in it, all of whom looked even less excited to be there than I was. A middle-aged man leaned awkwardly on the teacher's desk. His ass barely grazed the wooden surface, the same way cautious girls hover over public toilets. Maybe it was the stiffness of his pressed slacks that wouldn't allow his legs to bend. He was the kind of tall that constantly invites strangers to comment on how tall he is.

> **TALL GUY**
> The weather is fine up here, thank you.

> **JS**
> I wasn't going to say anything.

> **TALL GUY**
> Cool.

He's also the kind of guy that makes me cringe every time he says something remotely modern. Even "cool."

> **TALL GUY**
> As I was explaining to everyone else here, when we started at three —

Yes, I know I'm late. Thanks for the reminder, though.

> **TALL GUY**
> — you can call me Mr. Dubs. That's short for Mr. W, which is short for Mr. Wickershnitzel.

That's probably for sure not his real name, but he didn't expect me to remember it anyway.

> **JS**
> Nice to meet you.

> **MR. DUBS**
> Likewise, Ms. . . .

> **JS**
> Sinner. Jane Sinner.

Anyone who addresses me as "Ms." or "Miss" is automatically someone I would rather not talk to. I resisted the urge to check my phone to see if the hour was up yet.

Mr. Dubs explained that he's the Youth Reengagement Program Admissions Coordinator and High School Integration Adviser. Or something to that effect.

MR. DUBS
You should have all received an email with links to our new website, Facebook, Twitter, Pinterest, Tumblr, and Instagram accounts. Here at Elbow River we believe in building a sustainable community, materially and mentally, so I'm excited to let you know we've recently committed to a paperless future!

The students broke into scattered applause. Just kidding. They didn't.

MR. DUBS
However, we still have a ways to go, and for now I'm required to hand you this piece of paper. I apologize.

The girl in front of me passed the paper back. Under the Elbow River logo the hashtags #COMMUNITY #SUSTAINABILITY and #FREEDOM were printed. I couldn't wait to make fun of this place to Bonnie. Mr. Dubs spent the next hour going over the school philosophy ("We believe in philosophy, not policy"). I started a tally of how many times Mr. Dubs used the word *sustainability* in his talk but gave up after sixteen. He also reviewed the logistics of completing a certain number of high school credits over the spring term. He said it's possible to study through the summer term as well, if we're interested in earning college credits too. But if I attend community college, I'll want to get out as quickly as possible.

After the talk came the application form, which was broken down into three sections: name, address, and credit card information. I didn't fill it out. I got the feeling Elbow River was the Venus flytrap of last-resort education and it would clamp down on any student with a pulse. Even students like me. I was half-afraid Mr. Dubs would pull me aside to discuss my "history." But I can't be the only one with a "history" here. The other prospective students seem normal enough, but they're all here for a reason, too.

The required aptitude test came last. Maybe I'd discover a hidden talent for Sustainable Basket Weaving or Intergenerational Social Media Communications. A girl can dream. It took Mr. Dubs more than twenty minutes to troubleshoot the Wi-Fi so we could do the test online. I browsed the bulletin board outside the classroom while we waited.

Three flyers for Recreational Ceramics. Four for a car share with a picture of a man holding a cat under each arm. One handwritten Post-it note saying "smile, ur beautiful!" I can't stand that sort of senseless optimism. And one flyer for Optimism Club. I might have trouble fitting in here. The only notice that caught my interest was for a reality show:

ARE YOU A STUDENT LOOKING FOR CHEAP RENT AND A FREE CAR???

My name is Alexander Park and I'm a film student. I'm looking for new and returning Elbow River students to compete in my YouTube reality show: *House of Orange*!

Three guys and three girls live in a Big Brother type house and compete to win my five-year-old VW Golf (perfect condition)! The house is located near the campus and has separate bedrooms. Rent is only $200 a month (utilities and internet included). Meet some new people, do some crazy things, win yourself a car! For details and to fill out an application, go to www.houseoforangeshow.com.

Students must be over 18 and enrolled in full-time studies for both the Spring and Summer terms.

Maybe Bonnie and I can fit *House of Orange* in with *America's*

Next Top Model and *The Bachelorette* this spring. I stuffed the flyer into my bra because these jeggings don't have pockets. The ladies also made room for the *Tracy's in Trouble!* pamphlet. Maybe community college could teach me something after all.

I spent the bus ride home trying to figure out how to tell the parents what I'm going to do. I have to play my cards right, or it won't work.

As soon as I walked into the kitchen, Mom turned toward the stove and began rapidly stirring a pot.

MOM
How'd it go, then?

She is really quite terrible at pretending to be casual about things she cares about.

JS
All right. Not great. I don't know.

DAD
Well, don't-a-worry, we're making-a-curry!

JS
Curry is not Italian, Dad.

DAD
You think you're so smart, don't you?

I opened a cupboard and grabbed some clean plates for the table.

MOM
So, Jane? Do you think it's . . . a possibility?

DAD
You know, Jane, when God closes a door, he —

JS
He opens a window, I know.

DAD

No need for that tone, Jane.

JS

I just don't know if it will work.

MOM

If you decide that education is no longer a priority for you, we could discuss other options. Like pitching in more around the house. Maybe paying rent.

I set down four shiny glasses next to four shiny plates. Hiccups of doubt followed me around the table, but I said it anyway:

JS

I'll go to Elbow River. But only if I move out.

Mom set her spoon on the counter with a sharp click.

DAD

That's not happening.

MOM

You could go back to James Fowler in the fall.

JS

But all my friends will have graduated already.

MOM

You can always make new friends! You can be such a nice girl when you make the effort, Jane.

This is why I can't talk to the parents. They think you can get friends in high school the same way you get chips from a vending machine. Put in a little niceness, and some kid pops out ready to double-check your homework and paint your nails at a slumber party. Niceness is not a valid currency in high school.

JS
It's not that easy, Mom. I'm not going back there.

Friends or no friends, the Legend of Jane Sinner will linger in the halls of James Fowler for years to come. All I want is to put some distance between myself and that story. Between myself and anyone who thinks of me that way. All the parents want is for me to stabilize, to become the girl who used to exist but doesn't exist anymore, for everything to stay the same forever and ever, amen.

MOM
I suppose you could study online.

And never have a reason to leave this house? I've wasted far too much time here lately.

JS
I don't think so.

MOM
We're just concerned for you, is all. It might be too much for you right now, what with —

JS
I know. And I appreciate your concern. But I really need some space . . . to focus on my studies.

It's not easy being diplomatic. As if on cue, they looked at each other, took a deep breath, and exhaled my name.

PARENTS
Jane . . .

I wonder if they know they've slowly merged into the same person in two different bodies.

I can't believe I said this, but—

                    JS
I'll go back to youth group.

They immediately softened. I was hoping I wouldn't have to play the Prodigal Daughter card, but as far as I know, nothing can trump it.

                  PARENTS
Oh, Jane. That would be so good for you right now. Good friends, Christian support—

                    JS
Only if I move out.

Awkwardly trying to fit into conversations that aren't the right size or shape for me while dying of boredom every other week is not ideal, but it's a sacrifice I'm willing to make for my freedom. Mom picked up her spoon and resumed stirring, turning her back to hide the tiny smile inching across her face.

                    DAD
Well, that's something to consider, isn't it? Why don't we sleep on it?

                    JS
Sure.

Obviously I'm not going to tell them about *House of Orange* just yet. One step at a time.

This is what I sent to Alexander Park:

PART A: THE BASICS

   NAME: Jane Sinner

AGE: 18

DOB: June 6

PROGRAM/ COURSE: psychology

HOMETOWN: Calgary

DO YOU HAVE ANY ALLERGIES? no

DO YOU HAVE ANY SPECIAL DIETARY RESTRICTIONS? no

DO YOU HAVE ANY MENTAL OR PHYSICAL CONDITIONS THAT WOULD PREVENT YOU FROM COMPETING IN HIGH STRESS LEVEL CHALLENGES? not really

PART B: PERSONAL RESPONSES

ARE YOU IN A RELATIONSHIP? HOW LONG? no

DESCRIBE YOUR CURRENT RELATIONSHIP: no

DESCRIBE YOUR RELATIONSHIP WITH YOUR FAMILY: no

DO YOU HAVE ANY SINGING, ACTING, OR PERFORMING ASPIRATIONS? god no

WHAT DO YOU DO IN YOUR SPARE TIME? draw, eat, watch substandard television programming

WHAT IS YOUR GREATEST STRENGTH? brevity

WHAT IS YOUR GREATEST WEAKNESS? no

WHAT (OR WHOM) DO YOU VALUE MOST IN YOUR LIFE?

competence, autonomy, absurdity, abstract nouns in general, steak, the people who slaughter cows so I don't have to

WHAT REALLY ANNOYS YOU? poor grammar, penciled-in eyebrows, most displays of emotion, ballpoint pens

FAVORITE TV SHOW? America's Next Top Model

FAVORITE BOOK? the internet

WHAT ARE YOUR THOUGHTS ON POLITICS? I'm happily apathetic

WHAT ARE YOUR THOUGHTS ON RELIGION? my thoughts are too profound and complex to be adequately dealt with here

WHAT ARE YOU AFRAID OF? pain, middle age, the bottom of the ocean

WHAT GOALS DO YOU HAVE FOR YOURSELF? to become a well-adjusted and self-aware individual

PART C: THE SHOW

ARE YOU A PRIVATE PERSON/ HOW COMFORTABLE ARE YOU ON CAMERA? privacy is a state of mind

ARE YOU WILLING TO COMMIT TO LIVING AT HOUSE OF ORANGE FULL TIME (SPENDING AT LEAST 30 HOURS A WEEK AT THE HOUSE BETWEEN 8AM AND 11PM)? yes

ARE YOU A COMPETITIVE PERSON? yes

HOW DO YOU PLAN TO COPE WITH THE STRESS OF SCHOOL AS WELL AS A REALITY SHOW? I plan to not get stressed in the first place

WHAT MAKES YOU A GOOD CANDIDATE FOR *HOUSE OF ORANGE*?
I don't know

WHY DO YOU WANT TO PARTICIPATE IN *HOUSE OF ORANGE*? to
win the car, obviously

WHAT ELSE CAN YOU TELL ME ABOUT YOURSELF?

```
        @ . . @
      (--------)
    ( > _____ < )

      ^^ ~~ ^^
```

Technically I'm not eighteen yet, but almost eighteen should be close enough. I don't know if high school students qualify for the show, so psychology seemed like as good a fake area of study as any. I'll do that program or whatever that allows me to take college courses too. If that's not good enough for some shitty community college show, it's not like I have anything to lose. And if I'm going to be spending my spring attending some shitty community college, I might as well become a shitty reality show superstar. Move over, Bachelorette.

I filled out and submitted all three sections of the Elbow River application. It left a lot less to creativity than the *House of Orange* form, although it did make an effort to at least appear interesting. All the titles and headers are typed in what looks suspiciously like the Twitter font. I swear, their marketing department must be run by the kinds of parents who think wearing a baseball cap backwards and having a Hotmail account will help them fit in with their children. Is this really the sort of establishment I want to entrust with my future?

Well, what else are you going to do with yourself, Jane?

For starters, I can revise my history. That's what I'm doing here,

isn't it? Rewriting my story so it no longer revolves around the Event. So it no longer stars some washed-up nihilist too uncomfortable in her own skin to do anything worthwhile. People already talk about me behind my back. Maybe it's time I give them something new to talk about.

WedMar9

The parents made another attempt to persuade me to live at home. It was just a formality, really. They know as well as I do what happens when I make up my mind. "Why would you ever move out when you could have free room and board plus family support right here? You shouldn't be alone. Let us do your laundry and provide you with furniture and cook you macaroni and cheese with REAL CHEESE and chew your face off every time you come home later than we think you should and let you know when you're actin' sassy and love you more efficiently by seeing you EVERY DAY and living in the same house FOREVER." So. Pros and Cons of moving out:

<u>PROS</u>	<u>CONS</u>
freedom	macaroni and unreal cheese

The decision basically made itself.

I guess they do have a point about money, though. I'm no mathematician and I'm certainly no economist, but I think this formula is on point:

$$\text{reduced standard of living (student loans + part-time job)} = \text{affordable housing}$$

Two hundred dollars a month is all I can afford to pay for rent, and as far as I know, two hundred dollars won't get me anything besides a room on *House of Orange*. Unless, perhaps, I'm okay with living in

some hoarder's closet, smothered in poorly trained cats and breathing musty thrift store air until my lungs collapse.

ThuMar10

I met Alexander Park today and saw the house. He emailed me back thirty-two minutes after I sent him the application, asking for an interview. This means that either I am incredibly awesome or Alexander Park is desperate for people. When I got the reply I still wasn't sure if this was all a joke, and if it was serious, just how seriously it was being taken. *House of Orange* could mean nothing more than a lonely fourteen-year-old with a GoPro. I don't know how old Alexander Park is, but he has more than one GoPro. He also has four cameras on loan from the school, several computers, and a team of fellow film students wearing orange baseball caps embroidered with the letters HOO. Alexander Park introduced me to each one, but I don't remember all the names. I took a tour of the house, and it's not too bad. The house is a ten-minute bus ride from the school, and it's located in a reassuringly mediocre neighborhood. AP's parents own the place and usually rent it out to students. It's not a big house, but there are six "bedrooms," three up and three down. I have to admire the creative use of curtains and large shelving units. Not exactly conducive to privacy, but privacy's not the point. There's a bathroom on each floor, a living room, a large dining room, and a tiny kitchen with counters possibly made from recycled pylons. Also, orange shag carpet. Everywhere.

The team asked me the sorts of questions one asks on a first date, then talked for a while about the technical aspects of the show. They said enough to convince me it's legit. At least, as legit as a group of film students can make it.

ALEXANDER PARK
So, do you have any other questions?

JS

Well, where exactly are you going with this?

AP

What do you mean?

JS

You said the show would air on YouTube.

AP

Right, episodes every two weeks.

JS

For whom?

HOOCAP 1

Anyone.

JS
(That's lazy marketing.)
Don't you have a target audience, like other college students?

HOOCAP 2

Yeah. Those.

AP

We're going to promote it within the school—advertisements in the paper, commercials at basketball games, things like that. Elbow River has been quite supportive of the idea. This show is our baby. I'm going to make sure it's done properly.

JS

So how can you afford to give away your car?

AP

I'll just get another one.

                    JS
        [thinking]
I see.

                    AP
So what do you think?

                    JS
        [hesitating]

                    AP
The car is the grand prize, of course, and to win it
you simply have to be the last person standing, but
there will be other incentives along the way. Movies,
hockey tickets, books. Things students normally can't
afford.

                    JS
. . .

                    AP
Pizza, home-cooked meals . . .

                    JS
OKAY.

                    AP
Really? Great! That's great. I'll give you some time to
look over the paperwork, etc. . . .

I've told the parents I've found a place, but I haven't mentioned the
"conditions." I'll do that later. They asked if I'll be living with girls,
because of course college-age boyz (and even worse, college-age
men) have no place intruding on a young woman's personal space. I
told them I'll be living with girls, which is true enough.

FriMar11

I got a call from Mr. Dubs today.

> **MR. DUBS**
>
> Good morning, Ms. Sinner. This is Mr. Dubs from Elbow River calling. How are you?

> **JS**
>
> Fine, thanks.

> **MR. DUBS**
>
> Cool! That's great. Well, I have some great news. Your application has been approved!

> **JS**
>
> What? Oh. Good.

> **MR. DUBS**
>
> I'll be your adviser. I've sent you a friend request on Facebook — feel free to message me anytime, you know?

Speaking of Facebook, Bonnie only had a few minutes to chat before her class started, and I needed to know if she was coming over after school or if I should just catch up on *America's Next Top Model* without her.

> **JS**
>
> Yeah. Sure. Hey, I've got to go —

> **MR. DUBS**
>
> You know, we're really happy to have you as a student. We think you have great potential. Elbow River is such a cool place to really grow as a community-oriented individual, you know?

> **JS**
>
> Yeah. Sounds cool. But right now I'm in the middle of . . . making . . . lunch . . .

MR. DUBS

How about I send you a T-shirt? We just reinvented our mascot to better reflect our evolution as a community.

JS

Okay, sure.

MR. DUBS

What are you making for lunch, Ms. Sinner?

JS

Uh . . . donuts.

MR. DUBS

Cool! That's great. Well, you're officially a Greaser now!

JS

Sorry?

MR. DUBS

An Elbow Greaser! Ha-ha.

JS

My donuts —

MR. DUBS

We're going to have a great year, Ms. Sinner.

JS

They're ... burning —

MR. DUBS

Oh, and Ms. Sinner?

JS

Yeah?

MR. DUBS

Like us on Facebook and you'll get ten percent off your online textbooks!

The last basketball game of the season at James Fowler means nothing to me, but Bonnie, Tegan, and a couple other people I could probably stand for an hour or two were watching and I said I'd join. Tom was busy with homework, but he said we'd catch up later. I hadn't been to any games since the Event, and I was really hoping it would be different. That I would be different. That I could sit comfortably in my own skin without the need to censor myself for everyone but Bonnie. But it didn't feel that way. The gym was full of the same squeaks and echoes and unflattering fluorescent lights.

BONNIE
It's been a while, hey Jane? Not since Before.

Bonnie sees things the same way I do: Before and After.

JS
So I'm going. To community college.

BONNIE
No shit! Congrats, I guess?

JS
Thanks, I guess?

BONNIE
So you're really going to do this? The reality show?

JS
Why wouldn't I?

BONNIE
You're not exactly the in-front-of-the-camera type, Jane. What's your game plan — to sit there quietly, popping Prozacs while everyone else has fun?

I'm actually not on antidepressants at the moment. Besides, I was never on Prozac. It was Effexor. It kind of sucks that Bonnie doesn't think I'm serious about this. She's always had my back. But maybe I should cut her some slack. After all, I'm the one who wasted years of friendship refusing to stick up for her sexuality because I thought that was the "moral" thing to do.

JS
It would be nice if you believed I can do this. You're the one with faith, after all. Not me.

BONNIE
Don't be stupid, I know you can do this. It's just . . . different. You having an adventure without me.

Maybe it's time to have an adventure on my own. To be good at something on my own. To show the world I'm more than Bonnie's shadow. It's definitely time to move past James Fowler. I had only been at school for exactly two minutes and three seconds, and already heads were turning my way. I recognized one of the girls looking at me, walking in our direction. Jenna. I was surprised to see her there — she graduated last year. I've run into her once or twice before. More like run behind her. Our jogging paths intersected every now and then, but we've never really talked. I couldn't keep up.

Jenna stopped in front of me.

JENNA
You're that girl.

She wasn't referring to our brief jogging history. Yeah, I'm that fucking girl.

JS
You want my autograph or something?

JENNA
No.

And then she left. Either the joke went over her head or I was devastatingly unfunny. Which doesn't add up, because Jenna is no idiot and I am obviously hilarious. Bonnie's laughter helped calm my heart rate, which for some reason had skyrocketed. I'm trying to build up my resistance to other people's reactions by forcing myself to speak my mind more often. Perhaps Jenna was not the person to test this on.

                    BONNIE
    It's good that you're sticking up for yourself now.

Now, as in After.

                      JS
    Yeah, well, what's the worst that could happen?

                    BONNIE
    That's the spirit.

She craned her neck to follow Jenna.

                    BONNIE
    Why is she back at school?

Bonnie never forgave Jenna for being chosen to hang her artwork in the atrium last year. Jenna's portrait of Nietzsche won out over Bonnie's rendering of Céline Dion. Bonnie still mutters, "She's a motherfucking *national treasure*" every time a Céline song comes on.

                      JS
    I think she used to play. She probably still knows half
    the team.

                    TEGAN
    Don't worry about her, baby.

Tegan placed her hand on Bonnie's knee and ran it up and down her thigh. I threw up a little in my mouth and diverted my eyes. I really didn't want this to turn into a third-wheel situation yet again.

JS
She's still staring at me.

BONNIE
[distracted]
Who?

JS
Jenna!

Jenna is, without a doubt, one of the prettiest girls I have ever come across. I barely know her, but she seems like the kind of girl who does everything with a certain level of intensity, confident in what she wants. I envied that Before. Maybe I still do.

JS
Fuck, she's coming back.

Jenna had a determined look, like she had made up her mind about something.

JENNA
[offhandedly, to Bonnie]
I thought you weren't interested in basketball.

Bonnie was never one to keep her dislikes to herself. She was only at the game because Tegan wanted to go.

BONNIE
And I thought you graduated. What's it to you?

Jenna shrugged and nodded at Bonnie and Tegan's intertwined hands.

JENNA

Nothing. Your girlfriend's pretty good. I thought she'd make the team.

I think Jenna meant it as a compliment, but I can't blame Bonnie for getting defensive about Tegan. The number of passive-aggressive comments Bonnie's received from the church would be enough to keep anyone on edge.

BONNIE

She is pretty good, actually. I don't need you or your team to tell me that.

JENNA

I'm not trying to — never mind. Jane, can I talk to you for a minute?

Bonnie snapped her head toward me, suspicious.

JS

Uh. Okay?

I had no idea what Jenna could possibly want to talk to me about. My heart rate did that skyrocketing thing again. Whatever. I wasn't a high school student anymore. Stupid high school politics no longer applied.

I stood up and followed Jenna to the top of the bleachers, where we grabbed a seat away from everyone else.

JS

What's up?

JENNA

I hear you're going on *House of Orange*.

JS

Uh, yeah. You know it?

I really didn't think the show would be a big deal. Especially not here.

> **JENNA**
> Yes. I know Alexander.

> **JS**
> Ah. He seems cool.

> **JENNA**
> He has his moments.

Then it hit me. Jenna knew about the Event. She was a link between James Fowler and *House of Orange*, and I did not want any links between James Fowler and *House of Orange*. I wanted a clean break, a runaway lane, a tits-to-toes, all-in, no-chance-of-backing-out Jane Sinner Extreme Makeover. Starring Jane Sinner out of context. Out of years of uncomfortable context.

> **JENNA**
> Relax, Jane. I just want to help Alexander with the show.

That confused me. Jenna didn't seem like the type to care about reality TV. Or helping others.

> **JS**
> . . . Why?

> **JENNA**
> I owe him one. To be honest, I was surprised when you signed up. Didn't think you were the type.

> **JS**
> What do you mean, not the type?

> **JENNA**
> I mean, you always seemed like . . . not a goody two-shoes, exactly. A goody one-shoe, maybe.

I should have told her to fuck off. But I'm not Bonnie.

JENNA
Your parents are cool with this?

JS
My parents don't know. Yet. Do you want something from me, or . . . ?

JENNA
Look. The show is an interesting idea. Like I said, I'm just trying to help out Alexander, and that means helping you. You seem a bit out of your league.

She was right. I am out of my league. I hated how obvious it was.

JS
I'm trying to branch out. Away from James Fowler.

JENNA
If you want to talk about it, or you need advice with the show, let me know. If you don't, that's fine. Your call.

My instincts told me to smile politely, thank her for her interest, and run away from the conversation as fast as possible. I ignored myself.

JS
Okay. There's a way you can help. Two ways, actually.

If I'm really going to do this show, I need to be able to talk to people like Jenna. I need to be bold, to borrow her confidence.

JENNA
I'm listening.

JS

The first is that you don't mention this whole situation to Alexander. Including my age.

I waved my arms at James Fowler in general.

JS

The second thing is — wait, do you live on your own?

JENNA

Yeah, I have my own place. Why?

JS

I need a cover story. You don't have to do anything, just let me tell my parents I'm living with you. I don't want to tell them about *House of Orange* just yet. Or that I'll be living with boys.

JENNA

The show hasn't even started, and you're already lying to everyone around you? Nice.

JS

It's not like that.

JENNA

No judgment. And okay. I'll help.

Jenna stood up. I wasn't quite convinced this conversation had actually happened. If she saw through my false confidence, she didn't show it.

JENNA

See you around. Oh, and Jane? Watch out for college boys. Even the good ones can be pieces of shit sometimes.

JS
Well, technically they're only community college boys.
How bad can they be?

Jenna didn't answer.

Some girl I didn't know came up to me after the game.

GIRL
Wow, Jane, it must have taken a lot of courage to come
here. It must be so hard coming back.

JS
It would be a lot easier if you stopped telling me how
hard it is.

I hate how that place puts me on edge. Still.

SatMar12

Bonnie wasn't in the mood to hang out this morning. She said she had
homework, but something about her text — "You should call your new
BFF Jenna so you can talk about where you're going to hang pretentious portraits of overly mustachioed philosophers in your hypothetical dream home together" — made me think she was a tad bitter. Or at
least hungry. I suppose she resents me for consorting with her sworn
enemy after said enemy insulted her in public, if only in her mind.

Relevant text from Bonnie: Sorry for the text earlier. I'm on my period. Also I'm just a bitch sometimes.

I came home from work to find a nice dinner in honor of my tran-
sition into college. Dad barbecued steak and Mom assembled a pre-
packaged salad. The steak was really all I wanted. We ate on the deck,
and Carol and I lay on the spiky brown grass after. Our yard is small,

and unless you are lying down, all you can see is James Fowler High School looming over the fence. I'm sick of looking at it. We lay there for a while and listened to the parents bicker.

MOM

We should have invited her. She's my sister; why can't you learn to get along?

DAD

Jane, be a darling and get me a Coke?

JS

Nah.

DAD

Carol?

CAROL

Okay.

DAD

This is why Carol's my favorite.

JS

Ha, ha.

MOM

Don't change the subject.

DAD

I don't dislike Gina. We just don't have much in common.

MOM

You've never made much of an effort to get to know her.

DAD

So?

MOM

That's not very Christian of you.

DAD
I never trust a woman with more than two cats.

SunMar13

The family keeps acting as though going to community college is a big deal, as though I'm taking a step forward, not backward. As though this makes me an adult. If I'm an adult, what happened to my childhood? What have I accomplished with my youth? It seems like plenty of people my age have record labels, publish autobiographies, go on round-the-world sailing adventures, and win impressive scholarships. What have I done? I certainly haven't found true love, and as far as I know, I did not come into any supernatural powers on my sixteenth birthday. I suppose this is how the "real world" operates. I'm all for hard work and perseverance, but if I have to wait until my youth fades and my energy level drops and my body turns against me before I experience some measure of success, then WHAT IS EVEN THE POINT?

MonMar14

Bonnie and I were supposed to go to a movie tonight, but she canceled last minute to study for a test tomorrow. I'd offer to help, but I know she'd rather study with someone who knows what they're talking about. Like Tom. So instead I said it was fine, we'd catch up later, I have to work tonight.

I don't have to work tonight.

WedMar16

The T-shirt Mr. Dubs promised came in the mail today. It's white and light blue and has ELBOW RIVER HASHTAGS on the front. On the back is #JANESINNER. Below that, in smaller print, is #HASHTAGS. That's their new "mascot," I guess. Trying to be all connected and trendy and shit. But it's the worst thing I've ever seen and I hate it.

I wonder if it's too late to apply to a different community college in a different city in a different country.

FriMar18

Carol barged into my room as soon as she got home from her youth group, probably because she knew it was the last time she could. She flopped onto my bed, limbs spread out as far as possible, like she was trying to anchor the bed in place. Her leggings were an assaulting mess of hot-pink kittens riding frying pans. She really needs to find someone other than Bonnie for fashion inspiration.

> **CAROL**
> But why do you have to move out? Why won't you stay home and go to school?

> **JS**
> Don't tell the parents, but their heavy-handed approach to religion and my inability to fit into their narrow, conservative framework is crushing my delicate and blossoming identity as an autonomous individual.

> **CAROL**
> Sorry, what?

> **JS**
> They're killing my buzz.

> **CAROL**
> But they're gonna miss you.

> **JS**
> They'll get over it.

> **CAROL**
> But what about me?

                          JS

You'll get over it too.

                        CAROL

You've changed, Janie.

                          JS

So?

Poor, sweet Carol. She wouldn't know an existential crisis if it punched her in the face. Carol doesn't have any shameful secrets to hide, unless you count the collection of One Direction posters under her bed she thinks I don't know about.

                        CAROL

You used to be nicer.

                          JS

"Nicer"?

                        CAROL

Well . . . happier. You used to be happy. Right?

                          JS

It's a work in progress, kid.

Carol sighed and kicked her feet against the covers. I'll never resent her for not understanding. I just hope she never experiences first-hand what it's like to fall apart and not have the strength or energy to put yourself back together.

                        CAROL

You promised you wouldn't leave me again.

                          JS

No, I promised I'd be there for you. Which I am. In here.

I gave her heart a tender pat.

CAROL

Jaaanie. This is serious.

JS

I'm serious. You'll love me more when I'm gone. I promise.

She didn't look convinced.

SatMar19

Officially moved in.

Didn't take long at all, despite the storm that insisted on snowing on our parade. The parents helped load all my stuff (which didn't seem like a lot) into my bedroom. I made sure to unload everything when Alexander said no one would be home. I spent the whole morning making up answers to a million dumb questions about Jenna and her four other "friends." Jenna can probably look forward to a card and handmade sweater in her favorite color (which is . . . purple?) for Christmas this year. I'm looking forward to some time away from all these questions.

I've been assigned a basement room. It came with a twin-sized bed, a wooden dresser, and a nightstand with one small drawer. I made sure the parents saw me place my meds inside. Discreet but accessible. I'm still not sure what to do with them, or if they really work in the first place. I have the biggest bedroom in the house, but it doesn't have any windows and the door is a curtain. The parents weren't too thrilled to find only a thin sheet of fabric separating my vulnerable person from whatever college-age boyz might stop by. Of course they assumed the boyz would be here for Jenna and friends, not me.

Everything is clean but old, and the carpet is stained with god knows what. Possibly cat pee, since an overweight cat named Hinkfuss lives here too. The whole basement smells like old vegetables and must. It could be worse.

The girl in the room next to me listens to Meghan Trainor and Iggy Azelea and Nickelback. I could forgive the first two, but we share a cardboard wall. Chad Kroeger has no place in my room. Maybe she is cleverer than she looks, and this is all part of her game plan. In which case: credit where credit is due. She wears a thick layer of orange foundation, and every time I look at her I want to scrape it off with a credit card and vomit. Also, her name is Chanel or Shawntel or Chaunt'Elle or something else unnatural. I don't think we can ever be friends.

The guy across the hall seems all right. He's very alert. And physically unbalanced. Maybe it's the puffy vest and the skinny jeans over toothpick legs and the isosceles triangle nose that sticks out like a sail. I think one strong gust of wind will tip him over. We'll see.

I haven't seen much of the other roommates yet — everyone has been coming and going all day. Which is fine with me. When I wake up, the cameras will be on. I want to be ready.

SunMar20

CAMERAS ON.

We had the official introductions today. Alexander Park insisted we wear Elbow River shirts. I thought he meant the #HASHTAGS shirts, but no. These ones had that We Can Do It! woman from old war propaganda posters, along with the words #ELBOWGREASE printed in bold letters. The shirt is the worst kind of cheap: lumpy, thick cotton with a too-tight collar and stiff graphic that will bend and crack in a million places before the end of the night. I never thought I'd rather drown in a puddle of my own vomit than wear a T-shirt. But I wore it.

All six of us (plus Alexander Park and a couple of HOOcaps) crowded into the living room after AP showed us where all the cameras were. There is a camera (a GoPro, really) in each bedroom, but only half of each bedroom is in the shot. AP explained when exactly we have to be home, and for how long. The first voting ceremony and the first episode won't take place for a few weeks. Whoever is voted out will have to pack up and leave the next day. Sometime before the voting ceremony, we'll have a prize challenge and an immunity challenge. He won't tell us what to expect, though people kept asking, but I'm not worried about challenges yet.

My goal for now is simple: not to be the crazy bitch/douchebag/whiner/girl who cries at everything. Every reality show has one. That person never makes it to the end.

Besides Chaunt'Elle and Nose (whose name is actually Robbie), there is Marc, Raj, and Holly.

Raj and Holly are returning chemistry students in an advanced year-round program, Chaunt'Elle is taking general studies (she's new to Elbow River as well, but she must be in her mid-twenties), Robbie is a new commerce student apparently planning on summer school because he "likes" it, and I have no idea what Marc's deal is. He looks nearly forty, so he should be too old for this shit. I have a feeling he's the crazy bitch. I told them I want to study psychology but I have to upgrade a few high school courses at the same time. I don't know if it works like that, but no one said anything.

One of the HOOcaps made spaghetti, and the six of us ate together for the first time. Alexander Park was clever and bought a case of beer beforehand, but even with the alcohol, things were subdued. I doubt he'll have much usable footage of that dinner, unless he was hoping for awkward silences and embarrassing eye contact. I think Chaunt'Elle was nervous. She talked quickly and fingered her hair and was unnaturally neat eating her spaghetti. She's acting like a high school kid excited to hang out with college boyz. I would know. But of course I don't want to act like I'm the youngest one here, because I definitely am.

Holly seems ridiculously shy. The color of her cheeks speaks for her half the time, and it's almost painful to watch. I don't know what she has to be shy about, though. Raj won't shut up about how smart she is. Raj is quite the charmer.

I think the only other person here as cautious as me is Robbie. He ate neatly too, using a fork and knife on his garlic toast, sitting quietly. Watching. He's the one to look out for, I think.

After supper we watched TV and played card games. More beer came out, and the ice finally broke. I suppose we have Marc to thank for that. He chipped away at it all night, flirting with the jittery Chaunt'Elle and making us laugh with stupid, self-deprecating jokes. He may be a crazy bitch, but at least he's an amusing one. I can't dislike someone who doesn't take himself seriously.

Marc got drunk, of course, and Chaunt'Elle, Raj, and Holly were a little tipsy. I can hold my liquor, but I don't want everyone to know that yet, so I only had a couple. I was also afraid the alcohol would set my cheeks on fire, nervous as I was. Like poor Holly. Robbie didn't drink at all. It felt like a high school party (or at least like the only high school party I was brave enough to attend, thanks to Bonnie), with beer cans littered on the shag carpet and food everywhere and nervous stupidity floating around.

AP pulled each of us aside to a den he calls "the Elbow Room" and did a confessional-style interview, getting our first impressions. I didn't have much to tell him.

Before I went to sleep I spent an hour chatting with Bonnie on Facebook. I think she's more interested than I am in watching this show. She said she's excited for me and wants me to ruthlessly destroy the competition. I miss seeing her every day.

Marc just came downstairs complaining about the asshole who clogged the upstairs toilet. Complaining way too loudly to be innocent. I made the mistake of leaving my curtain open this evening and caught a glimpse of Marc in nothing but his briefs. It was quite startling.

He's been in the bathroom for half an hour now, and I can hear everything, including his plea for someone to bring him a roll of toilet paper.

I don't know what to do.

Some instinct tells me to turn on Hillsong or MercyMe, close my eyes, and pray until it's over. Perhaps if I spent more time in my childhood socializing with secular children instead of praying when I felt uncomfortable, I'd be better equipped to handle this situation.

It's only my second night here and already I'm wishing I had a proper door and window, because whatever Marc did to our bathroom didn't stay in our bathroom.

MonMar21

A HOOcap had to tell Marc to put on his mike twice this afternoon. Half an hour later Raj ordered pizza. He flirted with the delivery girl for a good five minutes before Marc slid next to him like a greasy-ass uncle and assaulted the poor driver with his eyes and weird chin nods.

> ### RAJ
> *[whispering]*
> Come *on*, bro!

The moment was ruined when the HOOcap asked the delivery girl to sign a release form so they could use footage of her on the show. She declined.

Nothing else especially interesting happened today. Or yesterday for that matter. I wonder how long this will continue before the Gamemakers set a fire to flush us out of our rooms so we'll fight to the death in the common area. I mean, interact in the common area.

TueMar22

I have to work tonight. It will be my first shift while living here, so I'll have to figure out which bus to take. Stocking groceries isn't the most exciting job, but it will pay for rent and cake. Now that I'm a college student, I wish I had a job that's a little more romantic. Like a barista or waitress or librarian. Maybe one day.

WedMar23

AP officially launched the *House of Orange* website today, complete with an episode schedule, bonus material, comment forums, and a brief bio of each contestant.

For each bio, he used the headshots he took yesterday, info from each application form, and individualized taglines he pulled from his ass.

Holly

High school valedictorian and field hockey captain. The all-Canadian girl-next-door who has nothing left to prove. Or does she?

Robbie

Quick thinker with a good head for numbers. Cleans his soccer cleats daily.

Raj

Chemistry badass. Like Walter White but less of a dick. Great smile. No meth.

Chaunt'Elle

Loves animals and only eats the ugly ones. Sugar and spice and usually she's nice.

Marc

Self-proclaimed hedonist. Disliked hipsters before they weren't cool.

Sinner

Budding psychologist with unclear motivations. Existential angst in its purest form.

He used a photo of me mid-laugh. One of those rare gems that capture my sparkling eyes and bubbly personality.

ThuMar24

Holly and I went out for lunch. I invited Raj, too, because I was worried Holly wouldn't talk otherwise, but Raj was in the middle of a computer game. Halo or Minesweeper or something.

> ### JS
> So. Any idea how you're going to play the game?

Holly blushed.

> ### HOLLY
> Oh, I don't know. You?

I saw a little bit of myself in her nervousness. So I pretended I was Bonnie, just to break the ice.

> ### JS
> Flash my boobs to the camera and hope for the best.

She gave the tiniest of obligatory laughs.

> ### JS
> You and Raj seem close. Have you known each other long?

> ### HOLLY
> Um. A year.

Holly reminded me of the way I feel when I'm with a friend of Bonnie's, when Bonnie goes for a smoke and I panic inside because I can't think of a single thing to say that doesn't sound like utter trash-crap. The last thing I want to do is tell Holly how quiet she is. People tell me that and it makes me want to punch them in the face.

> ### JS
> So, are we getting dessert?

41

HOLLY

No, thanks.

Her response sounded automatic. I realized she had ordered the cheapest sandwich on the menu, and I've only ever seen her eat no-name-brand food at home. Maybe this is none of my business, but Holly's got to have a reason for attending community college while signing up for a show that provides cheap rent.

JS

My treat.

HOLLY

Oh, Jane, you don't have to! I'm okay, really. It's so nice of you to offer, though.

I'm not nice. Holly's the nice one, which means she's not going to last on this show. There's no way I'm going to let her last longer than me. Especially not until I've had the chance to prove I'm not like her. Not now.

I went grocery shopping with Chaunt'Elle and Robbie after they came home this evening. The experience of choosing and paying for all my groceries was extremely satisfying. I bought cereal and orange juice and apples and a discount cake that reads HAPPY BIRTDAY JIMMY. Hurrah for breakfast foods!

ROBBIE

You're buying that cake for everyone?

JS

No.

ROBBIE

You're going to eat all that yourself?

I tried to come up with something sassy to say, but somehow my brain had become a mess of thick and tangled thoughts.

                              JS
Yes.

                            ROBBIE
You don't think that's kind of . . . gross?

I got the feeling that Robbie thinks a lot of things are gross.

                              JS
Who cares? I just moved out of my parents' place, and I'm ready to embrace my newfound freedom by exploring new dietary options.

That's not actually what I said. What I said was "No."

FreeForAllFridayFridgeMar25

I went for a run this morning in my old gym shorts, with a Tim Hortons gift card (a parting gift from the parents; they believe in well-caffeinated students) tucked inside my hoodie. I ran for half an hour, stopped for coffee, then took my time walking home. It's odd to think of this house as "home." It was about noon when I got back, and I was planning on having a piece or two of BIRTDAY cake for breakfast.

The fridge was empty.

Several icing-smeared plates sat innocently on the counter, and half of the plastic container stuck out of the garbage can.

Just then Raj walked in and placed another icing-smeared plate on the counter. I glared at him. He gave me his most charming smile.

                              RAJ
What?

JS

. . .

RAJ
Fair's fair. It's in the rules.

JS
What rules?

RAJ
On the fridge.

I closed the fridge and quickly read the small printed note pinned under a magnet.

FREE-FOR-ALL FRIDAY FRIDGE
In the interest of space conservation and the prevention of food expiration, EFFECTIVE IMMEDIATELY anything in the fridge is fair game on Fridays.

JS
So everyone helped themselves to a piece of my cake, because Alexander Park said so.

RAJ
Right. Actually, I had two pieces.

He shrugged as if to say, "Oops!"

JS
(You bastard.)

I know I signed away my right to peace and quiet and a bedroom door. But I draw the line at food. At *cake.* If Bonnie were in my place, she'd have it out with Raj here and now and let that serve as a warning to everyone else. I can't afford to act like that; I'm in this for the long haul. I don't want to come across as unstable. I didn't say anything else. I just looked at Raj again (I hope I told him "If you touch

44

my food again, I'll cut you" with my eyes) and went downstairs to shower. Game on.

I spent the afternoon playing video games with Raj and Holly. In all fairness, they're not the worst people I've ever met. We might even be friends, under different circumstances. But I'm not here to make friends. Shouldn't be too hard.

SatMar26

I got paid yesterday, so I bought Bonnie lunch for driving me to and from the northeast to pick up a used mini-fridge I found on Craigslist. I wanted to invite her over afterward, but that would involve paperwork and awkwardness. Bonnie is the only person I've told about *House of Orange* so far. I'm still not comfortable with everyone from James Fowler watching my life play out on the internet. *HOO* is for the people who don't know my backstory.

I was hoping to use that forty dollars I spent on the fridge for more cake and coffee and granola bars, but I think it's wise to invest in a little food security. I wish there was another outlet in my room so I could keep it downstairs, but I only have the one, and there is no space on the power bar. The mini-fridge fits in the corner of the kitchen, which is fine.

MonMar28

The Day Before Classes Start. I've got to psych myself up. Lols lols lols pun. The parents called, and I went outside, away from the cameras, to talk to them. Would have felt weird otherwise. They're concerned and proud and worried that living on my own while starting college might "just all be too much for you right now," but they're praying for me. Thanks.

TueMar29

What I'm enjoying most right now is the anonymity, which I haven't experienced in a while. I'll enjoy it while it lasts. No one here knows who I am or what I did in high school, and so far no one treats me differently from any other glassy-eyed freshman. When the students here learn my name, it won't be for the wrong reasons. This almost feels like a fresh start.

All together I have Intro Psych, Western History, Intro Sociology, and Math, as well as Bio. Might as well get that one over with. But in general, looking good.

I took strange pleasure in sitting at the back of a tiered lecture hall. I don't think that will ever get old.

WedMar30

This afternoon I sat on a wooden bench and read a textbook in the dappled sunlight while drinking chocolate milk and talking to students who don't act like they are five years older than me, even though they are. I spent three hours like that and loved my life. Well, not really, but close enough.

I need to psychoanalyze myself for Intro Psych. I'm not sure how that's possible; the prof was rather vague on the specifics in class today. I was also caught up in a doodle of my hand. I outlined my hand on my notes because the notes were ugly and otherwise useless. I layered the inside with different-colored gel pens until the outline was fairly thick. In the middle of the hand I drew toasters and toast. The whole thing came together really well. One of my better efforts. But I'm not sure how to psychoanalyze myself. I suppose I'll have to be both the doctor and the patient. Maybe the two of me can come up with some profoundly insightful insight.

A middle-aged man with thinning brown hair and a cozy sweater vest motions for Jane to lie down on the sofa. He takes a seat on his overstuffed leather armchair and crosses his legs like a girl.

THE DOCTOR

Hello, Ms. Sinner.

JS

Hi.

THE DOCTOR

Where should we begin?

JS

Don't ask me. That's your job.

THE DOCTOR

Please don't be getting sassy with me, Ms. Sinner. This won't work if we don't maintain a certain level of seriousness.

JS

Understood.

THE DOCTOR

It's interesting that you imagined me as a middle-aged man.

JS

Well, I assumed you'd be in a sweater vest. We both know men look better in sweater vests.

THE DOCTOR

That is a good point. Tell me about your childhood.

JS

Whoa there, Doc. Buy me a drink first.

The doctor lowers his clipboard and scolds Jane with his eyes.

                              JS

Please forgive me. What I meant was, I'm not comfortable
with this sort of thing. I need some time to get to know
you.

                         THE DOCTOR

Ironic, isn't it?

                              JS

Yes.

                         THE DOCTOR

You don't trust therapists? Not even therapists who exist
solely in your imagination?

                              JS

Especially not therapists who exist solely in my imagination.

                         THE DOCTOR

Well, we'll have to work on this issue of trust.

                              JS

I guess.

                         THE DOCTOR

Where would you like to start, Ms. Sinner?

                              JS

Please, call me Jane.

                         THE DOCTOR

See, we're getting there already.

ThuMar31

I dreamed I was walking somewhere and tripped, and I woke up
right before my face hit the ground with my heart in my throat and a

brilliant idea in my brain. I don't know how these things were related, but so it is. Perhaps Freud can help me one day. The psychology experiment I am most familiar with is Pavlov's dog. Classical conditioning. The association of a response (salivating) with a stimulus (a bell ringing). I thought to myself, as the sidewalk rushed toward my face, what if that response was fear? And what if I could use that fear to not only establish my authority early on in the game but also protect my food? I need to go grocery shopping again.

I bought chocolate milk and sugary yogurt and Coke and discount trifle and eggs. I won't have any more money until the rest of my student loans come in, but I'm considering this another investment. I made sure to unload the groceries at 6 p.m. — during designated home time as well as most people's suppertime. So they would see. I'm assuming the sense of entitlement associated with Fridays will stretch out across the week and across fridges, if it hasn't already. Especially with the boys. It's common sense not to trust boys with your food.

I sat down in the living room next to the stereo, just within view of the kitchen. I made sure the stereo was off, turned the volume knob to max, pretended to read my history textbook, and waited. It didn't take long.

Within an hour, Raj walked into the kitchen with his dirty dishes. After placing them in the dishwasher he casually walked over to my mini-fridge. He glanced up at me to see if I was watching, and I wasn't — not directly — because I was looking at the stereo.

Raj opened the fridge. I pressed Power.

The blast of noise scared even me, and I was expecting it. Poor Raj might have shat his pants. I lowered the volume and turned to Raj, meeting his eyes.

JS

Sorry!

49

RAJ
[breathing deeply]
Yeah . . . it's okay.

Raj turned around and walked back to his room.
I smiled.

APRIL

FreeForAllFridayFridgeAprl

Tonight is the first challenge. No one knows what to expect, just that we have to be home at eight. I came home after Bio to chat with Bonnie on FB and keep an eye on the fridge situation. Nothing was taken and only Holly is home right now.

Holly went into the kitchen, so I got up to get myself a glass of water, following her. As she turned her back to me and bent down and opened my fridge, I dropped my glass. It didn't shatter on the linoleum, but it landed with a heavy thump and crack. Holly jumped up and water splashed everywhere.

JS
Sorry about that.

HOLLY
It's okay.

I grabbed a towel to clean up the water. Holly helped, and I almost felt bad.

As soon as we had all gathered in the living room, AP herded us outside. It was still light. Cool but sunny. The air smelled faintly of cow shit. The big field across the street was empty except for a few

HOOcaps, tripods, and a plastic bin. AP placed us in a neat row and dragged a line across the dead grass with his foot. We stood there for a few minutes while AP talked with a HOOcap. With his thick-rimmed glasses, pink T-shirt, and expensive-looking blazer, AP looked like a producer. Like someone who knew exactly how to make an impression, someone who always wore just the right amount of cologne. I wondered what he thought of us. Out of all the contestants, I think Chaunt'Elle looks the most like she belongs on TV. Maybe Marc too, if *Jersey Shore* still counts. Holly is too down-to-earth to stand out, even in that clever shirt (OBEY GRAVITY: IT'S THE LAW!). Raj might pull off a one-line role in a crime show or legal drama. Robbie, with his tight pants, knitted sweater, and scruffy facial hair, is like an indie dream boy.

Holly shivered, fidgeting and giggling with Chaunt'Elle, as we waited for AP. Raj stood with his arms folded. So did Marc, but he wasn't wearing a jacket. He wasn't even wearing sleeves. I suppose he expects the ladies at home to swoon at the sight of his well-muscled arms. Thankfully I am no lady.

When AP finally turned to face us, he pointed to the soccer post at the far end of the field. "Run," he said.

We all looked at each other. AP looked at his watch.

AP

Three. Two. One.

An air horn screeched. We jumped. Marc took off first, arms pumping. The rest of us followed. I ran hard. I couldn't bear the thought of losing to a guy who wears tank tops that are too small just to show off his muscles. I lost anyway. I finished just after Raj, but third place is a waste.

Raj was hunched over, his hand on the post. I stood gasping. Marc lay on the grass, clutching his side.

MARC

Uhhhhhhhhh . . .

RAJ / JS

[breathing heavily]

MARC

Why did I eat six burritos?

Everyone had made it by then. I think Chaunt'Elle would have been red and sweaty like the rest of us if her skin wasn't smothered in makeup.

MARC

My thighs. Five would have been enough. Why did I eat six? It's all going straight to my thighs.

RAJ

Guess you're not as young as you used to be, eh, bro?

MARC

Shut up.

Eventually AP made his way over, calm as ever. Marc rolled over to face him.

MARC

So, man. What did I win?

AP

Nothing. That was a warm-up.

MARC

Are you kidding me?

AP

Okay, good effort, everyone! I'm dividing you up into teams. You three over here, you three over there.

Raj, Robbie, and I walked over to the other side of the goal post.

Marc sulked on the grass for another minute before Chaunt'Elle and Holly pulled him up.

> **AP**
> Here's the challenge. This container is full of balloons. Some of the balloons are filled with water. Some are filled with Kool-Aid. You'll stand in two lines, the first person in each line facing the other line, and on the count of three, you'll throw a balloon at the person opposite you. At their feet, preferably. If the balloon you throw sprays your opponent with water, or doesn't explode at all, you go to the back of the line. The first person to hit their opponent with Kool-Aid wins.

Raj laughed. Chaunt'Elle and Robbie paled.

> **CHAUNT'ELLE**
> But won't that . . . you know . . . stain our clothes?

> **AP**
> Probably.

> **CHAUNT'ELLE**
> But what if . . . you know . . . our clothes get stained?

> **AP**
> Then . . . your clothes are stained. Who wants to go first?

I didn't really care about stains because I prefer to remain emotionally unattached to my clothing, but Raj beat me to the front of the line. Robbie didn't move.

> **JS**
> You coming?

> **ROBBIE**
> No.

I would have tried to convince him, but AP was already counting down. Raj and Holly didn't waste any time hurling their balloons. Holly took one in the chest. To her credit, she didn't shriek. Neither did I, when Marc hit me in the stomach five minutes later. Unfortunately the balloon was filled with lime Kool-Aid. Marc danced around the field like a douchebag while AP explained that he won a twenty-dollar gift card to a restaurant down the street. If I had known we were playing for FOOD MONEY, I would have . . . I don't know what else I could have done. Elbowed Raj out of the way? Doesn't matter now. I'm going to go make myself a pathetic sandwich to eat by myself in my room.

It's not just food money on the line. There's no point being here if I'm not in it to win it. No more goody-one-shoe act, no siree. By the time my old life catches up with this show, I'll be a new person. My confidence will be blinding.

I'm going to pretend I didn't just write "no siree."

Relevant text from Bonnie: I miss you

JS: I miss you too. I wished you were here with me today

BONNIE: Haha april fools

I'm sure what she meant to say is "I'm so lucky to have someone like you in my life and I will cherish our friendship always." Damn autocorrect.

SatApr2

Mom emailed me twice today, sent me three texts, and left one voicemail message. She says she hopes I'm doing okay, and that God wants her to pray for me today. She doesn't understand why I don't always reply, because she still doesn't understand that I flinch every time her pity touches me. She offered to take me shopping for shoes tomorrow. It's a nice gesture but not a selfless one. To her, buying shoes for me is a symbiotic activity. Unfortunately for my mother, I am not like my sister. With Carol, you get what you put into her.

new shoes +
"You can do anything because you're our special girl!"
+ \$20 per A =
undying thanks + visibly boosted self-esteem + tail wagging

I think my parents appreciate Carol's enthusiasm, especially since I don't always respond to external motivation. I don't need shoes right now, and if I did, I'd buy them myself. But I know that's not what she means.

Robbie and I talked tonight. I'm glad he spoke first, because I was about to call him out for being such a lame contestant last night. It turns out he doesn't like getting dirty. It's not just that — he can't deal with being dirty. He can't deal with dirt in general. He came to a house full of other people because he wants to work on this, but a Kool-Aid bomb to the torso would have been too much too quickly. The Unqualified Psychologist in me wants to diagnose him and perform a series of experiments (using desensitization? the placebo effect? classical conditioning to associate germs with benign ambivalence?). Probably I won't do this. I think I would rather be his friend than his shrink. Or at least his ally.

SunApr3
I met the parents for lunch today at a crowded Chinese buffet close to home. Close to their home, I mean. They're average-looking people, but too self-aware to blend into crowds. They had just come from church, and I could smell Dad's hair gel and soap and cologne the moment I saw him from across the restaurant. They asked me how I liked my classes, and how I liked being on my own, and if there was

anything they could do to help. I told them the truth — that I liked classes so far and I liked being on my own and no, there wasn't anything they could do to help — but I didn't mention *House of Orange*. I probably won't until I have concrete evidence of my ability to look after myself. I don't want them to worry more than they have to. I think they trust me. At least, they want to. It's too bad that one Event is enough to wipe out years of accumulated Good Kid credit. And I was a Good Kid. I never had any adventures or did anything unexpected (in their eyes, at least). Until New Year's Eve.

Carol was at a basketball game today, so their undivided attention was on me the entire time. I'm still not used to that.

DAD
You have enough to eat? Enough clothes? Do you need a refill on your prescription?

MOM
Sometimes I look down and see that everything I'm wearing came from Sears.

Fortune cookie: The smart thing to do is start trusting your intuition.
   (in bed)

Robbie is from Saskatchewan, but I don't hold that against him. His parents live in Saskatoon — his dad is an electrician and his mom is a hairstylist. They both emigrated from India twenty years ago. Usually around 9 p.m. I hear Robbie in his room talking softly in Punjabi for a minute or two. I assumed he had a girlfriend or something like that, but it turns out he talks to his mother almost every day. I don't know what he has to say beyond *hello* and *good night*, but I almost find it sweet.

MonApr4
Robbie, Chaunt'Elle, and I have officially formed the Basement

Alliance. Robbie texted us to meet him in the food court this afternoon so we wouldn't be overheard by the HOOcaps. That's the tricky thing about strategizing—we'll be watching the episodes as we play the game, so we don't know what Alexander Park will choose to show or when he'll choose to show it. Robbie's reasons for teaming up make sense. Our rooms are close together, we want to counteract Holly and Raj's friendship, and no one really wants to be responsible for Marc (except perhaps Chaunt'Elle, but she won't admit it). I don't particularly want be responsible for Chaunt'Elle either, but nonthreatening people are the best ones to have with you at the end. Seems pretty straightforward to me. It's amusing how seriously Chaunt'Elle took the alliance—she wanted to sign contracts and swear oaths and spit in handshakes. Robbie and I looked at each other. All we want is to be the last (wo)man standing. Or at least the last two standing. That's what his eyes told me, anyway, but I suppose there is room for error in the interpretation.

Almost all the food I put in my mini-fridge last week is gone, and I am 95 percent sure Raj and Marc have been eating it. Everyone else seems content to stick to Fridays. I applied the stereo technique to Marc, but I haven't been able to catch Raj at it again. I need access to the footage of the kitchen.

I found Alexander Park in the garage this evening. The garage is *HOO*'s headquarters; most of the cameras and several computers are stored there. Underneath the desks lies a collection of beat-up rugs, and several lava lamps are scattered across the room. There's a fridge, heater, coffeemaker, and couch on one side. AP said there is almost always a HOOcap in there, monitoring the GoPros and ready to bring in a proper camera when necessary. The couch had several blankets lying on it, so I doubt there is someone actually watching all the time. I suppose he wants someone in there to be accountable for all that equipment. AP showed us the security system once. It's pretty complicated.

AP was sitting at a desk with headphones on and his back to the door when I walked in. I thought I was being quiet, but he turned around as I closed the door behind me.

AP
Hey, Jane. Is there something you need?

JS
Hi. Yes, I need access to footage of the kitchen.

AP
How much footage?

JS
All of it.

AP
And what do you want to do with it?

JS
Just watch. Study certain habits.

He didn't seem surprised, so I bet he had already caught on to the experiment. He stared at me for a minute, sitting strangely still and looking very small compared with all the empty darkness hanging overhead. It's easy to forget Alexander Park is just a student like me. A much more experienced, attractive, and ambitious student, but a student nonetheless.

AP
You understand I can't give you special treatment. If I give you access to footage, I'm giving you an advantage over the other contestants. If that got out, the credibility of the entire project would be undermined.

JS
Of course. I won't tell if you won't.

I held eye contact as evenly as I could, refusing to be the first one to look away. After another minute, he laughed.

AP

All right. If you're doing what I think you're doing, I want to see how it plays out. But if anyone finds out — your mother or best friend or a pen pal in China — you could be disqualified. Got it?

JS

Yep. Thanks.

He played with the computer next to his for a minute, then pulled out the chair and motioned me to sit down.

AP

You have half an hour.

Half an hour was all I needed. The footage from the GoPro in the corner of the kitchen was open in a video editing program, and I could drag the cursor across the timeline and watch hours speed by. I saw Raj open the fridge once during lunch when everyone else was at school and once in the evening. Marc helped himself the past three nights just before midnight. Once I finished I thanked AP again and left. He raised his hand once as I opened the door to the house, but his eyes never left his computer screen. His single-minded focus reminds me of someone I can't put my finger on.

I've decided the best way to proceed with the experiment is to set up my own GoPro. I found an old model on Craigslist for fifteen dollars. I'll pick it up on my way to work tomorrow.

TueApr5

My support for the Basement Alliance is already crumbling. This afternoon I found a whiteboard in the kitchen, with (dear god) a note about cleaning dishes written on it in careful pink letters. There was even a sickeningly cute smiley face drawn at the end, perhaps meant to trick the rest of us into thinking the author wasn't being passive-aggressively bitchy after all.

Dear Chaunt'Elle:
I know we're on the same team and all which basically makes us BFFs, but I recognize your writing and I've read enough blogs to realize that this sort of "problem solving" leads only to more passive-aggressive notes and resentment all around. If this happens again, we are going to have a lil' chat, and your delicate, nonconfrontational nature will cringe at my bluntness.
Love,
Jane

Hopefully sending this won't be necessary, but today I just snorted in understanding with Raj as we made subtle adjustments with a dry-erase marker to set a slightly different tone.

Hey guys! I know we're all super busy, but if we could just look at the wishes we dream before we put them away, we wouldn't end up with so many dirty wishes in the cupboard. Thanks :)

In other news, I am already behind in my assigned readings by a total of fifty-four pages.

I bought the GoPro and set it up in the kitchen when I got home from work, around eleven. I put it on top of a cupboard, fairly well hidden. I doubt anyone will notice that it hasn't been there all along. I figured tonight would be a good night to try it out, as I'm sure everyone knows by now I usually stock my mini-fridge with newly expired yogurt (still good for a day or two, really) when I work evening shifts. I set the remote-controlled car Bonnie got me when I was in the hospital on the opposite cupboard. If I stand in the corner of my bedroom, I can control the car from the basement. I set up the car so that it would knock over the vase sitting on the edge of the cupboard without falling down with it. At least that's what I hope I did. The camera is working fine. It's almost midnight, so I'm lying low downstairs.

Holly's bedroom is right next to the kitchen, so she heard the crash and came out right away to help Marc clean up the glass. Marc still took a yogurt before heading back to his room, but seeing him jump after walking into the kitchen so smugly in his too small tank top was satisfying. Now I just need a bunch more clever ideas.

> *Jane reluctantly agrees to another therapy session. Apparently, she still has some unresolved issues.*

JS
I think I can save us some time here. I'll tell you my only motivation in life.

THE DOCTOR
And what motivation is that?

JS
The lols. It's the only reason I ever do anything.

THE DOCTOR
This is a good start.

JS
Yes, it is.

WedApr6
If I was still at James Fowler, I'd have a free period with Tom right

now. We'd be meandering through Nose Hill Park, Slurpees in hand, complaining about school and the weather and each other. I'd ask Tom for help on my math assignment, and he would ask me to make him laugh. I'd tell him to shut up, and he'd laugh at that. He laughs at anything, really.

I called Tom.

TOM
Jane! Hey!

JS
Hey yourself. What's up?

TOM
Nothing. Just walking to the park. You? You never call anymore, by the way.

JS
I know. I'm the worst.

He laughed.

JS
That wasn't a joke, Tom.

TOM
Yeah, sure. Hey, can you hold on a sec —

A loud truck or something drove past, and I couldn't make out the rest. I heard laughing in the background.

JS
Who are you hanging out with?

I realized too late I sounded like my mom, trying too hard to be casual when she asks for details about my life.

TOM

Oh, no one. Just a couple of people. A new transfer student and —

Laughter erupted again, drowning out Tom's voice.

JS

Uh-huh . . .

TOM

Hey, Jane, what are you doing Saturday night? We're going to Ashley's farm out in Balzac for the night. You have to come!

We've got a *HOO* challenge Saturday night. I don't know what it is, but I promised AP I'd be home.

JS

I wish I could! But I've already got something that night.

TOM

Like what?

JS

It's kind of a long story, but —

More shrieks in the background.

TOM

Jane? I can't hear you. Can you call back later?

I don't know if *homesick* is the right word, but I can't think of a better way to describe how I felt after he hung up.

Robbie's bedroom smells like bleach. It's empty and too well organized. One wall is carefully covered with posters of Stevie Nicks, and it seems likely that Robbie measured the distance between each one. The uniformity is unnerving. Robbie and I are in the same Intro Sociology class, and we worked on a paper analysis for two hours. And by "worked on a paper analysis for two hours" I mean exactly that, which feels odd. Robbie divides his time up as thoroughly as he divides his wall space. He wastes nothing, and I have to admire that. We got a lot done, before Hinkfuss came in. She meowed loudly and didn't shut up until she took a piss on Robbie's notes. Alexander Park told us she was named for a philosophy prof at the college. I've never met Dr. Hinkfuss, but I can only assume she is long-winded and has little respect for student work. Robbie was annoyed, of course. I'd have offered to lend him my notes, but I doubt Pokémon doodles are much more helpful than cat pee.

Mr. Dubs sent me three Facebook messages this afternoon. He wants to know how I'm adjusting to college. I figured I should reply, since I haven't answered the other seven messages he sent this week.

JS: It's going well, thanks. Classes are good and I'm learning a lot and making new friends.

I should have edited that to make me sound less giddy and breathless, but I wanted to get it over with. He replied instantly.

MR. DUBS: Great to hear, Ms. Sinner!

JS: Could you call me Jane?

MR. DUBS: Of course, Jane. How is everything outside of school?

I wondered if he knew about *House of Orange*. He seems like the kind of guy who would watch it religiously. I don't like the thought of Mr. Dubs watching me on the internet. So I won't bring it up until it's too late.

JS: Everything is good. I'm getting to know a bunch of people I wouldn't normally hang out with.

MR. DUBS: That's great! You know, Elbow River has quite an array of clubs you might be interested in. Stop by my office sometime, and I'll go over them with you!

JS: Yeah, for sure! Can't wait.

I creeped his profile page after. I didn't want to know more about him but couldn't help myself. His cover photo shows him in the middle of a group of students in McDonald's or something, grinning with 25 percent of his mouth and 100 percent of his eyes. I scrolled through a couple profile pics of him on a hike but stopped after thirty seconds. I knew he wouldn't have minded, but I can't help feeling uncomfortable every time I realize teachers and pastors and program counselors are people with lives, too.

I waited for Marc tonight, but he didn't show.

ThuApr7

I'm caught up on reading now, and I want to pat myself on the back/shoot myself in the face. It's strange how all my classes are so disconnected, yet all the profs end up assigning work due the same day.

Bonnie wanted me to go out for supper with her and some other friends. I told her I had assignments to finish, because if I told her I couldn't afford to go out right now, she'd try to pay for my meal.

Everyone in the house except Marc stayed in tonight and watched movies. Holly and Chaunt'Elle watched a romantic comedy upstairs, but I had already seen it, unfortunately. It's about a ruthless and independent businesswoman who GETS THINGS DONE. Eventually she meets a kind and disheveled middle-school science teacher. Her heart melts and leaks all over the place and makes a mess of things, and after discovering that romance is the greatest thing ever, PERIOD, she sells her share in the company and cofounds an orphanage in Mexico. The credits roll after her wedding. It's one of the most depressing movies I've ever seen. Raj and Robbie and I watched a horror film in the basement and had a much better time.

The Doctor has a question for Jane.

THE DOCTOR
Why did you tell Bonnie you couldn't hang out tonight?

JS
I couldn't afford to go out.

THE DOCTOR
Perhaps you were just using that as an excuse. Perhaps you were avoiding her by distracting yourself.

JS
I'm not avoiding Bonnie or distracting myself. Sometimes I'd just rather stay in and eat fuzzy peaches.

THE DOCTOR
Well, fuzzy peaches are quite good, aren't they?

JS
I know, right?!

FreeForAllFridayFridgeApr8
All I wanted was lunch.

I didn't ask for rituals involving secret locations and masks and chanting. I certainly didn't ask to spend the afternoon with Marc. Maybe this is what it takes to fit in as a "college student." And maybe Mom has a point when she says I should work on being more social. I should at least make it part of my game plan and all. She called me this morning to ask if I was making any friends. I don't want Marc to count as my friend. But I ran into him this afternoon and I was hungry and Marc was hungry and one thing led to another.

MARC

I'm going to the Donz.

JS

The Donz?

MARC

Just relax, Jane. I want to get in with these people.

JS

These people?

MARC

Yeah. Do what I do. Act cool. Maybe you'll get in too.

I am pretty sure Marc and I have incompatible definitions of the word *cool*. Still, I followed him out the front door and down the street.

JS

So who are these people? And what does it mean to get in? I don't want to "get in." I just want a quick bite.

MARC

Well, don't tell them that!

JS

Will you at least tell me what the Donz is?

I struggled to keep up with Marc's increasingly long strides.

MARC

Sinner, has anyone ever told you you talk too much?

Of course no one has. And I was quickly losing interest in Marc's cool-guy act.

JS
Whatever. I'm getting something here.

I nodded to the McDonald's in the strip mall ahead. Marc didn't say anything but veered across the empty parking lot ahead of me.

JS
You don't have to come with if you have somewhere better to be.

Marc ran his fingers through his hair while checking himself out in the window. Then he opened the door.

JS
Please tell me this isn't the Donz.

My heart sank when I saw the group of students sprawled around three tables in the back, some of them wearing tacky Elbow River shirts, and each of them wearing a plastic Hamburglar mask. Creepy as shit. In the middle of it all stood Mr. Dubs, sticking out like a gangly weed, his masked head towering over the students. The starchy crease of his slacks cut through the sea of sweatpants like a knife. I'd ignored his last two Facebook messages inviting me to stop by his office. What was he doing here? Before I could ask Marc what was going on, Mr. Dubs's too-long neck swiveled, and his Hamburglar eyeholes snapped on me.

MR. DUBS
Ah, Marc, you brought a friend!

I'm not his friend. I'm not a part of whatever shit show is happening here.

MARC
Yeah, she wanted to tag along. Hope that's cool?

"Tag along"? Really, Marc?

MR. DUBS

Wonderful. Glad you both came. If she proves worthy, Marc, you did well.

JS

Actually, I have to run. I've got to —

MR. DUBS

We always initiate new members here at the Alpha Location. If you pass, we'll let you in on the other Donz locations we visit each week.

I scanned the sea of Hamburglars for some sort of clue as to what in the hell was going on here, but all I saw were dark eyeholes and heads tilted in curiosity.

JS

Okay, but what — what exactly is this?

Marc looked at me like *I* was the idiot in this situation.

MARC

McNugz Club, Sinner.

JS

Sorry, what?

MARC

Chick-En Mc-Nug-Gets Club!

JS

So, you guys just . . . eat . . . Chicken McNuggets?

Marc crossed his arms.

MARC

Ugh, I thought you'd be cool about this, Sinner.

HAMBURGLAR 1

It's like . . . if you have to explain why it's a club, why are you even here?

JS

So what's this about initiation, then? You guys swear an oath or something?

Someone snorted.

MR. DUBS

It's more like a rite of passage. Each of us has done it. Now it's your turn.

I sensed a trap closing in.

MR. DUBS

Twenty pieces, twenty minutes.

Marc clapped his hands together.

MARC

Let's do this!

JS

And that's it? Eat a twenty-pack and you're part of the club?

HAMBURGLAR 2

You come back if you're still lovin' it.

If this was the price of social acceptance, the price was too damn high.

The sea parted as Marc took a swiveling plastic seat. He pointed with his eyebrows at the seat next to him. A million stares were on my back, pushing me forward. Before I knew it, I was sitting down too. I couldn't see Mr. Dubs's face, but I could *feel* his big eyes grow bigger and his weird little quarter smile twitch behind his mask. I didn't approve of his approval.

A Hamburglar with bright green nails placed a greasy container in front of both of us. Marc caught my eye and grinned, like being made to stuff his face with McDonald's in front of an audience was the best thing that could have happened to him.

I couldn't do it. This was not my life. I was better than this.

Who am I kidding?

I am a girl who was kicked out of high school after fucking up therapy, who has since decided that joining a reality show was the best chance of a fresh start.

I am not above the McNugz Club.

And hey, there were no cameras around. So I could always pretend this never happened.

GREEN NAIL POLISH HAMBURGLAR
Dipping sauce?

JS
Uhm. Uhm, honey mustard?

HAMBURGLARS
Ooooh, bold choice.

I was about to start eating, but everyone's eyes were on Mr. Dubs. Waiting. He stretched out the moment and probably stretched out his smile as well.

MR. DUBS
[whispering]
Begin.

It turns out that twenty McNugz starts to look like too many McNugz somewhere after five. I really started to slow down after ten. I gave up on sauce after twelve — I didn't have room, and the tanginess of the honey mustard burned the roof of my mouth. Bold choice, indeed. By then, Marc was dangling the last nugget over his mouth, head tilted back, reveling in the chant of *Nugz! Nugz! Nugz!* that had sprung up out of nowhere and kept getting louder. Marc swallowed his last mouthful, drumming his fingers on the table. The Hamburglars cheered. The woman at the till rolled her eyes.

The chanting didn't stop after Marc finished. I didn't want to keep going, but I did anyway — I lost myself to the rhythm of the Nugz.

Fourteen.

Fifteen.

HAMBURGLARS
NUGZ! NUGZ! NUGZ! NUGZ!

Sixteen.

Seventeen.

There was no stopping it. This is how it happens, isn't it? This is how radicals are born, how monsters are created.

MARC
NUGZ! NUGZ! NUGZ! Ha-ha-ha . . .

The passion in his eyes unnerved me.

The last few nugz were excruciating. I wanted to crush the last one under my heel and set its mutilated remains on fire. Instead, I dunked it in honey mustard. Then turned it over and dunked the other side. Total submersion.

HAMBURGLARS
Oooooooooh!

I ate it all. The crowd went wild.

Marc was way too happy about it, slapping my back like we were bros. Mr. Dubs took off his mask and formally shook our hands. Green Nail Polish Hamburglar high-fived me and invited us out for drinks later.

Look, Mom! I'm making friends.

And, yes. I'll admit it was a little fun to have a crowd cheering me on, although I would have preferred it to be for other reasons. Maybe Bonnie and Jenna were wrong about me not being extroverted enough for the show. This doesn't mean I'm one of the Hamburglars now. I'm not saying I'll go back. All I'm saying, I guess, is that the idea of eating McNugz again at some point in my life isn't completely repulsive.

A little bit of research has shown that the McNugz Club is the third-most popular club at Elbow River, after Recreational Ceramics and Coupon Club. McNugz Club is sponsored, of course, by Mr. Dubs. Dubs's Nugz. They sell T-shirts online.

SatApr9

POKER NIGHT.

Texas Hold'em. Winner takes immunity.

Everything was set up in the garage. Cards, chips, converted billiards table, beer. Gaudy table lamps and a chandelier cast warm light and black shadows everywhere. The best part was Alexander Park: hands resting on the billiard table, arms spread apart, sleeves rolled up. He wore a visor and suspenders, and a lit cigar dangled from his lopsided grin.

AP

Welcome to House of Poker.

Before we got started, a makeup artist powdered our faces to soften the glare of the chandelier. Marc seemed to enjoy that the makeup artist took longer with him than with any of the other guys. Maybe he felt like a movie star. I guess he didn't understand that it was because he has more wrinkles than anyone else.

The makeup artist also had a selection of leather jackets, lipstick, sunglasses, and hats to choose from. Robbie chose a pair of oversize plastic sunglasses. Chaunt'Elle grabbed a leather jacket and fake eye-lashes. Raj took a well-worn leather vest. Holly took a pink bow for her hair. I put on a neon purple baseball cap and bright red lipstick. Marc chose to take off clothing instead. AP stopped him at his box-ers and undershirt. A HOOcap went over the rules while we adjusted our wardrobe. For the most part we looked good. By the time we sat down, we were all ready to play. AP set up the immunity idol (a Don Cherry bobblehead) on the side of the table as motivation.

Holly blew the first hand out of the water. No one saw it coming. Not even Holly. Raj took the next two. Seven empty Coke cans and two close-ups of the sweat trickling down Marc's neck later, AP upped the stakes.

AP
All right, listen up. Whoever takes the next hand wins a
pair of movie tickets.

AP dealt me the three of clubs and the eight of diamonds. The four and the queen and king of hearts turned up in the river. I decided to make everyone believe I had an amazing hand. I really don't know much about poker, but if it's supposed to be all psychology, I should have an advantage.

I studied everyone as subtly as I could. I didn't know them well enough to understand which subconscious behaviors indicated lying, but I had a fair idea of who was uncomfortable. I couldn't figure out Robbie, though. I saw why he chose to wear sunglasses. I'm pretty sure he was watching me, too. I kept my face relatively still, except for a tiny, smug smirk. I'm good at those. Or so Bonnie tells me.

I played the round confidently but reserved. Near the end, only Robbie and I were left. For some reason I was glad it was the two of us facing off, and I let it show, just a little. He kept his chips in tidy, sym-metrical stacks. I called his two and raised him ten, knocking over my own stack. I stared into his sunglasses. He backed down. I showed my cards and half the table swore. Marc was offended that I lied about my hand. I restrained myself from making fun of him openly.

I had three tens the next hand, and played it the same way. Raj thought I was bluffing and raised the stakes substantially. Before calling his bet, I stared at him. I did my best to smolder, but Bonnie has never told me I'm good at that. I wanted to see how Raj would react. He didn't do much, but Holly blushed. I won that hand too.

I dropped out early in the next hand, just to keep things interesting. I wanted the chance to observe Robbie without him observing me back. He won with a pair of twos. By now, Marc was pissed. He knocked over a Coke on Robbie's lap, possibly on purpose. I thought Robbie would run to the washroom, but he stuck it out. I learned that Robbie breathes tightly and rubs his thumb and index finger together when he's really uncomfortable.

I tried to match Robbie's discomfort on the next round. I played everything slightly slower, as if trying to make up my mind. I tucked my hair behind my ears several times and rubbed my thumb and index finger together. I didn't know if Robbie would unconsciously pick up on that, but why not try? He didn't back out, but he didn't raise the bet, either. I also teased Marc about his relative lack of clothing, asking if he was trying to build a fan base for himself by targeting a specific demographic. He kept getting angrier. After some deliberate deliberation on my part, I threw all my chips in. Raj, Holly, and Chaunt'Elle backed out, but Marc and Robbie went all in, too. I had a full house.

Marc had four queens. I swore, but I don't remember if I swore out loud. Marc just laughed insanely — the release after a long buildup. I didn't want to look at Robbie, but I did anyway. I think we realized at the same time that Marc had been playing with us all along.

Marc won the whole thing, of course.

Damn.

SunApr10

Last night I was scrambling for another excuse not to go to church with Carol and the parents when Jenna randomly saved me with a text, asking if I wanted to go for coffee. She had messaged me once or twice in the last month, but I didn't know how to keep the conversation going, beyond answering her questions. She's easier to talk to in person. We talked about her summer plans (now that she's pretty much done with her first year at U of C), which apparently involve staying in Calgary. She was quite interested in how the show was going, so I said she could come over for the afternoon and meet the gang. Which I thought was a good move on my part, because college-age people (like me, wink wink) know other college-age people. I'm pretty sure no one suspects anything so far, but I might as well play it up.

JS

You have to fill out paperwork before you can spend time at the house. Do you want me to let Alexander know you're coming?

JENNA

It's all right. I'll text him myself.

I was kind of looking forward to showing Jenna around the place. Bonnie never wants to come over. She says she prefers life on the other side of the screen.

JS

The house isn't too far from here. It's just —

JENNA

I know. I live down the street from you.

I did not know that.

Jenna didn't wait for me to lead the way up the front walk. She didn't bother ringing the doorbell, either. She just let herself in. I like how she does that. When I used to babysit for different neighbors, back when I was too young to realize that kids are the worst, I'd always triple-check the address and hesitate on the porch before ringing the doorbell.

Raj, Holly, and Robbie were studying in the living room.

JS
Hey, guys. This is Jenna. Jenna, this is Raj, Holly, and Robbie.

They looked at her. Then at me.

JS
Jenna is . . . a friend.

We weren't exactly friends. But "acquaintance" sounded lame. But hey, she's the one who invited me for coffee. Holly looked hesitantly at Raj, who smiled. Robbie looked like he was waiting for us to leave so he could get back to reading. Jenna looked amused by the moment of awkwardness. Playing host is still a new experience for me.

JS
Jenna and I went to the same school. High school. Last year. Jenna's going to university for —

HOLLY
Uh, Jane?

I was kind of surprised Holly interrupted me. I didn't know she had it in her.

JS
Yeah?

HOLLY
We . . . know.

ROBBIE
That's Alexander's sister.

JS

Uh.

Stupid Robbie. Stealing my words again. Raj laughed. Holly looked uncomfortable. Maybe she was empathizing.

JENNA

It's true.

Well.

JS

Uh. Right. You . . . want a beer or something?

JENNA

It's not even noon.

JS

Ah.

JENNA

Besides, aren't you a little young to be drinking?

She said it so casually, but the truth made my cheeks hot. I'm not some high school kid anymore. I have every right to be here. Don't I?

ROBBIE

She's eighteen. She's legal.

JS

(Thank you!)

Yup.

Jenna just snorted delicately — how is that even possible? — and left the living room. I followed.

JENNA

I didn't mean to make you uncomfortable back there.

I was over last week and met Holly and Raj. I think Alexander said you were at work. But I thought you knew.

JS

Uh, nope.

JENNA

I guess we still have a lot to learn about each other.

I nodded, not sure what she meant. I didn't have time to ask before we found Marc in the kitchen, half naked, drinking from the milk carton.

JS

Where'd your shirt go, Marc?

MARC

Oh, I didn't know you had company, Sinner.

JS

Ugh. This is Jenna. Stop violating her with your eyebrows. You're probably twice her age.

MARC

Hardly! Besides, I'm young at heart, babe. Nice to meet you, Jenna.

Marc took a swig of milk and extended his hand. To my surprise, Jenna shook it.

MARC

Will we be seeing you around, Jenna?

JENNA

Probably.

JS

Is that my milk you're drinking?!

MARC

Uh . . .

JS

You are actually the worst.

He took another swig.

MARC

Sorry, Sinner, but I'm pretty serious about my calcium intake.

Jenna laughed. And somehow I was okay again.

MonApr11

We found another note in the kitchen today.

> Sorry, just wanted to say that maybe the way the dishes are left in the sink isn't so great. Maybe we could all spend another 10 minutes when we're making supper to clean up after ourselves. Thanks! :)

Someone (Raj, I think) made this addition in thick, purple letters:

> dishes aren't cleaned and are left in sink; dishes can't be cleaned because sink is full
> maybe, if we all work together, we can overcome the vicious positive feedback loop of uncleanliness. thanks! :) :) :) :) :) :)

to which Holly replied:

> passive-aggressive notes are left on whiteboard b/c dishes aren't cleaned; dishes aren't cleaned b/c

passive-aggressive notes are left on whiteboard. vicious positive feedback loops FTW.

Chaunt'Elle was leaving the house just as I walked in, so I haven't had the chance for a lil' chat yet. Maybe we could have a house meeting. What am I saying? The first voting ceremony is tomorrow. Same thing. I just hope my ally stops being obnoxious long enough to vote the other three out.

I didn't wait up for Marc the past few nights because I've felt like sleeping at midnight. Tonight I made up for it. Around eleven forty I snuck outside with my laptop and waited underneath Marc's bedroom window. His light was on, so I threw rocks at the window and hid around the corner of the house. I was trying to set him on edge. The things I do for research. I watched my video feed, and sure enough, he came into the kitchen just after twelve. I stood at the front door, and as soon as he opened the mini-fridge I rapidly rang the doorbell three times. If I woke up anyone, I'm sorry. Marc spun around and even without the audio I could tell he swore loudly. He walked out of the kitchen, and I swore too as I shut my laptop and nearly tripped over myself running behind the house. Marc opened the door and shouted, "Fucking kids!" into the night air. I crouched by the back door and shook with adrenaline or amusement, I couldn't tell which. I let myself in ten minutes later. I wonder how long I'll have to keep this up before he flinches at the sound of the mini-fridge opening. I hope Alexander Park is enjoying this. I think he is.

TueApr12

I was late for Sociology by fifteen minutes today. I didn't have a good reason. Poor time management I suppose. Even though it's a big class, the prof doesn't let tardiness slide. She makes every latecomer sing in front of the class. Not many people are late. I swear, sociology profs mess with people all the time simply because they know how to. I sang One Direction and wanted to die. Everyone in my class knows my name and face now. I kind of knew this would happen, I just didn't know it would happen so quickly. If that wasn't enough, the prof brought up *House of Orange* as I walked to my seat. AND MADE WATCHING TOMORROW'S KICKOFF EPISODE AN AS-SIGNMENT FOR THE ENTIRE CLASS. Weird. I hope they don't just think of One Direction when they watch me on the show.

No one was late for the voting ceremony. We were all sitting down, ready to go, at 7:55. It took AP and a couple HOOcaps another twenty minutes to adjust the lighting and mikes. AP was very formal about the whole thing. He asked us a couple questions about the game first.

AP

What's the hardest part, so far?

HOLLY

Sharing a bathroom with two guys. Marc is in there all the time.

RAJ
[looking at Marc]

Sharing the TV with everyone else. I'm sick of home design shows.

AP

What's the best part?

CHAUNT'ELLE

So many new friends!

JS
(Barf.)

AP

How are classes going?

82

JS

They're not as bad as everyone said they'd be.

AP

Just wait another month. Okay, if we're all ready, we can start the vote. Marc, you're up first.

Each person went across the room to write down a name on a sheet of paper, *Survivor*-style. AP collected the papers and read them out, one by one. I'll admit, I was nervous. I wasn't afraid of being voted out. I knew I wouldn't be. All I kept thinking was, *My Sociology class is watching this.*

Final count
Chaunt'Elle: 2
Holly: 1
Raj: 3

So Raj is going home (or somewhere else?), which is fine. I think it will feel less surreal once he moves out.

WedApr13

Shit just got real.

We have a theme song.

A *theme song.*

It played over an intro montage of all the contestants. AP labeled me simply as "Sinner." Probably a good call—it's much more interesting than "Jane." He used the intro to make us all look good. Not attractive, necessarily, but appealing. Even Marc.

AP played up the friendship between Raj and Holly and the flirtation between Marc and Chaunt'Elle. Robbie and I look like loners. Maybe we are, I'm not sure yet. He also emphasized Chaunt'Elle's timidity and passive-aggressive tendencies, and put in the footage of Marc jumping in the kitchen when the doorbell rang at night. He didn't connect it to me. Not yet. I imagine it will be quite a victorious moment when he does. The whole episode looks legit, more so than I expected. People actually might enjoy watching this. They might enjoy watching me. I think I need to see it again.

It was strange watching myself. The parents were never big into video cameras. Or cameras. Or technology in general. I had to ask myself: Is this what I really look like all the time? If so, that's not so bad. I look odd next to Chaunt'Elle. Or she looks odd next to me. It's not that I despise makeup. I like the idea of it, actually. But I've never been able to figure out how to use it effectively.

I wonder what my class makes of all this.

ThuApr14

Mr. Dubs just called. I didn't answer because I didn't want to talk to him, so he left me a message. He needs to see me today after class.
Shit shit ugh.

MR. DUBS
Please, have a seat, Jane.

I had done an excellent job of avoiding his office before today. It's a large, clean room with white walls and a window overlooking the courtyard. Mr. Dubs sat behind a thin glass table, his knees bent at an alarming angle on either side of a large blue exercise ball. The hem of his slacks stuck out like tents suspended in midair. I shivered at the inch of skin exposed above his socks. I tentatively sat on a green ball.

JS
What's up?

Mr. Dubs stretched his arms out in front of him and began a series of squats on his exercise ball.

MR. DUBS

Elbow River has always been supportive of *House of Orange*. Mr. Park is a bright, creative young man, and his vision of bringing the community together though digital media is something I am personally quite interested in. I wholeheartedly encourage your participation in such a project, Jane. And while I hoped you would tell me about the show on your own terms, I didn't want to pry. I would never overstep personal boundaries.

I couldn't stop staring at his knees. Up and down.

MR. DUBS

However. After watching last night's episode, I couldn't help but notice some . . . discrepancies, I suppose the word is, between Jane Sinner the reality show star and Jane Sinner the student. Do you follow?

JS

Yes. I'm taking a psychology course this term. I'm hoping to focus more on that once I've earned my diploma.

MR. DUBS

Besides the . . . misunderstanding regarding your area of study, Jane, I believe you led Mr. Park to misunderstand your age. You are seventeen, are you not?

JS

At the moment, yes.

MR. DUBS

Every other contestant is eighteen or older. That makes you the only minor on the show.

JS

My mom always told me I was special.

MR. DUBS

I appreciate your sense of humor, Jane, really I do. But now is not the time or place.

How was I supposed to feel properly chastised when Mr. Dubs and his unnecessarily long limbs performed awkward spider aerobics mere meters from my face?

MR. DUBS

The problem is, Jane, Mr. Park unknowingly promoted footage of a minor wearing an Elbow River shirt drinking alcohol.

JS

(It was just one beer.)

Hmm. I see.

MR. DUBS

I'm sure you can appreciate the position this puts me in.

JS

I'm sorry. I didn't think about it. I should have been more careful.

MR. DUBS

I'm asking Mr. Park to recut that episode to not show anyone drinking.

JS

Are you going to tell him why?

MR. DUBS

That's for you to talk to him about. I can't make your decisions for you, Jane. I can only advise you to do the right thing.

JS

I won't drink on the show again. I mean, as a minor. I'll be eighteen soon.

MR. DUBS

Thank you, Jane. I really do want to see the show succeed. It's quite something, what Mr. Park is doing. It could really be good for Elbow River. I wouldn't want to see you disqualified, or see the show suffer, because of any dishonesty on your part. You're smarter than that, Jane.

JS

You're right. I don't want to mess this up.

I'm quite good at messing things up for other people. Just ask the kids at James Fowler.

MR. DUBS

And Jane?

JS

Yeah?

MR. DUBS

Good luck.

Jenna Park was here tonight. I walked into the kitchen after work, and there she was, talking with her brother over tea. She stayed in the kitchen after Alexander left. She asked me how the show was going these days. I told her AP knew what he was doing.

JENNA

I think you're going to win.

JS

Why do you say that?

JENNA
You're a survivor.

I'm still not sure if that was a joke.

I waited up for Marc again, but from what I heard coming from his room, he was otherwise occupied. I'm trying not to judge Chaunt'elle too harshly. I just hoped they covered the cameras.

FFAFFApr15

I am running out of black gel pens, which is too bad, because pencils smudge. I prefer crossed-out lines to erasing something and pretending it never existed.

I finally used the movie tickets I won at poker to take Carol for a night out. We watched some ridiculous action movie that technically Carol was too young to see. No one called her on it, and she was excited to break the rules and get home after the parents went to bed. She won't tell them. Even though we all know I am no longer a stable influence.

SatApr16

I ran for an extra half hour this morning because I woke up feeling lazy. Hurrah! Way to go, Jane! You can do it! Yeah yeah! Keep up the enthusiasm!

Robbie and I went to Denny's when I got back because we were hungry and I was still too lazy to cook. Breakfast tastes exponentially better the later it gets. After a shallow, sad attempt at discussing the benefits of multiculturalism to modern Canadian society, in order to prepare for a quiz, Robbie asked me why I wanted to do the show.

                                        JS
              To win the car, obviously.

        Robbie didn't say anything for a while. I assume he was looking for
        subtext that did not exist.

                                      ROBBIE
              Do you need a car?

                                        JS
              Not really. But winning one would be exciting.

                                      ROBBIE
              I suppose.

        I couldn't very well tell him I was using the show to reinvent my-
        self, because then he'd ask why. I'm not quite ready to tell him about
        the Event. I almost trust him, but late breakfast at Denny's wasn't the
        right time or place.

                                        JS
              How about you?

                                      ROBBIE
              You already know.

                                        JS
              You want to be able to cope with messiness/eat at a diner
              without sanitizing the table and utensils first?

                                      ROBBIE
              Something like that. Yeah.

        I stacked a pyramid of creamers on top of my overturned mug.

                                        JS
              What about privacy? Do you ever miss it?

ROBBIE

Yeah. All the time. It's nice to be talking to you without cameras around.

He laughed. I balanced a saucer on top of the creamers.

ROBBIE

We should do this more often.

I might have missed out on some subtext there. I'm pretty sure my mind was on food. I hope it was.

Likes: introverts.

The problem with introverts: no one initiates.

SunApr17

A question from my Bio assignment:

Imagine what would happen if you remained a single-celled organism throughout your life. How would your life differ from that of a multicelled organism?

I'm trying to have a positive attitude toward science, but it's hard. I'm not willing to suspend my disbelief. Not for this.

Marc has only shown up at midnight twice in the past two weeks, partly because I haven't bought many groceries lately. One night I waited outside with my laptop after coming home from work and slammed the front door shut when he opened the fridge. The other night I missed out because I was sleeping.

MonApr18

"The plot thickens."

Sometimes things look promising but something small is said

that could mean nothing or something bad. I know that's being vague, but so it is.

TueApr19

A note from Sociology that warmed my insides:

JS: What do you think of this class?

ROBBIE: John Rawls is an interesting philosopher.

JS: I guess. But I'm failing to see the practical implications of this information.

ROBBIE: The veil of ignorance could be applied to *House of Orange*.

JS: How so?

ROBBIE: Imagine you could design the challenges you'd be competing in, but you didn't know what competitor you'd be.

JS: You mean I wouldn't know if I'd be competing as myself, or you, or Holly . . .

ROBBIE: Yes. How would you design the challenges so that no matter who you were competing as, you wouldn't have a disadvantage?

JS: I would design all the challenges to involve swimming.

ROBBIE: But Marc can't swim. What if you ended up competing as Marc?

JS: I would deserve to lose.

ROBBIE: What if Marc wasn't competing?

JS: Um. I would leave everything to luck, I suppose. But luck is no fun.

ROBBIE: More fun than this class?

JS: Anything would be more fun than this class.

That wasn't exactly true. R has a way of making things interesting.

WedApr20

Sometimes, when school drags on, all I want to do is go home and journal about how sometimes, school drags on.

Favorite word to use in an essay: *significant.*

Nothing in the fridge is significant today.

A HOOcap just told me to wipe the Oreo crumbs off my boobs and answer the door. It was Mr. Dubs.

JS

Oh. Hey, there . . .

MR. DUBS

I was just on my way home from the school. Your McNugz Club hat arrived today. Thought I'd drop by to give it to you.

He held it out. It was yellow and red, with lumpy nugget-looking blobs and the words MCNUGZ CLUB on the front. Just as I feared, #JANESINNER was stitched on the back.

MR. DUBS

I guess you didn't get my Facebook message to pick it up from my office.

JS

Uh, no. Thanks.

He didn't look like he was planning on leaving anytime soon.

JS

Well, I don't want to keep you any longer. You must have
somewhere to be.

MR. DUBS

Ah, well. What's the point of rushing?

He was waiting for me to invite him inside.

JS

I'd invite you inside, but you'd have to sign a release
form . . . it's kind of a hassle.

MR. DUBS

I'm not in a hurry.

He's too tall to need to crane his neck to see past me, but he craned
anyway.

JS

Great seeing you! Thanks for stopping by.

I took the hat and stepped back.

MR. DUBS

Well, yes, you —

I closed the door.

This hat needs to be burned, but AP has cameras on the porch. The
damage may already be done.

ThuApr21

Tonight's the night I face the youth group again. I could only put it off
for so long. I've seen almost all of them in and out of school since it
happened, but not all together. And not at church. Bonnie's okay now,
and I can deal with Tom's refusal to acknowledge it ever happened,
but no one else knows me that well. They probably assume nihilism

93

is contagious and those infected with it should only be touched by a fifty-foot pole sanitized in holy water.

Either that, or they feel sorry for me.

I can't stand pity at the best of times. But it's so much messier when religious beliefs are involved. I wouldn't be going if it weren't for my parents, but a promise is a promise. They assume that because Carol is close with her youth group, I should be close with mine. I'm not. It'll be weird. The kind of weird I'm used to by now but will never get used to completely.

I like the church best at night. Hiding under the grand piano, savoring the emptiness of the black sanctuary, and blending into shadows. I'm pretty good at hide-and-seek. I definitely prefer it to truth or dare. Truth or dare makes me nervous. Or at least the truth part does.

> JS
>
> Dare.

> SARAH
>
> Are you sure you want a dare? Or did you mean date? It's just you and Tom in here . . .

Tom winked at me. One misplaced hand in a game of sardines two years ago, and I've never heard the end of it. And they wonder why I don't open up more.

> JS
>
> Dare.

> SARAH
>
> All right. I dare you to sing a Beatles song from the balcony.

The balcony is where the hand incident happened.

JS

What song?

SARAH

"I Want to Hold Your . . . Hand."

JS

Truth.

TOM

Too late for that now, Jane. You can't take it back.

Tom can keep his dirty winks. They don't get a rise out of me anymore. The parents were right—I do need more good Christian influences in my life.

Prayer circles are the worst. Somehow everyone assumes their prayers are only effective if their hands are touching some part of your body.

I know they mean well, but I don't get it. Prayer is just words floating through a room. Prayer is saying, *Yeah, we've got a problem here, but now that we've talked about it out loud, it's in God's hands and there's not much else we can do about it. Thanks for coming, Jane. See you next week.*

I stuck it out for the snacks at the end.

TOM

So, college already, Jane! Who knew you'd be leaving us
in the dust so soon?

If I had left them in the dust, I wouldn't have spent my Thursday night eating Timbits in a musty church basement. And if anyone will be leaving us in the dust, it's Tom. He has a decent shot at becoming valedictorian this year. As Bonnie would say (wink, wink), we've watched him grow into a well-rounded young man over the years. As if the friendship we invested in a knobbly-kneed fourteen-year-old with cargo pants full of ketchup-stained Nintendo DSs has finally paid off.

> **JS**
> It's not that spectacular. And it's community college, not real college.

I could have told them about the show. But I've managed to keep my James Fowler life and my Elbow River life separate so far (other than Bonnie), and I don't want to risk dragging the past into *House of Orange*. A clean slate doesn't stay clean forever, but I'll enjoy it while it lasts. Besides, Tom wouldn't get it.

> **JS**
> I mean, the classes aren't that different. I was expecting it to be harder.

> **TOM**
> That's what she said.

It doesn't matter how smart Tom is, he can still be the biggest idiot I know. Of course I don't want him to make a big deal about it. But some acknowledgment that things have changed wouldn't be uncalled for. I've been going to youth group for years, but somehow it's only tonight that I finally feel too old for this.

> **BONNIE**
> Jane? You want to come outside with me?

Bonnie only says she's "going outside" at youth group. Everywhere else she's "going for a smoke." Bonnie has her own reasons for not fitting in completely here, either. I followed her out, grateful for the escape.

She didn't light up right away, so I knew she had something on her mind.

JS

What's up?

BONNIE

What's up with you, Jane? You seem . . . distant.

JS

I don't know. I guess I'm not really feeling it tonight.

BONNIE

You used to love hide-and-seek.

Everyone always insists on telling me what I used to love, and they all think that if I just go back to loving the same things, we can all pretend the Event never happened. Too bad it doesn't work that way. Once a kid discovers Santa isn't real, reminding her how much she used to love Santa isn't going to make her believe again.

JS

Relax. I'm not depressed again or anything. I just don't fit in here anymore. I feel like I'm not on the same page.

BONNIE

I know you don't see things the same way anymore. I get that. But everyone is still super stoked to see you tonight!

Even Bonnie sees what she wants to sometimes.

JS

You don't understand. I don't believe what everyone else does. I'm a fraud.

BONNIE

Oh, please. Half the youth group still can't wrap their minds around a bisexual Christian, and the other half are only here for the donuts. You're not the only person who struggles with what they believe in. So what if you're confused?

Confusion is when your best friend converts to your lifelong faith, which by all accounts shouldn't interest her, and you have no idea why she's so much better at it than you are. So yes, I used to be confused. But that was Before. Now that we don't share the same faith, whatever divine mysteries may or may not exist are for Bonnie. Not me.

JS
I'm not confused. I'm just not interested.

Bonnie has forgiven me for many things, not least the time in ninth grade when I told her bisexuality was a sin and she was probably going to hell for it. But that doesn't stop me from cringing in the shower every now and then, paralyzed with the knowledge of what a little shit I used to be.

FriApr22

THE DOCTOR
So you've got your self-psychoanalysis paper due on Monday, eh?

JS
So it seems. I'm not making very good progress.

THE DOCTOR
So let's start with what you're feeling now. Or whatever.

JS
Wouldn't it be nice, don't you think, to not constantly compare everything you say and do to everything you've ever said and done and hope one day the good will outweigh the cringeworthy?

THE DOCTOR
I wouldn't know.

JS
Because you're not real.

THE DOCTOR
No. It's because I have my shit together. Brilliant psychotherapists are never plagued with periodic bouts of self-loathing. You wouldn't know.

JS
Oh.

THE DOCTOR
Just kidding; it's because I'm not real.

SatApr23

The five of us spent the afternoon together, studying in the living room. We shared highlighters and complaints and three pots of coffee. Holly told us how Raj had found an apartment with three other chemistry students. All girls. She seemed to want affirmation that a guy moving in with three girls was not a good idea. I had nothing to say. Chaunt'Elle agreed with Holly while assuring her that Raj was too smart to get involved with anyone else. Holly's cheeks turned their usual red as she buried her eyes in her textbook.

HOLLY
That's not what I meant.

ROBBIE
But didn't Raj move in with three girls when he came here?

HOLLY
That was different.

ROBBIE

No.

HOLLY

Yes it was . . .

CHAUNT'ELLE

Raj obviously likes you, he always made you dinner, blah blah blahby blah.

MARC

I knew this girl who made me dinner once. At first I was all like, WTF, quinoa?! But then she lit a candle and I'm like, wait. Wait a second.

Suddenly the room was too small for everyone. I closed my eyes but couldn't stop seeing the single gray hair sticking out behind Marc's ear. I needed to get out. Maybe this is where I start to crack.

JS

Anyone want to go see a movie?

Robbie looked up.

ROBBIE

Do you have something in mind?

JS

There's some psychological drama playing. I hear it's pretty dark.

ROBBIE

Yeah, let's go.

JS

Anyone else want to come with?

No one answered.

HOLLY

I have to study.

MARC

Sorry, that's not my jam.

ROBBIE

Really?

MARC

Yeah. Not a fan of dark movies. Or drama.

I shrugged and turned to leave with Robbie, catching Chaunt'-Elle's eyes on my way out. She gave me a knowing look, and I did my best to dismiss it with my eyebrows but ended up blushing like Holly instead.

The movie was really weird and depressing. I liked it. But we didn't get to see the ending because Robbie got a massive nosebleed. I waited for him outside the washroom to make sure he was okay. He emerged just as the audience began to trickle out of the theater. His face was red with scrubbing, and blood was splattered on his shirt and jacket. He said he was fine, it was just a random nosebleed. I believed him, because sometimes there are no reasons. Also the air was pretty dry.

JS

Are you hungry?

ROBBIE

No.

JS

Are you sure you don't want to split a pizza or something?

ROBBIE

I should probably go back home.

101

You're just saying that because you're feeling self-conscious.

ROBBIE

Yes.

His vanity was endearing but unnecessary. I took a long gulp of my Coke and dumped the remainder on my shirt. Thankfully I wasn't wearing potentially see-through material because I really didn't think it through.

JS

Now we can look stupid together. Let's go.

The pizza was worth it.

SunApr24

I wasn't prepared when Marc opened my fridge in front of me this afternoon.

MARC

Got anything good in here, Sinner?

I panicked. I threw my water at him. He swore.

MARC

What was that for?

JS

I tripped. I'm so sorry.

Marc swore again as he shook himself off and walked out. I toweled off the floor before making my own exit. A HOOcap asked for an interview right as I came out of the kitchen. I couldn't tell if I had been caught red-handed or not, but I was embarrassed anyway. I wish my cheeks were more reliable in situations like this. He sat me down in the Elbow Room and pointed some lights at my face.

HOOCAP

So, Sinner.

JS

Yeah?

HOOCAP

I can call you Sinner, right?

JS

Yeah.

HOOCAP

Tell me about the movie last night.

JS

It was good, I guess.

HOOCAP

And Robbie? Did he have a good time?

JS

I guess.

The HOOcap shifted to the edge of his seat and leaned in until his face was two feet away from mine. He'd look decent enough if it weren't for that ridiculous hat.

HOOCAP

You seem uncomfortable. Are you uncomfortable?

JS

(Yes.)
I'm all right.

HOOCAP

I noticed we seem to have less interview footage with you than with anyone else. Weird, hey?

JS

I guess.

He laughed.

HOOCAP

You're not very talkative, are you?

JS

No.

The rest of the interview was just awkward.

MonApr25

This afternoon I found my first sociology assignment returned to my student mailbox. It was a silly thing, all about goal setting and organization and dreams. The prof should have filled one out herself, since it's taken her more than three weeks to grade it. Got 6/10. Missed points on the career-planning section. Probably because the question asked where I saw myself in a year and I put "in the kitchen, barefoot and pregnant." Robbie got 10/10.

ROBBIE

Why do you say things like that? It's like you don't want people to take you seriously.

JS

I don't want people to take me seriously.

ROBBIE

But how will they know when you mean what you say?

JS

I don't think that's an issue.

ROBBIE

You can't always rely on irony to avoid saying anything meaningful.

JS

What if I'm being ironic ironically?

ROBBIE

Are you?

JS
(Please like me.)

No.

Robbie ran his fingers through his thick hair. The girl sitting behind him noticed.

I wonder what he'd say if I told him the truth about me.

Text from Carol: Hey janie come over 2nite for supper k?
JS: What's the occasion?
CAROL: Just want to see u. I'm making cake.
JS: Of course I'll come. What time?
CAROL: Asap please.

I walked in to find a lumpy, misshapen brown substance covering Mom's best serving platter.

JS

What's that?

CAROL

My second attempt.

105

JS

Nice.

CAROL

Can you help me with the pasta? How long do I need to boil it?

JS

As long as it takes.

CAROL

But how long does it take?

JS

Until it's done.

CAROL

Jaaane . . .

She rolled her eyes. Carol can be quite dramatic at times. I don't know where she gets it from — it's probably just the age thing. I must have been like that too when I was fifteen.

JS

Your hair looks nice today.

CAROL

Really?

JS

Yeah.

Carol tucked a smooth brown strand behind her ear and smiled. I wanted to pinch her cheek but politely refrained.

JS

So what's all this about? Trying to impress the parents?

CAROL

No! I mean, I just want to do something nice for them. Do you think they'll like it?

JS

Of course they will.

The parents were indeed delighted when they came home, half an hour later. Dad started on the garlic bread while Mom went to change out of her work clothes.

CAROL

I like your shirt, Dad. Purple is a nice color on you.

DAD

Actually, it's mauve.

He sighed at me.

DAD

You should invest in some more professional clothes, Jane. Now that you're in college, you need to show your professors that you're responsible and mature. They could be your references when you start applying for other jobs. I might be able to get you a receptionist job in the office this summer. Pays better than the grocery store.

JS

I'll keep that in mind.

CAROL

I like the way you dress. Like you don't care what other people think. Is that a stain on your shirt, though?

JS

Probably.

CAROL

Coffee?

JS

(Beer.)

Yep.

She put her hands on her hips, like a housewife on an old TV show.

CAROL

You drink too much caffeine.

JS

Don't judge me.

DAD

If she doesn't, I will.

JS

(Sigh.)

MOM

You couldn't wait five minutes for me to start eating?

Mom sat down at the table, wearing jeans and a shirt meant for yoga. She wears shirts like that all the time, although I've never seen her exercise. Dad shrugged and reached for more bread, his bald head reflecting the harsh overhead light. Before he could take a bite, the phone rang.

MOM

Hello? No, we just sat down, but it's not a problem. Uh-huh . . . yeah . . . you're sure it was her?

She looked at Carol. Carol withered.

MOM

Uh-huh . . . hmm . . . you can be sure I'll have a talk with her. Thank you for the call.

Click. Silence.

MOM
Would you care to tell me what happened today, Carol?

Carol looked down at her empty plate, her hair hanging in front of her eyes.

DAD
What's going on?

MOM
Apparently Carol was caught skipping class this afternoon. *Smoking a cigarette.*

Dad's entire forehead lifted up an inch. Maybe that's where Carol gets her drama from.

DAD
Excuse me?!

MOM
What on earth were you thinking?

CAROL
[to her plate]
I'm sorry.

Carol looked up at me, eyes huge. Asking for help.

JS
I bet it was science. Shitty class, am I right?

DAD
Jane! Watch your language!

JS
Come on, Dad. What does it matter if I say "shitty" instead of "crappy"?

DAD

You know very well what the difference is.

JS

They mean the same thing.

His forehead slid down an inch and a half.

MOM

Don't try to change the subject, Jane. Carol, would you like to explain yourself?

CAROL

Some kids offered and I didn't want to offend them — it was stupid, I know. But I've never done it before, I swear!

DAD

Go to your room, Carol. We'll talk later.

Carol kicked back her chair, stood up, and ran out of the kitchen. I'm surprised the parents didn't threaten to call Pastor Ron over this. Carol looks up to him almost as much as they do. The parents turned their eyes on me in unison.

DAD

This doesn't have anything to do with you, does it?

MOM

I'm worried, Jane. I thought moving out so soon was a bad idea. And this Jenna person — you hardly tell us anything about her, or what she does. What sort of influence is she?

JS

I know, you've told me several times. And no, I didn't put her up to this. It's just what kids do sometimes. Even the good ones.

I was actually a bit proud of Carol. For breaking the rules. It took me far too long to break any myself.

Dad sighed heavily.

> **DAD**
> Maybe it's something to do with Gina.

> **MOM**
> Oh, give it a rest. You know my sister quit years ago.

> **DAD**
> I just don't know what to think anymore.

I sighed, too. At that moment I was very glad I could simply get up and go. I wasn't stuck here anymore, like Carol. I began loading up my plate with pasta and salad. It would take a while for the parents to cool down, and I didn't feel like sticking around to watch it happen. I grabbed two forks before taking the plate to Carol's room.

I would have slept on her floor that night, but the parents didn't think it was a good idea. And I didn't want Carol to get into any more trouble. Before I left I told her she could sleep over at my place some night, and she smiled. I'll have to tell her about the show. Maybe I should have told her sooner. We're on the same side.

TueApr26

What is ridiculous: how many different scented products a girl could use in one morning. Shampoo, conditioner, body wash, shaving cream, face wash, hand soap, hand lotion, body lotion, facial moisturizer, lip balm, toothpaste, body spray, hair gel, hair spray, and deodorant. So I could, in theory, smell like tropical coconut, pomegranate, zesty lemon, raving razz-berry, apricot, peppermint, orange, green tea, chocolate strawberry, vanilla Coke, spearmint, Hawaiian ginger, cherry secret, and rainstorm ALL AT ONCE. Which is, of course, exactly what I want.

Today's prize challenge took place at school. AP and a HOOcap ambushed Robbie and me outside of Sociology when class let out. A couple students were curious enough to follow us to the atrium, keeping a step or two behind the camera. AP had set up a large booth with orange balloons and posters, where Holly, Marc, and Chaunt'Elle were already waiting. I can't describe the feeling of seeing my face on a poster. I wanted to take a moment to stare and reflect on what my life had become, but there was no time.

AP

Welcome to the second official *House of Orange* prize challenge!

A handful of nearby students clapped.

AP

Several *House of Orange* ball caps are hidden throughout the building. Inside each hat is a number of points. Once you pick up a hat, you have the option to keep it or put it back. You have fifteen minutes to collect five hats. The contestant with the highest cumulative point total wins a two-hundred-dollar gift card valid at the food court on campus. Sounds simple, right?

Chaunt'Elle nodded.

AP

But there's a catch. Some hats have low points but come with small prizes. And some have higher points but come with consequences. If you choose to keep one of these hats, you are also keeping the prize or consequence, no matter if you win or lose the challenge. Understood?

We all nodded. Robbie was already looking around for hats. Holly was looking at the growing crowd of students staring at us. Marc was grinning at a girl way too young for him.

AP

All right! The challenge begins in three ... two ... one
... Go!

We scattered. I headed for the food court, and Chaunt'Elle followed. I found my first hat sitting on a hard plastic chair. It had a sticker with the number 5 inside. I had no idea what range of points was available, so I grabbed the hat and moved on. I found two more in the area—I kept the seven-pointer and left the three. I wandered through the hallway, but Chaunt'Elle grabbed the next two hats before I could get to them. We saw the hat sitting in a plant at the same time, and I bolted. I just managed to grab it before she did. It was worth twenty points but came with a consequence: "Incriminating footage of you will be released on the website."

JS

Nah.

I put it back and headed down a different hallway than Chaunt'Elle. AP's voice screeched from a HOOcap's walkie.

AP

Two minutes remaining!

Something orange stuck out of a garbage can, catching my eye. I reached in to find a hat worth three points and the assurance that the television would be under my control for the next week. I kept it.

AP

One minute!

I still needed two more, so I started jogging. I found an eight-pointer tucked underneath some newspaper.

AP

Contestants, you have thirty seconds remaining!

I looked around, desperate. Nothing.

The only orange hat I could see was the one worn by the camera-man. I panicked and grabbed it off his head. Inside, it read: "1 point + 7 meals of free Chinese food."

JS

FUCK, YES!

AP

Aaaand . . . time! Contestants, please gather back at the atrium.

I made my way over, clutching my hats, relatively pleased with my-self. We all looked pleased with ourselves.

AP

Marc, you're up first. Let's see what you came up with.

Marc handed over his hats, grinning. His total was forty-three. He didn't have any consequences, but he managed to find a hat worth twenty points tucked into a ceiling panel.

HOLLY

How did you see that?

MARC

These blue eyes aren't just for looks. They're for looking.

Holly's total was twenty-eight, and she won exclusive access to the upstairs bathroom for a week, plus a coupon for two free ice cream cones. Chaunt'Elle ended up with a heartbreaking forty-two. She's re-sponsible for cleaning the kitchen every day this week. Robbie's eyes lit up when he heard that. She also had the hat promising incriminat-ing footage. I'm surprised she kept it. Perhaps Chaunt'Elle is less vain than I am?

AP counted my hats next. I came up with a pathetic twenty-two, but the prizes were worth it. Robbie won, with fifty-one points.

CHAUNT'ELLE
He had people helping him, though. He got random students to find hats for him. It's cheating.

AP
It's only cheating if it breaks the rules. I never said you had to do it on your own.

Chaunt'Elle mumbled something about playing fair while I caught Robbie's eye and nodded my approval.

AP
For the next five nights, Robbie, you have a curfew. Which means you have to be in your room, lights out, at eight p.m. You also aren't allowed to use anything in the fridge for a week.

ROBBIE
No problem.

AP
And just a reminder — if any of you choose to not follow through with your consequences, you forfeit the right to vote at the next ceremony. Thanks for playing, guys! I'll see you back at the house.

After he dismissed us, AP began handing out the collected hats to the crowd of students. Smart marketing. But now I'll instinctively assume all these people are pointing a camera at me. School used to be a HOOcap-free zone. Or maybe that was just wishful thinking on my part; it's not like the show doesn't exist outside of the house. That's not necessarily a bad thing. The less I focus on how weird it is, the more I can focus on being a strong competitor. Someone who deserves to win, who doesn't sit back and let other people tell her why she's in the spotlight. I can't forget that I'm the one in charge of how I come across. More or less.

Robbie and I headed outside, away from the swarming mass of HOOcap wannabes, and salvaged the remainder of our lunch together.

Robbie missed soccer practice tonight because of his curfew. It sounds like he spent the night talking to his family on the phone. He'll never complain openly about his curfew, but I feel bad for him.

WedApr27

The five of us watched the latest episode over pizza. It's only been a couple hours since it came out, and already it has two hundred more hits than the first. Maybe I haven't accomplished a lot with my life so far, but not many people can say they have a theme song. So I have that going for me, which is nice.

This episode focused mainly on the "will they or won't they" of Chaunt'Elle and Marc's relationship. I don't think Marc even knows he's in a relationship. And I was not thrilled to see my McNugz Club initiation make it in. I guess some cell phone videos surfaced after the first episode aired. I can't wrap my head around why footage of Marc hugging me against my will, my nauseated face speckled with flecks of honey mustard and nugz, would make Chaunt'Elle jealous. But I'm the first to admit I know nothing about the ways of love.

HOLLY
Oooh, Sinner and Marc! Sitting in a tree!

JS
I'm gonna throw up if you don't stop talking.

CHAUNT'ELLE
Yeah, Holly, don't be immature.

HOLLY

K-I-S-S-I-N-G!

I resisted the urge to punch Holly like I would have punched Carol, if Carol had been squished next to me on the living room couch instead.

CHAUNT'ELLE

Not funny, Holly.

HOLLY

Oh, but they're so cute together.

MARC

Ha. Sinner only wishes she had a chance with me.

ROBBIE

Yeah, right, Marc. Everyone knows it's the other way around.

JS

Let's not talk about this. Ever again.

CHAUNT'ELLE

I second that.

HOLLY

He's not your type, Jane?

Marc's probably twenty years older than I am. And he must be at least ten years older than Chaunt'Elle.

JS

Nah. He's too . . . Marc-ish.

No one needed to ask me what I meant.

HOLLY

[winking at Robbie]

That's too bad. But maybe your heart has already been stolen?

I wish Holly would go back to being quiet and shy. Girls can be the worst.

ThuApr28

THE DOCTOR
Tell me what happened on last night's episode, Jane.

JS
Chaunt'Elle asked Marc if he wanted to go see a movie with her. Marc said no.

THE DOCTOR
Go on.

JS
Chaunt'Elle stood there and told him she liked him. You know. And she wanted to "see if it could go anywhere."

THE DOCTOR
And what did Marc say?

JS
Marc told her to move because he couldn't see the TV. He was watching *Love It or List It.*

THE DOCTOR
And how did she react?

JS
She cried! Haha.

THE DOCTOR
I think you have some suppressed resentment toward Chaunt'Elle. Did you feel happy when she cried?

JS

Yes. Astute observation, Dr. Freudenschade.

DR. FREUDENSCHADE

I want you to tell me why you don't like Chaunt'Elle.

JS

I don't know.

DFS

Does she remind you of someone? Think about it.

JS

. . .

. . .

. . .

DFS

Have you tried to like her?

JS

Yes.

DFS

Have you tried trying harder?

JS

No.

DFS

Okay. I want to do some free association. I'll say something, and you tell me the first words that come into your head. Ready? Penciled-in eyebrows.

JS

Unnatural. Gross. Frozen burritos. Dinner. Burritos! Fridge. Burritos!

DFS

You're not taking this seriously, are you.

JS

No, I am not.

DFS

We'll try again another time.

FFAFFApr29

AP is out somewhere with his sister, and everyone is slacking off at the house. Chaunt'Elle and I played cards with two HOOcaps and Carol, who is staying over tonight. I told her a couple students might be filming me for some dumb school project, and she went along with it. I wanted to tell her more, but I can't be sure she won't slip up in front of the parents. I'm doing so well on my own, I don't want to fuck it up just yet.

I already talked with AP about having Carol over. Because she's underage and isn't signing any releases, AP can't show any footage of her online. Which meant we didn't have to censor ourselves all night. I censored myself anyway. Technically I'm a minor too. Oops. At least I've done my paperwork.

After cards we watched old Disney movies in the living room. I cleaned up Marc's empty beer cans beforehand, but I wondered if Carol might pick up on the smell and mention something to the parents. Then I realized I didn't care. The kid might not even know what alcohol smells like anyway. It's hard to tell how much she knows these days. Carol and Chaunt'Elle got along surprisingly well. They gossiped about boys and celebrities and TV shows while drinking chai tea and painting their nails flashy colors. Carol was delighted with everything. I have the feeling she'll start doing her hair like Chaunt'Elle's now, or, god forbid, her makeup. Carol tends to copy the style of girls she looks up to. Thankfully she doesn't wear as much neon as Bonnie now. The world needs only so many lime-green sweaters.

I texted Robbie (still living with his curfew) throughout the evening to keep him company but had to stop when Chaunt'Elle painted my nails. Normally I turn my nose up at this sort of thing, but it made Carol happy.

CHAUNT'ELLE
What color do you want?

JS
All of them!

CAROL
[rolling her eyes]
Don't be stupid.

JS
Most of them? A different color on each finger, at least.

They laughed at my poor taste.

SatApr30
Carol and I stayed up way too late last night, talking softly in my room.

CAROL
You don't have to sleep on the floor. We can share the bed, if you want.

She grabbed my hand.

CAROL
I don't mind.

JS
I'm not going anywhere.

Every now and then she worries that I'll disappear, and the way she squeezes my hand hard enough to break my fingers breaks my heart instead.

All work and no play makes Jane a dull girl.
All work and no play makes Jane a dull girl.
All work and no play makes Jane a dull girl.

I wanted to hang out with Robbie tonight, but he still has one more night to go. Technically I could have visited him in his room — AP didn't say I couldn't — but Robbie had to have his lights out by eight. It would have looked like something I didn't want it to look like. So we chatted online instead. Robbie has been spending more time than usual on Facebook these days. I don't blame him. He's getting a bit restless though. I created a fan page for him on Facebook and got a bunch of people to like it. So at least he has some stupid viewer questions to keep him occupied, but I think he's over it now. His latest status on his personal profile reads:

This status is a passive-aggressive plea for attention.

To which his mom commented: "oh Robbie, keep your spirits up! your father and I love you and are so proud! you will do great!" (I hit the LIKE button as soon as I saw it.)
    His aunt commented underneath: youre right jasmeet, he will be fine. how are you doing by the way?
MOM: just fine thank you for asking! and yourself?
AUNT: cant complain. took the twins out for a bike ride around the park today. they are getting so big already!!
MOM: tell me about it

Message from Robbie: Moms and irony don't mix.
JS: But moms and ironing do.

ROBBIE: I miss her though. Now and then.
JS: Understandable.

MAY

SunMay1

Raj was over at the house today, hanging out with Holly, flaunting his first piece of fan mail. It read:

> I think you're awesome. It sucks that you were the first voted out. Don't worry about the other contestants, they're all wizards. Let's hang out.

I recognized Bonnie's handwriting right away but didn't tell Raj I knew her. She probably meant it, anyway. Chaunt'Elle complained that she hasn't received anything yet, and I think it's time to do something about that.

MonMay2

Chaunt'Elle's shit hit the fan today. I forgot about the incriminating-evidence hat until I overheard a couple classmates talking about the new video on the *HOO* website. Apparently Chaunt'Elle has brought home a Man of the Night at least twice this month. AP either didn't have permission to show the guy's face or thought it would be fun to keep his identity a secret, because it's hard to tell who it is. Let the speculations begin. AP is such a tease, he wouldn't show anything more than some late-night flirting over open textbooks, half of it off-screen, but the implications are there for anyone to pick up and take to inappropriate places. I'm surprised that I'm surprised, considering we share a cardboard wall. I have a feeling she will be upset about this. But it's hard to feel sorry for her when WE ARE ON A REALITY SHOW AND EVERYTHING WE DO OR SAY AND ALL OUR

CHOICES END UP ON THE INTERNET BECAUSE WE ASKED
FOR THIS.

Yeah, she cried. I asked her why she was upset when she knew what
she was getting into, but she cried some more and said, "It's not
what they think!" So I put some ice cream in front of her in hopes
of keeping her quiet. It worked for a few minutes. Marc was super
nice about it and did the dishes for her and made fun of himself to
cheer her up. Normally this would have delighted her, but under the
circumstances it increased her embarrassment. Marc had no idea
why.

JS
Why were you so nice?

MARC
Because she's a good girl and doesn't deserve this shit,
and I know she'd do the same for me. I believe in being
kind to people who need it. Why were you nice?

JS
Because tears make me uncomfortable.

TueMay3
Went for a run today as usual. It started snowing. Gross.

Chaunt'Elle came into my room this afternoon. Usually she knocks
on the wall beside the curtain before coming in, but today she was too
disoriented.

CHAUNT'ELLE
Jane. I got this stuffed cow in the mail today.

She held it in front of my face. I snorted. It was small with freak-ishly large eyes and big lips.

CHAUNT'ELLE

What does it mean?!

JS

Someone likes you?

She sat down on my bed and stared at the thing in her hands.

CHAUNT'ELLE

Are they trying to say something?

JS

Like what?

CHAUNT'ELLE

Well, it's a cow . . .

JS

I don't get it.

CHAUNT'ELLE

Jane!! Don't make me spell it out!!

Robbie poked his head through the curtain.

ROBBIE

Spell what out?

JS

Chaunt'Elle has a fan.

CHAUNT'ELLE

A guy wouldn't send this, right?! But why would a girl send it?

JS

It's not from Man of the Night, is it?

CHAUNT'ELLE

Man of what?!

ROBBIE

Did it come with a note?

CHAUNT'ELLE

It said, "Best of luck with the show. Robin."

I never meant to insult Chaunt'Elle, only mess with her. Robbie met my eyes, and I kept my face perfectly still and he understood me. I love that. With the slightest of smiles, he took the cow from Chaunt'Elle.

ROBBIE

This looks pretty serious.

CHAUNT'ELLE

I KNOW.

Tonight's immunity challenge was laser tag. It was no surprise— AP has been promoting it throughout school for days, trying to get other students involved in the game. The five of us piled into a van, and AP drove us to the arena himself. It was a good turnout; the arena was packed. The objective was straightforward. The *House of Orange* contestant with the highest score at the end of the night wins immunity. The person (contestant or not) with the highest total score wins a gift card to some restaurant. I have strong feelings about free food, but I resolved to get the highest score for the glory, not the gift card. I have strong feelings about laser tag, too. I finally had a chance to shine.

As we strapped on our heavy electronic vests and put guns in our holsters, I prepared myself mentally. Chaunt'Elle was giddy with excitement and nerves. She wore heavier makeup than usual, probably so it would show up through all the smoke. She asked if I wanted to team up.

JS
No.

CHAUNT'ELLE
Why not?

JS
You'll slow me down.

CHAUNT'ELLE
But we have an alliance.

JS
I know. But I take laser tag very seriously.

Chaunt'Elle rolled her eyes and went to stand next to Robbie. The lights went out and an electronic voice began the countdown. I ignored the chatter and laughter around me and focused on the metal doors as they swung open.

We had thirty seconds to position ourselves before the guns were activated. I ditched the others and ran up the nearest ramp. The arena had three levels, all of them filled with smoke and barricades and flickering lights. It looks like a maze at first, but Carol and I come here so often, I know the place inside out.

The contestants all had to wear HOOcaps — I suppose to make us easily identifiable. I had no desire to be easily identifiable. As soon as the thirty seconds were up, I let myself get hit. While I waited for my gun to reboot, I congratulated the girl who shot me.

JS
Way to go. You're the first person to hit me, so I'm supposed to give you this hat as a prize.

GIRL

Really? Cool, thanks!

She had nowhere to carry it except her head.

JS

Good luck!

I shot her in the back as she walked away.

In laser tag, there are no rules. There are no friendships. There is something wonderfully violent and free about it all that makes me feel invincible.

I made my way to my favorite corner at the top of the arena. I had to climb through a narrow hole to get to it, but once I did so, I had a good view of everything below. It was excellent for sniping. I stayed there for a good ten minutes, making shot after shot, before a HOOcap found me. Security cameras gave me away I guess. The camera couldn't make it through the hole, so the HOOcap stuck it out around a corner at an awkward angle. I knew it would attract too much attention, and I didn't want anyone to find the spot. So I left, running faster than the camera could follow.

I figured if I looked for the cameras, I'd find the other contestants. Shooting them would help me more than shooting everyone else. Marc was the easiest to find, jumping over barricades and running between windows like fucking James Bond. I shot him from behind, then ran up from another angle before his gun rebooted.

JS

Hey, Marc!

MARC

Hey, Sinner. How are you making out?

JS

Not so good. Want to work together for a bit?

MARC

Yeah, I guess. I'm doing pretty well from here, but you can guard my back.

JS

Sure.

His gun flashed and he took aim outside the window, his back turned to me. I shot him.

MARC

Shit.

JS

I think it came from the corner over there.

MARC

Yeah, I think so.

I fired behind us, hitting a target for bonus points, while Marc kept his attention on the corner. I waited until a couple students ran out from another barricade, firing at us, before shooting him again.

MARC

Shit.

I kept this up until Marc's frustration grew so loud, it attracted more attention than I could handle. I quietly left Marc fighting a losing battle and found higher ground. Not long after, the buzzer screeched to end the game. I made my way back to the entrance, tired and sweatier than most people, but I won that round.

Normally after winning a round I'd buy Carol a pop or something to ease the pain of losing. She loves laser tag as much as I do, although I've never let her win. She knows she has to earn it fair and square — it's one of the reasons she keeps asking to come back. I didn't care about anyone else's feelings after this round though. I knew what was coming. People would start to gang up on me, fueled by resentment and poorly formed conceptions of injustice.

Robbie was the first to approach me as the doors opened for the second round. We trotted up the ramp side by side.

ROBBIE

Jane!

JS

Yeah.

ROBBIE

Let's work together this round.

JS

You know I won't.

ROBBIE

But we have an alliance.

JS

I know.

The buzzer sounded. I shot him in the heart. I didn't linger to see his reaction.

As soon as I was alone again, I took off my long-sleeved shirt. I wore a black tank top underneath. I put my hair in a messy bun and hoped I looked different. At least at first glance.

I thought I did well that round, but I came in third. The last and final round was make-or-break for me. I played my heart out, desperate to win.

The final scores came in as we gathered in the lobby, sweaty and tired and sober with the knowledge that not all friendships escaped this ordeal unscathed. I came in second overall. I don't know who Topher M. is but I hate him with the intensity of a thousand fire-breathing dragons. I did win immunity, though. Hurrah.

Second place is a letdown. I wanted to be the best at something, even something as stupid as laser tag. I wanted that tiny bit of recognition from others. I just wish wanting it didn't make me feel so small.

WedMay4

Chaunt'Elle called a Basement Alliance meeting between classes today. I showed up right after Bio, hungry despite the smell of formaldehyde lingering on my clothes, and annoyed with the red marks the goggles had left around my eyes. Robbie showed up a minute later, with chocolate milks for all of us.

> **CHAUNT'ELLE**
> We need to discuss strategy, now that Jane has the immunity idol.

> **ROBBIE**
> Okay.

> **JS**
> Sure.

> **CHAUNT'ELLE**
> . . . So?

> **JS**
> So, Marc is going home.

> **CHAUNT'ELLE**
> Well. I was thinking we could vote off Holly instead.

> **JS**
> *(Are you thinking with your feelings again?)*
> Ugh. Marc is the worst.

> **CHAUNT'ELLE**
> He's not that bad!

ROBBIE

But he's not that great.

I slurped my chocolate milk noisily, waiting for Chaunt'Elle to make her argument.

CHAUNT'ELLE

But that's the point. Holly is super nice. Everyone likes her. What if, in the end, the public votes for the winner? I mean, when it's just two people, we can't just vote ourselves. It wouldn't work. Right?

ROBBIE

It might come down to one final challenge instead. Marc seems to be lucky at those.

JS

Lucky people are the worst.

CHAUNT'ELLE

I don't think that's how it will end. I'm pretty sure Alexander wants to get the public involved at some point. And I know Holly would get more support than Marc would.

Chaunt'Elle was being rational. It didn't make sense.

CHAUNT'ELLE

Well?

I scrunched my eyebrows together. Robbie looked to me.

JS

All right.

I wasn't entirely convinced, but Marc made a convenient scapegoat. And I had a psychology experiment to finish.

Carol was devastated when she found out I'd played laser tag without her. She called to ask where I was the night before, because I had forgotten to show up to her school play.

> **CAROL**
> Janie, you promised!

> **JS**
> I know! I know. I completely forgot. I'm sorry, Carol.

> **CAROL**
> You can't just promise someone something and then not follow through on it. It's not right.

> **JS**
> Thanks for the wisdom, Mother Teresa. But you weren't actually in the play, right? You were a stagehand?

> **CAROL**
> Supportive roles are just as important!

> **JS**
> That's the spirit.

> **CAROL**
> I'm serious, Janie. I barely see you anymore. You promised.

I did promise I'd be there for her. Not just for the play.

> **JS**
> You're right. And I meant it. So how can I make it up to you?

> **CAROL**
> You could come live at home again.

Carol had really gotten the short end of the stick with this whole situation. The Event had hit her harder than anyone else. Then I moved out as soon as I could, and left her alone with the parents.

I can't live there again, though. Not even for her.

JS

Or I could just buy you an ice cream cone.

CAROL

Really, Jane?

JS

How about a round of laser tag next week? Just you and me. I'll even let you win.

CAROL

Yeah. We could do that.

JS

I'm not actually going to let you win, though. You know you don't stand a chance.

CAROL

Just watch me!

ThuMay5

I made supper with Chaunt'Elle this evening because she asked me and I couldn't come up with an excuse not to.

CHAUNT'ELLE

What do you want?

JS

Um. Fettuccine alfredo? I think if we combine our food supplies, we have the ingredients to make it.

CHAUNT'ELLE

What about the sauce?

JS

. . . We make it.

CHAUNT'ELLE

But I don't know how!

JS

Come on, Chaunt'Elle. The internet exists. There's no excuse for ignorance.

Marc heard us talking and came into the kitchen and asked if he could have some.

JS

Do you have any ingredients to contribute?

MARC

Uh, no.

JS

(We have enough food for three people, but you eat for two.)
Do you want to go pick up some?

MARC

Uh, not really.

JS

Then . . . no.

Marc pouted. I bent down to reach my mini-fridge, and as I opened it, a beautiful thing happened. Marc flinched. I almost peed myself, I was so delighted. I told Chaunt'Elle I'd be right back and ran to the garage. AP was there.

JS

Did you see that?!

AP

Yes! I can't believe it worked!

JS

I can.

AP

I need to use this in the next episode. If you have any other fridge shenanigans planned, I suggest you use them before it airs.

JS

I'll think of something.

AP

Good.

JS

. . . Alexander?

AP

Yes?

JS

I'm so happy.

AP

Me too.

FFAFFMay6

This afternoon I hung out in the kitchen, washing dishes and waiting for Marc. He walked in with his eyes glued to his phone, then spent a minute rummaging through his cupboard.

JS

Can I see your phone? I'm thinking of getting a new one and yours seems cool.

MARC

Yeah, sure.

He handed me the phone, and I looked it over, walking back to the sink.

JS

By the way, I think I still have yogurt in my fridge. You can have some if you like.

MARC

Oh really? Thanks, Sinner.

He bent down and placed his hand on the door. I held a small plate above the soapy water. When he opened the door, I let the plate fall.

JS

Oh shit. I dropped your phone in the water.

Marc spun around frantically.

MARC

What?!!

JS

Just kidding! Here it is. It's super nice, by the way.

MARC

Don't do that to me, Sinner!

His pupils were dilated and his face was flushed. I had already succeeded with the experiment. I didn't need to keep messing with him. I felt bad, until he walked out of the kitchen with the entire container of yogurt.

SatMay7

Bonnie wanted to see the new exhibit at the art gallery, I wanted to see Bonnie, and Tom wanted to see me, so the afternoon kind of fell into place. Bonnie knows I still haven't told Tom about the show, so she couldn't bring it up.

BONNIE
Remember the last time we were here?

JS
When you got so excited about that photo of Céline Dion, you nearly broke down in tears?

BONNIE
Passion is not something to be afraid of, Jane.

JS
I'm not afraid of passion.

BONNIE
You're super awkward around it, though. Do you ever get excited about anything?

JS
Well, I got a call from an American number this morning. Turns out I won a cruise. That was pretty cool.

Tom's laugh echoed through the gallery.

BONNIE
Relax, Tom. You're being loud.

TOM
So, Jane, the youth group is doing a fundraiser later. A bottle drive. You in?

JS
No.

TOM

Why, are you busy? I thought we could grab a bite or something after. I mean, all of us. Bonnie too. If you want.

JS

I'm not busy. I just don't want to.

TOM

Come on. The old Jane would be up for it.

Yeah, well, the old Jane would have felt guilty if she didn't go.

BONNIE

Jane can do whatever she wants. She doesn't owe you anything.

She might never fully understand what I want (which is only reasonable, if I'm not sure myself), but Bonnie will always defend my right to want it. I found that photo of Céline on a magnet in the gift shop and bought it for her. She teared up.

SunMay8

I decided to tell him today.

Robbie and I went to the playground across the street to get a break from the cameras. It was one of those rare evenings that feel like a stretched-out afternoon, with the orange sun low in the sky and the air warm and thick. The sort of evening that reminds you of being a kid with a sunburn and the taste of dirt in your mouth, and something about that makes you feel sad, but you can't quite figure out why. Robbie didn't want to sit on the swings at first, but I spent a good five minutes wiping down the seats and chains with my sleeve. I sat down and looked at Robbie until he sat down too. I watched the light hit his dark Roman nose and turn his face into a sundial while he waited for me to speak.

Then I told him I tried to kill myself in high school.

He asked me why, and that was a bit harder to say.

I wish I could blame it on something easily identifiable — like divorce or a death in the family or a traumatic childhood experience — something I could point to and say this is what went wrong. But it's not that easy.

Last October I sat with my parents in church. Everyone was singing. It was a contemporary worship song, one of those three-chord power ballads designed to manipulate the congregation into feeling emotion. A blandly attractive woman with knee-high leather boots stood at the front, mike in hand, arm outstretched, and sang:

My everything, I give to you
My whole life is yours
I love you more than life itself
My whole life is yours.

The parents stood on either side of me, staring at the woman and her boots, singing. I couldn't tell what they were feeling. I sang too. Then I realized I didn't mean it. I had never meant it, and there was no point trying to convince myself of something I didn't believe. I couldn't look at the woman on the stage, I couldn't look at my parents, I couldn't look at the lukewarm sea of half-raised hands. And just like that, I was different. Insincere. A hypocrite.

It took me a few days to realize what that meant. I didn't believe in God. Everything I knew about who I was and what was true became irrelevant. It felt like I was on a roller coaster, sitting at the peak and waiting to drop. Like my chest was a hole and my heart was falling through it, indefinitely. I kept waiting for it to hit the bottom. I wanted it to land, to splatter on something hard and be done with it, but it didn't. It kept falling.

I didn't tell my parents. I knew it wouldn't make sense. I argued with myself instead, telling myself what they would have told me.

They would have fallen back on theological catch phrases, trying to reassure me that everyone went through "spiritual dry spells." That God "tested our faith." That God recognized two types of people, saved and unsaved, and that the saved went to church, and the unsaved went to hell. I tried to understand the argument, tried to see the black and white. I just couldn't. And I couldn't respect a God who damned the majority of humanity to eternal suffering for questioning him.

I kept to myself for a few weeks, thinking. All the questions I'd managed to avoid until then came crashing down on me, prying my mind awake at night. If I never really believed in God, what *did* I believe in? Was I broken, defective, falling apart? Or was my entire family delusional? I didn't see the point anymore, of going to church, of studying and playing by the rules and never being brave enough to speak my mind. Of being Jane Sinner. That person was a shell, a pretender, empty and drifting.

I knew I was clinically depressed, but I never thought I was actually suicidal. I didn't look forward to death, and I didn't hate my life, though I wanted to. Hatred or love — either would have been enough to keep me going. But the slushy indifference I felt for everything and everyone wasn't on the hate/love spectrum. The indifference is what I couldn't stand. And buried somewhere in all that indifference was a tiny black crevice I could never bring myself to look at, because I knew if I did, I'd get sucked down into an infinite void and never find my way out. I told myself life was either all or nothing. At the time it made sense.

I jumped off a small cliff on an acreage at a New Year's Eve party, a spur-of-the-moment decision, thinking the rocks below would be enough to kill me. In retrospect I was tired of being the girl who sat quietly in her best friend's shadow, who didn't know what to do in social situations, who behaved herself and bored herself, who now had trouble getting out of bed and eating and being decent to her own family. I wasn't thinking of any of that on the cliff, though. The only thought I had was "I wonder what would happen."

I never did have good depth perception.

I hit the water instead, or at least most of me did. The chinook saved my life — if it hadn't been so warm that day, the cold water would have done me in, even after I half crawled up the bank. They told me Ben Hwong's dad found me and drove my limp body back to his house in his one-person tractor while shouting at quasi-drunk stragglers to get off his property. I would have liked to have been conscious to be amused by it all. Instead I woke up in a hospital bed a few hours later.

I remember the anger I felt when I woke. Not just anger: hatred. Hatred for the sterile hospital bed, hatred for the numerous hands that had touched my unconscious body, hatred for screwing up something as simple as death, hatred for the inevitable pity and compassion I knew I'd have to face. The hatred made my muscles quiver, and I felt stronger and more alive than I ever had before. It was beautiful. It didn't last.

Next came the parents, the flowers, the visitors I refused to see, the rumors I imagined spreading beyond my room. I spent a few days there, frustrated and bored. Carol was too angry with me to visit, at least the first couple days. Once I saw my dad almost cry. His eyes were red and wet, and as I looked at him, something sharp poked a tiny hole in my numbness. A little bit of pain leaked out. I don't think I've ever believed in regret, but that moment I came close.

I read something in a book once. It said, What if you could look back on your life so far, on every mistake, every triumph, every painful or horrifying or happy or embarrassing moment, and say to yourself, I'm glad for every one of these moments. What if you could say, I wouldn't change a single thing about my life because each thing has made me who I am now. There is no divine plan, no destiny, no life after death, and no compensation for what you lose. There is only here and now. There is only what you've done and what you are going to do. And if you can own up to every moment and take responsibility for your life and shape it into something beautiful and kind and generous — if you can do that, you've discovered what it means to be strong.

Those might not have been the exact words, but it was how I felt like remembering them. I repeated these words to myself over and over and hoped one day they'd sink in. And if they didn't, maybe I could stuff them into that black crevice so I wouldn't accidentally fall in.

This is what I wanted to say to Robbie. What I told him, I'm sure, didn't make enough sense. It's frustrating because he's the only person other than Bonnie I've ever wanted to explain myself to. Of course, I could just hand over my journal and he could read everything I've written in the past year. He'd understand then.

I meant that as a joke, but it's possibly the least amusing thing I've ever said to myself. I can't think of any person — real or hypothetical — with whom I'd willingly share this journal. Especially what I wrote in December and January, before I gave up writing altogether. It would be like standing naked in front of a stranger. They would see how sickly and wrinkled and flabby I really am. They would see every pore on every love handle and would make fun of me for it. I'm not strong enough to withstand that kind of scrutiny. For now, only I can laugh at all my flaws.

I suppose this means Robbie and I share a secret. It used to be my secret, then it belonged to my parents, then my high school. Robbie and I share it now. I can't tell if I'm relieved or not. The nice thing about Robbie is that he doesn't talk too much. He didn't tell me everything was all right, or that I was completely selfish, or that I should get help, or that he understood. He didn't offer empty condolences or say that everything always works out for the best. If Robbie had told me God obviously has a plan for my life, I might have broken his beautiful nose. But he didn't. He just listened. Even though I didn't tell him what happened afterward.

There is one thing I despise more than anything else in existence — more than stupidity, penciled-in eyebrows, or the episode of *Glee* that made me cry — and that is pity. I can't stand it when someone feels sorry for me. It's like touching a hot stove; it hurts, my hand snaps back, I'm self-conscious, and angry for feeling self-conscious.

Pity from my family is slightly less awful, if only because I know they genuinely love me and want me to be happy. But 99 percent of the students at James Fowler High School did not know me. They only knew they should feel sorry for me because my life must have been so terrible, I tried to end it.

Part of me wanted to stay home the rest of the semester and finish my assignments quietly in my bedroom, take my meds each day, shut up, and wait for it to all blow over. I could have done this; several people suggested it. But I didn't want to. It was like a massive bruise had formed in the back of my stomach, and every time someone mentioned what happened or every time I thought about what I had done, something punched me in the gut. Hard. I could have stayed home, and the pain would have eased into a dull ache that throbbed every now and then, but I wanted it to go away completely. So I went back to school and forced myself to look each person in the eye. I listened to all the gossip and felt the pressure of a hundred glances on my back and didn't deny anything that was true. I let countless people I didn't know tell me they were sorry or ask if they could do anything. They all said the same thing, if not with words, then with uncomfortable silences. I let them, and hated every moment of it. If I had stayed home, whatever was wrong with me would have stayed inside my head. I couldn't very well drown myself in introspection and hope for the best (although that's easier said than done). Fixing myself was not something I could do with no one watching. It's kind of funny when I think about it, considering how little regard I have for most people.

By the end of the first day back, my stomach was so sore I couldn't tell the difference between physical and mental pain. I threw up twice in the girls' washroom. The second day was worse. Students I didn't know or didn't like made an excruciating effort to be nice to me. Bonnie wouldn't tell me what she'd heard behind my back until I asked her four times. My classmates thought I was unstable, desperate for attention, pregnant, depressed. They said I ruined senior year. Bonnie always stood up for me, on principle if nothing else. I don't think she understood what had happened, not really. I think it was easier for her to pick a fight with other students than it was to pry details out of me. I don't blame her. It's taken almost half a year for me to figure out how to explain myself, and I'm not convinced I'm doing a good job of it.

I might still be at James Fowler if it weren't for the therapy. I wanted to grit my teeth and force my way through school, not sit with the therapist for hours and try to come up with words that didn't exist to explain why I did what I did. So I skipped therapy. And I skipped a couple classes when it all got too much. The school didn't like that. If I had been someone else, a star athlete or star student, they might have given me a second chance. I wasn't a star anything. The principal talked with my parents, and they all decided for me that I should take time off. They said I was ignoring the problem. I said I was trying to work through it in my own way. I'm still trying.

MonMay9

Hinkfuss woke me up this morning. I don't know why she chose today to pretend we are friends. She rubbed her face on my arm and purred and fell down on my stomach and writhed there. If I had a valid door, I'd have a way to prevent this sort of thing from happening. I don't dislike animals, really. I just can't relate to them.

R and I watched *Armageddon* at his cousin's house tonight. An older movie. Full of heroic people sacrificing themselves for the greater good. We were supposed to write about it, for Sociology—I forget why—but we just talked afterward, instead.

R
[absently]
Ever wonder how you're going to die?

He realized his slip instantly. It was rather funny, how wide his eyes opened.

R
I'm sorry, Jane! I didn't think before speaking. I'm being insensitive.

JS
Sure, I think about it. Everyone dies at some point, whether they want to or not.

R
Yeah.

JS
I suppose dying in my sleep is a good way to go.

R
I guess.

JS
You're not convinced?

R
No. I mean, you only die once.

JS
That's true. So how do you want to go? Saving the world?

He laughed.

R

No. Maybe. I don't know what I'm trying to say.

Suddenly I realized R's cousin had left the room. It would have felt like privacy, if it weren't for the HOOcap standing by the door. I wondered what would happen if the HOOcap left too. Maybe R and I wouldn't be sitting ten inches apart. Maybe our shoulders would brush against each other. The thought of his shoulder touching mine terrified me. As if he could hear my thoughts, the HOOcap put down the camera and the little red light went out.

HOOCAP

Can I use the bathroom here?

R

Yeah, it's at the end of the hall.

I held my breath, then let it go too quickly. *Stop it, Jane. He's competition he's not interested you're not interested.*

R

Can I ask you something?

Breathe.

JS

Yes.

R

I want to be with you, Jane. At the end. Promise me we'll stick together. For immunity, challenges, everything. You and me.

In and out.

JS

Yeah. Okay. I promise.

R

Good.

He smiled, and I swear the distance between us was down to three inches. I don't remember either of us moving.

The toilet flushed down the hall. Whatever moment we were having was about to end.

JS

Robbie?

R

Yeah?

JS

Thanks for not patronizing me. About what I did.

We were down to an inch and a half.

The HOOcap walked in and picked up the camera.

TueMay10

Voting ceremony tonight. Full of waiting and lighting adjustments and awkward silences. I wished AP would have played some dramatic music, either to increase the tension or to turn the whole thing into a parody. But music would have "compromised the production audio," so we suffered through in boredom. I don't envy the editors.

Everyone voted for Holly tonight, except for Holly, who voted for R. Holly cried and Chaunt'Elle cried and Marc and R and I just sat there, feeling vaguely uncomfortable. It's only the second voting ceremony, and already it feels like I've done this a thousand times before.

WedMay11

R passed this to me in class this morning:

Robert T. Patel's Comprehensive Guide to the Individual's Ideal Exit Strategy

Everyone dies at some point: complete this quiz to find out which way is best for you!

Scientific Accuracy Is Possible

(But Not Guaranteed)

1. What is your favorite movie?

A. *The Notebook*
B. *The Godfather*
C. *Fight Club*
D. *Braveheart*
E. *The Lion King*

2. If you could change one thing, what would it be?

A. your quality of life
B. other people
C. yourself
D. the world
E. nothing

3. What is your ideal sport?

A. Wii bowling
B. any sport involving balls
C. martial arts
D. something at the Olympic level
E. watching hockey

4. How organized are you?

A. just enough to get by

B. relatively organized
C. you have your own shit together, but you're not responsible for anyone else
D. very organized; you are able to see the bigger picture
E. not at all

5. How would you describe God?

A. good guy
B. judge
C. irrelevant
D. absentee father
E. it would be nice if he existed

If you scored:

Mostly As: You'd be happy to die peacefully in your sleep after a long and comfortable life. How convenient.

Mostly Bs: A shot to the head; you'll get what's coming to you, as long as it's quick, bloody, and effective.

Mostly Cs: Why leave it up to fate? Fate isn't even a thing. You want control over your life, and you'll decide when to end it.

Mostly Ds: We have a revolutionary! A martyr! It doesn't matter how you're executed, as long as your death changes the world for the better.

Mostly Es: This quiz was a waste of time. Que sera, sera.

Tie: Freak accident. Drive-by shooting? Random allergic reaction? Struck by lightning? It's better not to know.

It *is* better not to know.

The four of us crowded around Chaunt'Elle's computer to watch the new episode tonight. I started laughing as soon as the theme song began, and I might have never stopped, if it weren't for Chaunt'Elle's glare. It was a good episode. Super good. My favorite part was the fridge montage AP put together. He intercut Marc's reactions with footage of me setting everything up and ended on a slow-mo replay of Marc's flinch. Hilarious. Finally I've done something clever, something that will get me one step closer to winning, something worth watching. My second-favorite moment was R's face when Marc dropped a slice of pizza on the floor in the living room and walked away, accentuated with a well-timed zoom. My third-favorite was the montage of passive-aggressive notes left on the whiteboard, intercut with unrelated yet timely reaction shots of all of us. I really need to have that chat with Chaunt'Elle. My fourth-favorite moment was when I told Chaunt'Elle I take laser tag very seriously, and my face when I came in second.

> **CHAUNT'ELLE**
> I can't tell if you're a no-nonsense kind of girl or if you're full of nonsense.

> **JS**
> Full of nonsense. Probably for sure.

> **MARC**
> Seriously, Jane? You were messing with me the whole time?! What the hell!

> **JS**
> Seriously, Marc. You were stealing my food the whole time.

> **MARC**
> Yeah, well . . .

I looked to R for support, but his face was inscrutable.

> **CHAUNT'ELLE**
> I wonder how Holly is doing. It must be hard for her to watch.

MARC

She'll get over it. Why do you keep writing those notes on the whiteboard?

CHAUNT'ELLE

Why do you assume I'm the one writing them?

R

This is bizarre. This whole show.

MARC

Well, who else writes like that?

CHAUNT'ELLE

I don't know. Holly?

MARC

How convenient!

R

Don't you guys think this is weird?

JS

Super weird. Especially the fact that Marc has apparently worn the same tank top for two weeks in a row.

MARC

Shut up, Sinner. I buy them in bulk. It's cheaper.

CHAUNT'ELLE

Don't try to change the topic. Why don't you believe me?

MARC

Who says I don't?

R

Yeah, I have to go. I saw these cute tank tops online, I'm going to order some.

JS

Me too.

MARC

Shut up, Sinner! And what was that bullshit you pulled in laser tag?

JS

The same bullshit you pulled at poker night.

CHAUNT'ELLE

Stop changing the subject!

JS

Good night.

If it weren't for the lack of proper walls in my room and Marc and Chaunt'Elle's bickering, I'd be asleep by now.

ThuMay12

Dear Chaunt'Elle:
There IS NO LEGITIMATE REASON to start the majority of your sentences with "Sorry, I just wanted to . . ."
Love,
Jane

Someone said hi to me today. Not just hi, but Hi, Sinner. Someone I don't know. I suppose that counts for one of the six hundred hits on YouTube. I keep forgetting real people use the internet. Weird weird weird. I guess I'm not coming off as a complete idiot. The show is working then, I suppose.

• • •

DR. FREUDENSCHADE
It would seem you are acquiring a fan base. How does that make you feel?

JS
That question's getting a little old, Doc.

DFS
Just today someone asked to take a selfie with you.

JS
Who cares?

DFS
Like I said, you're gaining quite the fan base. With great power comes great responsibility.

JS
I don't want more responsibility. I'm struggling enough as it is getting to class on time.

DFS
You should probably spend less time taking selfies, then.

JS
Being ambushed by my program adviser doesn't count.

FFAFFMay13
Another note from Sociology.

R: Are you going to Jenna's party tonight?

JS: I didn't know she was having one. I thought we had a challenge tonight.

R: After the challenge. It's Alexander's birthday.

JS: I didn't know he was having one.

R: You should stop living under rocks. It can't be too

comfortable.

JS: Yeah, maybe.

R: I don't usually like parties, but I hear this one is going to be interesting.

People who are going to be there:

1. Alexander
2. All the crew
3. Alexander's cousins
4. Alexander's friends
5. Jenna Park
6. Everyone else.

JS: Lists make everything more epic.

R: Even Jenna?

JS: . . . Jenna Park came out of the womb at maximum epic capacity, which means there was never any room for improvement. I stand corrected.

I have fifteen minutes to kill before AP is ready to interview me. I think Marc is in the interview cupboard now. Everyone else is supposed to sit in their room and wait quietly. AP just finished explaining the rules for the prize challenge. We're watching an episode of *The Bachelor*. Every time the bachelor says

- — incredible woman
- — being open
- — I can see a future with this woman
- — here for the right reasons

or

- — I'm developing strong feelings for some of these women

each team has to take one shot and eat one mini-hamburger between the two of them. The same goes for every time a contestant turns the date activity into a metaphor for her relationship (e.g., falling for him, diving in, taking steps), every helicopter tour, and every time Chris Harrison makes an appearance for no reason.

Bonnie and I watch *The Bachelor* all the time for fun, so I know this will be INTENSE.

After *The Bachelor*, we'll play a game of spoons. We'll sit in the living room holding four cards each, passing one card at a time to the person on the left. As soon as someone gets two pairs, they try and grab a spoon. And as soon as the first person tries to grab a spoon, all the spoons are fair game. Whoever doesn't get one (there are only three) loses. The loser and his/her partner don't get two tickets to the hockey game tomorrow night. The winners do. Also, the spoons will be in the basement.

I won and I won last time too, so I got to choose my partner this time and I chose Marc. Robbie thought we'd be partners because we made an agreement, and so did I, the way his eyes looked at me. Neither of us has been to an NHL game, and I want to go because it's ABOUT TIME. I couldn't drink on camera, but they didn't know that, so I ate burgers. But Marc is a tank and tanked his way through *The Bachelor* and held my arm past Robbie and into the basement. Robbie didn't get a spoon, but that's okay because I did. Robbie ate most of their hamburgers because he didn't drink much either and doesn't want the hamburgers to make a mess on the floor. We're at Jenna's party now because Jenna is an INCREDIBLE WOMAN AND NO ONE WANTED TO LOOK AT CHAUNT'ELLE'S VOMIT ANYMORE. No cameras here, all off-duty, so I had a beer or two. I'm hiding in Jenna's bedroom now because of all the noise. I just realized I'm sitting next to a condom wrapper. I think Robbie hates me.

SatMay14

The only thing worse than admitting to being a jerk is being a jerk and not admitting to it. I didn't choose Robbie because I wanted to win. And I won. I am a jerk. But writing that in here isn't admitting much. At the time, winning was what I wanted more than anything, and I did what was necessary to make it happen. I should feel proud. And I do. But I also might be feeling something else: guilt. It's too bad, really. I thought I outgrew that months ago.

All I want is to watch the Flames beat the shit out of the Black-hawks in a crowded and incredibly loud arena, then congratulate the captain in person and maybe go for a few drinks. Possibly bear one or two of his children. We'll see. But I don't think I'll do any of that now. It seems the shriveled-up, stunted corner of my mind known as my conscience still receives blood flow.

Robbie left Jenna's house before I woke up. Whoever said that I could hold my liquor is an idiot and deserves to be shot. Lifting my head off the couch cushion (and holding it upright for the next hour) was the hardest thing I've done in a while. Someone left Advil on the coffee table (a kind and generous HOOcap, no doubt), and I swallowed a few before splashing water on my face, pulling my hair into a knot, and borrowing one of Jenna's shirts. She won't mind. I discovered several bruises on my arm. I remember Marc pushing Robbie and Robbie falling as we were running downstairs, but I can't remember falling myself. When I left Jenna's house, everyone else was still asleep. No cameras followed me.

I walked in the door to find Hinkfuss licking a half-eaten hamburger on the stairs. The house was a lot messier than I remembered. *Trashed* would be a better word to describe it. I wanted to find Robbie — I assumed he would be in the sanitary haven that is his bedroom — so I could give him my ticket for the game. Symbolically, of course, because Alexander Park still had them. He was too clever to give them to us last night. I was debating how to apologize as sincerely and quickly as I could so I could get back to Jenna's house and fall asleep again (our house smelled terrible) when I heard something move in the kitchen. I walked through the archway, and there was Robbie, on his knees facing the wall, bright yellow rubber gloves up to his elbows, scrubbing god knows what off the baseboards.

Every word I was planning to say died on its way to my mouth. He looked up at me for a moment, expressionless, before turning back to the wall. Not even half the kitchen was clean, and for all I know he'd been there for hours. I tried again to say something — even if it was only "sorry," I wanted to spit it out — but I couldn't. I watched his arm move up and down, up and down, and realized how much it must be eating away at him. Sure, the house was disgusting, but Marc or Chaunt'Elle or I could live with it. I could only guess how incredibly frustrating it was for Robbie to hardly ever feel comfortable in his own home. It struck me how unfair it all was. I wanted to punch something for him.

I gave up trying to say anything. Instead I looked under the sink for another pair of gloves. I filled an ice cream pail full of scalding hot water and disinfectant and set to work on the stove. Every now and then I'd look back at how Robbie was cleaning — I wanted to do a good enough job so he wouldn't have to clean my area again. Following his lead, I scrubbed the stove twice, emptied and refilled my bucket, and scrubbed it again. I scrubbed the cabinets, the countertops, the windowsill. I removed all the food from the fridge, threw some of it out (every item of Marc's may or may not have ended up in the garbage), scrubbed the shelves twice, put everything back. I disinfected each magnet on the fridge and cleaned the doors underneath. The cleaner got inside my gloves and made my knuckles bleed, so I washed my hands and put rubber bands around my wrists to keep the water out. When we finished the kitchen, we started on the living room. Neither of us was hungry. Neither of us said a word.

Nearly all of the food-stained clothes and magazines and dog-eared textbooks and half-eaten bags of processed food in the living room were Marc's. We picked it all up with our rubber gloves and held it with outstretched arms and threw it into Marc's room. We closed his door and didn't look back.

The dining room came next. Walls were washed and chairs wiped down, the vomit cleaned up, and the carpets sprayed. While I vacuumed upstairs, Robbie started on the hallway and bathroom downstairs.

We didn't notice the cameras until the sun went down. They might have been there for hours. It's funny how easy it is to forget them now.

When the basement was vacuumed and the trash taken out, I scrubbed my hands till they bled again, loosely bandaged my knuckles, and sat down next to Robbie on his bed. I was about to say something—the first words I'd spoken all day—but just then the front door slammed shut, shaking the entire house. We could hear Marc from downstairs.

MARC
Holy shit, man! I thought we trashed the place! What happened? Did the producers do this? Fucking awesome! *[And so on.]*

JS
(Is there anything you don't make worse by existing?)

Two loud thumps sounded above us, and I could FEEL the mud where his boots hit the wall. We cringed.

R
He goes next.

I just nodded.

Marc gave Robbie his ticket when he figured out what had happened. And by figured out, I mean one of the HOOcaps had to tell him *No, I am not your maid, and you couldn't have paid me enough to clean up that shit.* Chaunt'Elle was grateful too, I think, but all she did was say thank you.

R and I went to the game tonight and took as much pleasure as was appropriate in winning a playoff game. I didn't even miss not getting knocked up by the captain because I had such a nice time with Robbie. The cameras were only around for postgame burgers and shakes at Peter's Drive-In, so we even had a bit of privacy. We didn't talk about the show, or bitch about Marc, or plan anything. We mostly talked about each other.

I came home to find cat pee on my bed, but I can wash everything tomorrow. I grabbed a sleeping bag from the closet, and I'm comfortable on the floor. Hinkfuss is sleeping beside me, and I don't even mind.

TueMay17
Note from Sociology:

> **R:** Why does the prof keep bringing up the show in class?
>
> **JS:** I don't know. Likes reality TV, I guess.
>
> **R:** HOO is substandard. Even for reality TV.
>
> **JS:** Ha. Yeah. It's no *Survivor.*
>
> **R:** A used car isn't bad, but it's no million dollars.
>
> **JS:** I wish.
>
> **R:** What would you do with a million dollars?
>
> **JS:** Pay off student loans. Buy twenty pairs of jeggings with pockets. And a steak dinner. You?
>
> **R:** Several steak dinners. Maybe a modest house with a

mountain view where I could sit alone and ponder the empty space in my heart that money can't reach.

JS: Ha.

R: I'm not kidding.

JS: Oh.

R: Of course I'm kidding.

JS: Right on.

R: But not really.

Our souls are made of the same stuff.

I had to take the Myers-Briggs personality test for Psych. The results:

Introverted
INtuitive
Thinker
Perceiver

Apparently, as an INTP, I have "trouble appearing warm and supportive to those around me. I tend to devalue emotion in other people as well as myself. Intimate relationships do not come easily to me. I often overlook simple maintenance tasks, such as managing finances and dressing appropriately."

This sums everything up nicely. My hypothetical psychology studies might be redundant.

FFAFFMay20

The parents wanted me to go to youth group tonight because they were doing something or whatever, but I said no because there was an Elbow River costume party and I went to that. The other contestants and several HOOcaps were there too. Bonnie and Tegan came. I invited Tom as well, but it wasn't really his scene. Bonnie dressed as a burly hockey player, and I love her. Of course I didn't want to wear a costume. Of course I had to — so many contractual obligations! I bought a dragon tattoo from the dollar store, but I fucked it up somehow, so I went as the Girl Without a Dragon Tattoo. No one got it. Some girl dressed as a taco won for best costume. Chaunt'Elle came in second as a slutty dentist. I couldn't drink in front of the cameras because I promised Mr. Dubs, so I had to be suuuuuuper sneaky about it. Bonnie is a good friend. She distracted AP while I filled a water bottle with tequila. We did shots in the bathroom. Just the sneakiest. We almost got kicked out. Not because we weren't sneaky enough. It was because Jenna came across Bonnie and Tegan making out after I told her they were missing youth group to be here. At least I think that's how it started. All that I really heard Bonnie say was *"She's a motherfucking national treasure."* Whenever Bonnie starts going on about Céline, it's usually time to go.

SunMay22

Pulled my first college all-nighter, and I've aged ten years in ten hours. I feel good about what I wrote, but maybe I'm only happy to be finished.

JS
HELLO, ACADEMIC SUCCESS!!!!! PLEASED TO FINALLY MEET YOU.

ACADEMIC SUCCESS
Fuck off.

MonMay23

Sister fish and blue bird fly,

Trees devour cups of pie,
Born as velvet, steel I die
— word magnet poem by me, on the fridge

Went out for supper with R and a couple people from school. Two academic-looking guys and one generically pretty girl. The girl was flirting with R all night. I couldn't tell if he was flirting back. I'm clever enough to recognize when I'm jealous, but it makes me feel stupid all the same.

TueMay24

I got my first piece of fan mail today. So many new experiences this week. A postcard from the Elbow River gift shop with the #hashtags logo on the front. The back read:

> Hi Sinner! Just thought I'd say the show is all right. If I was a betting man I'd bet on you. I can't tell if you're quiet and crazy or mysterious and level-headed. It's cool that I can't tell. But I was wondering, what does a typical day look like for you? It's hard to say from the show. I'm not a creepy stalker I swear, but I'm interested in psychology and the effects a reality show would have on a competitor. Any illumination you would care to share with me would be appreciated.
>
> Sincerely,
>
> a Fan (James)

I bought a pack of stationery from the gift shop between classes and wrote my reply:

> Dear James,
> Thank you for your interest in my personal life. I've

never had a Fan before, and I am moderately pleased to have you. As requested, below is a somewhat accurate account of an average day in my life. From one budding psychologist to another.

7:00 a.m.: Wake up.

7:05 a.m.: Go for a run. Run run run.

7:33 a.m.: Wait for Chaunt'Elle to get out of the shower. Tell myself I'll wake up earlier than her tomorrow. Realize I'm lying to myself. Realize inauthenticity is not a good way to start my day.

7:35 a.m.: Existential angst.

7:45 a.m.: Shower.

8:00 a.m.: Get dressed.

8:03 a.m.: Change my clothes for the third time. Bemoan my vanity.

8:05 a.m.: Existential angst.

8:10 a.m.: Coffee and chitchat with Chaunt'Elle and Robbie.

8:30 a.m.: Catch a bus.

8:55 a.m.: Arrive in class.

9:00 a.m.: Pay attention and doodle.

12:00 p.m.: Have lunch. Answer fan mail.

1:00 p.m.: Class. Pay attention and doodle. Daydream about food.

4:15 p.m.: Catch a bus.

4:45 p.m.: Arrive at work.

5:00 p.m.: Work.

5:30 p.m.: Arrange display of soup cans.

7:00 p.m.: Assist the elderly with heavy bags.

8:30 p.m.: Work. Work work work.

8:50 p.m.: Time stands still.

9:30 p.m.: Arrive home and put recently purchased food items in mini-fridge. Wonder how long they will last before someone eats them. Bemoan the transient nature of food items.

9:40 p.m.: Existential angst.

9:50 p.m.: Interview for the show.

10:00 p.m.: Intensive and uninterrupted studying.

11:30 p.m.: Chat with Robbie.

12:00 midnight: Sleep.

Regards,
J. Sinner

WedMay25

I grabbed a coffee with Bonnie and Tom after classes. We've been meaning to get together for a while now, but if I'm not busy with the show, they're busy with school and youth group. Our lives are slipping out of sync. Bonnie is trying to start a food drive at the school to help the homeless, and Tom is overpreparing himself for university in the fall. Once again, I considered telling him about the show. But I didn't. I don't even know why. Anyway, they were too excited about grad to pry the details of my life from me. I was kind of hoping that if I didn't think about graduation, it would go away. But I can't ignore it completely, now that I've promised them I'd go. It's next week already. All the conference centers in the city are booked up with grad ceremonies at the end of June, so James Fowler books theirs earlier. Anticlimactic, I know. But I'll be there. Yahoo.

> **BONNIE**
> I'm so pumped. You have no idea.

> **JS**
> Yeah, it might be fun, I guess.

> **TOM**
> Don't sound too excited to celebrate with us.

> **BONNIE**
> It's gonna be awesome. I promise.

> **TOM**
> Do you have a date? I mean, have you found someone
> to go with?

> **JS**
> You mean, in the last five minutes? No. But if you look

out the window, you'll see the boys come running. Any second now.

Tom laughed, loudly enough to turn heads in the coffee shop. I not easy being so hilarious.

The fourth episode aired tonight. We all squished together on the couch to watch, as usual. This time, AP focused on R and me. We'r both way more cautious than Chaunt'Elle and Marc, but somehow A found the pieces to put a friendship together. Kind of cool to watch but it makes me nervous. Alliances make good targets.

R and I had a private strategy meeting later. We debated what w should do about our alliance, now that the cat's officially out of the building. We talked about playing up our friendship to generate pub lic support as the only sane people in a house full of batshit. The im plication neither of us was brave enough to admit was a showmance. I'm not okay with pretending to be in a relationship to get people I don't know to like me. I have principles, even if I don't know what they are. He does too, but I'm pretty sure he values honesty for its own sake. I value honesty as a means to an end. I told him yeah, there's no point denying we are on the same team. In a way it's us against Chaunt'Elle and Marc. He said yeah. So we didn't really figure out a new game plan. But we did eat donuts and talk about television.

R

You all right, Jane? You seem a little distracted.

JS

Hmm?

R

Everything okay?

JS

Oh. Yeah. It's nothing.

R

You know, you can tell me. I'm on your side, remember?

I could tell him. I hadn't really considered that option before —
my secrets are my business, not anyone else's. But he already knew
about the whole suicide situation. No one else from HOO knows
about that. What if R knew about my high school situation, too? I
decided to tell him before I overthought it and lost my nerve.

JS

Well, Robbie — the thing is, I'm still in high school.
Not *in* high school, obviously — I dropped out a couple
months ago — but I'm taking high school courses here.
To finish my diploma.

R

Shit. Does Alexander Park know?

JS

No.

R ran his fingers through his hair. Agitated.

R

Shit, Jane. You can't just — you can't just lie about that.
To everyone. And expect no one to notice.

JS

Well. No one did notice.

R

That's kind of messed up, you know? Don't you see that?

R wasn't the first person to call me messed up, and he won't be the
last. But since when did he have the ability to make me feel like I'm in
trouble?

JS

Yeah, I get it. I know this is fucked-up. And now everyone is graduating next week, and they want me to go to grad, too. I said I would, even though I'd rather stab myself in the eye than watch everyone I know graduate without me.

I wanted R to yell at me so I'd get angry too. But he didn't yell.

R

I'm sorry, Jane. That must suck.

JS

A little.

R

What if . . . would it help if . . . I go with you? As a friend? So you don't have to go through it alone.

I had to pinch my arm under the table so hard that my skin broke in order to keep from tearing up. I couldn't stop the tiny smile, though.

JS

That . . . would be great. Really. Thank you, Robbie.

R's smile was much more generous than mine.

ThuMay26

AP called a meeting tonight to announce the next immunity challenge.

It's fucked-up.

Simple, but fucked-up.

We're all getting into a van tomorrow. The last person to leave it wins.

That is all.

The only conditions are staying within city limits and not doing anything illegal. The challenge will continue as long as it takes. Hours. Days. It will be streaming live on the *HOO* website, 24/7.

AP

> And besides immunity, the winner will receive five hundred dollars cash! Thanks, Chrysler!

Once upon a time I used to read novels and run around in the sunshine and watch substandard television programming and draw pretty pictures. Now I sit at my desk in my basement room and read academic articles by artificial light, and all my previous social behaviors have been reduced to distant memories.

On the bright side, I get to live inside a van tomorrow.

I can hear Jenna and AP argue in the kitchen right now. She's been popping in and out of the house lately. Sometimes to see me, even when AP isn't here. I can't make out what they're saying, but I've never seen either of them less than composed before. I feel like I'm eight years old, listening to the parents bicker when they think I'm asleep. I thought Jenna might have told AP about my age, but she wouldn't do that. And why should I assume they're arguing about me?

JUNE

WedJune1

I'd like to say I'm a fairly resilient person, but I don't know if I can recover from what happened in that van. Words cannot begin to describe the horror. I'll have to try anyway, as I'd rather have these images stuck on paper than running free in my head.

It started well enough.

I considered myself prepared. I had my books, homework, iPod, laptop, notebooks, and enough gel pens to decorate the Sistine Chapel. I had mouthwash, deodorant, extra clothes, and pads. It was not my time of the month, thank god, but I couldn't very well pee in a bottle. I ate a big meal the previous evening and took a big shit Friday afternoon before I climbed into the van. God, I hate that word. If I never sit in another van again, it will be too soon. But the first day was all right.

It felt like a road trip. The four of us laughed, drove around the city, stopped at drive-thrus. We caught up with the McNugz Club, and Chaunt'Elle was pressured into completing her initiation. She finished her nugz faster than I did, but her motivation to impress Marc was significantly higher than mine.

There were small cameras in the van and a HOOcap trailing us wherever we drove, and who knows how many people watching us from home, but it still felt like we were on our own. Robbie did an unexpected and hilarious impression of Alexander Park. He flattened his hair with his fingers and put on the perfect serious expression.

R

RUN. Three, two, one.

After that, we counted down before doing anything. It really was quite funny. But maybe you had to be there.

The first night was uncomfortable but not unbearable. We drove back to the house and parked on the driveway. Once the sun went down it got chilly, but we had blankets. Chaunt'Elle and I slept on the bench seats, and the boys reclined up front.

When we woke up, Chaunt'Elle was gone. Normally I'd make fun of her for losing yet another challenge, but apparently she got her period. I can't blame her for this one.

The second day went by quickly. We watched TV shows on my laptop until the battery died. Robbie did really well, all things considered. He even peed in a bottle, wrapping a towel around himself for privacy and "to avoid splashing." We kept the van tidy, filling a bag with garbage and throwing it out the window onto the front lawn. Alexander Park came out and cleaned it up, which for some reason we found hilarious. I think he's trying hard to appease the neighbors and bylaw officers by keeping the outside of the house well maintained. Maybe he thinks it will make up for all the noise. After the first bag, we threw out garbage piece by piece. Robbie would count down, "RUN. Three, two, one," and we'd watch the HOOcaps scurry across the lawn like the boys who retrieve tennis balls during matches. Eventually the HOOcaps caught on and only came to collect the garbage when we weren't waiting to make fun of them. Considering that we had nothing else to do, this wasn't often. A few people came by the house to stare at us. We threw crumpled paper at them until AP came out and told us to stop. We threw paper at him when he walked away.

We didn't drive much that day because no one wanted to pay for gas. I took some notes from my Bio textbook, then doodled over them. Marc listened to the hockey game on the radio. Robbie sat quietly and slept. We ate a late supper in a Walmart parking lot. I didn't eat much. By this point the van did not smell good. It smelled like old french fries, urine, feet, and unwashed boy. Just when I thought I was getting used to the smell, someone would move and I'd catch a new whiff. Marc kept farting that evening. It was terrible. We had to choose between opening the windows and staying warm. We chose to freeze. By now Robbie was very grumpy. I told him to hold on. He did, until Marc took a dump out the window. Robbie didn't say anything — he just got out of the van and left. Marc put his pants back on and called out, saying he'd drive him home, but Robbie climbed into the HOOcaps' Civic without looking back. I would have taken us to a car wash, but everything was closed. Instead I drove the van to the opposite end of the parking lot. I climbed past Marc and over the back seat and fell asleep in the trunk. Then the music started.

I hate country music. Marc knew this. In a way I'm glad that's what he chose to play. If he had been clever he would have played a song I liked. He would have ruined Radiohead or Metric or the Beatles. But Marc is not clever and I doubt he has ever read *A Clockwork Orange*. So when the twanging started, I knew it could have been worse. After the fifth repeat of "Achy Breaky Heart" I was doing all right. After the tenth repeat I was getting a headache. After thirty plays, I climbed over the back seat and was ready to use violence. Marc was prepared for that. He was wedged between the front seats, staring at me. I tried to reach behind him. I tried to throw a shoe at the radio. He just laughed and pushed me back. I'm not a small girl, but Marc is bigger than me. And quite a bit stronger. I knew in my heart it was useless to fight him like that. And I didn't want to make a bigger spectacle of myself than I already had. So I retreated to the trunk and lay there, covering my ears and humming to myself. My iPod and headphones were still up front, so that wasn't an option. I told myself that Marc was listening to this too. It had to be getting to him. When I checked on him an hour later, he was reclining on the driver's seat, wearing my headphones.

Mr. Dubs was sparking interest on social media with tweets like "#houseoforange looks like #sinner and #marc could use a little more #elbowroom" and "#houseoforange really tickles the funny bone! #elbowriver." Other faculty and students got involved too, and the replies distracted me for a while, but I didn't sleep that night. Eventually Marc started the van and left it running for a while so the battery wouldn't die. Around midnight he turned up the volume until my chest vibrated with the noise. I held my head and rocked back and forth. For hours. It had to be getting to Marc, too. It had to. It had to. Maybe this is what would make him crack. It had to. This is the only thought that went through my brain that night. The sun was rising when he finally turned off the music. It didn't help much. The song kept playing in my head.

I didn't eat the next morning. My head was aching and I felt sick. Skipping breakfast was fine with me. I was still doing my best to eat as little as possible. I would not take a dump out the window. I would not.

As we pulled out of an automatic car wash, AP called. He told us to be at Fish Creek Park in an hour for an interview with the *Calgary Sun*. Dear lord. We were not happy. It would take at least forty-five minutes to get there, which meant we didn't have much time. Marc wanted aspirin, so he took us to a gas station. We pulled up to a full-serve pump, and Marc rolled down the window to talk with the attendant.

ATTENDANT
Do you want me to fill 'er up with regular?

We were pretty low on gas, but we were also in a hurry. And cheap.

MARC
No. Could you go inside and get me some aspirin?

ATTENDANT
Sorry, sir. Can't do that. You'll have to get it yourself.

MARC
Unfortunately I can't do that. Could you please make an exception?

ATTENDANT
Sorry, sir. If you don't want gas, I'll have to ask you to pull over. Other vehicles are waiting.

MARC
Look, I'll give you money. Ten bucks. Twenty!

ATTENDANT
Sir, please pull over!

Marc made a strange growling noise. He opened the window on the passenger side and leaned over me, yelling at a kid walking into the store.

MARC

Hey, kid! Yes, you. Come here for a second. I just want
you to do something for me. I have money.

I'm not even kidding. He yelled those things to a kid. From a van.
God knows I wanted aspirin too — I was lightheaded and still nauseous — but I couldn't help myself.

JS

Run! Run, kid! Three, two, one. Hahaha. Don't listen to
him! Tell your parents!

The poor kid ran inside, and our tires squealed as Marc shot
away.

MARC

What the hell, Jane?! I would have shared! What the
hell! What if they tell the cops?

At this point I was laughing uncontrollably. I hoped they did call
the cops. And that the cops would ask Marc to step out of the vehicle
first. I laughed all the way to Fish Creek Park. Tears were streaming
down my face. As we pulled up next to Alexander Park, I realized
what a mess I was. I brushed my hair with my fingers and dabbed my
eyes with my sleeve, still chuckling softly to myself.

AP

Sorry for the short notice, guys. But it's really great they
agreed to do this. Any exposure is good exposure, right?

Exposure. Newspapers. My parents read those. I still haven't told
them about the show. I will, eventually, but not like this.

JS

Look, we'll do your interview. But they're not printing
my last name or a clear shot of my face. All right?

AP

Jane, it's in the contract. I have the right to —

JS

Then I'm not doing the interview. I will wrap myself in
a blanket and wait it out in the trunk.

I started laughing again as I said this. The whole situation was getting to me.

AP

[Sigh.]
Fine. They won't use your last name or face. How about
you, Marc?

MARC

I've got nothing to hide.

AP

All right. Be honest but interesting. Talk up the show.
Mention the prizes. Got it?

We nodded.

The interview went well. For the most part. I didn't start laughing
again, which was good. I did throw up at one point. Thankfully I had
a bag handy. The journalist was so kind as to run it to the trash can for
me. It's not the sort of thing I'd want to throw around.

We had enough gas to make it home. We spent the rest of the
day on the driveway. Jenna came to visit me, bless her heart. She
brought me candy and magazines. We talked for a while, through
the window. AP said visitors were fine, as long as they didn't touch
the vehicle.

Robbie came outside too. He charged my laptop and my phone.
He also promised to film Sociology class for me, if I hadn't won by

Tuesday. We laughed for a good ten minutes about the gas station incident while Marc sat there sullenly.

Some of Marc's friends were having a house party at an acreage just within city limits. Marc thought it would be a good idea to go. I disagreed but couldn't physically move him off the driver's seat. He texted Chaunt'Elle to bring out a case of beer, which she did. Silly girl. I suggested we stop to get gas first, but Marc thought we had enough to get there.

We ran out of gas at 11:43 p.m. on a dark gravel road, a good five kilometers away from everything. We figured the HOOcap in the Civic behind us would get us a jerry can. He didn't. Or maybe Marc's friends would come. They didn't. I didn't want to bother Bonnie, because she lived on the other side of the city and she had school tomorrow morning. I didn't know of anyone else with a car. So we sat there. Marc opened the case of beer and had two. I threw the rest out the window because I did not want to spend the night in a van in the middle of nowhere with a drunk Marc. He was pissed. He turned on the CD player, and as soon as "Achy Breaky Heart" came on, I leaned out the window and threw up. As soon as I threw up, Marc opened the door. At first I thought he was getting out, but no, he was throwing up too. Most of it landed on his pants. He swore and took them off and threw them on the road as I climbed into the trunk. It was a long night.

I woke up extremely cramped. Every part of me hurt. I wanted nothing more than to stand up. And run. And join every sports team possible. Then shower. Part of the terrible smell in the van was my own body, and that annoyed me. I wondered how much longer it would take for Marc to leave.

Two more days passed. Four words, but they represent ETERNITY. A HOOcap eventually brought us gas because we were too stubborn to ask for help. It didn't really matter to us where the van was parked because we were ALWAYS IN IT. The need to stand up and move became almost unbearable. Almost. Whenever I thought I couldn't handle it anymore, I closed my eyes and retreated into myself and screamed inside my head. It sort of worked. I tried to keep up with homework, but it was almost impossible to concentrate. We ended up parked on our driveway most of the time. People came to visit us, but they never stayed long. Probably because we were in such a bad mood. I kept wondering when AP would call the whole thing off. This couldn't be fun for anyone to watch.

Marc and I couldn't avoid talking completely. We talked about school and movies and stupid things. Apparently he comes from a very close family. He grew up in Millet, which is just outside of Edmonton. That explains a lot. And his sister is getting married in July. Hooray for her. Sometimes we turned on the radio. A couple of times I caught myself wanting to sing along, or punch Marc in the face, or twitch and yell certain words over and over. When this happened, I reminded myself that the cameras were still on. It didn't make me feel any better, but at least I didn't embarrass myself as much as I could have.

One night we talked about the game. Not out loud, of course. We passed notes the cameras couldn't see.

JS: So are you seeing anyone?

MARC: None of ur bizniss, little miss nosy.

JS: Just making conversation.

MARC: Who do you want to vote off next?

JS: *(You, bitch!!!!!)* Whoever annoys me the most.

MARC: Haha. I get it.

JS: What about you?

MARC: Robbie.

JS: Why?

MARC: Because he's a clever little shit.

Part of me was offended that Marc didn't consider me to be a clever little shit. Stupid, I know. But I hadn't been thinking clearly for days.

JS: Maybe. But he hasn't won that many challenges.

MARC: I know. But I can convince Chaunt'Elle to vote him off. It would be harder to get her to vote for you. I think she wants another girl to stick around.

I think he was telling the truth. Whatever alliance Chaunt'Elle, Robbie, and I held, it wouldn't last forever. And it was obvious that Chaunt'Elle liked Marc more than she liked me or Robbie. If I won this thing, there would be a good chance that Marc would go home next. But if he won, it could be Robbie. Either way it will likely come to a tiebreaker. I don't trust tiebreakers. I hate vans. I don't trust Marc. I don't want Robbie to leave. I hate vans.

I'm almost always happy to see Bonnie show up in her plastic yellow sunglasses with a six-pack in her hand, but I felt and smelled like a piece of shit on Tuesday evening. I wasn't in the mood for anything but my own misery.

BONNIE
So how's life in the van?

JS
It's the worst thing that's ever happened to me.

BONNIE
Lucky for you, I brought beer.

MARC

I'll take one of those, thanks.

JS

They're not for you.

MARC

Gonna drink them all yourself, Sinner?

Even if I could have had a beer without getting in trubs from Mr. Dubs, I didn't want to. I felt nauseated enough as it was.

JS

No. I don't feel like drinking.

BONNIE

Lighten up.

Bonnie cracked one open herself. From the look of her, it wasn't her first that day. Bonnie is eighteen, but I couldn't explain why drinking was a bad idea for me, as privacy was not an option.

JS

Can we not drink, Bonnie?

BONNIE

Come on, Jane. We're celebrating.

JS

It's a little premature for that. I don't know how much longer I'll be stuck in here with this asshole.

MARC

I can hear you, Sinner.

BONNIE

You know, not everything revolves around you and your show. Other people have lives too.

Her words came out thick and messy.

JS
Can we not do this now? Here?

BONNIE
Yeah, I want to do this here. Just pretend Marc doesn't
exist.

MARC
I have feelings too, you know!

JS/BONNIE
Shut up, Marc.

Marc crossed his arms and turned the other way in his seat.

BONNIE
Are you even going to make it to grad? Or are you too
busy pretending to be a college student?

Bonnie was starting to make me nervous. She was dangerously
close to blowing my whole cover, and I wasn't nearly sane enough to
talk my way out of anything.

JS
Yeah, I'm coming to grad! Relax. We'll talk when I get
out. But for now, can you please —

BONNIE
We can talk about it now! Or is living in a fucking van
more important to you than your best friend?

JS
Of course not! We'll hang out as soon as this is over.

Bonnie threw her can of beer at the van. It dented the door, just
inches below where my arm rested on the open window.

MARC

Come on, Sinner. She can't do that.

BONNIE

Just fucking watch me!

She picked up another can and drew her arm back sloppily. A HOOcap put his hand on her arm and gently lowered it.

HOOCAP

All right, Bonnie. Time to go.

BONNIE

Are you going to let them take me?

JS

What do you want me to do, Bonnie?

My head was pounding. As much as I love Bonnie, all I wanted was some peace and quiet and time away from everyone.

BONNIE

I don't know. Maybe get up off your ass and come with me? Maybe I have shit I want to talk to you about, too!

JS

I can't get up! Not yet! You said yourself that you want me to destroy the competition.

Bonnie, of all people, should know how far I'd come. Why would she expect me to throw away everything I'd been through the last few days to talk, when we'd talk soon enough?

Bonnie didn't reply as the HOOcap slowly guided her back, away from the van. I wanted to go with her. She had no idea how much I wanted to. But I had spent more than four days trapped in that van, aching and filthy and miserable. I wasn't about to let it all be for nothing. Bonnie shouted one last *Fuck you!* over her shoulder — to me, to

Marc, to everyone on *HOO*—before she disappeared around the corner.

I don't remember how it ended because it happened while I was asleep. I've watched the footage several times since then. It's probably a GIF by now. It was dark. Marc was behind the wheel; I was sitting in the passenger's seat. Dozing against the door with my mouth half-open. He moved very slowly, reaching across me. Leather squeaked, but I didn't wake up. Once his hand reached the handle, it was over. In one swift motion he opened the door and pushed me out.

I was a wretched mess splattered on the driveway. The first few seconds were very confusing. I was half asleep, half full of adrenaline. Half in shock, half in pain. A HOOcap stood next to my head and stared down at me with a camera. Someone else jogged up and stuck a hand in my face.

MARC

Sinner? You all right?

I hurt. Not just my twisted ankle or my face where it scraped the pavement. My whole body was cramped and aching. I had spent the last five days imagining how glorious it would feel to emerge from the van, stretching my muscles in the sun. Smiling. Triumphant. I don't think I seriously entertained the idea of losing until it happened. I lay still for a while, organizing my thoughts, breathing cautiously to see how well my lungs still worked.

MARC

Sinner?

The pavement smelled nice. Like dirt and rocks and rain.

MARC

Jane? You okay?

I stretched out my legs and they hurt like hell. I flexed my hands, and I could feel some of the tiny pebbles embedded in my palm fall out. My head throbbed.

MARC

Jane? Jane? Jane?

JS

Marc?

MARC

Yeah? Look, I hope you're okay. I'm —

JS

SHUT THE FUCK UP, MARC.

Then I remembered this was still streaming live. I didn't know how late it was or how many people were watching, but it wasn't over yet. I lay still for a few more minutes and ignored Marc's voice. I hated the sound of it. Eventually a paramedic helped me up and wiped the blood off my face. She asked me a couple questions — I don't remember what they were — but I think I responded. I didn't respond to Mark, or the HOOcap. I wanted to, but all I could come up with were profanities.

Most of the attention was on Marc after that. Chaunt'Elle and Robbie came outside. AP was already there. He might have been standing there the whole time, I don't know. Chaunt'Elle and AP went to Marc. Robbie sat down next to me on the curb.

R

He's a dick.

JS

Yeah, well, we already knew that.

R

I don't think it's legal. What he did.

JS

It is, I'm sure.

R

You must be pissed.

I was. Extremely. Mostly I was pissed at myself, for not thinking of this before Marc did. I would have done the same thing. Robbie reached for my hand, and I let him hold it. I figured the cameras were off me for now.

When I woke up, Alexander Park was standing in my bedroom with a camera on his shoulder.

AP

I know you must be tired, Jane. But could you turn over so your bandaged cheek is showing? And just pretend I'm not here. You can go back to sleep if you like.

I didn't move.

AP

It will only take a second, Jane. We don't have to start the interviews now. We can do that after you've showered.

I closed my eyes. Rage swelled up within me.

JS

Look. This is a reality show. I signed up for this. I get it. But for Christ's sake, I just gave you the last five days of my life! I gave up my privacy, my classes, my dignity. Possibly my best friend. And all for nothing. So if you don't get out of my room right now — if you don't let me have just one goddamn day to myself — I am going to kick you in the nuts. I am going to slash your tires. I am going to piss on your hundred-thousand-dollar camera. And if you use any of this footage, I swear I will destroy everything you love! I'll run over your balls with that fucking van! I'll set fire to this house!

I don't know how long I had been yelling to myself, but he got the point. When I opened my eyes he was gone.

After he left I took a shower, since I was already up. I may have cried a bit while I washed the thick layer of grease out of my hair. It could have been from my aching body, the disappointment of losing in front of everyone, or even the sheer joy of being clean. Most likely it was the humiliation.

Needless to say, I've been in a bad mood all day. In the morning I watched the footage of me falling out of the van, over and over, then I helped myself to whatever was in the fridge. It's not Friday, but I didn't care. Everyone stayed out of my way. Eventually I grabbed my sunglasses and journal and left the house. The weather was shitty, so I didn't want to stay outside. I ended up walking to a coffee shop a few blocks away. I ordered a large brewed coffee with the change I had in my pocket and sat down and wrote. It helped, getting all this out. Catharsis. It's been a couple hours, and I'm starving, but I'm out of money. I don't want to go back to the house for my wallet, and even if I do, my bank account is empty. I spent it all on fast food. It will stay empty for a while, since I traded three shifts to stay in that fucking van. Refills are free, so I'm just drinking more coffee. Maybe I'll stay here and live off coffee forever. It might not be so bad. At least I can stand up.

I've been hoping for and dreading a text from Bonnie. Maybe she's waiting for me to apologize, instead. Should I? If I do, I'm admitting that I chose the show over her. No, I'm overthinking this. All I know is that neither of us wants to go to grad this weekend mad at the other. Bonnie is the only person outside of the show I can actually share *House of Orange* with. She's on my side. Maybe I'm forgetting to be on her side, too.

Also, I'm just a selfish bitch sometimes.

I'm calling her now.

ThuJun2

A lot of people were angry with me at school. Maybe not at me, but they were angry. Apparently, quite a few bets were lost because Marc won. I suppose it's good to know that people are betting on me, not Marc. I'm still in a bad mood today, so I just ignored everyone. I have a lot of schoolwork to catch up on. Robbie photocopied his Sociology notes for me, and I'm surprised how helpful they are. Maybe I should start taking decent notes instead of drawing over everything. I should, but probably I won't.

I spent the day trying to figure out how to cheer myself up. Most of what I came up with involved food, which I can't afford right now. Then I remembered Carol. I've realized how much more I appreciate her, now that we don't live together. I didn't want to go home, so we met at Elbow River after she got out of school. Carol was excited to be there. She wanted to read my assignments and visit the lecture halls and meet my friends. I texted Robbie to meet us for supper later. He bought Carol a marshmallow milkshake and an extra-large poutine, which was quite nice of him. Carol was certainly impressed. He offered to buy me supper too, but I told him I'd already eaten. The practical part of me screamed, JANE, WHO ARE YOU TO TURN DOWN FREE FOOD? but I ignored it.

It was dark by the time we left the restaurant, so I rode the bus with Carol back to the parents' house. I would have turned around and left right away, but Carol insisted I come inside and say hi to them. I couldn't figure out how to tell her no, so we went in together.

They were happy to see me of course. I was happy to see them too, actually. Then they brought out the guilt. They asked me why I didn't visit more often, why I rarely called, how I was doing, why I wasn't going to church, and a thousand other questions I didn't want to answer. I wanted to ignore them and walk out the door. I really wanted to. It would have been easier than telling them the truth. But I still care what they think of me. So I told them I was sorry, I'd call more, it's just that I've been busy. Mom gave me a Tupperware container full of homemade cookies before I left. I really should call them more.

FFAFFJun3

Marc offered to take me to a fancy steakhouse tonight. Actually, he offered me a gift card so I wouldn't have to sit with him, which was surprisingly thoughtful. The only thing right now I want more than filet mignon and expensive wine is the chance to rehabilitate some of my mangled dignity, so I politely declined. Everything still hurts.

I've never seen Alexander Park so happy. The challenge was a big hit, and not just with the college. Students told their friends, who told their mothers, who told their hairdressers, who told their therapists. The comment forums on the *HOO* website have seen quite a lot of activity recently. I spent an hour reading the comments, even though R advised against it. I didn't find anything unexpected — just the usual mix of ignorance, rage, and sincerity. But I didn't know that AP had set up a viewer contest! People submit photos of themselves with our van in the background, and the best photos will win a *HOO* sweater and mug. Since when do we have sweaters and mugs?! Most of the photos so far involve Marc and me sleeping in a Walmart parking lot.

AP also gave me a copy of the newspaper. I had forgotten about the article. I'd just assumed nothing that happened last week counted. It's not a bad article, although it leaves the reader with the impression that Marc and I are two nugz short of a twenty-pack for living in a van for days. Fair enough.

"Yeah, it's all about the money, for me. I'd do pretty much anything

for money. (laughs) I kind of hate it though."
— Marc P., full-time business administration student

"Yes it's uncomfortable, but I could really use the cash. School isn't cheap, you know."
— Jane S., full-time psychology student

I always assumed if I ever made the paper, I'd tape the article to my bedroom wall and feel good about myself whenever I walked past it. Probably this won't happen.

AP set up new GoPros in the house this aft. It seems the school is investing more money in the show these days. I asked AP if he could carry the upgrades a bit further and get me a door. He said he'd get back to me. Which means no.

A fortune cookie from last week that I found in my pocket today as I was (finally) doing laundry: Humor is an affirmation of dignity.
    (in bed)

Watched hockey tonight with Hinkfuss. She's all right, I suppose. For a cat. I might as well get used to her. A cat is probably the closest thing to a child I'll ever have.

SatJun4
I half let myself believe he'd show up at my curtain door in a fitted T-shirt and skinny jeans. Holding a textbook or something, not a corsage. A bubble of anxiety has been rising in my chest all day, and it only got bigger at the sight of him in a suit. Threatening to lift my heart right up through my throat.

He's waiting for me now, probably sitting on the sunlit concrete steps outside our front door. I told him I needed a few minutes to finish getting ready. Really I'm just trying to stab this anxiety bubble hard enough to pop it.

The corsage he slipped on my wrist is white, which he thought would go with whatever I wore. I decided on a long green dress, simple, smooth, and slim enough for me to slide through the cracks and slip away from unwanted conversations. Bonnie thought I should wear the ELBOW GREASE shirt to the ceremony to show I don't care what people think. But I care. I don't want to make a statement, I don't want to stand out. I want to make myself very very small. I've already ruined one party for the James Fowler kids. I don't want to take this away from them too.

He complimented me on my dress. I knew I looked pretty, and it made me feel unsteady and pretentious. I hated that.

We could have taken the bus, but R booked a cab instead. He knew without me telling him that I needed privacy tonight. Besides, limos are tacky. The ceremony and dinner took place in a swanky convention center downtown, and I made sure we arrived just as the ceremony started so we didn't have to make awkward small talk with anyone. We sat near the back with the parents and families. My own parents didn't come because I neglected to mention the occasion to them.

Observing all the people I've gone to school with for years graduate without me is not the most fun I've ever had on a Saturday night. It took an hour and a half to watch every student walk across the stage and collect a diploma. Two hundred ninety-nine names were called. My name would have made it three hundred. R started a game of Xs and Os on the program to pass the time. I'm glad he came with me, despite how surreal it was for me to have R see my high school life. Like mixing colors in with the whites. And that's a laundry metaphor, just to be clear.

I wasn't expecting Tom to make the valedictorian speech, because why didn't he tell me he'd made valedictorian?! His speech was hilarious. Or at least the other students seemed to think so. Half the inside jokes went over my head.

As soon as the ceremony ended, I rushed through the crowd to find
Bonnie, dodging eager parents like bullets in slow motion. I hugged
her longer than I've ever hugged anyone before. Long enough for Tom
to spot me and latch onto us. I congratulated everyone, telling them
how excited I was for them, how awesome tonight would be, smiling,
always smiling. They were all happy I came. And very interested in
R, once he caught up with me. The novelty of a College Boy was soon
distraction enough for me to slip away.

I knew the girls' washroom would be a shit storm of giggles and
lipstick, so I had to find an alley outside to cry in.

Crying is stupid. I know that. If I didn't graduate today, it's my
own goddamn fault.

I wished I smoked cigarettes so I'd have something to do other
than trying not to think about how red my eyes must be. No rain fell,
no thunder boomed dramatically, no one followed me outside.

Just Jane Sinner and the sunset.

Bonnie, Tegan, Tom, and a couple other girls I used to hang out with
reserved a table for us. Normally they wouldn't all sit together, but I
guess the friendship of Jane Sinner is like magic glue or something.
They weren't expecting me to bring a plus one, so I stole a chair and
the plate under Jenny Gunther's name card to make room for R. Jenny
borrowed my pen last year and didn't give it back. Also, I just don't
like her. Bonnie and Tegan held the table in case someone ratted me
out to Jenny while the rest of us waited in line for punch and an extra
breadbasket.

TOM
How's Elbow River?

JS
Pretty good, actually. I'm —

TOM
Hold on.

Tom placed a hand on the side of my face, tilted it up to meet his, and rubbed his thumb across my cheek. For fuck's sake. Did I not wipe off all the mascara tracks?

TOM

Just a bit of Elbow Grease.

I moved away from his hand.

JS

Fuck off, Tom.

TOM

Still got a dirty mouth, I see. At least the rest of you cleaned up nice.

He didn't wink as he said it. Behind me, R grew even more still. I don't know how I felt that, but I did.

TOM

What's Elbow's motto again? Success is just around the bend? We're the coolest joint in town?

JS

Good thing you're going into engineering, because you could never make it as a standup comic.

TOM

Yeah, well, I used up all the good material in my speech.

JS

It was a nice speech, by the way.

TOM

Thanks. I'm just ... I'm glad ... it's good that you're doing ... good, Jane. In community college.

He glanced at R as he said it.

R
She is doing good. Jane's the smartest person in our Sociology class.

TOM
Yeah. Like that means a lot at Elbow River.

Well, we can't all be engineers.

JS
The fuck is wrong with you, Tom?

TOM
Nothing. Punch?

We waited in silence while Tom filled all seven glasses, ignoring me the same way he ignores everything he doesn't want to deal with. A well-rounded young man, indeed.

Back at the table, Bonnie pulled out a flask from the depths of her neon-orange tulle and passed it around. I didn't take any. My emotions were hobbling around in stilettos, sore and unsteady. No need to make it worse.

BONNIE
[to me]
I'm going out for a smoke. Keep me company?

JS
(Thank god.)
Sure.

We didn't think to bring jackets, so we shivered and huddled together the way underdressed girls do when they're standing outside at night.

JS
So . . . what's the deal with Tom?

Bonnie sighed — the same long-suffering sigh she gives when I ask her to finish my food for me. Which I haven't done in a while, actually.

BONNIE
Jane. Dear, sweet Jane. You're living with college boys. Dating college boys.

Maybe Tom wasn't the only one ignoring things he didn't want to deal with.

JS
The fuck I am! What, did he expect me to sit through the ceremony and watch you all get your diplomas by myself? And how does he know I live with Robbie? Did he find out about the show?

It wasn't an accusation — I know Bonnie would never tell anyone if I asked her not to.

BONNIE
He has access to the internet, Jane. Things get around.

I made a weird growling noise and scuffed my feet on the pavement.

JS
What am I going to do when you leave in the fall?

BONNIE
Actually —

Bonnie took a drag and turned her back to me to exhale.

BONNIE
— I'm leaving sooner. In July.

JS
Wait — July? Already?

BONNIE
I got into a summer program: mixed media sculpting. It happened so quickly. I tried to tell you, Jane, but you're always wrapped up in that dumb show.

What happened to us? Nobody tells each other anything anymore. I watched Bonnie finish her cigarette. The unnaturally bright orange of her dress nearly glowed in the dark, and the trail of smoke smeared across the air made it seem like she was on fire.

R and I didn't go to the after party, although (almost) everyone insisted loudly that we both come. I wasn't in the mood. I wanted to go for a walk around our neighborhood by myself, to clear my head. R gave me his suit jacket so I wouldn't be cold, even though I could have run inside and grabbed my own.

JS
Robbie . . . thanks. For coming. And I'm sorry Tom was such a dick.

R
Don't worry about it. He doesn't get to make fun of Elbow River. We do.

Maybe Elbow River isn't so bad after all.

I texted Tom when I got in, only because I knew he was one of the few kids not already drunk on cheap beer.

JS: I'm sorry I didn't tell you about the show.

He hasn't replied yet.

MonJun6

An email from Bonnie:

Dearest Jane,

Please accept my hearty congratulations on being born exactly eighteen years ago today. I hope your day is filled with excitement, tasteful treats, and general well-being. I regret that I am not with you in the flesh to purchase you beverages and/or food items for your pleasurable consumption, as my evening tutoring session is inescapable, what with exams next week. I am grateful to have you as a friend and correspondent and wish you every happiness this special day.

Sincerely,
B.

My reply:

Dearest Bonnie,

First I would like to sincerely thank you for the warm wishes. They were received with much gratitude and rejoicing.

Second, I would like to tell you a story. Here it is.

I didn't tell anyone about my birthday because you know how I feel about vanity and self-indulgence: discretion is key. I was having a lovely day, holding onto my birthday like a secret. Like an inside joke between myself and I. However, I forgot I put my birthday on my *House of Orange* application and Alexander Park is not one to overlook details. I showed up at the on-campus pub at 7, hoping to get through the scheduled interview as quickly as possible, daydreaming about the bag of M&M's sitting on my desk at home. I walked into a three-camera setup, a large crowd, and a spotlight.

CROWD

Happy birthday, Jane/Sinner!

JS

. . .

AP

You wouldn't believe how hard this was to keep from you.

Naturally I resented AP for exploiting my secret day for dramatic purposes. I smiled cautiously, aware of the three cameras focused on me.

JS

I don't know what to say!

That's always a safe thing to say.

MARC

Have a drink; they're on Alex! Just for contestants, though. Sorry, everyone else.

I searched for Robbie as I followed AP and Marc to the bar. I couldn't find him. People I didn't know kept wishing me happy birthday, patting me on the shoulder. I tried not to flinch. As soon as AP gave the sign, one of the makeup and hair people rushed in for touchups. The cameras had to move in closer and pull focus before I was allowed to drink. I made polite conversation with everyone around me for what I assumed was two hours but turned out to be twenty minutes. I wished you were there. This is the sort of event we'd be good at avoiding, or at least leaving early. Unfortunately there were no opportunities for graceful exits.

At one point I was cornered by a boy I sit next to in Psychology. His name is Will and he has a beard, and he sat down and tried to buy me a drink. I told him to save his money because I already got drinks for free. He was distracted and didn't listen.

WILL
Listen. I've been meaning to tell you something.

JS
Um. Kay.

WILL
It's been hard for me to watch the show.

JS
Um. Kay.

WILL
Because I get jealous every time I see you talking with another guy.

JS
(WHOA THERE! HOLD UP! THIS IS NOT THE TIME OR PLACE!)
Pardon?

WILL
It's pretty obvious you aren't like other girls. You're different. I mean, you're so confident. And weird. But I mean that in the best possible way. And you have really cool hair.

JS
(Obviously I am a fucking snowflake, but don't you see the cameras around? Don't you know there is a boom mike hanging over your head?)
. . .

WILL

I really like you, Jane.

At this point Will put his hand on my thigh. If my mouth had been full, I would have choked. If my glass hadn't been empty, I would have dumped it on him. Maybe not. But maybe. Beer was free, after all. I blushed stupidly and scrambled for an appropriate response.

JS

I don't know what to say.

I picked up his hand, holding it like I'd hold my father's underwear when it was my turn to do laundry, and placed it on his own lap. Will seemed unaware of the awkward angle his elbow now stuck out at.

WILL

It's all right. You don't have to say anything now. We'll talk more in private.

Will stood up.

JS

No!

I motioned for him to sit back down. There was no way I was going to let this moment dangle in an ambiguous place where an editor could do something unnecessary with it.

JS

I'm sorry, but I don't feel the same way.

WILL

It's okay, I know you're not one to talk about your feelings in the open.

JS

I don't have feelings. For you.

Now, Bonnie—I know you are probably feeling a little sorry for Will at this point, and maybe that's fair, but you have to understand that Will is not the sort of guy I'd want the world to assume I'm dating. I know you are probably thinking I'd say that about almost any guy, and again, that's fair. But Will is an unfortunate combination of sensitivity and stupidity, and it freaks me out at the best of times.

WILL

You know, I've always been one of your biggest supporters. I know it must be tough to have your life scrutinized, and I just want you to know that I'm always around to talk. If you need to. I'm here.

JS

I have nothing to talk about.

WILL

Of course you do.

He put his hand on my arm. Unconsciously, I think.

JS

No.

I removed his hand once again.

JS

I have to go now.

WILL

Where?

JS

I don't know. Elsewhere.

WILL

I know the cameras are on and everything, but you don't have to be so dramatic.

He paused before calling "Happy Birthday, Jane!" as I walked away. I knew Alexander Park would enjoy that little episode of awkwardness. That's not the story I wanted to tell you though. That was just the context.

Another hour and a couple conversations later I was able to duck outside. I was hoping for some time alone to regroup mentally. I found Robbie out there instead, which was also nice. We talked for a few minutes. I don't remember what we talked about, exactly. Doesn't matter. I relaxed for the first time tonight.

Then Will came charging down the sidewalk and punched Robbie in the face.

My first thought was to see if the cameras caught it. They didn't. No one saw. My second thought was simply *What the fuck?* I froze. I'm pretty sure my face was stuck in resting bitch position, like a movie paused on the worst possible frame. The three of us stood there for a very uncomfortable moment before Will trotted back down the street. R wasn't bleeding and there were no teeth on the ground — he must have turned away at the right moment. I had no idea what to say to him.

JS

I'm sorry this happened to you.

I hated myself for saying it as soon as the words came out. R touched his forehead.

R

Yeah. It's all right.

I didn't have a clue what he was thinking. I was watching him closely, struggling to figure out what to make of all this, when the door opened and a HOOcap came out.

HOOCAP
Jane, Alexander needs you back inside. We need at least one more interview.

JS
I don't think . . . I'd rather . . .

HOOCAP
I'm not supposed to say anything, but there is a cake, too.

JS
[Sigh.]

R
You should go back inside. Really. You should go.

And so I went back inside and ate cake like the gluttonous coward I am.

When I got home, Robbie had his door closed and his lights off. I went outside and tried calling you, but I guess you were busy. Now I'm sitting at my desk, eating M&M's, wondering what I should be feeling because I'm not nearly as drunk as I'd like to be. I suppose the story ends here. Tidy endings are overrated.

Sincerely,
Jane

PS. If you feel, as I do, that these events (although quite eloquently accounted for in the above description) require further discussion, call me.

In retrospect, I should have asked if he was okay.

At least the house is quiet tonight. Chaunt'Elle fell asleep as soon as she got home, and I don't think Marc is here. He probably took full advantage of the free drinks and passed out on a bench somewhere.

TueJun7

Bonnie called this morning and we had a nice chat, but Robbie won't talk to me. He said he was running late as he ate breakfast, and of course it was bullshit; he's never run late in his life. Maybe he thinks I'm dangerous to be with. Maybe he doesn't think dangerous is sexy. Maybe he blames me. I don't think that's fair, but if I can't talk to him, I can't explain myself. Do I have anything to explain? Bonnie and I ended up laughing about the whole thing on the phone, but I feel like shit now.

It took me longer than it should have to think it through. AP didn't answer his phone all day, and the HOOcaps wouldn't tell me where he was. I went to the film department and asked around, but he didn't have class today. I thought about going to my own class, but the echo of Will's fist hitting Robbie's face was too distracting. Eventually I found AP lounging in Jenna's living room.

JS
You took things way too far last night.

AP
It was just a party, Jane. Don't tell me you don't like parties.

JS
I'm talking about Will.

AP
Ah.

JS

What did you say to him? Did you bribe him or something?

AP

I didn't have to bribe him. He was sincere. He just wanted a chance to talk with you. You could have been nicer to him, but it's more interesting when you're not.

JS

I could have been nicer? You're the asshole who got Robbie punched in the face.

AP

What?

JS

Don't tell me you didn't set that up.

AP

I did not set that up.

JS

. . .

AP

If I set it up, where were the cameras? Where was the reaction from the crowd?

JS

. . .

AP

I never told Will to do that. What would the point be, if I didn't film it?

I hated that AP made sense — it deflated my righteous indignation.

AP

Is Robbie okay, though?

JS

Probably. I think he's pissed at me.

AP

That's too bad.

    I doubt he meant that.

I went for another run tonight. Ran for kilometers and didn't get anywhere.

We all spent the evening in our own respective rooms. R is definitely pissed at me. It sucks. I love drama, but only when it happens to other people. R and I would be having a great time with this story if someone else had been punched for some other reason.

WedJun8

I think we're okay now. He said good morning to me, at least.

There was supposed to be another episode tonight but things are busy with the end of the term coming up, so AP is delaying it to next week. R and I took the opportunity to go on a Slurpee run instead. We came home to find a large box sitting in the middle of the living room. The label on the box read:

WALLACE & BEANZ
Instant Coffee Ind. Packs x 1000

    Robbie wanted to get an X-Acto knife from his bedroom to open the box, but I told him that would be a waste of thirty seconds. I butchered the box with my house key. He was worried I'd damage whatever was inside, because at that point we didn't believe the box contained one thousand packets of instant coffee. Turns out it did. After we took out all the packaging and opened the clear plastic bags, we dumped everything onto the floor, because why not? I handed Robbie one packet at a time, starting with the red packets and ending with purple, and he laid them all out on the living room floor in a beautiful and massive spiral. Each packet was placed the same exact distance from the next. Robbie has a good eye for symmetry. There were only 988 packets in the box, but they covered a good part of the floor. We sat there and stared at them for a while. It was nice. Robbie sat with his skinny elbows resting on his skinny legs, wearing a cable-knit sweater and red pants. His hair was messy, though I could tell he had tried to tame it.

After we stared at the floor for a while, Robbie made us tea because we were sick of the idea of coffee. We left the mega-spiral and went downstairs and sat on my bed. The basement was empty except for us. Robbie made my tea too sweet, but it was nice all the same.

R
Marc has the immunity idol, so someone from the Basement Alliance is going home.

JS
I know.

Robbie held his teacup in his lap and looked at his feet.

R
Who are you voting for, then?

JS
Chaunt'Elle, of course.

R
Why "of course"?

We made eye contact and held it for a couple seconds or a couple minutes. It doesn't matter. We looked away at the same time.

JS

I always assumed it would be the two of us at the end.

R

Me too.

Robbie placed his teacup in his saucer and wiped off a bead of tea with his thumb. I should have cleaned up the dishes and dirty bras scattered across my desk before inviting him into my room.

JS

Is it very hard for you, living here? With all the people and all the mess?

R

Yeah. But it doesn't bother me as much as it used to.

JS

Really?

R

I take it each day at a time. It's better to face the things you don't like. Get them over and done with so you can move on with your life.

JS

I agree.

Hinkfuss jumped on the bed and sat between us, rubbing her face on R's pants. R picked off the cat hairs and rolled them between his fingers.

JS

Just throw them on the floor.

He walked to the garbage can instead.

R

I just don't think it's unreasonable to ask that people clean up after themselves. And I can't be the only one who doesn't like a dirty kitchen.

JS

Oh my god.

R

What?

JS

It was you! All the notes on the whiteboard!

Robbie grinned sheepishly.

JS

And you made everyone believe it was Chaunt'Elle.

He shrugged.

JS

How aggressively passive-aggressive of you.

R

I suppose.

JS

It's mostly Marc, of course. The mess.

R

I know. If only we could vote him out on Friday.

JS

Well, he can't stay around forever. If Marc wins this thing, my life will have been in vain.

You've got him pretty well trained. Maybe you can condition him to lose challenges. Or do the dishes. At least his own dishes.

Hinkfuss stretched, climbed onto R's lap, and rubbed her face up and down his sweater, leaving a trail of cat hair. R just petted her and gave me a tiny smile.

Robbie is the sort of boy I'd admit to having a crush on, if I were the sort of girl to admit to having crushes.

ThuJun9

Some guy from Wallace & Beanz came by the house this morning. He gave me a yellow T-shirt with the W&B logo on the front and offered me fifty dollars to wear it all day. I said sure. I could use some new shirts. When he left I put a hoodie on because I'd never agreed to specific conditions like visibility. It's an ugly shirt.

Classes went okay. I handed in my history paper and my Bio lab report. After Bio I spent the money on some new shirts.

The end of the term is almost here, thank god. I couldn't handle another term of formaldehyde and ridiculous terminology and safety goggles. If I have to retake Bio, I'll kill myself. For real this time.

AP called a mandatory house meeting tonight. Said he had some big announcements. Marc and Robbie and Chaunt'Elle and I sat in the living room, confused and apprehensive, while AP explained (very happily) that Wallace & Beanz is our new sponsor! Hurrah!

AP

Wallace & Beanz grinds premium coffee beans into superfine powder that dissolves instantly in water.

You get to enjoy one thousand packets of delicious and locally produced instant coffee! Yum!

R

Nine hundred eighty-eight. Nine hundred and eighty-eight packets.

CHAUNT'ELLE

OMIGOD I LOVE COFFEEEE!

AP

Wallace & Beanz is proud to be a Canadian-owned company. And to celebrate their twentieth anniversary, they're offering a two-thousand-dollar scholarship to the winner of *House of Orange*!

JS

What?

R

What?

MARC

What now?

AP

[smiling]
Thanks, Wallace & Beanz!

After he said what needed to be said, AP quickly dropped the happy-advertiser act. He told us the more we drank the coffee and talked it up, the happier W&B would be. There's a chance W&B will increase the scholarship amount, depending on how well the show does.

AP

Which brings me to my next announcement. City Television has picked up *House of Orange*, and the next episode will air on Monday at three p.m.!

MARC
You mean, on TV?

R
[looks thoughtful]

CHAUNT'ELLE
OMIGOD we're going to be on TV?!

JS
(Shit. My parents watch television.)

Three p.m. is early. The parents will be at work then. Probably. Do they watch City Television? Do they even like reality shows? Once I caught Dad watching a rerun of *The Bachelor* on his day off. I don't think I had ever seen him blush before. Sweet mother of god. What if they hear about it from someone else? Like Aunt Gina? Sweet mother of god.

I've thought of something.

I didn't tell Robbie my plan, because I wanted to keep the guilt to myself. But I made him promise to be the first person to get up and have breakfast tomorrow morning. The nice thing about Robbie is that he trusts me.

I snuck into Marc's room around three a.m. There was shit everywhere. I could barely walk without stepping on something. I used the glow of my cell phone to look around. This was the part of the plan out of my control — not being able to find the immunity idol. I figured Marc would have tossed it somewhere and forgotten about it. I spent a long time checking under clothes and magazines, and it was quite a stressful experience. I was afraid he'd wake up and see me every time I made a noise. I was afraid of what I'd find growing on dishes buried under socks. I was also afraid I'd never find the Don Cherry bobblehead and Robbie would be voted off. Maybe I was even afraid of being alone in this stupid house.

I think Marc did wake up when I stepped on a bag of chips. He sat up and grunted, and I shrank back against the dresser. I crouched there for what might have been an hour trying to convince my heart to return to my chest before I stuck my head out to see if he was asleep, which he was. I found the bobblehead a minute later. It was hidden under an open book on top of the dresser. For some reason, my heart started beating faster when I picked it up. I tiptoed outside and tried not to look too excited as I walked into the kitchen.

I wasn't that surprised to see a HOOcap with a camera waiting for me. I guess they are watching us at night. Or maybe AP anticipated this. I ignored the camera and headed to the fridge. I read AP's note once more just to be sure.

FREE-FOR-ALL FRIDAY FRIDGE

In the interest of space conservation and the prevention of food expiration, EFFECTIVE IMMEDIATELY anything in the fridge is fair game on Fridays.

Sweet, sweet ambiguity. Maybe I'll be disqualified for this. Probably not. I placed the bobblehead next to the milk and smiled as I closed the door.

FFAFFJun10

Robbie texted me a pic of the bobblehead sitting in the fridge, with "lol" in the subject line. I think that means he literally laughed out loud. R sent another text afterward, asking me to tell Chaunt'Elle that Marc is next. I really hope she still believes in the Alliance. I'm pretty sure she does.

Exams start next week. I have two on Tuesday, two on Wednesday, and one on Thursday. I meant to study more this week, but I've been busy finishing all my assignments. And trying to deal with this stupid show. Sometimes I forget the only reason I'm at Elbow River is to get my high school diploma, but I spend way more time with *House of Orange* than I do with my schoolwork.

W&B is all over campus now. I did a promotional interview for W&B/Alexander Park before Sociology today. W&B gave me a box of instant coffee to hand out to my class. I would have stood on the roof and thrown packets at people as they walked by and been done with it, but a HOOcap talked with the prof and was there to film me handing out seventy-two packets to seventy-two students. Then I stood at the front of the class and explained that next week's episode would be airing on TV. Yes, by TV I mean television. Which is not the same thing as the internet. No, this does not make the show a big deal. Honestly, I have no idea why this is happening. Robbie grinned like an idiot next to my empty seat. His turn is coming, I hope. I gave up answering questions and sat down when someone asked for my autograph. THE THINGS I AM CONTRACTUALLY OBLIGATED TO DO.

I don't really mind being watched.

I just prefer not to watch others watching me.

Robbie and I got three minutes of studying done in Union Hall before the Students' Association asked us for an interview. I can't remember what I said, because the whole time I was thinking about enzymes.

ENZYMES!

I can't even remember what, specifically, about enzymes I was thinking about, which is a waste of half an hour of thought. I'll try again tonight, after the ceremony.

R and I skipped our afternoon classes. The last classes of the term don't mean much anyway. We brushed off the wet leaves from a stone picnic table in the courtyard and drank coffee. Real coffee, not the instant shit. When the coffee ran out we got more. I almost started to relax.

It's nice to know that no matter how bad things get, no matter how many exams I have to take or how many truths I have to hide, after tonight I'll still have the show and I'll still have R. I'll still have a decent chance of winning this whole thing.

I expected the voting ceremony to be interesting tonight, and it certainly was. I also thought Marc would be upset when he figured out what happened, but he wasn't.

MARC
I guess I deserved this, Sinner.

Robbie held the bobblehead and didn't say anything. He just looked at Alexander Park, as if daring AP to say Don Cherry didn't belong to him.

AP
Welcome to the third voting ceremony. Robbie is safe this week, so either Sinner, Marc, or Chaunt'Elle is going home tonight. Normally I would ask you all a couple questions, but I think we'll skip those tonight. After everyone has written down their votes, each person will hold up the paper and read the name out loud.

I was the first person to get up and write a name down, and I crumpled the paper with a sweaty fist while I waited for everyone else to finish. I let out a deep breath when the last voter sat down. Please please please be on our side, Chaunt'elle.

AP
We'll start with Chaunt'Elle and go clockwise. Who did you vote for?

CHAUNT'ELLE
Marc.

Thank god.

JS

Marc.

MARC

Sinner.

ROBBIE

Sinner.

It felt like the dream I had a while ago. The one where I tripped and fell and woke up right before my face hit the pavement. I looked at Robbie to see if he was laughing, if this was a joke, but it wasn't. We stared at each other, and his face didn't move.

AP

We have a tie, for the first time in *House of Orange* history.

Alexander reached into his pocket and brought out a coin.

AP

Heads, Sinner is leaving. Tails, it's Marc.

JS

Are you serious? That's it? A coin toss?

AP

Yes, that's it.

AP tossed the coin in the air. I wanted to do something. I wanted to scream at Marc. I wanted Will to charge down the hall and punch Robbie in the face again. I wanted to fight the entire crew of *House of Orange* with one arm tied behind my back. Anything. AP caught the coin and slapped it onto the back of his hand. He turned his hand slightly so the camera could see.

AP
The third person voted off *House of Orange* is Jane Sinner.

I sat there for a moment, trying to think. Trying to think of anything. Nothing came to mind. So I got up, took off my mike, and left the room.

I grabbed my jacket, headed outside, and started walking. It was hard to say if I couldn't feel anything because I was in shock or if I couldn't feel anything because I had nothing to feel. The farther I walked from the house, the more I believed the latter. It worried me. But even then I couldn't feel it directly. It was like I was watching someone else worry. Eventually the worry settled at the bottom of my stomach like a heavy rock.

I didn't want to think about Robbie, because I knew I wasn't able to summon the appropriate amount of righteous indignation. Part of me admires him for playing the game so well. I'm pretty sure that part of me will turn on myself when I'm able to feel things again. It will tell me I'm a stupid girl for trusting him. I'll probably believe it.

I kept walking. I took streets I had never been down before and wandered through neighborhoods I didn't know existed, but everything was all too familiar. The last time I took a walk like this I walked right off a cliff.

I wanted to do the show because it was different. Because I thought I could be different. I didn't want to see the same people every day, the same high school looming over my backyard. The same routine, the same pity, the same nothingness. I thought if I saw new places and met new people, I'd feel new things, too. It didn't work.

There weren't any cliffs around, or even any tall buildings. Not that I would have tried again. I'm pretty sure I wouldn't have tried again. But of course the thought crossed my mind.

It also occurred to me to pray. When I was in Sunday school, years ago, I heard the story of Moses. Moses led his people out of slavery after Egypt was destroyed by plagues. God sent the plagues because Pharaoh wouldn't let the Israelites go. And Pharaoh wouldn't let the Israelites go because God hardened Pharaoh's heart. What am I supposed to say to a God who does this to people?

I ended up at the parents' house. It was late, and the lights were off. I let myself in the backyard and climbed the ladder into the treehouse. Every year on Carol's birthday she and I spend the night up here, eating junk food and gossiping about anything we think the parents wouldn't want us to talk about. Tonight I just sat on the wooden floor and looked down at the house. It surprised me how badly I wanted to go inside. I wanted to smell Pine-Sol and clean linen and scented candles. I wanted to let Mom make me supper and listen to Dad complain about Quebec and to play video games with Carol. I wanted to ring the doorbell. They would let me inside. They would let me move back in. But if I stayed, they would want me to play nice and go to church and pray to a God I don't believe in and/or like before every meal. I can't do that. But if I didn't play along, I'd have to tell them the truth and let them believe I will burn in hell for eternity. I really want to find some middle ground, but I don't know where to look. There is only cold, dark air between me and the parents' house.

I don't know how long I spent there, but eventually I gave up on ringing the doorbell. At least for tonight. I've decided to move in with Jenna. If she'll have me, that is. She hinted as much a couple weeks ago, but I don't know how far her altruism extends, now that I'm off the show. If it doesn't work, I'll ask Bonnie if I can stay a couple nights, although she's busy getting ready to go to Edmonton. It can't be that hard to find a new place. There is always Craigslist.

I cried. I hate myself for crying.

Fuck him.

My iPod was in my pocket, so I listened to music on the way back to the house. Music filled up the lack of everything else as only music can do.

I run for half an hour every day because I hate it. It never gets any easier. Each day I dread going outside or to the gym, and each day I try to talk myself out of it. But I always go. I hate running, and I've run each day since starting the show to prove that I am stronger than my apathy. That I am stronger than the girl who gave up on life. The sidewalks were too dark and my jeans too tight for me to run, so I walked back to the house. It took two hours.

SatJun11

I was up at seven this morning, packing. AP says I have until tomorrow to leave House of Orange, but why wait? It didn't take me long. All the furniture belongs to the house. I just threw my clothes into a couple garbage bags and everything else into a suitcase. Chaunt'Elle helped. I think she was genuinely sad to see me go. She stressed that she had no idea they were planning to vote me off; she told me over and over that she was sorry. I believed her. She was the only one who helped me pack, the only one who meant what she said, the only one who didn't give my name to Alexander Park last night. I was actually glad to spend time with her this morning. The irony was interesting, but obviously I couldn't share it with her. Of course Chaunt'Elle ended up bursting into tears, which washed away whatever friendly feelings I was having for her. I hugged her — for her sake, not mine — then dragged all my shit upstairs and outside.

I was wondering how I'd get everything to Jenna's house when I remembered seeing a kid's wagon in the garage. I went in through the side door. Alexander Park was sitting at his desk, looking unusually unproductive. A couple of HOOcaps were sitting beside him, glassy-eyed and clutching crumpled coffee cups. I doubt they've had much sleep recently. I wanted to throw something at them to see if they'd respond, but somehow I restrained myself.

> **JS**
> Can I borrow the wagon?

> **AP**
> What? Oh. Yes, I suppose.

> **JS**
> Thanks.

I walked across the garage and pulled the wagon out from under a pile of camping equipment. The squeak of plastic wheels and the crunch of pebbles underneath were the only things we heard for a while. I piled my bags into the wagon. Alexander Park opened the garage door, and I stoically faced it with my back to the house, the daylight hitting me as the door rose. It must have looked very dramatic. I hope AP has cameras in the garage so he can use that shot. If I can't end this show as the winner, at least I can go out with dignity.

> **JS**
> *(Goodbye, viewers. I hope you remember me as the girl who should have won, not the girl who was outplayed by an asshole named Robbie.)*
> See you.

I grabbed the wagon and left.

Jenna is an INCREDIBLE WOMAN. She is letting me stay until the end of the summer, possibly longer if she doesn't hate living with me. Fair enough. Her house smells like spearmint and leather. It reminds me of Mom's purse. I don't feel like unpacking just yet. I might not bother at all. But it's such a relief to sit in a house and know I'm not being filmed. I've forgotten how much I love privacy! I don't have any money, but I'm going to use my credit card to buy Jenna a bottle of the second-cheapest wine I can find.

The doorbell rang at 8:03 p.m. I answered because apparently Jenna is the sort of person who showers in the evening. A neon-green hoodie stabbed me in the eye. When my sight adjusted, there stood Bonnie. She hugged me.

JS

How did you know I was here?!

BONNIE

I talked to Jenna's brother.

JS

You just . . . talked. To him.

BONNIE

Yes. He reached out to me, actually. Told me what happened and asked me to make sure you were okay. Jenna told him you were here. But you could have saved me an hour if you had just answered your phone.

JS

Oh. I'm not sure where it is right now.

BONNIE

Why the fuck did you come *here,* by the way? You could have stayed with me.

JS

It was closer. I was walking. And you're leaving soon, anyway.

BONNIE

Whatever. Where is he?

JS

                    JS
Who?

                BONNIE
Robbie.

                    JS
He's not at the house?

                BONNIE
No. I'm going to find him, then I'm going to kill him.

I smiled and motioned for Bonnie to come in.

                    JS
We'll find him. But if anyone is going to kill him, it will
be me.

SunJun12

Bonnie woke me up at six this morning. I have, in all seriousness,
never seen her awake this early. We had to be in and out of House
of Orange before anyone woke up. We found out through AP/Jenna
that Robbie stayed over at his cousin's house last night. Couldn't
handle being at the house I suppose. Good. I hope he feels like a
bag of trash. We had his room to ourselves. I forgot to give back my
house key when I left yesterday, so getting inside wasn't a problem.
After we grabbed the box of coffee and scissors from the kitchen,
we headed downstairs. A HOOcap was waiting for us, camera on
her shoulder. I knew they wouldn't interfere without seeing what we
were up to first.

Approximately nine hundred packets of instant coffee were emptied in Robbie's room. On his floor, on his shoes, on his clothes, on
his bed. Nine hundred is a conservative guess, but we left the empty
packets on his floor too. I bet he'll count them.

Bonnie took me to an all-you-can-eat brunch buffet. I love her. She had to go study this afternoon. Bonnie has exams tomorrow, and she can only stand being in Jenna's house so long. I have to study hard tonight as well. I can't very well throw away my education a second time because of some stupid asshat on some stupid show. Monday's episode will air at three p.m. It might be the worst day of my life.

> *After politely knocking and receiving no answer, Jane cautiously opens Dr. Freudenschade's door. The doctor's chair is empty, but a polished brown loafer peeks out from beneath his desk.*

JS

Hello? Doctor?

> *The silence is broken by a muffled cough coming from the floor.*

JS

I know you're here.

DFS

Perhaps you should act as though I'm not.

JS

I don't follow.

DFS

I'm going to sit this one out.

JS

Just come out already.

DFS

No. It's for your own good.

Jane sighs noisily.

DFS

Good day, Ms. Sinner.

She rolls her eyes as she leaves.

MonJun13

Jenna watched today's episode with me. I'm glad she did. We sat on her leather sofa and watched the show on her wide flat screen. I like the way she decorates her house. Everything is so clean-cut, bold, and intentional. It's comforting.

AP didn't hold anything back this episode, except for R's thought process. R is too clever to confide things to the camera. The HOOcaps managed to fit in the coffee incident and R's reaction. Priceless. I hope that's a GIF by now. Jenna laughed when she saw what Bonnie and I had done. Her amusement wiped out the shadow of regret my conscience had been threatening me with all day. Also — AP does have a camera in the garage. I'm pleased I came across so stoically. If I had cried at any point, my tears would be all over the internet.

TueJun14

Carol called. She wanted to know why her friend's brother's friend saw me on TV yesterday. I told her I'd explain later. She promised to never tell the parents. I figure that means I have two days. I'll think of something.

Exams were not so great today. I didn't sleep much last night. Or at all. I suppose this is stress.

AP called. He said I owed him an exit interview because I left the

223

house in such a goddamn hurry. I told him I preferred to think of my departure as efficient. He snorted.

AP

We're putting together one more webisode before exams are over. It's going to be simple — just one final interview from you and the remaining contestants.

JS

Why did you wait four days to ask for another interview?

AP

You're not the only one with exams. Also, I thought I'd give you some time to cool down.

I snorted.

AP

Don't tell me you don't care at all. Even you must have felt something.

He was trying to get a rise out of me.

JS

Save it for the interview. I'll give you fifteen minutes, and then I'm done with the show.

AP

How about Friday? Three o'clock?

JS

All right.

AP

Great. And let's make it half an hour.

So much studying. So many words. When the family goes to the

Rockies in the summer, we spend a good seven hours driving past trees. Hundreds of kilometers. Millions of trees. Every one of those trees is a word, and I'm supposed to know all of them. But I only have a couple seconds to see each word. That makes no sense. I wish I could think more clearly right now because I feel there is a good analogy in here somewhere. Something is buzzing, and I can't eat, and I never want to eat again.

I don't know what's happening to my brain. It's not good.

WedJun15

They know.

It wasn't Carol. Aunt Gina told them. Her best friend's son's girl-friend recorded it on PVR.

Aunt Gina also showed them the YouTube channel.

Never trust a woman with more than two cats.

It doesn't matter.

What matters is the two-minute-and-forty-three-second voice-mail message weighing down my phone. They are

- — shocked
- — disappointed
- — worried
- — befuddled (their word, not mine), and most of all,
- — upset that I lied to them.

I don't know if I lied to them. I never denied participating in a reality show. That probably doesn't matter as well. They are upset, and I am nervous. I don't know what, specifically, I am afraid of. Very unpleasant emotion. I think I need to bury my head in the proverbial sand tonight and wait this out.

Nope. Didn't work. I did, however, check my Elbow River email, and I got a shitload of messages. Three cheers for popularity. Some were angry, some were outraged, some were sympathetic, some were resigned, some were optimistic. It was nice to read them, because it saved me the trouble of going through those emotions myself.

hey sinner. sorry you were kicked off. not cool. robbie is such a douche. call me?
—Tim S.

Jane!!! What a Bastard!! You totally deserved to win!! Life's not fair I guess . . . Keep you're chin up!!!
—Sara

Hi Jane,
I just watched today's episode. I must say I am disappointed with the result of the voting ceremony, not only because I thought you deserved to win. I just lost $50 to another professor. The whole faculty is rather impressed with the show in general, though. Would you consider giving a presentation in one of my classes next term? Enjoy your break.
—my sociology prof (DELETE! DELETE! DELETE!)

You were my favorite.
—Spencer M. (I think this guy sat behind me in Bio. I could ask and find out, but the ambiguity is preferable.)

It's about time. No offense.
—Maxxx935

you are kind of a bitch so I'm glad you aren't going to win.
—Tina Blenheim

hi sinner,
you probably don't know me but i've watched your show.

226

it's really good. i enjoyed the classical conditioning. the use
of fridges in general was outstanding. well played. maybe we
can go for coffee sometime . . .
— Kris (Kristin? Kristopher? Kristofferson?)

IM SO ANGRY AND I DONT KNOW WHY!!!!!1
— CARL

I wish Carl would have asked me to go for coffee. I could use more passion in my life.

ThuJun16

I am done with exams, but I don't feel any better. My stomach is a little tender right now. Like that bruise is resurfacing. I want to punch it back down, but I don't know how. That's not true. I know what I have to do because it's the last thing in the world I want to do.

I had already made up my mind to talk to the parents when Bonnie suggested it. She thinks I should have told them from the beginning. Bonnie has always been the good kid dressed up as a bad one. I think I'm the other way around.

How I wanted the conversation to go:

JS
This is what happened. I tried and I lost and I am okay.

THE PARENTS
Hmm. Interesting. Well, look at you go, taking risks and being independent! We're so happy that you are okay; of course we knew you would be. We trust your judgment. Do you want to come live at home again?

JS
No, thank you.

THE PARENTS

Why not?

JS

For some reasons.

THE PARENTS

Fair enough. As long as you have a safe place to stay.
Here are some cookies. See you at Christmas!

This is not how the conversation went.

I felt incredibly flimsy and exposed as I walked up their driveway, as
though one gust of wind would blow right through me and scatter my
organs across the lawn.

They were not happy to see me.

I let them talk first to get it all out. It took a while.

MOM

What were you thinking? Why didn't you tell us?

DAD

What else haven't you told us?

MOM

We are trying to help you, trying to support you. Why
won't you let us?

DAD

Would you at least talk to the doctor again? Or Pastor
Ron?

MOM

Have you been taking your prescription?

They paused for an answer then, so I gave them one.

JS

No.

DAD

Why not?!

The doctor said to take pills; the parents said to pray. Neither option seemed to have done much.

JS

It didn't seem like they were helping.

DAD

Why wouldn't they?

JS

Because I'm not convinced there was anything physically wrong with me.

DAD

What about your depression? Where did that come from, then?

JS

(cognitive dissonance/existential crisis)

DAD

Well?

And then I told them I don't believe in God.

They yelled and threw their hands in the air and asked a hundred questions at once, but I could tell they were afraid. Terrified. It really unsettled me. My stomach turned to jelly and wouldn't stop quivering. I didn't know how to explain myself to them. Even now I don't know what I could have said to calm them down. I had several rational arguments lined up in my head, but no one was in the mood for rationality. The only thing they were thinking was: *My daughter is going to hell, and there is nothing I can do about it.*

All I wanted was to hug them and cry. It hurt, how much I wanted that. But I couldn't. Eventually I left. I walked back to Jenna's on shaky legs, hoping that by the time I got there they would solidify. They didn't.

I wish Hinkfuss were here. I don't know why.

I haven't heard from R at all. Not that I expected to. I thought we were friends. That seems like a stupid thing to say, but it's what I thought. I really want to know what he thought. I haven't heard from anyone else today. Even Jenna is gone. All this solitude is weird. I don't know what to do with myself.

FriJun17

For some reason I am more nervous about this interview now that I'm off the show than I ever was as a contestant. Butterflies are attacking each other in my rib cage. Or maybe they are attacking me? I can't tell. Why am I spending an hour getting ready? Is this stress again? Will I have to talk with him? Yes, I hope so. I will. I'm wearing lipstick, my tightest jeans, and a push-up bra. My confidence needs all the support it can get.

I walked up the steps at 3:05. AP was waiting for me.

AP

Hey. Thanks for doing this. One more interview and we'll leave you alone, I promise.

JS

Sure.

He lingered on the steps, blocking my way inside. He fidgeted with his collar.

AP

I don't know how to tell you this, but I thought you should know.

JS

Thought I should know what?

AP

Well, I was going through footage of last week, and . . . I saw Robbie in your room. I think he was looking at your journal.

JS

(WHAT.)

AP

[throws up hands defensively]
I didn't get a look at what he was reading, and I've never read it myself. I respect boundaries. But I couldn't help noticing you spent a lot of time writing.

I've never told a single person about my journal, other than my therapist. I've never hated a person as much as I hated Robbie in that moment.

JS

Thanks for letting me know.

I was so close to being done with this show. Being done with R. Now I didn't know what to do, besides focusing on getting through this last interview.

Everyone was in the living room. I took a seat on the armchair farthest from the sofa where Marc, Chaunt'Elle, and Robbie sat. I made eye contact with each of them. Marc and Chaunt'Elle looked vaguely uncomfortable, but R sat there impassively. His lack of emotion annoyed me, but I refused to let his stoicism outmatch mine.

AP

Welcome back, Jane. How are exams going?

JS

Fine, thank you. How are yours?

AP

Good, thanks.

AP paused. I think he was trying to figure out how to convert the quiet tension in the room to something more obviously dramatic.

AP

We'll do a group interview first, then I'll interview each
of you separately. Robbie, why don't you start? What
would you like to say?

R

I didn't come here to make friends. I came here to win.

He turned to me.

R

I'm sorry, Jane, if I led you on. It's nothing personal.

He paused for me to reply. I had nothing to say, so he continued, leaning in slightly.

R

I know you've been through a lot in the past year, but
you'll get through it.

I snorted.

R

I think you'll be fine. You're a smart girl. You're good at
a lot of things.

His voice was drenched in condescension. I lowered my arm and clenched my fist. Where the camera wouldn't see.

R

You're also good at manipulating people.

Marc grunted.

I could feel my face redden with embarrassment and anger. Knowing that I was on camera made me even more embarrassed and angry. I kept my face as still as possible and hoped I looked sunburned and indifferent. Not like I was ready to carve his heart out with a spoon.

R

You think no one noticed that you treated the show like one big psychology experiment? Like we were all your lab rats?

I focused on breathing. In and out.

R

Maybe you can see why we couldn't keep you around. You were a threat.

Robbie leaned back and smiled.

R

It's a compliment.

At that moment I knew Robbie would win. He'd win the car and the scholarship and the right to say he played the game better than all of us. Better than me.

R

I forgive you, by the way. For what you did to my room.

The room was silent and still. Even the HOOcaps held their breath.

AP

Jane, is there anything you want to say to Robbie?

JS

(I don't care if I'm not a contestant anymore. I'm still in the game, and I swear on my grandmother's future grave that I will destroy you.)

No.

After the group interview, I wanted to go outside and be alone and compose myself. And think. Before I could, Robbie grabbed my arm.

R

You know this is all part of the game, right? No hard feelings?

JS

Of course.

I peeled his hand off and walked out the door. AP followed me outside.

I leaned against the house and closed my eyes. I had to be calm for my individual interview. It's the last one I'll ever have. I might as well face it with some dignity. I imagined swallowing my anger. I didn't want it to go away completely — it felt good to be angry — but I didn't want it to show. I wanted to keep it to myself.

By the time Chaunt'Elle came outside a few minutes later, I was back in control of myself.

CHAUNT'ELLE

Hey.

JS

Hey.

CHAUNT'ELLE

How are you doing?

JS

Pretty good, actually.

CHAUNT'ELLE

I hope he didn't hurt your feelings.

JS

He didn't.

CHAUNT'ELLE

You don't seem upset.

JS

I'm not.

CHAUNT'ELLE

. . . Don't you care?

JS

I do. It's just not the same thing as being upset.

CHAUNT'ELLE

Sorry, no offense, but sometimes I think you can seem a little bit cold-hearted.

The individual interview went well. And by that I mean I didn't humiliate myself further. Before I left, Marc asked me if I wanted to go out for drinks later.

JS

(WTF?)

. . . No thanks, I have plans.

MARC

All right. We're cool, right?

                                    JS
Yeah. Good luck, Marc.

   I think he meant it as an apology. He's the sort of asshole who feels
bad for being an asshole. Eventually.

                                    JS
I hate him.

                                   DFS
You should calm down, think through this.

                                    JS
He's dead to me. I could have forgiven him for voting
me off. Maybe. But not this.

                                   DFS
Has it occurred to you that you might be acting a little
melodramatically?

                                    JS
Robbie Patel is the worst person to ever exist, and I will
see his head roll, or so help me god.

SatJun18

Mom called this afternoon, and I answered. She apologized for "the
way she handled our conversation the other day." I apologized too. It
was a brief conversation; neither of us could figure out what needed to
be said to make things better. She still wants me to come to the family dinner on Sunday. She didn't say anything about Dad, and I know
what that means.

Jenna and I didn't leave the house today. We cleaned and made enchiladas and watched old Hitchcock movies. I learned I'm not a fan of Hitchcock. Maybe I wasn't paying enough attention.

                              JS
            Hey, Jenna?

                            JENNA
            Yeah?

                              JS
            What would you do to someone who pissed you off?

                            JENNA
            Could you be more specific?

                              JS
            Someone who betrayed you.

                            JENNA
            Is this about Robbie?

                              JS
            No. Yes.

                            JENNA
            I thought you handled it pretty well, with the coffee.

                              JS
            Yeah, but . . .

                            JENNA
            Did something else happen? Alexander said Robbie was
            a bit provocative yesterday.

                              JS
            You could say that.

I didn't want to tell her about my journal because I don't like admitting to other people that it exists. Even hidden among my dusty high school science notebooks it feels vulnerable.

> ### JENNA
> You don't want to talk about it, do you?

> ### JS
> No.

> ### JENNA
> Well. I'd make sure he didn't win. And I'd make sure he knew it was because of me.

> ### JS
> That's what I was thinking.

FB tells me it's R's birthday today. Not that I didn't already know.

SunJun19
I've got a family dinner to look forward to tonight, my first time seeing the parents since I dropped the bombshell on Thursday. I'll finish work early enough to attend. Dad assumes I've been working Sundays because I'm a misguided youth who has succumbed to secular temptation. Or maybe those were my grandparents' words. It's hard to keep track of which family member is judging me these days. Time to catch up with the other aunts and uncles. Hurrah.

Dinner was at Uncle Hank and Aunt Flora's. They live on Upper Signal Hill with a lovely view of the city and mountains. No one knows (or will tell me) where their money comes from. It probably has to do with their lack of children. They don't normally have family over, because they feel the same way I do about family dinners. They also make wine in their basement. Obviously they are my favorite relations. The parents left shortly after dinner. Dad said he had an early meeting tomorrow morning, but I think they just don't know how to deal with me yet. I was afraid my bombshell would devastate them, but they seemed more uncomfortable than anything. Here I was thinking they'd show up on a righteous crusade to reclaim their daughter's soul, with a Bible and a speech prepared for the meal blessing. Instead, Dad spent the meal scrutinizing every aspect of the weather this week and Mom picked at the homemade label on a wine bottle. Maybe they think I'm beyond their help. Or maybe hell no longer feels real to them, either. Either way, I'm on my own now. I guess I asked for this.

Aunt Gina brought up *House of Orange*, and of course everyone wanted to watch it. We were a couple bottles of wine in, so I didn't mind. Anything is fun to watch in their theater. It was the first time I've thought of *HOO* as only a reality show. Pure entertainment. We had a great time, ripping everything apart. Aunt Gina was especially hard on Robbie, bless her heart. She had already seen the whole thing, so she knew what was coming. Everyone else was appropriately amused, disgusted, and outraged. They made fun of me, too. Specifically how pissed off I looked at the last group interview.

I threw my popcorn at the screen every time Robbie came on, but I felt bad afterward and cleaned it all up.

MonJun20

I stumbled into the kitchen this morning with pillow lines on my face, several elastics stuck in my hair that I knew I'd have to cut out later, and no pants. AP was waiting for me at the table. He looked short on sleep but sat up straight with a focused, single-minded air about him. He looked like his sister.

JS

Gooood morning.

AP

Sit down, Jane.

You didn't put a pot of coffee on by chance, did you?

AP

We need to talk.

JS

Okay, but I already told you. I'm done with the show.

AP

I got a call from the dean last night, Jane. He wants to know why footage of an Elbow River minor drinking alcohol ended up on television.

Uh-oh.

AP

You lied to me about your age, Jane.

This was probably the sort of conversation I should have worn pants for.

JS

I know. And I'm sorry. But I'm eighteen now. I only drank on camera on my birthday.

AP

And what about the recap we showed at the beginning of the episode? You think the cameras never recorded you intoxicated before? What about the costume party? Or how hung-over you looked when you cleaned the place with Robbie? And the first episode I had to recut —you think you can just erase something from the internet?

I was at a loss for words. AP was a thundercloud.

AP

The show was finally getting somewhere, Jane. Our ratings on Monday were better than we could have hoped for. And now that all this attention is finally on the show, the dean is on my ass because whoever put together our profile on the Elbow River website finally noticed that something didn't add up with your records.

JS

Look, I didn't know this would happen. I just wanted to do the show. I thought I was being careful about drinking.

How was I supposed to know that people would make a big deal about some girl having one or two beers on a shitty little web series about a shitty little community college?

AP

It's not even the drinking, Jane. You lied about your age on the contract you signed. Your entire participation on the show was built on a lie.

JS

It's not your fault; it's mine. I'll take all the blame. I'm already off the show.

AP

You don't get it, do you? I exploited a minor on the show. The dean wants to cancel *House of Orange*. I could be expelled.

Shit.

JS

Does he . . . want to expel me, too?

AP

I don't know.

Motherfucking shit on a stick. Jane, you idiot. First the suicide attempt, then high school, then the only real friend you thought you had in the house, then your relationship with your family, then the entire show. Why not add community college to the list of fuckups?

JS

So what do we do?

AP

I'm going to beg the dean not to expel my ass. As for you —I don't know.

Jenna found me sitting in the same chair an hour later. She placed a latte in front of me.

JENNA

It's not too late for coffee, I hope? It's definitely not too late to put some pants on.

JS

Thanks.

She took a seat next to me.

JENNA

He told me what happened. It really sucks.

JS

It does, doesn't it?

On top of the humiliation of being expelled, as well as being the one responsible for bringing the show crashing down, is the massively unsatisfying prospect of what happens to R. If the show is canceled, R can't win, but I don't want him to simply not win. I want him to *lose*. I want to see him humiliated, too. He can't violate my privacy like that and simply get away with it.

JS
They can't really expel him, can they? He didn't know.

JENNA
But it was his job to know. He should have checked his facts.

JS
So what can he do to save the show?

JENNA
Nothing. I'm going to save it.

JS
How?

JENNA
I don't know yet. But haven't you ever wondered why a guy like my brother ended up at Elbow River? I'm in university, but he's the better student. And don't tell him I said that, or you'll no longer have a roof over your head.

JS
So why is he here?

I was starting to sound like a broken record with all these questions.

JENNA
He started off at the U of C. Spent a year there. But he was kicked out. Like you.

I never thought of AP as someone like me. Someone looking for a second chance at Elbow River.

> **JS**
> Did he jump off a cliff too?

Jenna smirked.

> **JENNA**
> No. And I'm not telling you what happened. All you need to know is, he didn't deserve to be expelled then, and he doesn't deserve to be expelled now. So we're not going to let that happen.

I'm dying to know what happened, but I can't very well be annoyed with Jenna for keeping secrets when she's kept mine for so long.

> **JS**
> We?

> **JENNA**
> This is your mess, Jane.

I never thought I'd say this, but I have to call Mr. Dubs.

He's out of town for a few days, so we'll meet on Thursday. Until then I guess I'll sit in this corner and think about what I've done.

TueJun21
Not even Bonnie and Tom could cheer me up today. They're all caught up with the show and the drama and my uncertain academic future. I know Tom thought the show was a bad idea, but at least he had the grace not to say "I told you so." I wish their summer break didn't start

when mine ends next week so we could go on a road trip or camping or something.

> **TOM**
> Actually, Jane . . . I'm going to Edmonton for a week in July. With the youth group. There's gonna be a bunch of concerts there.

Edmonton is possibly the worst place on earth, but I'd go with them if I could. I never received the invite. Probably because they knew I'd have school. Or maybe it's because I haven't shown up at youth group since April.

> **TOM**
> And in August I'll be on a missions trip to Colombia.

South America? I really am out of the loop.

> **JS**
> That sounds like fun.

> **TOM**
> I wish you could come too.

I don't know if I believed him.

ThuJun23

Jenna and I discussed the fate of *HOO* over cereal.

> **JS**
> The school needs the show. Even if they don't know it yet.

> **JENNA**
> So what you have to do is make them understand. Explain to your adviser today what *House of Orange* can do for the school.

JS

I think he knows what it can do. He's already a fan.

JENNA

That's not enough. He has to believe the benefits
outweigh the risks. That the attention on Elbow River is
more positive than not. And as for you — Elbow River
is full of people looking for second chances.

JS

I think I'm on my third chance now. But who's counting?

It's hot out today. I bought a Slurpee on my way to the school but
dumped what was left of it before walking into Mr. Dubs's office, in
case it made me seem too flippant about my future. Maybe I should
have worn my #JANESINNER shirt to show school spirit or whatever.
Mr. Dubs sat on his exercise ball, wearing shorts and sandals with
socks. His new glasses, big, square lenses rimmed in thick hipster
black, gave me hope. This was a man trying to fit in with Kids These
Days. Always one step behind, but trying nonetheless. All I had to
do was convince him this reality show was even better than hipster
glasses.

MR. DUBS

Good to see you, Jane.

JS

You too. Nice glasses.

MR. DUBS

Thank you. You don't think they're a bit much?

JS

Not at all.

A tiny, necessary white lie. I rolled up an exercise ball.

MR. DUBS

So, Jane. We have a bit of a situation here, don't we.

JS

I suppose we do.

MR. DUBS

You understand the consequences of your actions, of your . . . misrepresentations?

JS

I do. And I'm sorry things got so out of hand.

Mr. Dubs began a series of squats on his ball.

MR. DUBS

This puts the school in a tight spot. Elbow River can't condone underage students drinking.

JS

But you knew all along. You knew how old I was. You could have done something.

Maybe it's risky implicating Mr. Dubs, but if we're on the same sinking ship, he's more likely to start bailing. He sighed.

MR. DUBS

Yes, I knew. I thought it would be best for you to deal with your participation on the show and Mr. Park on your own terms. I misjudged the situation.

JS

So what do we do? I mean, canceling the show seems a bit much, don't you think? Especially since my friends at high school are really getting into it. You know, a couple of them are thinking of coming here in the fall.

Yet another little misrepresentation. Forgive me, Lord, for I am a Sinner.

MR. DUBS

Is that so? Well, that's good to hear. Really. Maybe we can send them T-shirts. Do you think they'd like that? But as for the show . . . well, it's really not my decision.

JS

Maybe you could talk to the dean about it. I'd hate for *House of Orange* to end on a bad note. You know? I mean, the show could do so much more good for the school. We could really put Elbow River on the map.

MR. DUBS

I see your point. But we can't let this . . . incident . . . happen without consequences.

JS

I agree. But don't expel Alexander. Without him, the show would fall apart.

MR. DUBS

And what about yourself, Jane? What happens if you're expelled?

JS

That would really not be a good thing for me.

MR. DUBS

Maybe you should have thought of that before you decided to casually lie about your age.

This guy must have kids.

MR. DUBS

Jane, I really don't want to see you go. But maybe Elbow River is not the healthiest community for you right now.

I couldn't let this happen. As much as I found it revolting, I had to open up to Mr. Dubs. Maybe I could pretend this was like *The Bachelor*. If I didn't open up when I had the chance, I wouldn't get a rose. But that would make Mr. Dubs the bachelor, and the thought almost made me choke on a laugh. Pull yourself together, Jane.

JS

Mr. Dubs, can I tell you something? Something I haven't told many people here?

MR. DUBS

Of course, Jane. You can tell me anything.

JS

The reason I'm here — the reason I was kicked out of high school — I was going through kind of a rough period. The doctors called it clinical depression.

MR. DUBS

I'm sorry to hear that, Jane.

JS

I tried to kill myself on New Year's Eve. It was a dumb thing to do. But it kind of messed things up for me. And if I can't finish my high school diploma — if I can't even handle community college — then I don't know what I'll do.

I couldn't read his face. But he was no longer bouncing up and down on that stupid ball.

JS
I'm asking for another chance.

MR. DUBS
Thank you for telling me this, Jane. I know it wasn't easy for you.

JS
So . . . can I stay?

MR. DUBS
I hope so, Jane. But it's not up to me. Tell you what: I'll talk to the dean and see what he says.

I had to readjust my legs to keep them from shaking.

JS
Thank you.

MR. DUBS
Or you know what? I could talk with both Mr. Park and yourself. If the show does in fact go on, maybe he could use the conversation on the next episode. You know, part of the drama.

JS
I don't think that's necessary.

MR. DUBS
I wouldn't mind if he filmed it. If it would help the show.

JS
(No way in hell.)
Right. Good talk.

FriJun24
Thank God for Jenna. Without her I'd have nothing to do but sit on my

ass, waiting for the phone call to find out if I'm going back to school on Monday. I didn't realize she had such a big following over social media, but she's using it to promote the show. She's reblogging GIFs, commenting on the *HOO* Facebook page, tweeting #SaveHouseof-Orange.

I've been answering some fan questions on the *HOO* website (which AP has been asking me to do for weeks, but I hadn't gotten around to it before now). I'm very cautious and repentant in my answers: "I've made some bad decisions; I regret if my actions negatively impacted the show; Robbie is an asshat, and if I never see him again it will be too soon," etc. I told Aunt Gina I'd steal her the hat from AP's head if she talked up the show in her office. I even called the newspaper and gave the journalist who threw out my bag of puke a ten-minute interview over the phone. So it's not like I'm not trying.

No phone call. I'm not in the mood to party tonight. I told Bonnie I had a hot date with Netflix, so she'll have to celebrate the end of her exams without me. She assumes I want to hang out with Jenna instead, but I think Jenna's the one with a date tonight.

No phone call.

It's 1 a.m. on a Friday night and I'm on Facebook, accepting friend requests from people who gladly watched me suffer through a term of humiliation so they can continue to watch the humiliation of other contestants, all the while checking my phone, because even though it's late, the dean might call, and who knew I'd end up so desperate to attend community college? This is probably not what my therapist meant when she said, "Half a year from now, Jane, you could be doing things you never dreamed of."

When my phone did ring, my stomach did a backflip.

It was Carol.

JS

Isn't it past your bedtime?

CAROL

I'm not a kid anymore, Janie.

JS

So what are you doing up? Drinking alcohol and flirting with boys?

Carol sighed dramatically.

CAROL

Don't be so immature, Jane. I was *reading.*

JS

Mm-hmm.

CAROL

Why are you up? And posting so much stuff on Facebook? I thought you weren't on the reality show anymore.

JS

And I thought you were *reading.*

CAROL

I can take breaks, you know!

JS

Mm-hmm. I'm trying to help out the show. I don't want it to get canceled.

CAROL

Why would they cancel it?

JS
Because I did something bad.

CAROL
What did you do?!

JS
I skipped science class and smoked a cigarette.

CAROL
That's not funny!!!

JS
Then why am I laughing?

CAROL
But what did you do? Really?

JS
It's a long story. But I lied about my age to get on the show. Now other people are in trouble because of it.

CAROL
You shouldn't lie.

JS
Thanks for the advice, Tips McGee. Do me a favor and don't tell the parents?

CAROL
You want me to lie for you?!

JS
Not lie. Just don't tell them before I do.

CAROL
Fine. Well, you should go to bed. You need to get some rest.

JS

Thanks, Mom.

CAROL

I'm serious, Janie.

JS

I'm serious, Janie.

CAROL

Stop that!

JS

Stop that!

CAROL

GOOD NIGHT, JANIE.

JS

GOOD NIGHT, JANIE.

She makes it too easy.

SatJun25

Bonnie and I were stuffing our faces with poutine from a food truck near her house when the dean finally called.

BONNIE

Answer it!

I pointed to my face, my cheeks full.

BONNIE

Want me to get it for you?

JS

MMMph.

254

I forced myself to swallow the half-chewed fries, coughing as the lump made its way down my throat. I answered the call just in time.

                    JS
Hello?

                    THE DEAN
Is this Ms. Sinner?

                    JS
Yes, it is.

I burped softly into my sleeve.

                    THE DEAN
This is Horace Bates, the dean at Elbow River. How are you?

                    JS
        (A mess of nerves and gas.)
Fine, thanks. Yourself?

                    THE DEAN
I'm well, thank you. Ms. Sinner, I've thought long and hard about your future at Elbow River. And I've decided that we'd like to have you back for another term.

                    JS
        (Thank you, Jesus.)
That's great.

                    THE DEAN
However. You'll be on academic probation. And I hope you won't give me reason to reconsider — you're an ambassador of Elbow River, Ms. Sinner, and I hope you'll act accordingly.

JS

Yes, of course. Thank you. And if I might ask: What will happen to *House of Orange*?

THE DEAN

That remains to be seen. It keeps getting more and more attention — my daughter loves it. But Mr. Park and I still have a few things to discuss.

JS

I understand.

I hung up, put on my best nonchalant face, and told myself I wouldn't spend my last weekend with Bonnie talking about myself. Besides, it's not so much a victory as it is a lack of failure, but I'll take it. I took the rest of Bonnie's poutine, too. For once I was hungrier than she was.

DFS

So. Academic probation?

JS

Yes. Kind of sad that I nearly got kicked out of school twice. Who knew getting a high school diploma would be so hard?

DFS

It is sad, isn't it?

JS

Woe is me.

MonJun27

First day back at school. It's almost like I never left. Random people said hi and wanted to talk about the show. For the most part I answered their questions, even though I'm no longer contractually obligated to do anything.

The guy who punched R in the face last term now sits behind me in three classes. He tried to corner me after our first class wearing an oversize U of C hoodie, sweatpants, and too much facial hair, but I just happened to be walking too fast for him to catch me.

This term I have English, the second halves of Intro Psych and Sociology, as well as Creative Writing (ha!) and Intro Philosophy — with the original Hinkfuss (and Marc)! I wanted to take Vintage Gunsmithing and The Carbon Footstep of Twitter, but my program has its limits.

TueJun28

A text to Carol: Hey you is my jacket at the parents house?
CAROL: I don't know, is it?
JS: Just tell me if it's there
CAROL: I don't know if I feel like it.
JS: Do it or I'll rip the heads off all your dolls
CAROL: Is that you trying to be funny?
JS: Kids grow up so quickly these days.
CAROL: I'm not a kid.
JS: Is my jacket there, kid?
CAROL: Maybe it is, maybe it isn't!
JS: Don't make me come over there and sit on you
CAROL: ACCEPT THE MYSTERY!

The internet just destroyed my life. I'm sure the internet destroys lives all the time, but it's so much easier to not care when it's someone else's. No no no: Robbie destroyed my life. The internet isn't capable of responsibility. R was the one who leaked a copy of my journal online. Not all of it, or any mention of my suicide attempt, thankfully, but enough. Most of it *HOO* related. And all the shitty parts where I come close to acknowledging warm and fuzzy feelings for a certain asshat. It had to have been him. This is worse than being naked in front of a crowd. Much worse. Good thing I'm so witty, and so far a quarter of the comments on the internet are distracted by this, but I want to jump into a proverbial pair of sweatpants and run the hell out of town. I feel worse than naked writing this now. Shit shit shit. It may be a silly journal full of silly thoughts, but they are my thoughts nonetheless.

> Dear Robbie:
> FUCK YOU.
> Sincerely,
> Sinner

WedJun29

I wanted to face the shit storm like a boss. I wanted to stare down the school and start a fistfight with anyone who suggested I was capable of sentimentality, or with anyone who suggested I wasn't capable of feeling emotion at all. I didn't get the chance because I woke up with pinkeye. Days like this I wish I believed in God so I'd have someone other than myself to blame for my life. It's hard to say what's more revolting — looking like a coward or looking like someone with an infectious face disease. I hid at Denny's the entire morning, eating waffles with sunglasses on, doing my best to redirect the energy I was wasting feeling sorry for myself into some more productive outlet. I didn't come up with any brilliant revenge plots, but I did end up feeling less pitiful. So that's something.

I practiced my nonchalance on Jenna when I got home from the doctor today.

> **JENNA**
> So it's not getting to you at all, then? You don't care that the boy you liked screwed you over completely?

JS

No. It's easy not to care when you don't have a heart.

JENNA

Oh, so that's it.

JS

Yes.

JENNA

What happened to it?

JS

When I was eight I was in a car accident. The doctors were going to perform a heart transplant, but when they took out my heart, they discovered I functioned just as well without it. Didn't bother to put a new one back in.

JENNA

Hm. I'm not convinced, but it's a start.

JS

All right then.

Possible revenge plot: rubbing my face on R's pillow.

Relevant text from Bonnie: Ever have one of those days when all the shortcomings of your life come together to form one massive hole?

ThuJun30

Woke up with my eyes glued shut with disease. Couldn't look at light for hours. Jenna is staying with a friend all weekend. I'm lonely but can't blame Jenna for her instinct to protect herself.

"Nobody can tell what I suffer! — But it is always so. Those who do not complain are never pitied."
— Mrs. Bennet (Jane Austen, *Pride and Prejudice*)

CAROL
[over the phone]
I hear you're not feeling so hot, Janie. I hear your face is riddled with disease.

JS
You shouldn't believe everything you hear.

CAROL
So how are you doing? With the new term and, you know . . .

JS
My public humiliation?

CAROL
Yeah. That.

JS
Splendid. Just splendid.

CAROL
You don't have to be all sassy with me. I genuinely want to know how you're doing.

Yeah, I believed that. She's always loved me more than I deserved. Maybe her love wouldn't be so unconditional if she knew half the things that went on inside my head.

JS
All right. You really want to know?

CAROL

Yeeeeeees.

JS

Well, as soon as I thought I was starting to get the hang of everything, of Elbow River and *House of Orange,* I was voted out of the house. I barely know anyone outside the show. The one friend I thought I had turned out to be a complete dickwad who was using me the whole time. It's not enough that he voted me out — he had to go and post my journal online, just to twist the knife. It doesn't even matter what I wrote. Those words were mine, and he stole them and gave them away and I hate him for it. People don't look at me the same. I'm used to stares by now, but if I'm going to be stared at, I just want to be in control of the reason why. Is that really too much to ask?

Fuck, my throat is probably going to be sore tomorrow from talking so much.

CAROL

I'm sorry. That sounds terrible.

JS

So, what would you do? If you were me.

CAROL

I'd do my homework and make sure I graduate. And I'd try to get back on the show to kick some ass.

JS

You're too young to swear, kid.

CAROL

I can do what I want.

I don't need to know God loves me. I just need to know that she does.

JULY

FriJul1

AP sent me a basket of muffins this morning. At first I assumed Jenna told him of my condition, but no.

> Dear Jane:
>
> Happy Canada Day, you hoser.
>
> I know you appreciate getting to the point, so I will. The dean has decided not to cancel *House of Orange*. In fact, CityTV now wants to air episodes weekly. Jenna tells me you've been making an effort to promote the show. While your efforts wouldn't have been necessary had you not lied in the first place, they have been appreciated. The latest episode received strong ratings and just hit 100,000 views on YouTube. This is a result of strong editing, camera work, and producing. It is also a result of a strong cast. I understand you have had a harder time than others, but I wanted to let you know your strategies, relationships, and sassy attitude have been duly noted. Thank you for helping make the show a success, and I hope you will exemplify honesty (when appropriate) in future endeavors. Enjoy the muffins.
>
> — Alexander Park

A peace offering, eh? Well, AP knows just as well as I do that "honesty'" doesn't make for good television. At least now I know the show will continue on swimmingly without me. Not that I wanted to hear that. I was feeling practical, so I ate the muffins instead of throwing them at Robbie's basement window. I did save one to light on fire and place on their doorstep. Raisin bran.

I wonder if AP feels any sort of responsibility for my journal ending up online. How would R know I had it, unless AP gave him footage of my room and R saw me writing? Now, that's a creepy thought. Even AP wouldn't go that far.

Aunt Gina's house tonight. No one wanted Canada Day at her house, but we went anyway. The entire family was there, minus the extended Edmontonians. No great loss. Thankfully my face has returned to normal.

I was in a bad mood this afternoon. I don't know why. Yes, of course I do. Gillian's boyfriend ate the last seven chocolates. Not just the last one but *the last seven*. Who is this person, and why did they have to keep touching each other at a family dinner? My claim to those truffles was stronger than his.

The kids' table was overflowing with barbecue sauce and elbows. I had to sit next to Jack and Gill. Jack is probably not his real name, but who cares? If I had a love interest, I would never touch him in public. Especially not at family dinners. I might never touch him at all. Kids these days.

SatJul2

Bonnie's relieved the show won't be canceled. I know she'll still watch every episode from the godforsaken cultural black hole that is Edmonton. She's not enjoying her first week of class as much as I thought she would. It's the first time she's been away from Tegan for more than a day, and sixty-three texts and/or phone calls a day just isn't the same. Bonnie says I wouldn't understand, and she's right. I can't stand the thought of talking to the same person that many times in one day, never mind every day. Bonnie once told me that she thought Tegan was dead or pissed off or unconscious when she hadn't heard from her in three hours. I once told Bonnie that I didn't know my dad had gone on a business trip for five days until my mom asked me to pick him up from the airport.

I sent Bonnie a postcard of Calgary with the Rockies in the background to remind her of better days and nicer places. If only I could still win AP's Jetta — the first thing I'd do is drive it to Edmonton and bring Bonnie back.

SunJul3

Had lunch with the parents and brought them up to speed with my life, minus the parts about academic probation, nearly getting expelled, and my journal ending up online (god knows they would snoop). Besides, I think we've all had enough "honesty" for now. They took it rather well, which means they have considerably lowered their expectations of me.

MOM

Thank you for being honest with us, Jane. And your exam results were actually not bad!

I tried not to hold her surprise against her.

DAD

See? A little academic discipline is good for you. We're ... proud, Jane. That you've been able to keep up your grades despite everything else you've chosen to take on.

JS

Yes, well. I'm trying to turn over a new silver lining.

DAD

It's "turning over a new leaf."

JS

Oh. I guess I really dropped the bag with that one.

DAD

Jane, come on now. If you're going to say something, please say it right.

JS

Sorry, Dad. I was just playing devil's avocado.

I had to stop myself there. Any more improper idioms and Dad would never forgive me. It's still up in the air, as it is.

MonJul4

First day back at school after the Journal and Pinkeye Incidents. Awkwardly walking down crowded hallways wondering if it's just your imagination or if every other student is looking at you gets old after a while. I want to hate every person I see, because for all I know they've spent the last week amusing themselves with my angst.

I have to keep reminding myself who is really to blame so I don't lose perspective.

I shared my sonnet with the class today because sharing is part of our grade. I might have liked this class if it involved significantly less social interaction. But someone under academic probation has to play by the rules, especially when she just missed several classes due to pinkeye. Anyway. This one's for you, posterity.

<u>Now My Feet Can Touch the Ground</u>

Attraction; everything is drawn to you.
Resistance is heavy-handed, like too
much at once. What else could disgruntle you?
Nothing but groundless instability.

I'll listen to you drone steady nothings;
privacy's not required, but still inclined

to happen if they resolve to close doors.
But what we do is done for them, as well.

If I have forgotten you, forlorn and
static, I'm sorry. But satisfaction
runs all the deeper for the tardiness.
And what we do is sure to be done well.

Beauty might be the visible motive
if underneath is just as well exposed.

The class had to discuss the meaning of each poem after it was shared. I couldn't help but notice the half smiles and knowing glances my classmates exchanged between themselves after I shared mine.

TRAVIS
Is it about . . . you know . . . a breakup?

I waited a couple minutes until everyone agreed on the same thing before telling them it was about vacuuming.

JS
It's about vacuuming.

TRAVIS
Really?!

JS
Really.

We all had a nice laugh about it.
I don't need a TV show to lead an interesting and fulfilling life. Right?

After Creative Writing, a girl stopped me in the hallway and told me how shitty it was that my journal was online.

I know.

GIRL

I'm so sorry. I don't believe what everyone says about you, if it helps.

JS

(WTF do people say about me?! Don't tell me don't tell me; god, I want to know.)

Thanks.

The day is so much worse in retrospect. Usually I'm curious enough to browse social media and eavesdrop on conversations. Can't handle it today. Too much sympathy. It's gross. I'm hanging low in the linguistics section of the library, doing my best to blend into a stack of books that happen to match the color of my sweater.

Text from R(?!): You busy?
JS: *(So busy.)*
R: Can we meet up to talk?
JS: *(Actually I have to go home now and think about my life. Perhaps suffocate myself with self-reflection.)*
R: Please just respond. I need to talk to you.
JS: *(Why don't you go stick your head in a dumpster?)* No, thank you.

Jenna and AP were fighting in the kitchen again last night. All I could make out was AP saying "not here," and then they went outside. I shut my eyes and tried not to listen for their muffled voices outside my window. Tom ended up calling from some concert in Edmonton, but I couldn't make out anything beyond distorted guitars and sober excitement.

TueJul5

A fan sent flowers to my house. That's all the card said:

To: Sinner
From: A Fan

No idea if I know this person or not. And I'm not sure if I care.

ThuJul7

I saw R eating his lunch on a window seat today. Almost a silhouette, with the pale sunlight outlining the far side of his face. HOOcaps would have liked the lighting. He sat with his knees up, leaning against the wall with eyes closed and chocolate milk in one hand. It was one of those moments that specifically feel like a moment. Or a memory. Something bittersweet. I couldn't help but see how well I would fit next to him, the warm pressure of his sweater on mine, how nice it would be to enjoy the silence together. Of course, this will never happen now that I know what he is.

He texted me again. I told him to fuck off.

FriJul8

R ambushed me outside of English today, holding out a chocolate milk and surrounded by a cluster of HOOcaps. I ignored the chocolate milk but did consider dumping it down his shirt. But Academic Probation Jane restrained herself. So I gave him the coldest of shoulders and left him standing awkwardly on his own. You're welcome, AP.

Really. What is *House of Orange* going to do without me?

Jenna and I were talking tonight. It was late and the TV was on, but we had stopped paying attention when a legal drama began and we couldn't find the remote. God, I hate legal dramas.

JS

I have a question for you. It's for a philosophy assignment.
I want to know what you think.

I fished around in the sad, disorganized sack that is my shoulder bag. It had been sitting next to me the whole night. Anyone who thinks that homework + television = effective multitasking is lying to herself. I found the assignment from Hinkfuss and showed it to Jenna. It read:

> **Jane Doe is tied to a railway track, just within reach of a switch. A train is coming down the tracks. It will crush her, unless she pulls the switch. But if she pulls the switch, the train will be diverted to another track, where it will crush three senile eighty-year-olds. Jane does not have enough time to free herself — only to pull the switch. What is the moral thing to do? (Defend your answer using either utilitarianism, deontology, or virtue ethics.)**

JENNA

The only immoral thing I see here is Hinkfuss using a whole sheet of paper to print one stupid question. And the illustration — I assume it's meant to be an illustration — is nothing more than a giant blob of black ink. What a waste.

JS

I've always thought the gloves come off when you're facing death. At least that's what everyone seems to think. Anything goes when it comes to self-defense, or survival.

JENNA

That's bullshit.

> **JS**
> Maybe. Why?

> **JENNA**
> Because that way of thinking means, at the end of the day, it's everyone for herself. It means individual life is the only thing that is sacred. Not conscious, active, feeling life. Biological life. The state of being not dead. The same life that all animals share. And if this is the only thing worth doing anything for, then it means we're just animals, too.

Sometimes Jenna opens her mouth and words float out and I feel like an ignorant child.

> **JS**
> But aren't we just animals?

> **JENNA**
> Of course. But we're also human. And being human means believing in something bigger than the life of one person.

> **JS**
> Hmm.

I found myself intuitively agreeing with her but didn't want to say so until I had thought it through more.

> **JS**
> I have another question. Do you ever find yourself irrationally afraid of burning in hell for eternity?

> **JENNA**
> No.

> **JS**
> Didn't think so.

TueJul12

Enough of this. I'm going to see Alexander Park.

He wasn't in the garage when I got there. The HOOcap on duty said he was on a date or something. I don't know why that made me feel jealous. I sat on the couch and made the HOOcap uncomfortable by staring. AP woke me up around 2 a.m. He smelled pleasantly of candles. The HOOcap was asleep at his desk.

> **AP**
> Why are you here, Jane?

> **JS**
> I want back in.

> **AP**
> Blunt as usual.

I held eye contact.

> **AP**
> Come on, Jane. Even if I *could,* it's a terrible idea, considering the mess we're in.

> **JS**
> You miss having me on the show. This is the best idea in the world, and you know it.

AP groaned. He hates being wrong almost as much as I do. We're more alike than I thought.

> **AP**
> Do you have any idea the sort of headache that would cause me? What would I say to the dean? I can't just let you back on the show. You know I can't change the rules halfway through.

JS

I'll help with the headache, I promise. But you've managed to get Elbow River a weekly spot on TV — the dean will fold your underwear and powder your balls if you ask him to. And I'm not asking you to change the rules. I'm asking you to announce a surprise twist.

AP

What twist?

JS

After Thursday's voting ceremony, you'll be down to the final two.

AP

Yeah?

JS

At the end of the next episode, you could announce that one of us is coming back. Voted in by the public.

I watched him digest the idea.

AP

But I couldn't guarantee you'd make it back in.

JS

You wouldn't have to. I'd get the votes.

AP

You're pretty confident.

I shrugged. Confidently, I hope.

JS

Think of all the publicity. The four of us would be campaigning across the school, as well as outside of it. We'd be doing the work for you. And you could drag out the show until the end of August.

AP

I have a contract with CityTV . . .

JS

Renegotiate.

AP looked me in the eye.

AP

Why do you want back in?

JS

You know why.

I'm not finished with the show, and I'm not finished with Robbie. I have a debt to pay, a car to win, fans to awe, and everything to prove.

AP sighed.

AP

Let me think about it.

JS

When will you make a decision?

AP

Watch Monday's episode. You'll know then.

As I left, AP smacked the sleeping HOOcap with a newspaper. I smiled.

WedJul13

I left a bottle of aspirin addressed to AP outside of the house before going to class. For the headache.

My mind has been a bit buzzy today, thinking about how I can get back on the show. I sat by a window in Philosophy and did my best to daydream, but my eyes had nothing to hold on to. Hinkfuss called me out on my inattention.

HINKFUSS

Jane? Would you care to join the rest of the class?

JS

Hmm? Oh. Sure.

HINKFUSS

If you don't want to be here, Jane, please don't let me waste your time.

JS

I'm sorry. I want to be here.

HINKFUSS

Wonderful. Thanks for playing with us.

Marc passed me a note five minutes later.

MARC: Come on, Jane. This class is the best. Don't make her hate me because she hates the show because of you.

JS: I'm sorry, Marc. I was being immature. It won't happen again.

MARC: Okay. You know, you shouldn't let them get to you. It's part of being on TV.

JS: Haha. I don't.

MARC: Freedom is when you don't take anything personally.

JS: WTF, Marc?! That's really clever.

MARC: Ha.

JS: I'm not being sarcastic. You should mention that to Hinkfuss.

MARC: I can't. I'm shy.

JS: I'm rolling my eyes at you.

ThuJul14

Jenna and I had crepes for dinner. We lit used Christmas candles and listened to contemporary jazz and didn't change into sweatpants until after we finished eating. Once the dishes were cleaned up, I sat down cross-legged on the couch and pulled out my English notebook. Jenna made fun of me for the Pokémon doodles on the front. It was hard to focus on homework when I knew Chaunt'Elle was probably being voted out right then.

JENNA
What are you working on?

JS
We have to write a mythological explanation of the nature of love.

JENNA
What are you going to write?

JS
I don't know. Some bullshit, probably.

JENNA
I went to church on Sunday.

JS
What?

I thought Jenna was the kind of intellectual who looked down on religion from a lofty perch. She'd mentioned Christianity once

or twice before, and her interest struck me as curiosity, not condescension. Still, I didn't think she'd be curious enough for a ground-
level approach. Jenna waited a moment before continuing. I hoped
I didn't look too confused. Or blank. Or bitchy. My face does that
sometimes.

JENNA
Supposedly God loves us. But what is his one com-
mand? "What you do unto others, you do unto me.
Love others: and above all, love me."

She stared at me as though the intensity in her shiny dark eyes
could make me understand.

JS
. . . And?

JENNA
What's it to God if we love him or not? What does he
get out of it?

I thought for a minute.

JS
He gets us.

JENNA
He gets all of us. If this is love, it's not a "feeling." It's
more than that. It's possession.

JS
That doesn't make sense. Doesn't love involve self-
sacrifice?

JENNA
Think about it. The more I sacrifice, the more you owe
me.

JS

But what if the other person doesn't love you back? How can you possess them?

JENNA

It's not about them. It's about you.

I was beginning to wonder if I was clever enough to follow her thought. It's not fair how some people can be so good-looking, smart, and badass. I struggled to think of something to say while maintaining a thoughtful appearance.

JS

Why were you at church?

JENNA

Because sometimes I feel my life is one big meaningless hole.

JS

You too?

JENNA

I wanted to try something new. See what the big deal was.

JS

And did you find out?

JENNA

No.

FriJul15

Dear English 205:
Please accept this mythological explanation of the nature of love. It may be the most brilliant thing I've ever

written. It certainly has shed illumination on my own experiences.

Sincerely,
Jane Sinner

The Sky was the biggest, most powerful god, but also the emptiest. She was so big and empty that there was nothing in the way of her seeing everything that happened, both on the earth and outside it.

One day she looked above her and saw the Sun. When he passed by her, he filled her with his brightness and warmth and made her feel bigger and fuller and more powerful than before. The Sky liked the feeling so much that she decided she had to keep it, and to keep the feeling, she had to keep the Sun. She complimented him, calling him beautiful and radiant and strong. The Sun was flattered and couldn't resist going to her.

At first he was happy to stay; no one had ever appreciated him so much. But it wasn't long before he found that he couldn't move, and he became restless. His heat dried up the clouds and smothered the wind. The Sky felt her clouds dry up and her winds stop, but she refused to let him go, because she found that she could see her own self, her own strength and power, better in his light. She reproached him for wanting to leave, saying he was ungrateful. She reminded the Sun that he could never find such a welcoming, appreciative home anywhere else.

The Sun didn't want to cause her pain, but he couldn't remain still much longer. He told the Sky that he wouldn't leave her until every part of her was warm. The Sky agreed, not because it would make him happy but because she knew he could never leave. To this day, the Sun keeps moving round and round the Sky, always

278

bringing his light into the darkness and cold where he has
already been.

The End

I watched some behind-the-scenes footage on the website and found
out that R went on a date with a very pretty girl last weekend. Seems
like they had a good time. I saw her at school today, and we made
eye contact. She had the decency to look embarrassed. I hope I wasn't
glaring at her, but I probably was. He's mine. In a purely vengeful sort
of way. I bet he doesn't even know I'm coming for him.

SatJun16

We're not supposed to take home the overripe produce that gets
thrown out at the end of the day. Sometimes it ends up in my backpack anyway. Oops. Most of it is still decent — Jenna and I made some
fajitas. It's nice to have a roommate wealthier than I am but still practical enough to eat from a dumpster now and then. I'm glad the dinner went so well; I had something to ask her.

> ### JS
> Jenna, I've been thinking.

> ### JENNA
> Oh?

> ### JS
> I talked to your brother the other night, and I believe
> there is a possibility I'll end up back on the show.

> ### JENNA
> Yeah, I know.

> ### JS
> If I'm going to make it back on, I'll need the public to
> vote for me.

JENNA

So?

JS

So.

I swirled the juice in my wineglass as I chose my words.

JS

I'm not sure I'd get the votes. I want to win. So I figure I'll need a plan.

JENNA

What sort of plan?

JS

A campaign. And I want you to be my campaign manager.

JENNA

Is this a paid position?

JS

Of course not.

JENNA

What's in it for me?

JS

A steady supply of freshly expired grocery products and secondhand glory.

Jenna kept a straight face as she thought about it. I wish I could keep my face that straight all the time. I also wish my face was that attractive. Razor-sharp cheekbones! NVM I'm wasting words here.

JS

You're an efficient, objective, intelligent, and ruthless

business student with no patience for stupidity. I admire all those qualities. You also have over a thousand Facebook friends. That's got to count for something.

JENNA

Don't you think there'd be a conflict of interest? Since I'm the producer's sister?

JS

Who is going to know? Or care?

JENNA

I'll do it, but I don't believe in charity. If you win, I want a thousand dollars of your scholarship.

JS

Done.

MonJul18

Chaunt'Elle was voted off on today's episode. So many tears onscreen, so many smiles in our living room. I was kind of hoping Marc would go, but he had the immunity idol. Won it in a chili cook-off. I don't know what R did to get Marc to vote for Chaunt'Elle, but I think Marc felt bad about it. As she left, Marc gave her a kiss on the cheek. I've never seen him display affection like that before, and in any other context it wouldn't have made him look like a douchebag. R sat there like he didn't give a fuck. Cold and calculating. I won't be able to stand my life if either of these guys wins.

It's official. Holly, Raj, Chaunt'Elle, and I are in the running to get back on. AP announced the twist with his usual careful charisma. The rest of the episode was a little flat. It was mostly Robbie and Marc bickering about conflicting standards of cleanliness and hygiene.

• • •

DFS

Tell me what happened on last night's episode.

JS

Oh, you know. The show doesn't have the same level of psychological insight as it used to. Robbie is good at manipulating people, but he's too subtle for television. Other than the twist, last night was rather boring. I'd like to say this is because I left, so I will. The show is boring because I left.

DFS

Interesting. Very interesting. Do you hear yourself?

JS

Uhm. Yes?

DFS

You sound arrogant. I'd like to say I'm a good psychotherapist and I know what I'm talking about, so I will. I'm a good psychotherapist and I know what I'm talking about. You are arrogant. Why do you always think you are better than everyone else?

JS

I don't. Not always.

DFS

So walk me through your game plan here. You're going to get back on and humiliate R? And once you win the show, everyone will realize how clever and self-sufficient and totally-not-suicidal you are, right? All your dreams will come true, and you'll ride a unicorn into the sunset and live happily ever after?

JS

That is the general idea, yes.

TueJul19

Today is officially the first day of my campaign. We have one week. Here we go.

WedJul20

Jenna surprised me with a box of T-shirts with a stylized graphic of my face covering the front. I'm wearing one to school today because it amuses me. Tacky and vain? Or hilarious and ironic? It's a fine line sometimes.

Jenna had another surprise when I came home from work: a Facebook page titled "Win a Date with Jane Sinner!" I laughed out loud.

> **JS**
> Lol.

> **JENNA**
> I talked with Alex — every IP address gets one chance to vote someone back on the show. If someone votes for you, they get the option to enter their name to win a date with you. If you get back on the show, we draw a name. If a guy really wants to win, he can get his friends to vote for you and put his name in. Or her name. I assume you'd go out with a girl? I'd like to appeal to as many votes as possible.

I don't swing that way, but I'm okay with keeping options open.

> **JS**
> Sure. Give me a minute to think this through, though. So, this would take place after I'm back on? Is this a televised date?

> **JENNA**
> Of course.

JS

And it's just a one-time deal? Any specific contractual obligations I should be aware of?

JENNA

Nothing you won't agree to.

JS

Hmm. Well, if this is what it takes.

I admire Jenna's ingenuity, but I really don't know how effective this will be. I doubt I come across as very desirable date material.

JENNA

You're more desirable than you think you are. You've been on television, after all.

JS

Thank you.

A couple of Jenna's friends I had never met before came over tonight to design the Win a Date poster. Large text! Abstract patterns! Bold colors!

JS

Why are you doing this?

JENNA

It's part of the job.

JS

I mean, why put so much effort into this? What's in it for you? You don't really need the scholarship money.

JENNA

I like winning just as much as you.

That's it? You're doing this because you like winning?

JENNA

For the most part.

Jenna can be very ambiguous when she wants to be. It's frustrating.

ThuJul21

Marc let it slip on new website bonus content that I tried to kill myself in high school. Most likely R told him. So much for my attempt to leave that all behind at James Fowler. The worst part is that Marc played the Instability Card, and he probably has no idea that he did. Not the type of instability that results in entertaining reality television — the instability that results in emotional trauma, psychological scarring, and potential psychopathic tendencies. Obviously this is not the image Jenna and I want to present to the public. I hate the Instability Card. The parents play it too often.

I can see where Marc/R is going with this. If they can convince the public that I am a liar and returning to the show would be bad for my mental health, I won't get any votes.

This game plan will negatively affect me in the following ways:

- — My credibility as a strong competitor will be undermined.
- — Hundreds (thousands?) of people will feel sorry for me.
- — I might be tempted to feel sorry for myself.

Obviously we need to adjust our strategy. I haven't talked with Jenna yet, but I already have a couple ideas.

The first requires a substantial amount of instant coffee.

The second requires that I drop out of school and become an artist, playwright, philosopher, or some other profession that justifies obvious eccentricities. Like being a hermit.

The third involves a massive mud-slinging campaign funded by a sponsorship with Effexor or Prozac.

The forums on the *HOO* website are seeing a lot of activity. Most of it is bad news for me.

> "Jane Sinner shouldn't be on television. She obviously can't deal with stress. One day she is going to snap."
> —anonymous

> "WTF? why would she lie about everything?"
> —annie435

> "What an attention whore. But I guess shes cool."
> —2lowrider

> "My friend is a stay-at-home mom she makes over $2000 a week working from home click here to see how"
> —janelle45

> *Offensive material removed by moderator.*
> —leef tappynix

> "It's too bad, I thought I wanted her to win."
> —roxanne22

Jenna's plan of action is much better than what I had in mind. She thinks I should own it. The fact that I tried to kill myself. She says the public needs to see that everyone makes mistakes and everyone deserves compassion and a second chance. I'm not sure if she believes it, but if she believes it will get me back on the show, that's good enough for me.

Bonnie and I came up with a clever idea to make a video that addresses the suicide thing. I'm working on it now; should take a day or two to get right.

FriJul22

I went to McNugz Club today (they still email me the locations every week), only to find Marc and Chaunt'Elle already there. I wasn't exactly surprised to see her with Marc, even after he voted her off. No one wore Hamburglar masks. I guess those are reserved for initiations only.

CHAUNT'ELLE

Oh hey, Jane. Marc said you might come by.

Marc grinned smugly.

JS

Yeah. It's been a while.

MARC

If you want the votes, you'll have to earn them.

JS

How?

CHAUNT'ELLE

A nugz-off.

I knew exactly how that would go — Chaunt'Elle would kick my ass. She spends too much time eating junk food with Marc. I figured I'd cut my losses and let her have this one.

JS

Actually, I'm here to see Mr. Dubs.

He's never hard to spot.

MR. DUBS
What can I do for you, Jane?

We went outside so we wouldn't be overheard. Mr. Dubs waved the cameras that came with Marc to follow us, but I told them to go back in. I didn't like how happy Mr. Dubs was with cameras pointed on him.

JS
I know you know about the surprise AP announced. And my bid to get back on.

MR. DUBS
I might have heard something about it.

By that, he means he tweets about it every hour.

JS
Yeah. Well, I just wanted to keep you in the loop. I'm going to do this right this time.

MR. DUBS
Cool! That's great. Thanks for letting me know, Jane.

JS
So you think it's a good idea?

MR. DUBS
I think it's going to be much harder for you than the others to get back on. You betrayed the public's trust.

Yeah, well, I don't really care about the public's trust.

MR. DUBS
And I know you have your reasons for wanting to get

back on the show. But Robbie isn't a bad person, you know.

JS
How can you say that? He's the worst!

And here I thought Mr. Dubs was on my side. I almost told him R was the one who leaked my journal online, but I didn't want to acknowledge the fact that Mr. Dubs has probably for sure read it. I threw up a little in my mouth just thinking about it.

MR. DUBS
He's not so different from yourself, Jane. It's easier to hate someone than it is to open up to them. I'd hate to see you get hurt. Promise me you'll . . . play nice.

Yep. He's definitely a dad.

JS
I'm not going to do anything stupid.

Or at least undeserved.

AP released even more bonus content on the website today, much to the delight of the masses. Besides promoting the surprise twist, the new video is basically a teaser trailer for the upcoming man drama.

Cut to the living room destroyed after a night of Marc's shenanigans. Cut to close-up of an unidentifiable stain on the couch. Cut to Marc's eyebrows dancing when he said he was meeting a "lady friend" later. Cut to R in the interview room.

R
[deadpan]
He's possibly the worst human being I have ever met.

Cut to Marc's blond stubble covering the kitchen sink and floor. Cut to Marc's interview.

MARC
[laughing]
Bro needs to re*lax*.

Cut to Marc showing up at R's indoor soccer practice holding a six-pack. The ref shoos him off the field. In the background, R puts his head in his hands.

I told AP that if reality TV doesn't work out for him, he should consider sitcoms.

I just finished uploading my reapplication/suicide ownership video to the internet. It's not so much a video as it is a photomontage with text overlay set to a bumpin' eighties jam.

Jane Sinner: Talented Artist. *(photo of doodle of hand/toast)*

Jane Sinner: Sensitive Poet. *(photo of my vacuuming poem with "B+ Good Job, Jane" written on the top corner)*

Jane Sinner: TV Celebrity. *(photo of me doing a fist pump after I won the* Bachelor *challenge)*

Jane Sinner: Star Athlete. *(photo of me all sweaty after a run, catching my breath)*

Jane Sinner: Failed Suicide Attempt. No one can be good at everything. *(photo of me shrugging)*

Ninety-seven likes and counting! I wish I'd had time to get it done sooner. The live debate/public vote is happening the day after tomorrow. We'll do our thing at the school theater at one o'clock. Votes are accepted on the *HOO* website from two till seven. The winner will be announced *live* at nine. I'm nervous I'm nervous no I'm not.

Tweet from Chaunt'Elle: So grateful for the second chance!! <3 <3 <3 #HouseofOrange #InItToWinIt #AttitudeofGratitude

Who knew Chaunt'Elle's twitter account had so many followers?! My tweets would be so much wittier if they weren't all hypothetical. Jenna has been nagging me for a while to get an account — she thinks I'd get a lot of followers, and probably she's right — but I prefer to be more subtle about my egocentrism. My thoughts are more amusing as inside jokes between myself and I.

SatJul23

Chaunt'Elle threw a massive party at her friend's house tonight, a last-minute attempt to get support before the vote tomorrow. Jenna and I dropped by in lavish masquerade masks. It wasn't a masquerade party, but why not? I didn't drink because I don't want to be hungover for the debate tomorrow, but I had fun anyway. It's so much easier to appear in public these days with my face obscured by feathers and glitter.

SunJul24

How to deal with talking in front of crowds:

1. Eat breakfast and throw it up noisily.
2. Overanalyze the entire situation until it becomes so familiar it's no longer terrifying.
3. Drink three beers.

I'm no genius, but I think I might be a genius. When I stepped up to the podium I was not shaking, nauseous, or sweating uncontrollably, which sounds like success to me. I didn't take any notes because I planned to let Chaunt'Elle, Holly, and Raj do most of the talking. This was Jenna's idea. She is probably a genius as well. Chaunt'Elle was dramatically overprepared, with fake eyelashes, a carefully arranged messy ponytail, and a tight, low-cut shirt that said MCNUGZ, NOT DRUGZ. In what kind of world do sexy McNugz Club T-shirts not only exist but also receive a standing ovation from the entire school population?! Holly curled her hair and wore a T-shirt speckled with polka dot molecules. Raj looked clean and tidy in slacks and a dress shirt. I wore skinny jeans, lipstick, and an old T-shirt my dad got from the dentist with a graphic of a smiling tooth brushing its own teeth. Jenna and I agreed it's very meta. My hair did its own thing, which was fine with me. I wonder if the others have managers as well. If they have strategies and wardrobes with philosophical significance and campaigns fueled by a burning desire for revenge.

The auditorium was packed, and the stage lights were hot and uncomfortable. Four podiums were arranged in a loose semicircle facing the audience. AP sat at a desk, looking professional with a lamp and pitcher of water next to his notebook. He took his time introducing the show, the debate, each of us, the sponsors.

> **AP**
> First question. Why did each of you decide to come on the show in the first place?

> **RAJ**
> To win the car.

> **HOLLY**
> To challenge myself and overcome my shyness.

> **JS**
> For the glory. And the car.

> **CHAUNT'ELLE**
> To meet new people!

> **AP**
> Next question. What is the biggest obstacle you've had to face on the show?

> **RAJ**
> The swarms of adoring women.

HOLLY

Dealing with all the cameras and lack of privacy.

JS

Protecting my food, I guess.

CHAUNT'ELLE

I don't know. Relationships?

AP

Let's take a look at some of the highs and lows of the past six months.

AP played a ten-minute clip, showing everything from Chaunt'Elle crying for no apparent reason, to Marc flinching when the minifridge opened, to R washing dishes at midnight, to my face hitting the pavement, to Raj's rage when he lost at Mario Kart, to a time lapse of Holly studying all night. After the clip, AP opened the floor to questions from the audience. I could tell he planned it out ahead of time — HOOcaps distributed mikes through the audience efficiently, one step ahead of the questions.

STUDENT 1

[to Chaunt'Elle]

What's the deal with you and Marc?

CHAUNT'ELLE

It's complicated. We're friends.

STUDENT 1

How would you feel about competing against him, after he stabbed you in the back like that?

CHAUNT'ELLE

[flustered]

I don't know. I mean, it's just a game, but I still want

to win. I hope we can be friends though. It's just a game.

AP
Well said, Chaunt'Elle. It is indeed just a game. The lady in the back?

WOMAN
[to Holly]
Did your grades ever slip during your time on the show?

HOLLY
Not really.

WOMAN
How were you able to manage your time so well?

HOLLY
Discipline. And day planners.

I was impressed at how well Holly did in front of a crowd. Maybe the show was good for her, after all.

AP
The gentleman in the front row? What's your question?

TOM(!)
It's for Jane. Are you pissed that Robbie leaked your journal online?

I hadn't seen Tom since before Bonnie left, I think. I had no idea he'd show up. I stood with my mouth hanging open for a while before I remembered how to respond.

JS
Yes.

TOM

I would never do that to you.

JS

Most people wouldn't.

TOM

I'm not most people.

JS

Next question?

TOM

Is it true that Alexander Park's sister has been helping you get back on the show?

JS

We're friends, but she isn't part of the show. Who gets back on is entirely up to the votes.

TOM

Sure.

SOMEONE ELSE

You don't even have a high school diploma, Jane. What makes you prepared to take on a reality show?

JS

A diploma is just a piece of paper. It has nothing to do with me being prepared or not.

The questions went on for another ten minutes or so, and it was surprisingly exhausting. I was glad when AP moved on to closing remarks.

Holly, Raj, and Chaunt'Elle smiled and didn't say anything unsafe. We expected that. Which was why Jenna had arranged for me to go last.

I don't care if you like me or not. And it doesn't matter if you trust me. No one watches reality TV to see everyone get along. No one wants to see the nice guy finish first. You all want to see conflict. You want to see drama. You want arguments and hurt feelings and stupidity and tears. I don't want back on the show because I think I'm a better person than everyone here. I'm not. I want back on the show because someone I cared about screwed me over, and I am going to do what it takes to make sure he doesn't win. If that doesn't make for good television, I don't know what does.

I thought about thrusting a bloody sword into the air, shouting ARE YOU NOT ENTERTAINED? to the roaring crowd. It's hard to say how they reacted to my speech. The spotlights effectively blinded me, and the dull thump of my slightly drunk and adrenaline-fueled heart was all I could feel. AP thanked us and explained the voting procedure (open for five hours, one vote per registration, blah blah), and I'm pretty sure the audience cheered enthusiastically as we left the stage.

I felt like running a thousand kilometers while we waited, but I didn't want to reappear onstage even more red-faced and sweaty than I already was. I wasn't in the mood to face Tom and his inappropriate questions, so I left with Chaunt'Elle, Raj, and Holly. The four of us ended up hanging out at Denny's, no cameras. We talked about everything other than the show. It was nice enough, but my stomach was too queasy to properly enjoy anything.

We walked onstage together, single file. The lights were brighter than I remembered, and I couldn't see the audience, only hear them cheer. My palms were sweaty. Knees weak. Chaunt'Elle grabbed my hand

and I grabbed hers back, and then we were all holding slick hands together. Terrified. AP let the crowd work themselves up while we stood there. Sweat trickled down my back, and I questioned every decision in my life that had brought me to where I was standing now. I felt like the entire world was looking at me.

I felt like an idiot.

Alexander Park called my name.

I wasn't sure it meant what I thought it did until Chaunt'Elle hugged me and pushed me forward. The audience roared and the lights were relentless and my stomach couldn't figure out where it wanted to be. I smiled.

Jenna was waiting for me backstage, grinning, arms reaching for me. Neither of us is a big fan of physical contact, but I wanted to hug her because a chance like this might never happen again. I threw up into a garbage can instead. I could still feel the crowd buzzing through every inch of my body. AP's face filled a TV monitor next to me. I wondered how many thousands of people had just watched me on television, and I panicked. I closed my eyes and promised myself Netflix and chocolate and whatever else it took to get me through one more interview. The show has come a long way since the first YouTube webisodes.

Jenna, AP, and I had a celebratory glass of champagne at Jenna's place tonight. It took me a while to stop shaking. But eventually I did, and I feel ready to move back in next week. I'm only mildly terrified now.

Relevant text from Bonnie: I never doubted you'd make it back on. Time to kick some ass.

MonJul25

I've been flooded with congratulatory emails and mild threats all day. I don't care as much as I thought I would. I called the parents this evening when they got home from work. They were happy I called. I know they are still concerned, but they'd be concerned for me no matter what I did. I talked with Carol too, and she is full of youthful excitement and pride. Adorable.

TueJul26

Date night. Jenna won't tell me who won — she wants me to be surprised. So does AP. They really are the same person sometimes. I'm not nervous. I've been ignoring this night for too long for it to feel real. I'm wearing the shirt with the graphic of my face and a light cardigan. I'm hoping it will encourage my date to not take me too seriously. I'm also wearing lipstick and very tight jeans because it is a date after all.

I have twenty minutes before my ride gets here. Jenna did my hair. I feel like a slob already because there is no way this standard will be maintained. I promised Jenna I wouldn't be sulky and introspective tonight. This date is really for her, and I want her to feel like all her clever strategy is paying off. I turned on the Beach Boys, and now I just have to pick up some good vibrations. Yeah yeah — c'mon Jane, you got this!!!

I knew there was a strong chance my date would be Tom or Will, but I didn't want to admit it to myself. My stomach sank as I walked up to the restaurant. I wanted to kick myself for not seeing this coming. I should have insisted on the right to veto ex-classmates and potentially violent dates. I should have made a provision in the contract. I should have had my lawyer write the contract in the first place. I should have a lawyer. Why don't I have a lawyer by now? But it wasn't Tom or Will waiting for me across the candlelit table.

It was Robbie.

It was a punch to the gut. A series of punches. Uppercut uppercut jab cross left hook right hook. Roundhouse.

R

Hey, Jane.

JS

R

You might as well sit down.

Some paperwork lay on the table next to his skinny elbows. I didn't have to read it to know it was the contract.

R

I just want to talk. Jenna said you wouldn't run out on me.

Damn it. Of course I couldn't run out. I owed her. I owed all the people who voted for me to see this happen. I knew what I was getting into. I remembered that I promised to not be sulky and introspective, and a small laugh squeaked out of me. I sat down.

R

You look nice.

JS
(I hate myself for the effort I put into my app-earance.)
It's been a while. How have you been?

R

If you've been watching the show, you have a pretty good idea.

JS
Yes, I've been keeping up with the show.

R

Wine?

JS

(Oh god, yes.)
Yes, thank you.

A waiter promptly filled our glasses, and I promptly took a dainty sip. It tasted expensive.

R

Congrats on getting back on the show. I was hoping it would be you.

JS

Thank you.

Silence.

R

How have you been?

JS

Very well, thank you.

R

Come on, Jane. You can drop the act.

If the cameras weren't around, I would have chewed him out. And by chew him out I mean ignore him more severely.

JS

Please, call me Sinner.

Robbie sighed and readjusted his cutlery. I opened a packet of cream and dumped it onto a candle.

R

I want to tell you something.

R

I wasn't the one to post your journal online.

JS

(Your timing is very convenient.)
Your timing is very convenient.

R

I mean it. I don't know who did. I want you to believe
me.

I shrugged.

JS

I don't.

Robbie sighed again. I resisted the urge to check my cell phone for
the time. I knew I still owed him another three hours and fifty-five
minutes of my life.

JS

So how did you get this date? Jenna told me the whole
process would be legit.

R

It was. I convinced a lot of people to vote for you and
write my name down.

Something unpleasant twitched inside of me. I did not like the
thought of owing my success to Robbie.

JS

Why?

R

Because I wanted this time to talk to you. Just us. Before you moved back in. I knew you'd never agree to meet me any other way.

So he'd ambushed me.
Silence.

R

If we're going to be living together for the next few weeks, I don't want us to hate each other.

JS

If you don't want me to hate you, don't be an asshole.

R

Come on, Jane! It's just a game. It was just strategy. You said yourself that you didn't come here to make friends. I'm not asking to be friends. I just don't want us to hate each other.

I don't know what he could have said to change my mind. I trusted him. I liked him. Then he screwed me over, he lied to me, he made me look like an idiot. He invaded the only privacy I had.

Sometimes it's nice to hate someone.
Silence.

R

You don't get it, do you? How you can be an asshole too.

Three hours and fifty-three minutes? Who am I kidding? Jenna knew I'd never make it. I walked out, taking the bottle of wine with me.

Now he must hate me even more, and I'm scared of hating him any less.

302

I took my wine, walked around the city, and reveled in my anonymity. I found some paper to write down what happened so it would be on the paper, not in my head. I drank the wine. I also didn't want to go home because my hair looked so good, it would be a shame to let it go unnoticed. I ended up in a park; then I ended up home. Jenna had waited up for me.

JENNA
Jane, what happened?

JS
Come on, you knew I wouldn't make it! You set me up!

JENNA
I didn't set you up! He had the most entries, and his name was drawn. You agreed to this.

JS
You set me up.

JENNA
All you had to do was talk to him.

JS
I had nothing to say.

JENNA
Why do you have to be so stubborn?!

JS
I'm not stubborn!

JENNA
Of course you are!

JS
Well, I'm not going to pretend I'm wrong when I'm not!

Jenna rolled her eyes dramatically and left.

Tired and no longer as drunk as she'd like to be, Jane falls down onto Dr. Freudenschade's couch. She doesn't know why she's there.

DFS

Why are you here?

JS

I don't know.

DFS

It's rather rude, you know. Walking in here at two a.m, expecting me to make sense of your life for you when you can't even tell me why you're here.

JS

Meh.

DFS

You're extremely selfish.

JS

I know.

DFS

You say that as if self-awareness justifies it.

JS

Doesn't it?

DFS

Probably not.

WedJul27

Jane wakes up on Dr. Freudenschade's couch.

DFS

Good morning.

JS

I guess.

DFS

What do you want to talk about?

JS

I don't know. What do you want to talk about?

DFS

Robbie.

JS

Oh. What about him?

DFS

You didn't break your heart, obviously, but you cracked it.

JS

Don't you mean Robbie cracked it?

DFS

No. You did that yourself.

JS

Oh. It is rather brittle.

DFS

So what are you going to do about it?

JS

Reinforce my rib cage with steel. I don't want to talk about this right now.

DFS

We have to talk about it sometime.

                                JS

Go to hell.

                                DFS

All right. I'll see you there. We can talk about it then.

                                JS

All right.

Relevant text from Tom: Hope the date went well last night. You deserve a gentleman.

JS: It was not ideal.

TOM: I should take you out and show you how a girl deserves to be treated.

JS: I don't think I need you to tell me what girls deserve.

TOM: You don't know a good thing when you see it, do you?

JS: I do, actually. I'm staring at a bag of Twizzlers right now.

SatJul30

I wish it were possible to wash my brain out with soap and/or erase all memories of the past twenty-four hours.

I was going to stay at the parents' last night (I thought we'd be okay enough to spend a night in the same house) and watch a movie with Carol, but Carol just had to go and get food poisoning and ruin everything with her uncontrollable diarrhea exploding everywhere. But even witnessing that was preferable to what came after.

Jenna was obviously not expecting me to come home that evening. I walked in to find the house dimly lit and the radio blasting. That was fine. It was Friday night. I thought that meant Jenna was in the living room. I thought maybe Jenna could sit through *Harry Potter and the Half-Blood Prince* with me without shitting her pants. You never know.

Turns out she was in the living room, and the volume of the radio, loud as it was, was not loud enough to drown out the grunts of frenzied sex. Jenna is only human too, I guess. So she had a Man of the Night. Whatever. And they were going at it on Jenna's squeaky leather couch. Okay.

Pastor Ron can keep his theodicies and Christian apologetics. The strongest argument against the existence of a benevolent God I've ever seen came in the form of Marc's naked body violating the couch where I spend most of my evenings. Half a second was all it took for his red face, sweaty tattoos, and mass of pubic hair to burn themselves in my memory. And that was not okay.

JS
(There are no words.)

MARC
Uh, Sinner. What . . . what are you doing? Here?

JS
I fucking live here! What the fuck!

The only decent thing about Jenna at that moment was her decision to keep her mouth shut.

JS
Well, I'll be going now. Please tell me you'll disinfect that couch.

MARC
It's not what it looks like!

JS
(What are you doing, then? Baking cookies?!)
WHAT THE ACTUAL FUCK, MARC? No. Just . . . no.

I had lingered too long already. I headed back to the front door

—I'd take Carol's shit over this any day—and in the worst timing in the history of the universe, Alexander Park opened the door.

JS

Trust me, you don't want to go in there.

AP

Are you fucking kidding me? Marc's here again?

JS

AGAIN?

There was not enough disinfectant in the world to save me now. AP stormed past me as I hesitated in the doorway, caught between shit storms. Against my better judgment, I followed AP's yelling back to the living room. Something clicked. I've heard them yelling like this before.

AP

I TOLD YOU TO STAY AWAY FROM HER! GET THE FUCK OUT!

JENNA

What are you doing here?!

AP

Your *boyfriend* is supposed to be at a challenge right now.

JENNA

Ugh, he's not my boyfriend. Stop calling him that.

Jenna had wrapped herself up in a blanket. Marc was standing next to the couch, making no effort to hide his boner.

AP

[to Marc]

Put your fucking clothes on and get out, or so help me god.

I had no idea AP could be so terrifying.

JENNA
You had no right to barge in like this!

MARC
Yeah! What the hell, man? You need to chill out.

AP/JENNA
SHUT THE FUCK UP, MARC!

MARC
I'm sick of people telling me to shut up! If your sister wants to bone me, that's none of your business!

AP lunged at Marc, shoving him against the wall. Marc threw his hands up but not quickly enough to block AP's punch. Marc's head hit the wall with a crack. I ran across the room and grabbed AP's arm. He was stronger than I expected, but his shirt was surprisingly soft. Jenna was still kneeling on the couch, the blanket wrapped tight around her.

MARC
Is that it? Is that all you got, bro?

AP shook me off and grabbed Marc's shoulders, then pushed him to the floor. Marc stumbled up, grabbing his jeans. He caught my eye as he left, shrugging as if to say, "What's his problem?"

AP
[to Jenna]
What were you thinking? Of all the assholes you could screw, why *him*?

JENNA

Oh please. Like you're some sort of saint. You *want* Marc
to be an asshole. You use him just as much as I do!

I was starting to think I should back away slowly and leave it to the
two of them.

JENNA

You use him, you use me, you use Jane.

AP

It's not like that, and you know it.

JENNA

Oh, it's not? Then how do you explain what you did to
Jane?

They both snapped their eyes on me. I was halfway through the
door frame to the kitchen.

JS

Uh, I'm gonna make a sandwich or something . . . You
guys want . . . anything?

AP

Leave her out of it.

JENNA

She still doesn't know, does she? That you leaked her
journal online to get more attention for the show?

JS

Sorry, what?

For once, AP didn't know what the right thing to say was. His eyebrows did pushups on his forehead. I struggled to understand what
this meant.

It was never Robbie.

AP

Jane, look — I didn't mean for it to go this far. When you left, the show wasn't the same. I didn't want people —

JS

So you just let me believe it was Robbie? You all but told me it was him!

AP was red in the face, pacing the living room and waving his hands everywhere. Jenna quietly began putting her clothes back on.

AP

Viewers wanted a villain. You wanted to hate him, too.

JS

Don't you dare say this is my fault.

AP

Well, what do you want me to do, Jane? You need this show as much as I do!

I hated him for saying that. I hated him for seeing through me.

JS

You're sick. Both of you.

AP stopped pacing.

AP

Jane . . . I'm sorry. I shouldn't have done it.

JS

Right. Go suck a bag of dicks, Alexander.

Jenna snorted.

You too, Jenna. How long have you and Marc—forget it. Just . . . god.

I walked past the two of them and into my bedroom. Only one more night here, then I'm back in *House of Orange* with three of the worst human beings I've ever met. Not that I'd rather stay here with Jenna and that cesspool of a couch. I almost wish there were cameras around tonight. These asswipes deserve to know what it's like.

SunJul31

Move-in day. Again. This time it was just me and the wagon I'd forgotten to return to AP. Jenna offered to help me gather all my things, but I told her she should get her own shit together first. Actually I didn't say that, but I should have. Setting up my room felt so much different from last time. I feel older, more tired. I want to say I feel wiser, but I think it's just bitterness. The house was empty and quiet. R must have done a lot of cleaning recently, because it looks better than it did in the last episode. I forgot how much orange shag carpet there is—I can't tell if I missed it or not. Thankfully I didn't have to spend much time there before heading to work. Marc acknowledged my presence by saying, "Hey, uh, hey, Sinner," while refusing to meet my eyes. Robbie gave me a careful nod. He may not have leaked my journal, but he still stabbed me in the back. AP didn't show his face all day.

My mini-fridge was full of mostly rotting food and Coke. All Marc's, of course. I threw out the food and drank a Coke.

HOOCAP
So, Jane. How does it feel to be back?

JS
(Lonely.)
It feels emptier. Like something is missing.

HOOCAP

You mean Chaunt'Elle?

JS

No, that's not it.

HOOCAP

What's the plan now?

JS

I'm going to win the show by destroying Robbie Patel and everything he loves. And then I'm setting fire to this house. Jenna's house too.

HOOCAP

How very . . . spirited of you.

JS

Some girls just want to watch the world burn, you know?

HOOCAP

. . . Right. Well. Thank you for your time, Jane. I'll let you get back to unpacking. Welcome back, by the way.

JS

Thank you.

Maybe I should have just finished high school online.

AUGUST

MonAug1

It's good to be back, in a way. I'm in my element, no matter how shitty everyone around me is. I didn't expect to come back and find the house full of unicorns and rainbows. Still, thousands of people I don't

313

know voted for me to be here. I can win this. I know what to do and I'm angry. It's enough for now.

I came home after school to find a single rose on the counter next to a tiny envelope addressed to me. A HOOcap was there to film me open it.

It was from Tom, who said he misses me and I'm such a clever girl for getting back on the show and he wants to go for coffee tomorrow before he leaves for Colombia. The fact that he said "Let's go for coffee" and not "Let's hang out" is cause for concern.

JS
Meh.

HOOCAP
You should go. At least give him a chance.

Of course the HOOcap wants me to go. For all I know, AP put Tom up to this. Or at least hopes I'm petty enough to try and make R jealous. I texted him "sure" (with the camera pointing straight down on my hands in what the HOOcap called "Wes Anderson style"), but I'm regretting it now. Maybe it's time I draw a line between what I do for the show and what I don't.

AP was waiting for me after my evening run, sitting on the steps, drinking iced tea. Wearing a crisp button-down shirt and new shoes, his hair perfect. His skin smooth and even. Not like the last time I saw him. And not like me, with my damp T-shirt and wet hair clinging to red cheeks. Sometimes it's so easy to hate attractive people.

AP
Jane! Glad I caught you. Can I talk to you for a minute?

314

JS

Sure.

AP

Wait here. I'll grab you an iced tea. Nice evening out, isn't it?

JS

Sure.

I thought about going inside to shower first, but I assumed the reason AP wanted to talk outside was to avoid the cameras. He returned with a tall, cool glass and handed it to me with a smile.

AP

How . . . are you doing?

JS

Fine. What do you want?

His smile didn't flicker.

AP

I wanted to apologize. Formally.

I didn't respond. I wanted him to feel as uncomfortable as possible. We both took a sip.

AP

You must hate me.

JS

Something like that.

AP

I looked through your backpack to find your journal. At Jenna's. She didn't know.

But if she did, would she have stopped him?

AP

I only wanted people interested in the show again. I didn't want to hurt you.

JS

Say what you want. You knew exactly what would happen.

AP

I messed up, okay? I made the wrong call. I wish I could take it back, but I can't. I don't know what to do now.

I let the moment sink in while I sipped my iced tea.

AP

Did you talk to Robbie about it?

JS

No. I will tonight.

AP

That's what I wanted to ask you. I know I let him take the fall, but if this gets out — if people find out it was me, not him — the show will lose all credibility. It'll fall apart, and I'll be in deep shit again. I can't let that happen.

JS

You should have thought of that before.

God, I must have sounded like the parents. Or worse, Mr. Dubs.

AP

The unfortunate truth is, we both need this show.

JS

Why do *you* need it so badly?

AP

You're not the only one looking for a second chance, Jane.

Damn him for being a reasonable asshole. I'd rather he didn't make sense. I'd rather not depend on a reality TV show for redemption.

JS

So what are you asking? That I keep my mouth shut? Does Robbie know?

AP

I didn't tell him, but I think he suspects. I know I don't deserve this, but please don't say anything. At least not until the show is over. Just a couple more weeks.

I'm not interested in helping AP save face, but unfortunately he was right. We're in this together. What's one more lie?

JS

Fine. But after the show it's all coming out.

AP

I know. And please . . . I don't want to make a big deal about Marc and my sister. I really don't want people to know.

JS

I never want to think about that night again. Why would I talk about it?

I drained the last of my iced tea and stood up.

I need to go shower.

AP

My sister wanted to apologize. Although I don't blame you for not answering her texts. She thinks really highly of you, you know.

Sure.

It's all a mess. I've screwed over R, and I'm lying (or at least avoiding the truth) to protect the guy who screwed me over. R thinks I hate him, and I'm going to let him think that, because I'm too much of a coward to say otherwise.

Right now I have more public support than he does (or at least I hope I do — he did get me votes, after all), and I want to win. I need to win, because I have nothing else to look forward to. And if I lose, then I can't even justify my shittiness in retrospect. R let me believe all along that it was him. Why? No, he tried to tell me, I think. On that "date." And I didn't believe him. For obvious reasons, I think.

I doubt the parents would be proud of me right now. If they knew what I'm thinking, they'd tell me to visit a proper therapist again. Or talk with Pastor Ron. I'm too much of a coward to even be honest with my family. I'm barely honest with myself.

I thought about talking to R tonight, anyway. Off camera. But if I apologized (which I'm not ready to do), and if he wanted things to go back to the way they were (which I wouldn't, if I were him), then there's a small chance we might start getting along again. In which case, AP couldn't rely on our revenge story to carry the show to the final episode, in which case, he'd keep Marc around instead of R for drama. I can't live with the thought of Marc violating our furniture here any longer than necessary.

Besides. I doubt R is willing to talk again after I ditched our "date."

TueAug2

I met Tom at a coffee shop during lunch. He had to spread his legs awkwardly just to fit them under the tiny table. He reminded me of Mr. Dubs, and the mental image of Tom in fifteen years made me cringe.

> TOM
>
> Jane! It's been a while.

He pulled out my chair for me.

> JS
>
> I know. How have you been?

> TOM
>
> Really good, thanks. What's new?

> JS
>
> Well, I'm back in *House of Orange*.

> TOM
>
> Right. I voted for you, you know . . .

> JS
>
> Yeah, I figured you would. Thanks.

> TOM
>
> . . . even though I don't like the whole thing.

> JS
>
> You never did appreciate reality TV.

> TOM
>
> It's just so . . . worldly. What is our generation coming to?

> JS
>
> It's a means to an end. Something I have to see through.

TOM

What are you trying to prove, Jane?

JS

Nothing. It's just . . . well, I still worry about saying the wrong thing, but not as much. Not in the same way. Sure, I offend people now and then, but it doesn't scare me. I can be a whole new Jane.

I didn't expect Tom to understand what it's like on the other side of church.

TOM

And you can only be "a whole new Jane" if the world is watching?

JS

I don't know about the world. I'd settle for local viewers of substandard television programming.

TOM

You don't have to do this, though. You're better than this.

JS

(Right.)
Thanks, Tom.

TOM

I'm serious. You don't have to lower yourself on TV just to get revenge or, I don't know, impress someone. People like you for who you are, not for this new TV persona. I like you for who you are.

"Who I am" really wanted to smack him.

JS

So, all ready for Colombia?

TOM

Oh. Uh, yeah, just about. It's going to be incredible. What about you? Any plans for a missions trip?

JS

Nope.

TOM

How about traveling, at least? Once you're done with whatever you're doing at community college?

Yeah, because I've got so much money to burn at the moment.

JS

Well, my Aunt Gina was thinking of going to Ikea this weekend. Maybe I'll tag along.

TOM

That's not exactly what I meant.

JS

I could use a new rug for my bedroom. It would really tie the room together, you know?

TOM

Uh, I guess.

JS

You've never seen that movie?

TOM

What movie?

JS

God. What is our generation coming to?

TOM

Why do you do that?

JS

Do what?

TOM

Say "God" all the time. Take his name in vain.

JS

I don't know. Habit, I guess.

Tom sighed heavily.

TOM

You've changed, Jane.

Thank god.

Mom was happy to meet me for supper tonight. Just the two of us. We both knew without saying that it would be much less awkward without Dad. We went to a Thai place, and I think she had been waiting for a while before I got there, even though I arrived on time. She stood up when I walked in and crushed me in a hug, her massive leather purse and bony knuckles digging into my back. It's not easy hugging someone so much shorter than yourself. You'd think by now we'd have it worked out.

MOM

It's so nice to see you! I'm so glad you called. How have you been? How is school? Are you doing okay?

JS

Yes, I'm good.

When she finally released me, we took off our jackets and sat down. I took a sip from the glass of water she had already ordered me.

MOM

Are you sure going back on the show is a good idea? I mean, will you be okay? Will your grades be okay?

JS

Yeah, I'll be fine! Don't worry.

MOM

What about that boy? Robbie? Are you still friends?

JS

Not really. We're not exactly on speaking terms. But I don't want to talk about him right now.

The waitress came and asked if we were ready to order. We both said, "I'll have what she's having" at the same time before settling on pad thai.

JS

I saw Tom this afternoon.

MOM

Oh, Tom! How's he doing?

JS

Getting ready for his missions trip. Then it's off to school for engineering. Real school, I mean. University.

MOM

He's such a well-rounded young man.

JS

So I've heard. He watches the show all the time, even though he says it's "too worldly." The bonus stuff on the website, too. He . . . asked me if I was seeing anyone. And I told him yes, even though I'm not.

MOM

But why would you do that?

JS

I don't know. To get him off my back.

MOM

But you said Tom watches the show. He'll know you lied. You'll embarrass him on TV.

JS

Yup.

MOM

Doesn't that bother you?

JS

Nope.

MOM

Janie! Is this any way to treat your friends?

JS

Do you think there's something wrong with me?

MOM

Oh, Janie, I think there are several things wrong with you. But there is so much more that is right.

She reached across the table and grabbed my hand.

MOM

I don't know why you want to do that show again. You don't have to prove anything. But if it's what you want, I will support you. I'm always here. You know that, right?

I squeezed her hand back.

• • •

I can't concentrate, can't sleep. R walked into the kitchen around 3 a.m. I was making tea and cereal in my short shorts and T-shirt.

JS

Help yourself to tea.

R

No, thanks.

JS
(Please talk to me.)
I can't wait for all this to be over.

R

Me too.

He grabbed a box of cookies from his cupboard.

R

Want one?

He avoided eye contact as he said it.

JS
(I want to sit down next to you and put my head on your shoulder and pretend the last few weeks never happened.)
No, thanks.

R ate his cookie, slowly and neatly.

R

Why are you staring at me?

I looked away. It was dark; I don't know if he saw me blush. I felt the night air on my bare legs and the thinness of my T-shirt and the nakedness of my face and wanted him to look at me. He didn't.

JS
(I want to tell you everything, but honesty doesn't come easily to me.)
I'm sorry.

I think it was Mr. Dubs who said R was like me. As in not great, but not the absolute worst. Damn Mr. Dubs if he's right.

R bent down, picked up a minuscule crumb, walked over to the sink, and dropped it in.

My useless, freeze-dried, goody-one-shoe heart gave a shudder.

Don't you do this to me, Robbie Patel. You've already taken enough from me. You can't take my self-righteous anger, too. You can't take my burning desire for revenge.

R
It's your turn to do the dishes, by the way.

He left.

Fine. If that's how he wants to play this, that's how we'll play. If AP wants a rivalry, I'll give him a rivalry. I don't need R to be my ally anymore. Or whatever.

Honesty: I've been taking my meds again since I got back on the show.

WedAug3
I spent the evening at the kitchen table staring down a stack of textbooks, armed with a pot of coffee and a single highlighter. The textbooks won. Alexander Park showed up around ten, carrying books of his own.

JS
The Cinematographer's Handbook?

326

AP

Thrilling material.

JS

Naturally. Help yourself to coffee.

AP

The pot is empty.

JS

Well, never mind then.

AP sat down across the table and neatly arranged his books and pens in front of him.

AP

I can't concentrate at home. Hope you don't mind if I study here.

JS

I guess.

I ignored him until it was obvious he wasn't interested in studying.

JS

So where do you live?

AP

My parents own a few restaurants downtown. I live with them right above one, on Seventeenth Ave. It gets pretty noisy at times.

JS

Jenna said your parents bought your car. And that they pay for her place. Why wouldn't they pay for a place for you?

AP

Who do you think pays for this house? But I hardly spend any time at home anyway, so there's no point moving out.

I had never thought about AP having a home outside of House of Orange. He spends as much time here as I do. It was odd to have him sitting at the kitchen table with me, doing homework. So informal.

Something hairy brushed past my legs. Hinkfuss meowed loudly as she jumped onto the table. She licked the half-eaten toast sitting on my (lack of) English notes. I didn't bother moving her.

JS

Why did you pick me, by the way? For the show?

I knew it had to do with Jenna, but I wanted him to admit it.

JS

Of course, I am an Incredible Woman. Maybe it's obvious.

AP

You are one of the most sarcastic people I have ever met.

JS

You should take me more seriously.

AP

You have an interesting look about you. And Jenna knew about you. She thought you would have something to prove.

JS

But you must have had a thousand other applicants with troubled pasts and irresponsible hair.

AP

Two other applicants, actually. In total.

JS

Well, I guess I *am* pretty interesting.

AP smiled at me. A genuine smile — meant for me, not the cameras. It was unnerving.

JS

You have something to prove, too.

AP

Like what?

JS

I don't know. But why else make a school project your life? Why take it as far as you do?

Why be willing to destroy someone's privacy for it?
He sighed and rearranged his pens.

AP

Because filmmaking is a brutal industry. You don't get anywhere unless you work more than anyone else. Unless you're better than they are.

JS

You are better than they are.

AP

And I don't want to end up working at a Chinese restaurant for the rest of my life.

JS

I thought you were Korean.

AP

Exactly. I love my parents, but I don't want what they
have. Does that make me ungrateful?

JS

No. I get it. But I don't get why you're at Elbow River.
Jenna said you used to go to U of C.

He leaned back in his chair and crossed his arms.

AP

Yeah, well. Did she tell you why?

JS

No.

AP

I don't want to talk about it.

JS

Of course you don't. Why should I expect you to
open up to me? It's not like you know all *my* dark and
humiliating and shameful secrets.

I took a noisy slurp of lukewarm coffee to let my point sink in.

AP

Yeah. I guess I owe you. But you can't tell anyone. I
already turned off the cameras in here.

JS

Cross my heart and hope to die.

AP

Jenna was hanging out at my dorm one evening. Just
watching movies, like we'd done a thousand times
before. But this one night, she did lines of cocaine in my
bathroom.

JS

Huh.

AP

I bet she didn't tell you she did cocaine, either.

JS

The subject has never come up organically.

AP

So my roommate came back early and ratted me out. I sent Jenna home and took the fall. The school has a pretty strict no-drugs policy, and they made an example out of me.

JS

But why cover for her?

AP

Because she's my little sister!

He said it like it was the most obvious thing in the world. Maybe it was.

AP

She was young and stupid. My parents were pissed at me, but they would have been so much harder on her.

JS

Huh.

I've never heard anyone describe Jenna as stupid before. Although you'd have to be to sleep with Marc. But now I get why she's so eager to help out the show. She owes AP big time.

AP

I gave up a full scholarship. No other university wanted me. Yeah, I've got something to prove. I don't need a scholarship and experienced professors and expensive equipment to make something people want to watch. So here I am.

JS

Here we are. A school for second chances. Thanks for telling me, Alexander.

AP

Just don't tell anyone about your journal. Please.

JS

I already said I wouldn't. That doesn't make it okay, though.

AP

I know. Thank you, Jane. So what about yourself? I can't figure you out. Where do you want to end up?

I shrugged.

AP

You're too clever to have no ambition.

JS

I know it's a problem. I'm working on it.

AP

I'm happy you're back now, but ... whatever you want from all this, don't let it end with the show. There's always an after.

JS

It's not in your best interest to tell me this. I should stay focused on the show. I'm your contestant.

AP

Is that really how you want people to see you? Do you think that's all I see?

332

It's what I've worked so hard for the last few weeks: the chance to be a contestant again. This is what I'm good at. Yes, that's all I thought he saw. I didn't want that thought to hollow me out, so I didn't answer.

AP
Jenna says you're different now. That you've changed since she knew you in high school.

JS
Jenna didn't know me in high school.

We wouldn't have been friends if she did. Jenna didn't have time for girls who apologized for nothing, who relied on their best friends to do all the talking. The fact that I lived with Jenna, that I've argued with her, in my underwear, over the last slice of pizza, means I've changed for the better. I've grown a pair of lady balls.

Hinkfuss climbed onto my lap and purred. I absently scratched behind her ears, scanning through the open book in front of me, until a wet warmth spread across my leg. I threw Hinkfuss off and stood up.

JS
Where did you get this animal, anyway?

AP
Honestly, I don't know where she came from.

JS
Well, I have to go deal with my pants now.

I left my books spread out on the table and headed downstairs to change. AP called out after me.

AP
I'm sure you'll figure it out, Jane. What you want to do.

I know what I want to do. Or I did, until AP ruined half the fun of getting revenge on R by confessing he leaked my journal. I guess I'll have to settle for the other half of revenge. And winning. R isn't getting off easy.

As for the after — we'll see.

ThuAug4

R and I went for a run this morning. Not intentionally — just awkward timing. We nodded to each other once before heading off. We used to run together, weeks ago. In another life. We took the same route we normally do. We both knew neither of us likes to talk when we run, so the silence was natural.

Marc, R, and I met at the campus gym at nine for tonight's prize challenge. R and I brought our running shorts and T-shirts, but Marc was unsurprisingly unprepared. The bleachers were full of enthusiastic students wearing GO #HASHTAGS! shirts. AP motioned for us to join him in the center of the court. I concentrated on the familiar smell of rubber and sweat to steady my nerves as AP waited for the crowd to settle down.

AP

Welcome to tonight's prize challenge!

CROWD

Yay.

AP

We're playing dodgeball!

CROWD

Yay.

Marc put his arm behind his head and stretched, twisting his torso dramatically.

AP

We're going to change it up a bit tonight. Instead of

competing individually, the three of you are on a team.
Want to know who you're playing against?

CROWD

Yay.

AP blew his referee's whistle, and a dozen HOOcaps ran out, single
file.

AP

Since there are more crew than competitors, each of
you has three lives. If you get hit three times, you get
a pie in the face. Want to know what you're competing
for?

CROWD/MARC

Yeah!

AP blew his whistle again, and the house lights went off. The
Weeknd blared from the speakers while colorful spotlights danced
across the court. The main doors opened, and a busty girl in a short
skirt holding three new iPhones strutted in. This show is getting
pretty serious.

AP

If you don't win, the last three *House of Orange* crew
members get the phones. Losing team gets a pie in the
face. Is everyone ready?

JS/R/MARC/CROWD

Yeah!

Marc, R, and I walked to the edge of the court while a couple students placed rubber balls on the center line.

MARC

What's the plan?

R

Hit them and win.

JS

Works for me.

R

If we all aim for the center first, we'll have a better chance of taking them out quicker. We should spread out.

AP

Ready? Three, two, one.

His whistle shrieked and the lights came on and we bolted. After grabbing a ball, I retreated to the side closest to the bleachers, holding the ball in front of me as a shield. I briefly noticed a group of girls in the front row wearing the shirt with my face on it before taking aim. I threw at the center of the HOOcaps but missed. R nailed a girl in the stomach, and the crowd went wild.

I dodged a sloppy throw as I ran to pick up another ball. I hit the girl closest to me in the face. Her nose started bleeding. I didn't apologize.

A loud smack behind me almost made me jump. Marc swore.

AP

Two hits for the cast, one for the crew.

R was moving fast and hitting hard with beautiful ruthlessness. I made my first hit after getting pounded in the shoulder. The next ten minutes were a blur of rubber and squeaks and cheers. By the time we got the crew down to three, Marc and R had taken two hits each, while I only had one.

With a shrill yell, Marc ran for a ball near the center and tripped over his shoelaces. It was the most hilarious and pathetic thing I've ever seen. His arms and legs and tank top twisted in impossible angles as he lay sprawled on the scuffed-up floor. The last three HOOcaps raised their balls, grinned in slow motion, and took aim.

I raised my ball, too.

My shot hit Marc square in the chest with a satisfying *slap*. This one was for the couch. Marc lay there, confused, while I bent down to pick up another ball. Someone hit my back, but I ignored it and took aim once more. This one smacked him in the face. I'd been hit three more times by the time I found another ball, but I didn't care. Once again, I raised the ball into the air. Dimly, I heard AP's voice saying, "Just go with it! This is good." So I turned around and threw the ball at AP, knocking that fucking HOOcap right off of his fucking head. God, it felt good.

We didn't win.

The pie in the face wasn't even all that embarrassing. I must be a veteran of public shaming by now. By the time we left, Marc had already changed his Facebook profile picture to a selfie of him grinning through a thick layer of meringue.

On the ride home R complimented me on my aim.

FFAFFAug5

I had a dream last night.

House of Orange went on a camping trip, or maybe we were always in the forest. I can't tell. Chaunt'Elle said she was going for a walk, and I'm like, *fine*. So she walks up to this big black dog, only it's not a dog and I shout, "CHAUNT'ELLE THAT'S A BEAR!!!" and the bear swipes at her and takes off half her face. I punch the bear because who is he to mess with Chaunt'Elle?! and we run away. We were all a hundred feet away from the bear now, except for R. R kept running and didn't look back. Marc was out of breath, crouching down and looking at his feet, saying, "These old dogs are howling." Then the bear threw something at me. I forget what it was, but it smacked me in the head, and I was terrified, because WTF — bears can do that? The details are blurry, but I woke up irrationally mad at R.

SunAug7

Someone egged our house.
Good thing I have no window.
At least three dozen.

Relevant article from the *Calgary Sun:*

REALITY STAR FALLS

Local reality show contestant Marc Fletcher (39) was arrested Saturday night on multiple charges including public intoxication, property damage, disturbing the peace, and resisting arrest. He was competing, along with two other Elbow River Community College students, in a scavenger hunt challenge on the hit student-run show *House of Orange.* Witnesses say he was seen running naked alongside the gorilla exhibit at the Calgary Zoo, shouting, "I'm one of you!"

Zoo security was alerted around 8:30 p.m., when Fletcher attempted to climb over an exhibit fence. He did not make it over the fence, but officials say significant damage was caused. A vomit-covered tank top was found next to a nearby destroyed garbage can. Police suspect the incidents are related.

For the duration of the challenge, Fletcher reportedly drank from a clear plastic water bottle. After the results of the challenge were made known, Fletcher's drinking increased. The bottle was later confirmed to contain vodka.

Fellow contestant Robert Patel (20) suggests that

Fletcher's actions resulted from his disappointment at losing the challenge and, ultimately, his place on the show. "Normally we'd be competing for immunity in the next voting ceremony. The sudden death aspect of the challenge threw us all off. I don't think he expected to lose. I really don't. He's been a strong competitor throughout the show — in his own way, I suppose — and having to pack his bags and leave, after months of this — it must have been a shock."

The producer of the show, Alexander Park, gave a statement shortly after the incident. "On behalf of *House of Orange*, I would like to apologize for any distress Marc's actions may have caused. We deeply regret the incident, and would like to assure the public that it was never our intention to cause any damage, physical or psychological, to the residents of our city. We will be working closely with the city to repair all damages."

The scavenger hunt had the contestants racing across the city to find clues leading to their ultimate destination. The event tested stamina, knowledge of the city, and creative problem-solving skills. Patel and his remaining competitor, Jane Sinner (18), were neck and neck for most of the challenge, but Patel was the first to make it to the Canadian wildlife exhibit. As the winner, Patel secured his place on the show and received $200 worth of books donated by a local store. Sinner is also still in the running for the grand prize — a car and a scholarship — but chose not to participate in this interview.

Patel and Sinner are now finalists in the competition. The winner will be determined at the final challenge taking place on August 18, and the season finale is set to air August 22.

There was no way AP was going to let Marc stick around any longer.

• • •

I've got a psychology paper due in twelve hours. I've been struggling to get anywhere all day. Normally I'd be only mildly stressed, but the stakes are high. I am on academic probation, after all. AP set up the living room GoPros for live feed on the website, and I'm having trouble concentrating. My bedroom is way too messy to support any semblance of organized thought. I'm sitting with my back to the camera, doing my best to appear studious and boring.

Jane settles down on Dr. Freudenschade's couch. Her hair is a rat's nest and her eyes are bloodshot.

JS

Help.

DFS

Wow, I'm hungry. What's on TV tonight?

JS

. . . That's it? What happened to your "professionalism"?

DFS

You know it was all bullshit anyway.

JS

Lovely. My paper is due tomorrow, and all I have are the disorganized ramblings of a nihilistic psychotherapist whose metaphysical qualifications are questionable. At best.

DFS

Stop trying so hard.

JS

Stop not trying at all!

Jane gets up, but before she can storm out of the room,

*she slips on a banana peel and lands on her ass. Dr.
Freudenschade laughs.*

MonAug8

Marc moved out today. He asked for my help — he has a ridiculous
amount of stuff, including an entire box of hair products — but I told
him to go fuck himself.

> ### MARC
> What did I ever do to you, Sinner?

> ### JS
> Really, Marc?

> ### MARC
> You're not still mad about the whole Jenna thing, are
> you?

> ### JS
> Bye, Marc.

> ### MARC
> Well, fine! If that's how you want to be, I'm going to talk
> to Mr. Dubs.

> ### JS
> Why?

> ### MARC
> *[huffing]*
> To have you removed from the McNugz Club email
> list! You're dead weight, Sinner. And you have a lousy
> attitude.

> ### JS
> Oh no. Whatever will I do.

He hesitated at the front door, waiting for me to say something else. I turned to go.

MARC
So . . . are we still on for that thing tomorrow?

JS
I told you not to bring it up on camera!

MARC
Is that a yes, or . . . ?

JS
Yes! Goodbye, Marc.

TueAug9

Finally I can admit what I've been working on for the past week. I couldn't risk leaking any information before it happened. Private journals are not safe these days. I didn't sleep at all last night.

Stage 1
4 a.m.

I sneak into R's room and set all his clocks back one hour. I know the password for his phone because I asked AP for footage of R entering it. AP was onboard with the whole thing — that guy is always up for shenanigans. Also he doesn't want to risk pissing me off.

Stage 2
9:45 a.m.

As R gets off the bus to go to Sociology, Marc casually runs into him. Says something stupid like "Hey, dude. God, I'm so tired. I haven't been sleeping enough," to which R replies, "Yeah, me too." Marc walks off. As soon as he turns the corner, Marc whips off his tank top, throws a different one on, and jumps on his bike. He rides as fast as he can toward the building where R has class, throws his bike into another bush, and runs inside.

Stage 3
9:48 a.m.
Someone R does not know accidentally bumps into him and says, "Wake up." Said person walks away as if nothing happened.

Stage 4
9:52 a.m.
Marc walks out of the building and casually runs into R. Says something stupid like "Hey, dude. God, I'm so tired. I haven't been sleeping enough," to which R replies, "Didn't I just see you at the bus stop?" Marc says, "What are you talking about?" Marc leaves.

Stage 5
9:54 a.m.
R walks into Sociology class, only to find everyone already there and Dr. Benson in the middle of her lecture. Benson raises her eyebrows and says, "Thanks for joining us, Mr. Patel." R says, "But it's not even nine." The prof's eyebrows slide up higher as she tells him it's nearly eleven. After singing some ridiculous song to appease Benson, R takes a seat in the nearest chair and avoids eye contact with his classmates, who are all annoyed by the interruption.

Stage 6
11 a.m.
Class lets out. It's a good thing sociology profs love to mess with people, or Benson wouldn't have agreed to end class one hour early. R, having confirmed with several classmates, thinks it's twelve o'clock, although his phone tells him it's ten.

<u>Stage 7</u>

11:12 a.m.

Someone else R does not know accidentally bumps into him and says, "It's all a dream." Said person walks away as if nothing happened.

<u>Stage 8</u>

12:25 p.m.

AP calls R to ask where he is. R has no idea what he means. AP says, "The voting ceremony. Why aren't you here?" R panics and says he'll run back home. AP tells him the ceremony isn't at home: it's at the top of the Calgary Tower. R swears and says he's on his way. AP tells him they can't wait much longer because they have to be out of the building in half an hour.

<u>Stage 9</u>

12:58 p.m.

R jumps out of a taxi and runs into the building. He doesn't see me loitering behind a plant, texting AP. R tells the woman at reception that he's there for *House of Orange*. She gives him a pass. As he steps into the elevator, he gets another call. AP tells him he's off the show. Disqualified. R's eyes widen and his mouth opens in protest as the doors swallow him.

<u>Stage 10</u>

1:02 p.m.

R trots around the observatory, looking for the film crew. Instead he finds random people staring at him. A handmade banner covers a window, reading:

DEAR ROBBIE:

JUST KIDDING, LOL

REGARDS,

SINNER

R swears loudly and turns around to find a HOOcap with a camera behind him.

I'd like to thank Alexander Park and the crew of *House of Orange* for making this prank possible. I'd also like to thank Dr. Benson and my Sociology class for playing along.

I've never seen R so red before. He caught my eye as soon as he stepped out of the elevator. He opened his mouth to say something but quickly thought better of it, then shook his head and walked past me. I laughed.

It went exactly as I'd hoped. Better, even. There is no reason for me to feel anything but victorious and triumphant and happy, like the future *House of Orange* winner that I am.

No reason at all.

Except that maybe, just maybe, messing with R has only evened the score between us. Despite my best intentions, R still isn't the mustache-twirling bad guy I need him to be. A nemesis or a friend — either would be enough to keep me going. Because once this show's over, any shittiness on my part toward him no longer counts as strategy. It's just shittiness.

WedAug10

I came home this afternoon to find my room empty. No furniture, no clothes, nothing. No crumbs on the carpet. Of course he would vacuum. I checked the entire house, and nothing I own is in it. Even my mini-fridge is empty. I'm not mad, really. I'm annoyed but impressed. Well played, sir. AP wouldn't let me see any footage. I suppose it was R's turn to ask a favor. I'm pretty sure Jenna is home now, so I'm going over to her place to see if she knows anything. Good thing I had this journal with me in my backpack, or I'd be screwed.

• • •

I hadn't been back there since That Night. I've been trying to figure out why a girl like Jenna would go for some douche nearly twice her age. There must be some sort of plan. Some greater good, some suffering necessary for character development or whatever. But as much as I want to, I can't convince myself of any of that. Jenna is just some girl who wanted to get laid.

JS
Hey. Any chance you know where all my stuff is?

JENNA
No.

JS
You can't say? Or you won't?

JENNA
I promised Alexander I'd stay out of it.

JS
When you said you'd help me, back in James Fowler, you weren't doing it for me, were you?

JENNA
I —

JS
For the same reason you convinced him to pick me for the show in the first place. It's why you helped me to get back on. All you care about is an entertaining reality show, because you fucked up and Alexander took the fall.

Jenna leaned forward. She looked concerned, but I couldn't afford to believe her.

JENNA
Come on, Jane. You know I enjoyed living with you.

JS

Fuck, Jenna. If your brother is all you care about, fine.
You could at least respect me enough to admit it.

She didn't say anything. I didn't feel like waiting for her to come up with more bullshit, so I left.

The parents were happy to have me over tonight, once I explained what happened. Even Dad wasn't as awkward as he could have been. They'll never be completely onboard with the show, but I think they're relieved to know that it's not all booze and parties and rampant immorality.

DAD

It's all right, Jane. Just a bit of good, clean fun. Get it —because that boy cleaned out your room? You know, when I was your age, I used to replace my roommates' yogurt with mayonnaise, just to see what they'd do. It was a hoot!

JS

Obviously I'm way too mature for those kinds of shenanigans.

Carol insisted I stay in her room so we could watch Netflix on her computer and make it a sleepover.

CAROL

Soon you'll get your high school diploma and go off to real college and shit, and you won't have time for juniors like me. Are you busy this weekend?

JS

I don't know. And you're not a junior yet, kid.

> **CAROL**
> Close enough!

> **JS**
> And don't say *shit*.

> **CAROL**
> I can say what I want.

This is why I'll never have kids.

> **CAROL**
> Do you want to stay at Elbow River after the show? Or
> are you gonna go to U of C? And are you still going to
> study psychology?

> **JS**
> I don't know.

> **CAROL**
> But you're eighteen now, Janie! You're supposed to know.

> **JS**
> The next time anyone tells you that, do yourself a favor
> and drop-kick them in the tampon tunnel.

Relevant text from Jenna: Everything is in Robbie's cousin's garage.
You can borrow my car tomorrow if you want.

ThuAug11

Jenna left her keys with a HOOcap, and I drove to R's cousin's place
this morning. The HOOcap who followed me offered to help move
everything into the car, but I automatically declined. This was my
mess, I could deal with it. But I couldn't move my bed on my own,
so I had to swallow my embarrassment and ask him to help anyway.

I wonder if humble people ever feel embarrassed. Probably not. R left the bed disassembled, so we managed to tie it to the roof. Everything else barely fit inside.

After we got home and I set everything up, I went for a run. I told myself I'd run until I figured out what to do about R. I lost about five pounds, two hours, and three dollars on Gatorade but didn't come up with any decent ideas. I hate apologizing. No, that's not true. I hate being wrong.

I miss my anger. It was so nice to hold on to, so warm and full of energy. But it's deflating and I'm deflating; I'm a balloon leaking air.

Maybe I was wrong to think getting back on the show would keep me going.

FFAFFAug12

A letter that arrived in the mail this morning:

> Dear Sinner:
>
> You don't deserve to be back on the show. The whole thing was rigged. You are kind of an asshole to everyone esp. Robbie. He obviously still likes you, but you won't even talk to him. I hope you lose because I used to like the show but I'm sick of everything being about you.
>
> — ANONYMOUS

Fairly straight to the point. I prefer the postcard from West Edmonton Mall I received a couple weeks ago, which said, "Experience the best that Edmonton has to offer!" on the front and "die sinner" on the back. It's hanging on my wall.

SatAug13

So many papers.
Rough drafts are good enough drafts.
I have no patience.

So many cameras
Pretending not to be here
Watching empty rooms.

Poetry is a poor substitute for emotion. Good thing I only have a few more exams between me and the end of this term, because I'm losing my fondness for words.

Less than two weeks until I (theoretically) graduate. Feels like an eternity away. Once I have my stupid diploma, once this show is over, I can leave Elbow River and never look back. And then —
Well, what are you going to do with yourself then, Jane?

SunAug14
Nothing.

I was supposed to go to the parents' for lunch, but I canceled. I didn't have the energy to deal with the parents. Carol woke me from a textbook-induced coma with a phone call.

CAROL
How are you feeling, Janie?

Why does everyone keep asking me that?

JS
I don't know.

CAROL
Well, you must be excited for your final challenge this week, right?

JS

I don't know.

CAROL

I would be. You've got a good chance of winning. I wish I was on the show!

JS

You don't want to be like me, kid.

CAROL

Why not?

JS

You just don't. Listen, I'm sorry I didn't make it today. We'll hang out more when this is over.

Silence.

JS

Carol?

CAROL

It's always "when this is over."

JS

It's not like that. You don't understand.

CAROL

Because you never talk to me! You treat me like I'm a child.

JS

That's not true.

I know she's not really a child. Part of me wants her to stay the same forever, and part of me wants her to learn from my mistakes and do more with her teenage years than I did.

CAROL

Yeah, it is. And you're right — I don't get it. I don't get why you're making such a big deal out of this show. I don't get what you're doing or what you want, or why you don't think the people who love you can help.

Maybe she had a point. Maybe if I had done things differently, if I had listened to my best friend and gotten out of that fucking van before Marc pushed me out, I wouldn't be sitting by myself in coffee-stained underwear, arguing with the one person I need on my side no matter what.

JS

Carol, trust me. This isn't about you.

CAROL

Why can't it be about me, just for once? I wanted you to come over today, Janie. I invited someone else too, and I wanted you to meet him.

Carol has a boyfriend? No shit. She's growing up faster than I am.

JS

I'm sorry, Carol. I didn't know. Look, I'll come over as soon as I can, but I've got exams this week. And the challenge.

CAROL

Whatever. Just do what you have to do. I guess I'll see you when this is over.

Talking with Carol should have cheered me up, and yet it's done the

352

opposite. Whatever numbness crept up on me last year feels like it's creeping back. I don't know how to explain this to anyone — it sounds like bullshit, even to me.

MonAug15

Jane is dozing at her desk when a gentle knock wakes her up. Dr. Freudenschade removes his hat and sits on the edge of Jane's bed.

DFS

So what's going on, Jane? You're back on the show and have the support of your entire school. Why isn't this enough?

JS

I don't know.

DFS

That's not a reason.

JS

Sometimes there are no reasons.

DFS

Why don't you talk about it? Tell someone how you feel. Or that you can't feel anything. If you want to kill yourself, shouldn't someone know?

JS

I don't want to kill myself. I just want to stop existing. Take a break from myself.

DFS

Tell someone.

JS

I'm telling you.

DFS

I don't count.

JS

Then what good are you?!

DFS

I don't know.

I gave Bonnie a call this evening. I debated for half an hour before hitting the button, because we don't talk that much anymore. Not like we used to. And for the first time I can remember, I wasn't sure if she wanted to hear my voice.

Thank god she answered.

JS

How do you know for sure that you want to study art?

BONNIE

Easy. It's what I love. Why, are you feeling inspired? What do you want to do?

JS

After *House of Orange*, I want to go on *The Bachelor*. Then I want to go on *Bachelor in Paradise*. If that can't get me on *Ellen*, I don't know what will.

BONNIE

That act's getting a little old now, Jane.

JS

So my mom keeps telling me.

We didn't talk for a minute or two, but it didn't feel like silence. I didn't want her to hang up.

JS

Do you believe God has a plan for everyone?

BONNIE

Yes, I do.

JS

So what's mine, then?

BONNIE

I honestly don't know. But I believe one day we will understand more than we do now, and we'll be able to see how everything falls into place.

JS

So everything happens for a reason?

BONNIE

I think so.

JS

What about the fucked-up shit?

BONNIE

God works it all into the plan. Even the fucked-up shit.

JS

So it's planned.

BONNIE

No, it happens because we're so messed up. Our choices do that.

JS

But God didn't plan on us being messed up.

BONNIE

Well, he gave us free will.

JS

So he created us so that we'd fuck up, then blames all the shit that happens on us.

BONNIE

It's hard to understand how God works.

It must be nice to be so sure of someone in control. Taking care of things for you. Cleaning up your mess.

BONNIE

If it makes you feel any better, the church I started going to up here staged an intervention for me. They're worried about my lifestyle choices.

JS

Why would that make me feel any better?

BONNIE

So you don't feel like you're missing out. I know you. Church won't make you happy.

She should tell that to Dad.

JS

So why do you bother going? It's always been more of a hassle for you.

BONNIE

Because it means something to me. And I think so many Christians are focused more on hatred than on love, and the irony is depressing. I want to see that change. I'm not a quitter.

JS

Wish I could say the same.

Bonnie was quiet for a long time.

BONNIE

You don't . . . you don't think about . . . you know, what happened on New Year's . . . you wouldn't . . .

JS

Of course I think about it. What's the matter?

I could tell she was on the verge of crying.

BONNIE

Jane, I . . . please know . . . if anything happened —

She cut herself off with a sob. I didn't want to see her hurt, but the amount of emotion leaking out of her voice was fascinating. Bonnie never cries.

JS

I'm sorry. I didn't mean to upset you.

BONNIE

No . . . it's . . . I'm glad you told me . . . Promise me. Promise me you won't do anything. Please.

JS

I promise.

I had never told Bonnie this, but I always respected her faith more than my own. Her faith was a conscious decision, a hard-earned achievement, constantly evolving to deal with her family's agnosticism and her own bisexuality. I wore my own faith like the shirt I fell asleep in because I was too lazy to change.

TueAug16

I couldn't get out of bed today. A small part of me, neglected and tucked away in the back of my mind like an old science textbook, told me I was wrong. It told me getting up was the simplest thing in the world. Like the textbook, it was true. In a way. But also like the textbook, it was completely irrelevant to my life at that moment. I was supposed to work all day, but that didn't happen.

Hypothetical phone call:

SUPERVISOR
Good morning, Jane.

JS
I'm afraid it's not.

SUPERVISOR
Why not?

JS
I can't feel anything. I'm staying in bed because I have no reason to get up.

SUPERVISOR
Are you ill?

JS
No.

SUPERVISOR
Then what's wrong?

JS
I can't feel anything. I'm staying in bed because I have no reason to get up.

SUPERVISOR
We need you to cover your shift, though. People are counting on you. You have the opportunity to earn money. Why isn't that reason enough to come in?

JS
Because nothing has meaning.

SUPERVISOR

Sometimes, when I'm feeling down, I drink a cup of tea and listen to my favorite song. Sometimes that helps. Why don't you try that?

JS

I'm not feeling down.

SUPERVISOR

I make a list of all the things in my life I am grateful for, and I look at pictures of cats on the internet. The internet is full of cats, you know. There is no reason to feel down when there are so many cats on the internet. Why don't you try looking at some cats?

JS

I am dead inside.

SUPERVISOR

But have you seen the cat that talks about french fries?

Hypothetical phone call #2:

SUPERVISOR

Good morning, Jane.

JS

I'm afraid it's not.

SUPERVISOR

Why not?

JS

My grandma died. I'm not coming in today.

SUPERVISOR

Is everything okay?

No.

SUPERVISOR

Then what's wrong?

JS

My grandma died. I'm not coming in today.

SUPERVISOR

We need you to cover your shift, though. People are counting on you. You have the opportunity to earn money. Why isn't that reason enough to come in?

JS

Because I lost my grandma.

SUPERVISOR

Sometimes, when I lose someone I love, I check the last place I remember seeing them. Sometimes I find that person there. Why don't you try that?

JS

I haven't misplaced her. She's dead.

SUPERVISOR

Sometimes I take a moment to remember to keep my chin up. Death can't be so bad if it happens to everyone, right?

JS

. . .

Actual conversation:

SUPERVISOR

Good morning, Jane.

> **JS**
> Hi. I can't come in today.

> **SUPERVISOR**
> Why not?

> **JS**
> I'm sick.

> **SUPERVISOR**
> I am sorry to hear that. Feel better.

> **JS**
> Thank you.
> *[Coughs.]*

Unfortunately, the truth would have sounded too much like bullshit.

When AP noticed that I hadn't moved from my bed for twenty consecutive hours (except to pee and tell a HOOcap to fuck off), he called my parents. I guess he knew he couldn't call Bonnie or Jenna or Tom. When the parents showed up in the evening, AP disabled the cameras in my room and told the HOOcaps to give us space. The parents brought donuts and coffee and read ridiculous tabloids out loud like bedtime stories, just like they did when I was in the hospital months ago. And just like in the hospital, they didn't ask questions. I didn't feel better after they left, but I felt slightly less like nothing. So that's something. Almost.

WedAug17

I got out of bed. Exams are done. All right all right all right.

I am officially unemployed.

Technically I was laid off, not fired. "Cutbacks" and "quarterly losses" and "sincere regrets," but I find their sincerity questionable. I'd become a bit of a monkey in the past few weeks, with customers gawking and tweeting pictures of me.

I guess the largest grocery store chain in western Canada didn't feel like providing the backdrop to hashtags such as #longhairdontcare and #bitchesbaggingbread.

I could really use a scholarship right about now.

R mentioned he'd be staying with his cousin tonight, which was fine with me. Like the bride and groom spending the night before the wedding apart. Except we're not getting married tomorrow — just competing in the final challenge of *House of Orange.* Winner takes all. Sinner takes all, if all goes well. I'll find the energy somewhere.

When I'm the only person in the house, it's quite easy not to care about cameras. I didn't change out of my T-shirt and short shorts because today is just one big Who Gives a Shit. Instead of showering, I blasted sixties soft rock, lay down on the saggy living room sofa, and stared at the orange shag carpet for two hours. Eventually I made french toast. Out of boredom, not hunger. I put the plate of french toast on the floor next to the couch because I was losing interest in the carpet and had no intention of eating the food anyway. I lay there for another hour or two because I was starting to feel something. I couldn't tell what it was — it was like seeing a pinpoint of light out of the corner of my eye — but it was something. Excitement for the challenge tomorrow? Or maybe dread for what I would do with myself after? I was too busy concentrating to notice R walk in.

R

Are you all right, Jane?

362

Suddenly I was hyperaware of my greasy hair and the compromising position my short shorts had arranged themselves in. I tried to pull my hair back and my shorts down and stand up all at once. I fell off the couch. My hand landed in the french toast. When I pulled it out, my fingers bleeding maple syrup and cinnamon, I saw that my hand had left a perfect impression in the bread. Like I gave the bread a high-five. I started laughing. As though, for the past week or two, my brain had forgotten what it was like to feel things, then all of a sudden it remembered. I guess the meds are finally catching up, or something.

BRAIN
OH, I'M SORRY! LET ME MAKE IT UP TO YOU! HERE, HAVE SOME FEELINGS! HAVE SOME MORE! LOL ROFL OMG!

JS
LOL LOL LOL LOL LOL LOL

R
Jane, what's going on?

JS
IT'S LIKE . . . THE TOAST — I GAVE IT A HIGH-FIVE, AND NOW — SEE — IT'S LIKE WE'RE FRIENDS . . . AND —

R
Should I call someone?

A HOOcap was already there. I saw myself on television like this and found it hilarious. I mean, I'd signed up for a reality TV show. How was I expecting to come out of this not looking like an idiot? Something must have snapped in R, too, because he started laughing as well. Soon the two of us could barely breathe.

I wonder what . . . Alexander . . . what he'll make of all this —

JS

I hope . . . maybe he can't use . . . no context . . .

It took me a good half hour to calm down. Then I slept for five hours.

It's a good thing I was born with such a sunny disposition, or I might be dead by now. With so much metaphorical sunlight saturating everything, it's easy to look on the bright side.

I am a superhero! I am the Nihilist! My superpowers include logical detachment, emotional invincibility, and the ability to blend in anywhere. I work alone and am never compromised by romantic entanglements, and I don't have a costume because who the fuck cares?

Mom called tonight, making sure I was okay. I wished she would have spent half an hour giving me a million useless updates on Carol (like she usually does), but the fact that she said nothing about Carol told me Carol is still pissed. Mom cautiously suggested I visit my therapist again — maybe if I explain the situation, I can get in early tomorrow morning. If not, when the final challenge is over. I said yes, that is a good idea.

DFS

Hello, Jane.

JS

Hi.

DFS

I hear you have a stressful event tomorrow and your parents are worried about your mental health.

JS

Yes. My producer is also concerned.

DFS

Let's talk about this.

JS

Sure.

DFS

What are you afraid of?

JS

Sometimes I am afraid of being stuck in outer space. I'm very confident I wouldn't like it there.

DFS

You've seen enough movies to know that most people don't have a good time in space, but that's not what I mean because it won't happen. Real fears are frightening because they could happen. What are you afraid of?

JS

I'm afraid of oil spills, fascist governments, and balloons that pop unexpectedly.

DFS

Why can't you ever take a serious question seriously?

JS

Because sometimes I'm afraid that if I don't feel amused, I won't feel anything at all.

What I'm actually scared of is what I'll be tomorrow. Best-case scenario, I win *House of Orange*. What then? Instead of being the Girl Who Tried to Kill Herself, I'll be the Girl Who Won a Shitty Reality

Show. Either way, I'm a Girl Who Did a Thing. At this point, I don't know how I can go back to just being a Girl.

ThuAug18
Final challenge day.

Two slices of cake, two cups of coffee, yogurt, and an apple. Breakfast of champions.

We have half an hour to pack. We're told to bring a change of warm clothes and anything else we think we'll need for two or three days. No cell phones, no electronics. It all has to fit in a backpack. I'm throwing in leggings, T-shirts, sweaters, socks, underwear, toques, basic toiletries, a lighter Marc forgot underneath a couch cushion, a water bottle, Tylenol, instant coffee, pens, sudoku, garbage bags (for insulation and water protection because you never know), this journal, and a mickey of vodka. Whatever space is left over I will stuff with granola bars. Jenna lent me a compact sleeping bag that straps onto the bottom of my backpack. I'm not sure how much she knows, but carrying a sleeping bag with me makes me feel bold and terrified at the same time.

At nine forty-five we had our final interviews. I spent a little extra time getting ready for it. I had no idea what the final challenge would involve, but I assumed this interview would be the last chance I'd get to control how I look on camera. So I tamed my hair and used the last of my lipstick. I guess I've used more lipstick than I thought lately.

At ten we climbed into the van (which I am all too familiar with) and said goodbye to House of Orange. A HOOcap with no cap drove. She didn't answer any of our questions. There were no cameras in the van, no radio playing. The HOOcap turned onto Stoney Trail, then Sixteenth Avenue. We left the city and headed west. R and I sat in silence as the mountains rose on either side of us, creeping up the windows until there was nothing left of the sky.

We stopped a couple hours out of Calgary, near Lake Louise. We parked next to some familiar cars at a small rest stop a few hundred meters off the main road. A couple HOOcaps got out of a dirty Civic. After fitting us with our lav mikes, they strapped their cameras onto shoulder rigs. The HOOcap with no cap told us to use the outhouse here while we had the chance. R and I didn't move, so she handed us our backpacks and said to follow her.

The day was sunny but not warm, and the ground was a brown, soupy mess from yesterday's rain. Balancing our heavy backpacks while keeping our grip on the steep trail was neither easy nor graceful. We couldn't complain, though. The HOOcaps went slowly too, careful of their equipment. I'm in pretty decent shape cardio-wise, but I have limited experience with steep inclines. After an hour I started to wonder how high we were supposed to go. After two hours, I started to wonder what we'd find when we got there. I wanted to ask a thousand questions — the drawn-out anticipation was almost as agonizing as the fire spreading through my lungs — but if R could keep quiet, so could I.

Eventually we stopped for a rest. I sat down on a fallen tree, dumped my backpack onto the mud, and peeled off a sweaty layer. Someone handed me a Gatorade, and I finished it in three swallows. R drank his more slowly, but not until he had arranged a blanket over his side of the tree and sat down carefully.

R
What do you think we're in for?

JS
I don't know. Mountain biking, I hope.

R
I'd settle for bird watching.

My muscles relaxed and my lungs caught up to the rest of me. As the sun warmed my face I began to smile, if for no other reason than the absence of pain.

R

I just hope it's not bear wrestling. I hate bear wrestling.

JS

Did your parents make you do that, too?

R

Every other weekend.

I laughed before I could tell myself not to.

It was late afternoon before we reached the top. By then I had no idea what AP had in store for us, or why he'd want us exhausted before we'd even started. AP and his crew stood around a fire, drinking coffee and laughing. Relaxed. It was chilly up there — the HOOcaps had switched their ball caps for embroidered toques in an even brighter shade of orange. AP cracked a huge grin at the sight of us.

AP

Hey! You made it in one piece. Hope you're not too tired.
Help yourself to coffee before we get started.

I didn't need an invitation to head toward the coffee. It was the instant shit of course. Wallace & Beanz. I turned to make some comment to R, but he was still standing on the edge of the trail. Looking out at the most beautiful view I have ever seen.

Lake Louise stretched out below us, smoother than a sheet of ice and impossibly turquoise. Mountains framed the lake on all sides, the hazy sunlight casting hard shadows on prickly trees. The sky, free of clouds, was so saturated with color that the darkest blues were slipping down to rest on the jagged peaks.

R and I stood there in silence. Staring. I hoped we'd stay there until the sun dropped into the lake and the sky exploded and the stars flickered on. It wouldn't be too much longer. I snuck a glance at R to see if I could tell the time by the angle of the light on his sundial nose, but I was distracted by the purity of the expression on his face. Most people would have whipped out their smartphone to Instagram the shit out of that view. Somehow I knew that even if he had his phone, R wouldn't have blocked his view with a screen.

AP
Nice, isn't it?

I hadn't noticed AP creep up next to me.

JS
You do have a flair for the dramatic.

He laughed.

AP
We'll be ready in a couple minutes.

I turned around as AP walked away. I closed my eyes and focused on breathing in the sharp, thin air until I stopped thinking about the view, about Robbie's nose, about Jenna and Carol and the HOOtoques and the fact that I was about to win a car and/or humiliate myself in front of the largest audience I'll likely ever have.

Breathe.

In and out and in and out and in and out.

This was it.

What would I do with myself when this was over?

I was cold. And shaking.

In and out and in and out and —

AP
Jane? We're ready for you.

AP held out a steaming W&B mug, and I took it gratefully. He guided me to a clear patch of rock where a HOOtoque had dropped a mark for me to stand on. I let the mug warm my fingers while AP worked out some technicalities with a camera guy. Robbie took his place next to me, and we waited. I've waited like this a million times before, but it never felt like this.

DFS

What are you afraid of?

JS

(Not now, please. Can't you see I'm—)

HOOTOQUE 1

And . . . roll sound!

HOOTOQUE 2

Rolling.

JS

(I'm busy.)

HOOTOQUE 4

Final challenge intro, take one.

HOOTOQUE 3

Mark it.

R

You ready?

DFS

We have to talk about it sometime.

HOOTOQUE 3

Set.

JS

(Not now.)

Yes. Are you?

370

AP

Action!

In and out.

AP

Welcome to the final challenge of *House of Orange*! Joining us today to remind us of the prizes is a representative from Wallace & Beanz, Alan Burrows.

Alan had a distinguished-looking salt-and-pepper beard, a beer belly, and a crisp suit. I wondered if he had to change his clothes in the bush after climbing the mountain.

ALAN

Thanks, Alexander. As you both know, the grand prize is the car and the scholarship. Wallace & Beanz is proud to announce that the scholarship amount has been raised to five thousand dollars! We are also pleased to announce a cash bonus of two thousand dollars to the winner.

R and I looked at each other.

AP

Thanks, Alan! The goal of the last challenge is simple. The first person to make it back to House of Orange wins.

AP let that sink in while we waited for the catch.

AP

There are a few conditions. First, you are not permitted to use any electronic communication devices. No cell phones, no internet. Second, you are not allowed to spend any money. Third, you are not permitted to obtain assistance from any *House of Orange* crew member. Fourth, you are not permitted to use any motorized vehicles.

My mind raced. No cars? What did that leave?

AP

If you break any of the rules, you are subject to disqualification. If a crew member feels you are in danger, he or she has the right to call for assistance and you will be subject to disqualification. You two are free to work together or separately, your choice. There is no time limit. Any questions?

JS

(Yes. How?)

. . .

R

. . .

AP

Before we start, each of you will receive a safety pack.

A HOOtoque handed us each a large orange fanny pack.

AP

Included in this pack are an insulating blanket, basic first-aid items, a pamphlet on the dangers of interaction with the local wildlife, pepper spray, and three flares.

I did not feel any safer.

AP

You will also each receive a small DSLR as a personal camera, to use as you wish. Are you sure you don't have any questions?

What was I missing? How long would it take to walk back? How fast can I run? How far can I push the rules without getting disqualified? Is it too late to find a lawyer? How terrified do I look right now, and how can I convince everyone I'm not?

I strapped on the fanny pack.

JS
Yeah. When do we start?

AP
Three, two, one. Now.

I had to get off the mountain before the sun set.

I thought going down would be easier, and it was, until my legs turned into tight Jell-O doused in alcohol then set on fire. R was close behind, so I couldn't let myself stop. I fell a few times. But I always got up.

By the time I made it to the bottom, my body felt exactly how I'd expect it to feel after climbing a mountain and tumbling back down. I found a boulder and sat and pulled out my water bottle. At least the vodka was still intact. It was too early to drink it though; I still had nearly two hundred kilometers to go. Oh god. After two long swallows, I forced myself to get up and keep moving. Robbie would catch up any minute, and I didn't want him riding my shooting star all the way back to Calgary.

I needed to think. I needed a game plan. In order to win a car, AP made us find our way back to Calgary without one. The irony was delicious and incredibly frustrating. A HOOtoque walked beside me, but I ignored her. By the time I found the main road the sun was nearly down. I stood on the shoulder for a minute, deciding which way to go. Right was Calgary, left was Lake Louise. If my plan was to walk, I should get started right away. Unless . . . unless I found a bike. Or a skateboard, or Rollerblades, or a horse. A bike seemed most likely. I turned left. I couldn't spend any money, but I could borrow a bicycle. I hoped.

It took me a good hour to reach the town. I don't know for sure because I don't have a watch and I didn't want to ask the HOOtoque. I don't know if asking for the time means asking for assistance, and I don't want to take my chances.

I ended up at a small diner just as I was about to fall over with exhaustion and hunger. I'd already gone through half my granola bar stash. I spent only a couple minutes there, drinking water and discreetly tucking peanut butter packages into my pocket. I'd already taken advantage of the bathroom and changed into dry clothes. I watched intently as a googly-eyed couple pushed their half-eaten meal away from them and waved for the bill. I asked them if I could have their remnants. They looked at my messy hair and muddy backpack and the HOOtoque behind me with raised eyebrows but kindly gave up their plates. I inhaled the food. It's too late for me to feel shame now. If not, it will be soon.

I needed to find a bike. The sun was down and soon the town would be empty. I asked the waitress if she knew of any bikes I could borrow, but she said no and asked me to leave.

My shoulders cried as I strapped on my backpack, but I told them to shut up and headed outside, where two HOOtoques were waiting to switch with the first.

Lake Louise is small and full of tourists, so I bet there was a bike rental store around. I found one on the other side of town, three blocks away. I could see they were just about to close as I walked in.

EMPLOYEE
I'm sorry, but we're closing. Unless you know exactly what you're looking for, could you come back tomorrow?

JS
Actually, I'm looking to rent a bike.

374

The employee looked at the dark sky outside the window.

EMPLOYEE

Now?

JS

Yeah. My name is Jane Sinner — I'm part of a reality show called *House of Orange*.

I nodded to the HOOtoque holding a camera behind me.

JS

Maybe you've heard of it.

EMPLOYEE

No.

JS

Well. As our final challenge, we have to make our way back to Calgary without using cars.

EMPLOYEE

Hmm.

JS

I'm not allowed to give you any money now, but I can pay you later —

The HOOtoque coughed loudly and gave me a look.

JS

I can't pay you now or later, but my producer will reimburse you in a day or two.

EMPLOYEE

I'm sorry, but I can't rent you a bike with no money.

JS

But your store would be featured on television . . .

I don't much care for reality TV.

But . . . exposure . . .

Sorry, kid, I can't help you out on this one.

(Sigh.)
Thanks anyway.

Outside, the town was dead. I'd wasted too much time at the diner —I should have started looking sooner. I sat down on the curb, thinking. I wondered how much closer I'd be to Calgary by now if I had just kept walking. Probably I'd be dead—exhaustion or cars or wildlife would have gotten to me. No. I couldn't think like this. I had to think like a winner. Like a champion. At the very least, like a logical person. Where could I find a bunch of people right now who would be willing to lend a stranger a bike?

A bar, of course.

I'd seen one next to a cheap motel on my way into town. I stood up, swung my backpack onto my aching shoulders, and started walking.

The bar was relatively quiet but not empty. I paused after walking through the door, taking in my options. After a minute, people noticed the HOOtoques and stared. I didn't know what to do, besides feel like an idiot. My cheeks burned while I told my mind to think faster. It was obvious what to do when I realized I had the entire room's attention. I cleared my throat and inhaled as deeply as I could, leaving no room for butterflies to flit around my rib cage.

Excuse me? Hi. My name is Jane Sinner.

BAR

JS
I'm part of a reality show called *House of Orange*. Does anyone know it?

BAR

JS
(Does no one appreciate good television these days?!)
As part of our final challenge, I have to make my way back to Calgary without using motorized vehicles. So I need a bike.

Everyone continued to stare, but no one moved. It was a bit creepy. I wondered if my voice was loud enough.

JS
The thing is, I can't spend any money. So I'd need to borrow it. Does anyone have a bike they could lend me for a day or two? I promise I'll return it.

BAR

JS
This will be televised, so thousands of people will see this and hold me accountable.

BAR

JS
Please? If you help, you'll be on TV. I'll make you cookies after or something.

I was desperate and my face was on fire. I hated being at the mercy of strangers, but I didn't know what else to do. I didn't know what else to say. Unless — I still had the DSLR that AP had given me. I think his words were "use it as you wish."

JS
I can trade you for a DSLR.

BAR

Shit.

I figured I might as well use the washroom before leaving. I made my way to the back of the bar, humiliated and wretched and on the edge of a very dark mood, but I forced myself to make eye contact with as many people as I could. Maybe someone would take pity on me. Or at least feel ashamed of being cold-hearted. A tall guy in a black shirt walked in front of me.

TALL GUY
Excuse me, but do you have a permit to film in here?

I looked at the HOOtoques. They shook their heads.

JS
No.

TALL GUY
I'm going to have to ask you to leave.

JS
All right.

I turned around and walked out. Standing on the sidewalk with a cigarette in one hand and a beer in the other was a girl. Wearing the shirt with the graphic of my face on it. I almost cried with joy.

JS

Excuse me! Hi! Do you watch *House of Orange*?

The girl looked up and her mouth dropped open.

GIRL

Oh my god, are you . . . are you . . .

JS

Jane Sinner. Yeah.

The girl looked at her friends, at the HOOtoques, back to me.

GIRL

Oh my god! I love your show! What are you doing here?

I explained to her what the final challenge was, and how desperate I was to find a bike. I asked her if there was any way she could help.

GIRL

I don't know. I don't live here, I'm visiting my cousin.
She might have a bike though. I can ask her. Oh my god,
this is so exciting!

JS

Yes, it is.

Yes, it is.

While the girl called her cousin, one of her friends asked me for my autograph. I signed her phone cover with a pen.

GIRL

Jane! She has a mountain bike and she'll let you use it!!

JS

Oh my god! Thank you so much!

GIRL

She lives pretty close to here; we can leave now if you
want.

JS

Yes, please.

The girl led the way and the rest of us followed. I was giddy with
companionship and success. I chatted amicably to the girls, who were
visiting from Lethbridge to hike and camp. They asked a bunch of
questions about the show and about Robbie, and for once I didn't resent answering. When the girl with the shirt emerged from her cousin's garage with the bike, I hugged each of them.

OTHER GIRL
[to her friends]
I didn't know she was so nice.

I forgot the HOOtoques were still there until they made a call to
confirm the next shift. I don't know how they'll keep up with me, but
I don't doubt they will.

GIRL

I have a lock with a key and a helmet for you too. You
never know.

JS

I don't know how to thank you! Write your phone
number on my arm so I can return everything when I'm
done. Is there anything else I can do for you?

GIRL

Just win. That would be pretty cool.

JS

Okay, I can do that.

I strapped on the helmet, thanked them again, and pedaled off into the night.

I found the main highway and rode like the wind. I had no idea where Robbie was, but I knew I couldn't underestimate him. Thankfully the bike had a small headlight and reflectors so I could see the road and cars could see me. Not that there were many vehicles out. For the most part it was just the HOOtoques' dirty Civic and me. I rode until my lungs burned and my legs threatened to snap. When my vision blurred and I yawned more than I breathed normally, I pulled over. I spread the packets of peanut butter on granola bars and took a long drink from my water bottle. As soon as I finished, I got back on and kept going. I had no idea how many more hours it would take to get out of the mountains, but I couldn't wait for flat road again. Eventually my exhaustion numbed my aching body, and all I could feel was the darkness and the cold mountain air and the countless black trees rising up on either side of me. I don't know if I've ever been so vulnerable.

I'll sleep when I've won.

I'll sleep when I've won.

I'll sleep when I've won.

I turned the next bend to find huge eyes glowing in front of me. My heart screamed. I tried to turn away, but my blood was molasses. Adrenaline kicked in and my mind compensated for my lack of mobility. *Oh god not a bear not a bear I have pepper spray but it's in the safety pack what if it's a moose I hope the HOOtoques are getting this what if the moose's antlers impale me oh god not a moose—*

Crunch.

Antlers pummeled my rib cage. I twisted and fell and hit the pavement with another *crunch*. My bike wheel landed on my leg, but that was impossible because my bike was underneath me.

MOOSE

What the fuck?

JS

[Unintelligible groan.]

MOOSE

Jane? Jane, are you okay?

JS

Robbie?

Robbie slowly pulled his bike off of us and sat up. A car door slammed shut, and heavy footsteps ran toward us. I spent a confused minute looking for the moose before I realized there was no wildlife present.

HOOTOQUE

Jane? You all right? Robbie?

JS

(?)

HOOTOQUE

Just hold on. Don't move. I'm calling for help.

JS

Don't you dare!

HOOTOQUE

What?

I'd come too far to be disqualified now.

JS

I'm fine. I don't need assistance. I can get up.

I was definitely not fine, but I got up anyway to prove my point.

HOOTOQUE

Jane, it's okay. But you're not okay. We just want to make sure you're okay.

I picked up my bike and checked for damage. Surprisingly, it seemed all right. Robbie's bike took the worst of it. I got back on. The adrenaline was wearing off, and I was afraid if I didn't get going right away, I'd fall asleep. I felt better once I'd started moving again. R called after me.

R

Are you sure you're good?

JS

I'm good enough.

Somehow R's bike still worked and he quickly caught up. As we wobbled along the road together I allowed myself a brief look back. The HOOtoque was talking on his cell phone.

R

You know they're calling for help right now.

JS

Yeah. But I refuse to be disqualified for something as stupid as a bike crash.

R

I wish we could get rid of them.

The sky was clear. We didn't need the Civic behind us — between the moon and the headlight on my bike, I could see fine. After a few minutes of slow riding, we came to an exit for a rest stop. I took the exit, keeping my eyes on the sides of the road. As soon as I found a decent trail, I bolted.

The mountain bike handled the trail fairly well, and the excitement of ditching the cameras for a little while gave me a second boost of energy. I whipped down the trail as quickly as I dared. I couldn't go as fast as I would have liked, but unless the HOOtoques had bikes in the back of that tiny Civic, they wouldn't be catching up anytime soon. I had ridden for half an hour or so before I realized Robbie was still following me. I couldn't stop him and I'm not sure I wanted to. If I was going to win, I wanted to beat him fair. Not because the paramedics caught him.

I kept going longer than I wanted to—I expected him to fall off any minute. He didn't. Eventually I pulled over anyway. Robbie stopped too. As soon as I dismounted, everything hurt.

JS

Are you following me?

R

No. We just happen to be going the same direction.

I drained my water bottle. We were both breathing hard.

JS

So, what now?

R

What about a truce?

JS

Ha.

R

Temporary of course. Just until we've rested.

JS

How can I trust you to not ride off without me?

R pulled a lock out of his backpack.

R

You can have the key.

JS

And how can you trust me?

He shrugged.
I pulled out the key to my own lock.

JS

We could use both locks.

R

Okay.

We moved the bikes off the trail and hid them in some bushes, locking the frames together. I sensed a trap, but I didn't have the energy to outthink him. As we stood over the bikes in silence, it hit us. We were alone. No HOOtoques, no people, no lights, no cameras.

We had never been this alone before.

R

So, what now?

I didn't know.

JS

We sleep, I guess.

R

Yeah. We should get farther off the trail, though. They'll catch up eventually.

JS

Yeah.

We walked through the brush in silence. R led the way with a flashlight. I followed, shivering.

JS

Your bike. I saw some just like it at the rental place. You got there first, didn't you?

R

Yeah.

JS

What did you give him?

R

He just wanted to be on TV, I think. I told him I'd put a good word in for his store if he turned you away.

JS

And how did you get away from the crew?

R

Luck. They got a flat tire soon after I left town. About an hour before you rode into me.

JS

You picked a stupid place to stop.

We came up to a large rock wall that leaned in slightly — a good place to camp.

R

I never posted your journal online, you know. I never read it.

JS

Yeah. I know.

R

Then why do you still hate me?

I dropped my backpack to the ground with a heavy thud.

JS

Plenty of reasons. You stabbed me in the back, for one.

R

Yeah. I know. It was strategy. You would have done the same.

JS

No. I was the one who gave you the immunity idol, remember?

R

And yet you chose Marc as your partner in that prize challenge, after we made an agreement.

JS

I apologized for that! You never did! And it was only a pair of hockey tickets you lost, not the entire game. And you got the tickets anyway.

R

I tried to apologize, but you were too stubborn to listen. And you got back in the game, anyway.

I wished I had lost R on the trail. I wished the paramedics had gotten him.

R

What's the difference? Voting you out sooner rather than later? That's how the game works. Only one person wins. So why do you still hate me?

I sat down cross-legged on the grass, thinking about the vodka in my backpack. Hoping the bottle was still unbroken.

JS

I don't hate you.

R

You don't care at all, do you?

JS

R

Fuck, Jane. There are no cameras around.

No. But we still had our lav mikes. I turned around, pulled the mike out of my shirt, and switched it off. They must have been out of range, but it made me feel better anyway. R did the same.

JS

I care. I did.

R gave a short laugh.

R

You did? I don't get it.

JS

What don't you get?

R

On your birthday. Another guy hit me in the face because he was jealous. And you just stood there. You didn't do anything.

I stood up.

JS

I was in shock! What were you expecting?

R

I don't know, maybe a little sympathy? Maybe any indication at all that what happened was not okay?

JS

Of course it wasn't okay.

We faced each other, almost nose to nose. Too close.

JS

What does it matter now? Let's just go to sleep.

Robbie didn't reply. He stared at me, angry or hurt or full of contempt, before pulling the insulating blanket out of his backpack. He didn't bother sweeping twigs and leaves off the grass before lying down.

I collected a few dry branches and rocks and made a pathetic fire with Marc's lighter, then started writing in here. I am strangely awake for an exhausted person. Half of me wants to wake up R so I can argue with him some more. The other half doesn't know what it wants.

I was about to curl up in my sleeping bag and blanket when I noticed that Robbie was shivering. It was pretty cold out, and he didn't bring as much warm clothing as I did. I fished out an extra pair of socks, a toque, and a sweater and threw it all on top of him. As he sat up and put everything on, I tossed the last of the dry wood onto the fire.

R

Thank you.

JS

Don't worry about it.

I took a sip of vodka and offered the bottle to him. He judged me with his eyes but sat down next to me and drank anyway.

JS

I ran out of water.

R

Keeps you warm I guess. You're not cold?

JS

(Yes.)
No. One of the perks of being cold-blooded.

R

Why do you always do this?

JS

Do what?

R

Pretend like you don't have a heart. Like you don't care.

I took the bottle from him.

JS

Maybe I don't.

R

Why can't you ever say what you mean?

JS

(Who are you, my psychotherapist?)
I do. I've been told I'm very blunt.

R

Not when it comes to this.

I didn't know what to say to that. So I took another drink.

R

I like you.

I met his eyes for a brief moment. Long enough.

R

I voted you out because I knew I didn't stand a chance against you. When you left I thought it would get easier. But everyone kept talking about you. I didn't want to be distracted by you. Or hurt. But then I'd see you in the hallway and I'd give anything to know what you were thinking. But you always kept walking. I voted you out because I thought I wanted to win more than anything. *[Pause.]* I was wrong.

I wasn't sure what to say to that. Isn't that what I wanted too?

JS

You helped me get back on the show. Why?

R

Because you deserved another chance. You deserved to be on the show more than anyone else. Especially Marc.

JS

Good thing Marc lost the sudden death challenge.

R

Yeah, well. He had a little help.

JS

What do you mean?

R

I filled his water bottle with vodka. I encouraged him to drink.

JS

So you did it because you wanted it to be you and me at the end.

R

Is that what you wanted?

I wanted to make eye contact and hold it and hold my breath until my lungs smothered whatever else was happening inside my rib cage. I imagined my heart as something smooth that I could turn over in my hands, free of messy attachments. Something I could keep to myself.

It didn't work.

R

Please be blunt right now.

I had nothing to say and no way to say it. My mind forgot all the words I'd ever known. I wanted to be honest, though. I wanted to say what I meant.

So I kissed him.

He kissed me back.

We pulled away from each other, and it took me a while to notice everything else — the smell of smoke, the half of me that was warmed by the fire and the half that wasn't, the soft call of an owl. Everything that wasn't him. We sat together in comfortable silence, the warm pressure of his leg next to mine. He reached for my hand, and I let him hold it until we fell asleep.

I woke up with Robbie on one side of me and a camera on the other. I tried to get up, but my muscles wouldn't let me. Every part of me weighed ten times as much as it should. My mouth was dry.

JS
(It's not what it looks like.)
Uhhmphh.

I flailed around, slowly and painfully, until I was able to sit up. I reached for Robbie's backpack and grabbed a water bottle. It was empty.

Uhhmggh.

A HOOtoque handed me a full bottle. I let it dangle in front of my face.

HOOTOQUE
It's all right, you won't get in trouble for taking it.

JS
. . .

HOOTOQUE
I promise.

I grabbed the bottle and drank most of the contents. The rest fell on my sweater because my hands were shaking. I looked over at Robbie, who was still sleeping, then back at the HOOtoque.

JS
It's not what it looks like. We were cold.

HOOTOQUE
. . .

JS
(Sigh.)

After I managed to get up, I changed my sweater, popped some Tylenol, and restarted the fire. The HOOtoque gave me four liters of water, and I made coffee with Robbie's camping pot. I caught up in this journal, and now I'm waiting for him to get up.

He's taking forever.

DFS
Maybe we should talk about what happened last night.

JS

All right.

DFS

I think you are making progress.

JS

In what way?

DFS

In most ways. What are you afraid of?

JS

Looking stupid in front of the camera.

DFS

And yet you tripped and fell down a mountain. You finished a stranger's half-eaten dinner. You spoke to an entire bar. You woke up next to Robbie.

JS

You don't need to rub it in.

DFS

And then there's Robbie.

JS

What about him?

DFS

Don't tell me you're not afraid of him. Or afraid of yourself.

JS

I won't.

DFS

But you kissed him, for Christ's sake!

JS

Please keep your voice down.

I looked up at the HOOtoques in case they could see what I was writing, but they were still chatting softly on the other side of the fire, my back to their cameras.

JS

I'm still afraid of other things. Like losing.

DFS

All I'm saying is that you're making progress.

After Robbie woke up and had some coffee and granola bars, AP made a surprise visit. He was fresh and clean and smelled like cologne. It was annoying.

AP

Congratulations on making it this far! It's nice to see you two getting along.

Robbie and I kept our faces blank, but I hope he was laughing on the inside. I think he would also rather be amused than mortified.

AP

I have a surprise for both of you — a video message from your families.

We waited for the catch.

AP

No strings attached.

AP opened up his laptop and played Robbie's message first. His parents filled the screen, smiling. They told him how proud they were of how far he had come this year, how they were sending him a care package full of his favorite food and extra socks because he never threw his out when they got holes, how excited they would be if he won the car and could visit in the summer. How he should call as soon as the show ended. How much they loved him. Robbie smiled to himself as he watched, not saying anything except to ask if AP could play it again.

AP opened my message, and there was Carol, sitting on our living room couch. When did she start using lipstick?

CAROL

Hey, Janie. I have no idea what you're doing right now because they won't tell me, but I hope they're making you work for it. If you win the car, I call dibs on the first ride! That's not why I want you to win, though. You should win because you deserve it. Sorry, Robbie. If you win tonight maybe you can make it to my party tomorrow afternoon. A bunch of friends are coming over, and there's someone I want you to meet. I'm not naming names though because this is probably on TV and that would be super embarrassing. Um. The producers wanted to interview Mom and Dad, but I asked if I could do it instead. I wanted to say sorry for what I said the other night. I never want to be the one to make things harder for you. We're on the same team, remember? Anyway. I love you. GO TEAM SINNER! SINNERS ARE WINNERS! Has anyone else thought of that before? Um. Sorry. This is embarrassing. Okay bye.

By the time AP closed the laptop, my heart had fallen out of my chest and splattered on my feet. Carol's birthday was today, and I had completely forgotten. She must have recorded this message yesterday, which meant her party was today. Her sweet sixteen party.

I had never missed her birthday before.

JS

Hey, Alexander — how long will it take to bike to Calgary from here?

AP

At least nine hours. But since you're already tired and sore from yesterday, I'd say ten or eleven. Not including breaks.

JS

So I'd get there around . . .

AP

Around eleven, maybe. Then interviews.

JS

I see.

Robbie and I started again soon afterward. It was already past noon. I wanted to fly down the trail, but my body refused to cooperate. The Civic was waiting for us on the main road. We didn't stop. In a way I was glad we were going so slowly — I needed to figure out how to make it up to Carol. If that was even possible. We'd slept in the tree-house on her birthday every year since she was old enough.

Carol took my suicide attempt the hardest. She refused to visit me at the hospital. I desperately wanted her to come so I could see that some part of my life was still okay and innocent and the way it was supposed to be. I assumed she was mad at me because I did something I wasn't supposed to do. Like when we were young and she was angry that I kept my loonie instead of putting it in the offering plate because Pastor Ron would just *know,* and he'd *know* Carol hadn't done anything to stop me.

Eventually I realized she wasn't mad, not at first. She was scared. She wasn't sleeping, wasn't eating, couldn't go to school. "Do you know what it would have been like," she told me when I finally came home, "to lose your only sister?"

Then she punched me as hard as she could.

She hit me square in the shoulder, over and over. I let her.

My skin turned red and purple. I wore that bruise as a badge. Proof that however fucked-up I was on the inside, it wasn't all in my head. It was real, it was visible, and eventually, it would get better.

Carol slept on my floor that night and bombarded me with reality TV and sugary junk food so I wouldn't drift off to sleep and leave her alone. I'll never forget the relief of being with her and no one else, exhausted and hollow and scared myself, but okay. We were going to be okay. We were together.

We reached the exit for the Trans-Canada Highway. Robbie took the exit — it was the most direct way home. I stopped. When he noticed I wasn't following, he turned around and called back.

R

What are you doing?

JS

I'm taking a different route.

R

But you know this is the quickest?

JS

I have a plan.

Robbie looked uncertain.

JS

Go ahead without me. I'll see you there.

He hesitated before riding off, much faster than before. I watched him leave, then turned to the HOOtoque already standing next to me. I looked directly into the camera.

                              JS
        Happy birthday, Carol!

I never really needed a car in the first place.

I kept going a couple hundred meters down the road before stopping again. The HOOtoque stepped out of the car once more. My mind was already made up, and there was no point second-guessing myself. It's lovely to not believe in regret. I started waving at the oncoming traffic. After a minute, a gray sedan stopped in front of me. I gestured to the driver to hold on. He nodded.

I took off my safety pack and handed it, along with the lav mike and bike, to the HOOtoque.

                              JS
        Can you look after this bike for me? I'll come get it later.

                          HOOTOQUE
        I guess. Why?

                              JS
        I quit.

It wasn't enough. If I couldn't go out in a fiery blaze of glory, I could at least break all the rules.

                              JS
        Can I please use your cell phone?

                          HOOTOQUE
        . . . You sure? Are you sure you want to do this?

                              JS
        Yes. It's an emergency.

He handed me his phone, and I called Alexander Park.

JS

I quit.

I hung up before he could reply and sent him a quick email of res-ignation. I took my wallet from my backpack and fished out a ten, then held it in front of the camera, nodding to the driver, just to cover all my bases.

JS

For gas.

There was nothing left to do but nod meaningfully at the HOO-toque, throw my backpack onto the back seat of the car, and get in.

JS

Are you heading to Calgary?

DRIVER

Yeah. I'm Jeff.

JS

I'm Jane. Nice to meet you.

I asked if I could borrow his phone, and I texted his description and license plate to Carol, in case the HOOtoque didn't get it on cam-era. Exhaustion is no excuse for stupidity. I watched the HOOtoque fade from sight in the rearview mirror. I didn't see him turn off the camera, but I smiled at the thought anyway. That's right. Nothing more to see here. Move along.

I've shared my triumphs, my humiliations, my secrets, my jour-nal, and now my shocking departure with the general public. I'm a generous person. There's no reason why I shouldn't take what I want from the show and leave on my own terms. Sure, the online message boards will be full of speculations and outcries, but no one can say I didn't play the game well. The legend of Jane Sinner will linger on the

internet for years to come. Let the public speculate and cry out. They can't tell me anything new. Anyone with the balls to talk to me in person better put on a pair of shades, because this sunny disposition will not relent.

In the words of my dear little sister, "I can do what I want."

We reached the parents' house by midafternoon. I could see from the barbecue smoke rising up from the backyard that the party had already started. I pulled down the visor and checked my reflection in the mirror—I looked pretty gross, but that was to be expected. I probably smelled worse than I looked anyway. I handed the ten-dollar bill to Jeff and thanked him for the ride. Before I swung my legs out of the car I took a deep breath, suddenly nervous. What if bailing on the show was a bad idea? What if everyone assumes the worst—that this means I'm giving up on everything again?

I got out, grabbed my pack from the back seat, and walked up to the gate.

Carol was ecstatic to see me, and I couldn't help but grin back at her. Mom hugged me but Dad refused, telling me to shower first. Fair enough. They asked me about the show, and I said I'd talk about it later.

After scrubbing myself clean under the hot water—the second-best shower I have ever taken—I put on one of Dad's old T-shirts and a pair of Carol's gym shorts. Now that cameras weren't focused on my every move, comfort was a priority.

I had taken two steps through the patio door before Carol grabbed my arm and dragged me across the yard. A stocky, dark-haired boy sat on the bench, a plastic cup of lemonade in his hands. He stood straight up to meet us. Carol nodded at him the same way she used to nod at her artwork on the fridge. *See that? It's mine.* He wiped his hand on his pants before offering it to me.

CAROL
Janie, this is David. David, this is my sister, Jane.

401

DAVID
I've heard so much about you!

I took a small step toward him, my resting bitch face cranked up to eleven.

JS
Dave, is it? So you've heard of me.

DAVID
Yeah! Carol showed me *House of Orange.* I think you're awesome on it.

JS
I am awesome on it. That is because I have a very particular set of skills. Skills I've acquired over a very long career. Skills that make me a —

CAROL
OKAY, Janie. He gets it.

DAVID
[to Carol]
You're right. Maybe she does spend too much time on TV.

Carol laughed. Her laugh is one of my favorite sounds.

CAROL
Come on, the food's ready!

Carol grabbed David's hand like it was the easiest thing in the world to do and pulled him toward the barbecue. David glanced back and noticed me noticing their hands. *A nightmare,* I mouthed. *A nightmare for people like you.* He gulped appropriately. A bit of healthy fear never hurt anyone.

Everyone asked me how the show went, and I had to tell them I lost. I said they'd have to watch the show themselves to see how. There was no point making Carol feel guilty for being born just yet. For the first time in months, I didn't have to strategize. I don't remember the last time I felt this light.

A HOOcap showed up at the door a couple hours after I arrived. I said he could come in and have some cake if he didn't turn on his camera. He declined.

CAROL
You could have let him film, you know. I wouldn't have minded.

JS
I'm pretty tired of the show. I want a day off.

CAROL
I think it's kind of exciting though.

JS
That reminds me — I have a present for you!

I found my backpack, pulled out the DSLR, and handed it to Carol. I don't give a shit what AP thinks. At the very least he can let her keep it as a consolation prize.

JS
Sorry I didn't have time to wrap it.

CAROL
It's awesome! Thank you, Janie!

JS
I think you'll have more fun behind the camera than in front of it.

Carol grinned and pointed it at me before running off to point it at David. I called after her.

JS
You have to turn it on first, kid!

Dad thought I should turn in at a decent hour and sleep in a bed, but I disagreed. The night was cold, but we didn't care. Carol and I huddled in our sleeping bags, eating leftover candy and playing cards. I asked her about David, and she was happy to give me details, but those details are for her own journal, not mine. She fell asleep long before I did. I played with the flashlight as I waited to drift off. The light bounced around the rough walls and empty wrappers, throwing shadows on Carol's face. When the battery died, I pulled the sheet from the window and watched the clouds drift across the moon, wondering how Robbie was celebrating. Wondering if he called my phone, even though he knew I didn't have it with me. Wondering what I'm supposed to be feeling. The show is over. I have nothing left to be afraid of, no more competition to manipulate, no more secrets to hide. Not really.

The sky stretched out above me, deep and empty and dim. This is freedom, I suppose. Maybe I should be feeling happy. Maybe I am happy — it's hard to tell. If not, I'll settle for free.

SatAug20

The luxury of the parents' house wore off after breakfast. For the most part they mean well, but they don't understand why I still don't want to move back in, even just for a few months. I thanked them for their concern but left before our differences overshadowed the temporary oasis Carol's birthday had provided. I still had to face *House of Orange* one last time.

Robbie gave me a lopsided grin as I walked in the door. I stuck out my hand to congratulate him and get it over with. I knew I was responsible for his victory, but it choked me all the same to admit it. I held my hand out in front of him, slowly dying inside, but he let it hang there. Drawing out the moment as long as he could. Still an asshole.

AP

Jane! You came back.

I lowered my hand.

JS

Yeah. I still have some food in the fridge, so I guess I had to.

AP

I should congratulate you.

JS

For losing?

AP

Yes. I have to say, I didn't see it coming. I was sure one of you would make it back. I had balloons and everything. But the audience will love the surprise ending.

JS

What do you mean? One of us did make it back.

AP

Well, yes, you're both here now. But disqualified, of course.

What?
I looked at Robbie. He shrugged.

JS

And what the hell did *you* do?

Robbie opened his mouth, but the words didn't make it out.

AP

He had just made it inside city limits when he overheard the crew talking about you. We had figured out where you were, but up until then Robbie had no idea you quit. He had nearly killed himself riding to Calgary to beat you, convinced you had some trick up your sleeve. But when he learned you left the show to go to your sister's birthday party, he . . .

AP stopped, waiting for Robbie to pick up the story.

R

I borrowed a phone and called my cousin to come pick me up. We went to a bar and drank.

AP

The cameras followed, of course. It wasn't just any bar — it was the grungiest, seediest place I've ever seen. Robbie walked in and ordered a drink like he had done this a thousand times before. An appletini. Hilarious.

JS

Why?

R

Because they're delicious.

JS

But why did you quit?

AP

After a couple more, he starts buying drinks for the crew. Then he throws up all over his shoes and just laughs it off. Hilarious.

My mouth hung open while I waited for either of them to say something that made sense.

AP

It was chivalry, I suppose.

JS

What does chivalry have to do with anything?

R

I wanted to win. But I wanted to beat you fairly. Not win by default.

JS

That's stupid.
(But I get it.)

We were both stupid. And proud. And losers.

R

A part of me hoped if we were both disqualified, we'd split the prize.

AP

Unfortunately, chivalry gets you nowhere in reality television.

The first thing Marc did with his prize money was take Robbie, Chaunt'Elle, Holly, Raj, and me out for a drink. Marc has no moral issues with winning by default. He was quite pleased with himself, grinning like an idiot as AP handed over the keys and cash. It would have been easy to resent Marc, to let jealousy and disgust and contempt take over, but I knew it would be irrational. I should have handed the keys to him myself.

At the bar I asked Robbie if he wanted an appletini, but he shook his head and ordered a beer. I ordered an appletini, in part to let him know I wouldn't make fun of him, in part to make fun of him anyway. Once we finished our drinks, I ordered two more appletinis because Marc was paying. Also, they were delicious.

SunAug21

Marc offered to share his prize money with Robbie and me, but I declined.

> ### MARC
> Your loss. I'll use the money to get a new spoiler for the car.

I did ask him if I could borrow the Jetta for a couple days. I had to return the bike and visit Bonnie.

> ### MARC
> Sure. No hard feelings, right, Sinner?

> ### JS
> We're good.

> ### MARC
> Can I ask you something?

> ### JS
> Sure.

> ### MARC
> Do you think Chaunt'Elle likes me? I mean, still?

> ### JS
> Probably.

> ### MARC
> Well . . . what should I do?

He looked like a puppy. A pathetic, confused, overgrown puppy with floppy hair and a greasy tank top. I wanted to tell him I was no expert on relationships or girls or kindness in general, but the show was over. I had nothing to gain by being unhelpful.

> **JS**
> Ask her on a date. Go swimming.

> **MARC**
> But I can't swim. I don't know if she knows that.

> **JS**
> She knows. And she'll think it's cute if you ask her to teach you.

> **MARC**
> You think?

> **JS**
> *(Honestly, I have no idea.)*
> Yes. And when she takes off her makeup so it doesn't run in the water, tell her she looks pretty. And compliment her on her bathing suit. She'll feel comfortable around you.

Marc smiled. I hoped for her sake that I wasn't lying to him. But then again I could be helping her start a proper relationship with Marc. Gross. Ah well. The two of them can work it out.

MonAug22

House of Orange was full of people today — contestants, crew, friends. Carol was there. Most of us had to sit on the floor to see the TV. One last episode. It was more bittersweet than I wanted it to be. It was like waking up from a dream or coming home after a long holiday.

Jenna nodded to me from across the room. I don't think she's on good terms with her brother yet, although she did refuse to acknowledge Marc all day. We talked for a minute before the show started. She apologized, but I don't know where to go from here. I hate how much I miss her though.

Watching the show was a blast. Robbie and I both looked like idiots of course, but that was half the fun. Carol never missed an opportunity to point out anything remotely embarrassing. I threatened to sit on her to keep her quiet, but she didn't take me seriously until it was too late.

I watched the episode again as soon as I got home, but not because I'm vain. Well, I am vain, but mostly I'm in awe of the way AP put everything together. I know how much footage he had to go through, and it couldn't have been easy to narrow it down. But he knows how to tell a story, and I appreciate that.

AP and I went outside after the show, just the two of us. I felt strangely grown up. Like his equal. The air was clear and the shadows were sharp and the setting sun framed his profile perfectly. No cameras were in sight, and it was a relief to know this moment would never exist outside our memories.

AP
Jane, I want to ask you something.

JS
Shoot.

AP
The show turned out how I hoped it would, more or less.
Better than anyone else expected, though.

He took a sip of iced tea and turned the glass around in his hand, spilling some on his expensive shoes. It took me a moment to realize he was nervous. It was so absurd, I wanted to laugh.

AP

I've had an offer from another television network. They want to pick up the show for another season in the fall. We'd have more equipment, a proper budget, more exposure . . .

JS

That's great! You're going to do it, aren't you?

AP

I want to, but . . .

Oh god, no.

JS

No. I'm not coming back. I can't do it. I can't.

He laughed.

AP

That's not what I meant.

He met my eyes. I didn't realize until then that we were the same height.

AP

I want you to be my coproducer.

JS

What? No. Why?

AP

I'm serious. You'd be good at it.

JS

I'm flattered, but I don't know if I could.

AP

Part-time, of course. I know that you're thinking of

continuing psychology in the fall. And you can leave the technical stuff to me, but I want you to help plan challenges and do interviews and promote events. You'd be calling the shots.

It was weird to think about. Being on the other side of the camera? Holding all the power, watching other people squirm?

JS
I really don't think so.

AP
I know you haven't forgiven me for leaking your journal. If you want to tell everyone the truth and hold off making a decision now, I understand.

JS
I'll think about it.

AP
Thank you, Jane. It would mean a lot to me.

He smiled and we finished our drinks. Maybe I could get used to feeling like his equal.

WedAug24
After today, I'll be able to look strangers in the eye and introduce myself as Jane Sinner, high school graduate. Nice to meet you. Not to be confused with Jane Sinner, the Girl Who Tried to Kill Herself or Jane Sinner, the Girl Humiliated Repeatedly on Local Television. Please, just call me Jane. Jane is enough.

Watch out, future employers. You're about to meet an individual who isn't perfectly well adjusted, but let's be honest: who is? She excels at written communication, interpersonal strategy, and advanced doodling techniques. Her media-focused education at a trendy community college has equipped her for navigating high-pressure situations in the modern world. She can't give you any references from her previous employer, but officially she was laid off, not fired, so relax. She doesn't have a BA in anything but is definitely maybe considering getting one in the future.

My resume is going to be the shit.

> *Jane settles down on the tired sofa, hands on her lap, head tilted back. She has only a couple hours before she graduates high school. She closes her eyes.*

DFS
I wish you wouldn't put your feet on the table.

JS
Who cares? It's not real.

DFS
It's the thought that counts.

JS
So how long do I have to keep coming back here?

DFS
A while. The rest of your life maybe. Probably for sure.

JS
(Sigh.)

DFS
What did you expect? That at age eighteen you'd have all your shit together?

JS
Yes.

Silence.

DFS

So how's nihilism treating you these days?

JS

Oh, you know. It's not the worst.

DFS

Can I tell you something super enlightening?

JS

Yeah, okay.

DFS

The past doesn't exist. It's just a story we tell ourselves. And stories change each time you tell them.

JS

Oh, wow.

DFS

If you don't like what you've written, write something else.

JS

That's a bit heavy-handed, you know.

DFS

Doesn't make me wrong.

Jane absorbs this as she sinks farther into the couch. She closes her eyes once more, and the couch is now a lawn chair in her parents' backyard. Carol offers her a balloon, and she ties it around her wrist because the balloon is lifting her up and she wants to keep it that way. She floats above the house, above the high school, above the city, above the atmosphere. Space is cold, but at least she's

in good company. Her balloon pops but doesn't make a
sound. She floats.

Graduation wasn't much of a ceremony, but it still involved getting up on that stage again in front of a crowd. It was way less nerve-racking than the time Alexander Park called my name and I got back on the show. That says a lot about my priorities, I suppose. Still, I walked onto the stage with the odd realization that everyone there knew me (or at least knew of me), and knew why I came to Elbow River in the first place. They'd watched me study, socialize, manipulate, and embarrass my way through school. They knew I tried to kill myself.

The parents sat front and center, grinning stupidly. Despite whatever they thought of what I'd done to get here, despite how I'd scared or disappointed them, they came.

I expected the parents and Carol to be there, but I didn't expect Marc, Chaunt'Elle, Holly, Raj, Jenna, AP, and the whole crew of *HOO* to take up the rest of the front row. And Bonnie. Bonnie somehow made it down for the day; one look at her and I knew she wouldn't have missed it for anything.

I recognized a lot of faces from school, and it took me a second to register that both Elbow River and James Fowler students were there. Only fifteen other people received diplomas, but the auditorium was full.

We didn't have music or robes or roses, but AP made me a HOOcap with a tassel, and after handing me my diploma, Mr. Dubs moved the tassel from one side of the brim to the other with the biggest smile I've ever seen him wear. And that's saying something, considering how radiant he was at McNugz Club with two cameras pointed at him.

I turned to face the crowd. Everyone rose. Everyone roared. And there I stood, a pimped-out ball cap on my head, a GO #HASHTAGS shirt on my back, a piece of paper in my hand that had cost me way too much trouble to get.

I felt like a motherfucking idiot.

R wasn't looking at the hat. He wasn't looking at the shirt or paper. He was looking at me, cheering louder than anyone else.

Fuck it.

I had nothing to be embarrassed about. I had nothing to hide. No reason to act differently just because cameras were pointed in my direction. Cameras didn't matter today. I had done it. I saw this through. Sure, I was just a high school graduate a little sunburned after her fifteen minutes in the spotlight, but it was enough.

And yes, I can be a motherfucking idiot sometimes, but today I was something else.

ACKNOWLEDGMENTS

Thank you to:

My editor, Anne Hoppe. I never dreamed I'd find someone else who understood Jane Sinner so thoroughly and cared about her the way I do. My agent, Brooks Sherman: Jane's original champion. I can't thank you enough for guiding me through the new and overwhelming world of publishing, and for being the first to celebrate every success. The B-Team: agent siblings extraordinaire. You all inspire me more than you know. Tara Sonin, for your tireless enthusiasm. You're the best publicist a girl could ask for. All the unsung heroes at the Bent Agency and Clarion Books.

Becky Albertalli. You found me lurking in the obscure corners of the internet and encouraged, supported, and believed in me until I was ready to come out of the writing closet. I wouldn't be where I am without you.

My early beta readers and everyone who offered feedback on Absolute Write. The 2017 and 2018 YA/MG debut authors, for being such an incredible community in which to learn and ask dumb questions.

My parents. You took the late-night "Surprise, I wrote a book and it's getting published!" phone call rather well. Dad, thanks for instilling in me a love of fantasy. Mom, thanks for thinking I'm funny (though please stop with the joke about Egyptian food because I'm not that funny). Even when we don't agree with or understand each other, I've always known I'm unconditionally loved and supported. That means the world to me.

My older sister, Dana, who loves books just as much as I do. You're one of the strongest people I know, especially when you think you're not. Together we can do some pretty substandard things.

My younger sister, Goose, AKA Erin Bosker, the Second. Your truly bizarre sense of humor has inspired me, as has your life motto: "I can do what I want." You are one of the strangest people I'll ever have the pleasure of knowing.

Kevin and Evie and Toby and Sir Pips-A-Lot, for all your love. Thanks for letting me sleep in your basement.

Friends and family both in Alberta (shout-out to Andrea for her passionate and unhealthy love of McNugz) and Vancouver (if we've ever enjoyed an IPA or gone camping together, I'm talking about you). You all keep me sane.

Brian, the love of my life. You've supported me through every step of the publishing process, even if YA isn't your thing (although I'm glad you found "parts of my book entertaining"). I'm forever grateful for celebratory beers, movie nights, and epic outdoor adventures. One day we'll have our cabin in the woods.

And finally, thank you to Margo and Bitey and Alley and all cats for existing.